A Murderous Game

The Third in the Hippolyta Napier Series

by

Lexie Conyngham

First published in 2017 by The Kellas Cat Press, Aberdeen.

Copyright Alexandra Conyngham, 2017

The right of the author to be identified as the author of this work as been asserted by her in accordance with the Copyright, Designs and Patent Act, 1988.

All rights reserved. No part of this publication may be reproduced, stored, or transmitted in any form, or by any means, electronic, mechanical or photocopying, recording or otherwise, without the express permission of the publisher.

ISBN: 978-1-910926-40-6

Lexie Conyngham

A Murderous Game

Chapter One

London, June 1828

The crowd was horrible.

In normal circumstances, they would never come to something like this, never, and they could feel their shoulders contracting in revulsion. Beside them was a fat, self-satisfied woman in a let-out dress poorly cut to imitate the latest fashion, smelling of sweat and stale beer: she had her arm bound around a scrawny man who managed to ignore the stream of useless and erroneous gossip she was emitting. He spent his time yawning, sneezing, and swearing, in succession, wiping his reddened nose on his sleeve, as they shifted to avoid his energetic nasal projections. It would have been hard to ignore them, had it not been for the tall man on the other side who was giving forth in a voice of almost professional volume.

'Fourth woman that fellow has hanged this month, and no harm in that, when they're monsters like this one, eh? Getting to the day you can't hardly sell them chapbooks: nothing new to say in them, is there?'

They shuddered, and reached out to squeeze each other's hands briefly. This one was new to them, anyway.

'Though this one's a bit different, I suppose: this one didn't smother her baby, like the rest of them.'

No, she had not smothered her baby: there was no doubt of that.

'Stabbed her ruddy husband! That's the kind of thing ought to be put a stop to, and no mistake!'

It was enough to make anyone sick. They tried to move away a little, back towards the walls of the shops behind them. London was dusty and hot and out of season for the grand people, and those who were left, the not so grand and the downright humble, were happy for any distraction from their stuffy, sweaty work. The street was packed. They wriggled and shoved a little, not wanting to draw attention to themselves, but in the doorway where they sought shelter there was already a soldier, reeking of brandy, wrapped around a woman mostly, as far as they could judge, in place of her clothing. They met each other's eyes, disgusted. They longed for this to be over – but for this to be over, that would mean that it was all over.

He would not be here, of course. He would have moved on to other triumphs. He would not want to waste his precious time witnessing the outcome of some minor incident.

The crowd moved in some subtly different way and they stiffened. Was this it?

It was. They could hear the cartwheels, so heavy, such a contrast with her light form when they saw her at last standing there, her hair shorn, her hands bound in front of her with ropes that looked too heavy for her to bear. Their eyes swelled with tears but she was not crying: she looked as if every last drop of tears, and blood, had been drained from her, for she was whiter than the border of her shift. As the cart stopped, almost in front of them, they saw that she was shaking, and it was as much as either of them could do not to leap up and hold her tight.

The hangman guided her steps on to the gallows. The crowd were quiet now, every eye on her, waiting for a faint, a bid for freedom, a dramatic speech, a fervent prayer of repentance, some decent reward for their long vigil in the hot street. The hangman bent close to her, tender like a lover, and she seemed to whisper something. He nodded, half-shrugging. Whatever it was, he had heard it all before, the last intimate whispers of the about-to-die. A clergyman from the prison, a stranger, prayed familiar words that used to comfort, but now seemed bereft of anything of the sort.

They gripped each other's hands hard, now, though neither of them could remember reaching out to the other. They had promised, promised her they would see it through, though she seemed not even to know they were there. The crowd breathed slowly and heavily, like one large hungry creature, creeping softly on its prey. The crowd knew better than they did how these things happened, how the performance went.

The hangman gently propelled her on to the platform, where the noose waited. He laid it about her thin neck, arranging it with deft, tender fingers. Surely even now something would intervene? Thunder, lightning, a miraculous pardon? God's hand reaching down from the burning sky to lift her clear? She was so small, so light, so weak.

And then all too suddenly there was a thump, and a cry, and horror of horrors the hangman leaping to the ground to tug hard on her thin legs, to make up for her slight weight. Then they looked away, and the crowd, satisfied, dispersed; and round the corner they propped each other up, and were sick in the gutter as the tears flooded down their faces.

Ballater, Aberdeenshire, December 1831

Hippolyta Napier sat back sharply from the breakfast table.

'I am heartily sick of reading of parliamentary reform!' she declared, with a look of reproach at her husband's newspaper. Patrick Napier peered over it at her with gentle amusement.

'I thought I was the one reading about it,' he said mildly. 'You were reading your letters.'

'I was, but I ran out of letters,' she admitted. 'And if there is something in front of me to read, it must be read – even if it is the back of your newspaper. But it is all reform! Why can they not think of something else to argue about? How to stop this endless miserable rain? How to light the streets better? They have gaslight in Ellon, you know. How to make sure the children up in Glenmuick are getting hot food? And an education?'

'The children I've met up in Glenmuick have no desire for an education, not just at present,' muttered Patrick, whose medical duties had taken him that way the night before on a particularly irritating case. 'Though doubtless they would dispose of any food that came within their reach. I take your point: but there are those who would say that you cannot organise such things properly unless Parliament is organised properly.'

'What on earth has Parliament to do with it?' demanded Hippolyta, whose sleep had been disturbed too. 'I doubt half the members would know where Aberdeen was on a map, never mind Ballater.'

'What are your plans for the day?' Patrick asked, recognising the need for a diversionary tactic when he saw it. Sadly, he hit on the wrong one.

'That's assuming there is such a thing as day. Did ever you know such a dark winter? There is no sense in going anywhere, or doing anything. The snow has been and gone in a day, leaving us nothing but slush and depression. There is scarcely light to paint, the mud has blocked every road, and it seems that it will go on raining until the crack of doom. I daresay,' she said with a martyred air, 'that I shall go now and try to dry out the shawls I wore to go and feed the pig and the hens this morning. But they were scarcely dry from yesterday, and tomorrow, no doubt, I shall have to dry them out again. Will it never end?'

'Of course it will,' said Patrick, though he knew it was of little use.

'And Mrs. Riach says there isn't a piece of mutton to be had this side of Kincardine o'Neil, and even the kale in the garden is rotting on its stalks, and how is she supposed to cope? Well, how am I supposed to cope with her in that mood?'

'With your usual angelic composure, my dear?' Patrick suggested tentatively. Hippolyta scowled at him for a moment, then burst out laughing.

'That's it exactly! I shall have to,' she agreed. 'Now, I wonder where I left it? When did I last use it?'

'Every day, my dear, every day.' Patrick smiled, then sighed, and rose from the table, dislodging a tangle of comfortably warm white cats from his lap. He went round to kiss his wife on the top of her fair head. 'I must go, though, and leave you to it: I have a call to make up at Dinnet House.'

Their eyes met: their friend who had lived at Dinnet House was long gone, and it had been standing empty.

'Heavens,' said Hippolyta, not quite able to keep a quiver from her voice, 'who is calling you from there?'

Patrick made a face expressive of mild bewilderment.

'A Lady Pinner, apparently. They're up from – er, somewhere in the south of England, and have taken the house for the winter.'

'For the winter? That's not the usual pattern, is it? I hope it is not a lunacy case,' she added with a mock frown.

'No, but I gather she has not been well – she had a child six months ago and has not made a good recovery – and her husband is in need of a rest, apparently.'

'Still, a strange place to choose. I mean, my dear, an excellent choice, given our healthy air and outstanding local medical gentlemen, but it is not what people usually do.'

'No: the winter is usually a good time for us to recover from our summer hosts of spa visitors, and have a rest.' He went out into the little stone-flagged hall, and picked up his medical bag from the hallstand, checking its contents. Then he set it down again and began, with her assistance, the task of wrapping up warmly for the walk up to Dinnet House, in boots, hat, fur cape turned inside out to keep the sleety rain out, and both woollen and leather gloves. He grinned, eyes bright, from amongst the wrappings as he bade her goodbye at the door, and she waved him to the end of the garden path before shutting the wet cold out, and girding her own loins for the very thought of going out later. The cats regarded her with complete disdain from the comfort of the parlour where the fire was cosy. Why on earth would anyone go outside voluntarily?

She glanced at her letters on the breakfast table, and hurriedly picked them up, tucking them into her little desk in the corner of the parlour. That was something else to think about – something she had not mentioned to Patrick at all.

The Edinburgh apartment was smothered in a heavy blanket of stuffy warmth, and Elinor Broughton felt that at any moment she might simply stop breathing completely. Outside the window, the streets were a morass of mud and slush, with carters swearing and horses slithering. It was not quite what she had hoped from the Edinburgh season, having tempted her husband so far north: they darted in stiff, formal clothes and stupidly thin slippers from overheated parlour to overheated assembly room to overheated drawing room and back, busy with the conversations of half-remembered strangers, to some of whom she was related. The talk was all of politics: for herself she could not complain, for at least her mind was occupied, but she had hoped to keep Broughton clear of all that guddle for a month at least. That, and other matters.

But it was not to be. She knew the moment she entered his study that she had failed. His face had that set, smooth look that she was sure someone would carve in marble one day, but for her it was not a good sign. It was the sign that he was facing a problem for which he could see no solution.

'What is it, my dear?' she asked briskly, always one to face the worst. He turned stiffly to her, and she saw the other side of his face. His eye was puffy, and when he closed it she saw a line as thick black as India ink on his eyelid. And his lip was cut. 'Oh, no, not again!'

'I fear my business is known of even here, my dear,' he said, with a slight mumble.

'Someone of significance?'

'A lawyer. Young, idealistic, and with a handy fist.'

Edinburgh was not far enough, she thought to herself. I thought it would be, but it wasn't.

'Was it – was it very public?'

'Public enough.' He sighed, and tried to look apologetic. 'Well, my dearest, we knew this would come eventually. Word gets around when one is prominent in public life.' He made a face as if the words tasted bitter, then winced.

'Only one thing for it, then, my love,' she said.

'But there is nothing else to do! One must simply face these things!'

'There is an alternative,' she said firmly. 'There's a good deal more of North Britain left to go, you know. Let's move on – let's go north!'

'But where? Where could we go?'

'The Highlands?'

'The Highlands? Aren't they full of Jacobites and wolves?' But she could see that he was beginning to smile, lopsidedly: the idea was taking hold.

'Nothing better,' she said bracingly. 'Where there are Jacobites and wolves, who will dare to follow us?'

Hippolyta could not put off much longer her own reason for going out that morning, and assumed bonnet and cloak as soon as she had finished her own breakfast. Her pony was stabled at the inn, for they had no stable themselves, and every couple of days at least she went to visit him, to see that he was being fed and cared for adequately, and to apologise to anyone he had bitten. There was usually a list.

Outside the house, once she had darted beneath the dripping bushes by the gate, she was on the village green, with the solid centrical church of the three parishes dark brown and imposing opposite her. Beyond it, in good weather, one could clearly see the mountains, Lochnagar chief amongst them, to which Hippolyta constantly fought to do justice to with her paints, but today there was nothing to tempt her through the flat white mist. The street on which the church stood sloped gently down to her left, and she joined it, passing the low cottages that lined the main street and led down to the bridge over the river – or where the bridge had been. The floods of two years ago had destroyed it and no one had yet managed to agree how to replace it, to the advantage of the ferrymen who plied their trade across the Dee in its place. The inn, a rambling building with additions and outcrops in several directions, stood beside it just where the main commutation road from Aberdeen entered the village, and fielded the coaches that arrived regularly, usually bearing visitors to the spa on the other side of the river. The archway to the stable yard stood next to the road, of course, and Hippolyta, still huddled against the rain, scuttled inside and across the cobbles to the stables.

The pony was as usual not particularly excited to see her, but was reported by the stable boy to have spent an unusually placid couple of days staring out at the rain: Hippolyta was worried it might have fallen into a melancholy – worried, and sympathetic. The stable boy gave it as his opinion that the creature was sickening for something. Hippolyta decided not to take it out for a walk in case it became chilled, fed it a carrot, and bade it goodbye, promising to pop back tomorrow at the latest to see it again.

To her surprise, outside the stable the rain had eased just a little, and the sky had brightened. She breathed in the air and took a few steps to peer over the broken parapet at the river below: it was swollen and grey, and brought back bad memories of that flood in 1829. Across the river, the ferrymen squatted beneath the trees, their boats pulled up on the shore with canvas covering them: no one wanted to go anywhere much in this weather, but they would be ready to cross if they had to. She noticed someone else, though, on her side of the river, taking the chance to linger a little in the gentler rain.

'Mr. Worthy!' she called out, recognising him.

'Mrs. Napier!' He bowed, and a flurry of drips scattered from the brim of his hat. He put a hand up to remove it but she waved at him to stop.

'You'll be soaked – pray, keep it on!'

'Thank you, madam, you are most thoughtful!' He scrunched up his face in a kind of smile. 'The river is most ebullient today, is it not?'

'Ebullient is certainly a word for it. Are you out on business, to risk this dreadful rain, or do you take a stroll?' She smiled back at him. He was an oddity, she thought, with his almost poetic words and his half-English accent, and his face where all the features seemed to struggle at once to be most prominent.

'I take my morning constitutional regardless of the intemperate moods of the heavens,' he explained. 'And I find this spot most interesting for the purpose of observing how the river in its might has moved and carved its way through the apparent geological permanences of the landscape.'

'Of course,' said Hippolyta, nodding obediently. 'Well, I wish you joy of it, Mr. Worthy: I must carry on with my own duties for the day. No rest for the wicked, of course!'

'Yet I am sure you are not wicked at all, Mrs. Napier. That is,' he corrected himself, perhaps anxious that he had committed some indelicacy, 'I am sure there is very little wickedness in Ballater.'

'Hm,' said Hippolyta, but managed to contain any further observations she might have made on the wickedness that had visited Ballater on occasion. 'Nevertheless, the work is there to be done! Good day to you, Mr. Worthy.'

'Good day, Mrs. Napier!' he responded, and absently lifted his hat, spraying both of them with water from the sweep of its brim. She laughed, and returned to the main street.

The weather was in fact so much better – only drizzling, now – that she felt she needed to take the opportunity to stretch her legs. To breathe fresh air and to feel all her limbs moving – it was all she could do not to skip up the street, but she was fairly sure that would not be becoming in a respectable doctor's wife. She grinned to herself in the shelter of her bonnet, and returned to her own house to find out whether Mrs. Riach wanted anything fetched from Strachan's warehouse. Lingering to speak to the housekeeper only a moment or two, she was soon back outside again, and walking energetically up the hill, past the church to where Mr. Strachan's well-supplied warehouse took up the space of two shops already on the narrow street.

Inside the shop, the air was warm, thanks to a lively fire in the fireplace, and smelled of all kinds of delights: from the side of the counter further from the fire smoked meats, cheeses, tea and coffee and chocolate, a sharp note of brandy, and from the warmer end lavender and cloth and beeswax. A number of customers were already occupying the chairs by the counter and Hippolyta was happy to stop and gaze about her at the merchandise, not expecting anything much new in this weather and at this season, but hoping there was something her eye had not caught before. She nodded with satisfaction at the sight of some fabrics she had seen and liked previously, including one she had happily used to make up new curtains for their drab dining room, but there was nothing else of interest and she angled herself to see the meats and cheeses, deciding which to buy so as to be ready when her turn came. The wooden floor was polished to excess but slippery with rainwater, and everyone moved carefully: she was surprised, then, when there came a polite throat-clearing from around her elbow when she had not noticed anyone approach. She turned: it was the minister's wife, Mrs. Douglas, a woman who was rarely first to approach anyone and who stayed, if at all possible, somewhere in the shadows out of sight. As Hippolyta was, moreover, not one of her husband's flock, being Episcopalian, she was even more surprised at Mrs. Douglas' timid curtsey, though of course, Ballater being a small place, they were well enough acquainted.

'Good day to you, Mrs. Napier,' she whispered.

'Good day to you! I hope I find you well,' returned Hippolyta, sure that this enquiry would provoke an account of some medical emergency for which Mrs. Douglas required Patrick, but Mrs. Douglas nodded gratefully and smiled.

'Quite well, thank you. And you?'

'Oh, very well, yes indeed, thank you. What dreadful weather!' Hippolyta relapsed into the easy topic. 'Yet it is a little clearer this morning, I believe.'

'I think we have all hurried out to make the best use of it while we can,' agreed Mrs. Douglas. 'I am here with – with the lady at the counter.' She nodded across with what Hippolyta could only think was resignation.

The lady at the counter was not much older than Hippolyta herself, perhaps in her mid-twenties. She wore an outfit in a brownish, slightly shimmery fabric that Hippolyta knew with a thrill must be aventurine, the very latest in French fashion. It suited the lady, too: her hair was a rich brown and her complexion was fresh and fair, though she was a little too thin and sour about the face for true beauty, Hippolyta considered. Mr. Strachan himself, his black whiskers polished and sharp, was attending her in his most obsequious fashion.

'Dr. Napier told her she needed fresh air and exercise, and I happened to be visiting her when he called,' Mrs. Douglas continued in her low, scratchy voice, like a mouse at a wainscot. 'She asked me if there was an area with respectable warehouses in it, so of course I brought her here. There is nowhere else, really, is there?'

There were a few other traders in Ballater, more in the summer than in the winter, but it was true that Strachan's was the only possible place to take someone in a new aventurine carriage gown.

'But who is she? Is she the lady who has taken Dinnet House for the winter?' Hippolyta murmured, remembering Patrick's mission that morning.

'That's right – well, her husband has. He's Sir Holroyd Pinner, you know? Well, I didn't know, I must say.' Mrs. Douglas frowned, worried at her own ignorance. 'I try not to read the newspapers, they make me so anxious.'

'The member of parliament?' Hippolyta remembered. Sir Holroyd had made some very stirring speeches against Reform in the last session: some of them had taken up several columns of coverage in the newspapers. 'And this is Lady Pinner?'

'That's right – rather younger than he is, of course.'

'I see.'

She regarded Lady Pinner with renewed interest – the lady of a baronet and a patient of Patrick's, a combination guaranteed to arouse her curiosity.

'Dr. Napier said she needed more varied society, too,' Mrs. Douglas was saying. 'At present, you see, apart from her nurse-companion, I am her only visitor. And she requires quite a number of visits,' she added, her voice uncertain.

'I should be honoured to visit her,' said Hippolyta at once, 'if she would be kind enough to receive me.'

'Oh, may I introduce you?' Mrs. Douglas was suddenly eager, and Hippolyta absolved her of all devious plans to entrap Hippolyta into helping her. 'I shall ask her immediately.' And with a boldness rather unknown in the minister's wife, she marched straight back to her companion.

'Lady Pinner,' Hippolyta heard her say, 'I wonder if I might be allowed to introduce –'

'No,' said Lady Pinner, without looking round. Mrs. Douglas blushed from bonnet to collar, and Hippolyta's own blood surged in embarrassment for herself and for the little minister's wife. She beckoned Mrs. Douglas back over quickly, for it looked as if she might burst into tears.

'She is busy at present, no doubt,' said Hippolyta hurriedly. 'Perhaps another time, when she is less – busy.'

'Of course, of course,' agreed Mrs. Douglas.

'I think, too,' Hippolyta went on, 'that I might pop outside for a moment and see if the rain has stayed off. Would you care for a breath of fresh air?'

'I should like that above all things,' said Mrs. Douglas with feeling, and they left the shop together. Hippolyta was very pleased with herself for not quite slamming the door.

Chapter Two

Outside in the street, the rain had fortunately stopped altogether, though the bulging clouds promised more later. Mrs. Douglas took a deep breath, and Hippolyta unclenched her fingers, but before either of them could speak they were greeted by a small knot of people in the street.

'Mrs. Douglas! Away over here!' called one of them, a broad, solid woman with a wicked grin. The woman next to her, similar in build if a little taller, nudged her hard in the ribs.

'Ada!'

'Ach, away with you. I want to hear the claik!'

Hippolyta smiled despite herself, took Mrs. Douglas firmly by the arm, and went to join the others for a news.

'Mrs. Kynoch,' she said, to the third, quiet woman in the group, then to the broad sisters with their wiry hair, 'Miss Strong, Miss Ada.'

There was a round of shallow curtseys, the curtseys of those who saw each other every day and did not need to make a fuss about it. Hippolyta was the youngest by far. All the others were middle-aged, and she knew her slightly ambiguous level in this hierarchy: youngest, which dropped her down, married, which pulled her up, comparatively new to Ballater, which dropped her again, but married to the local doctor, which certainly gave her a cachet in gossiping circles. Besides, she liked all of them, Mrs. Kynoch in particular.

'Was that you away into Strachan's with the lassie from Dinnet House?' Miss Ada demanded, bonnet focussed sharply on Mrs. Douglas. The minister's wife wilted under the scrutiny.

'Aye, it was,' she sighed.

'How's she cried?' the interrogation continued.

'Her name is Lady Pinner.'

'Ha!' Miss Ada's cry of triumph caused her sister to nudge her hard again.

'Ada!'

'I knew it!' cried Miss Ada. 'She's the wife of yon Sir Holroyd Pinner, is she no? I thought I heard his name mentioned at the inn, but she – ' the bonnet jerked towards her sister 'dragged me off before I could find out more. The big Tory anti-Reformer, here in Ballater? Now there's a thing, eh?'

'You'd think he would have plenty to do in London,' agreed Miss Strong. 'Even with Parliaement prorogued.'

'Aye, there's no knowing when they'll be summoned back for the rest of the session,' her sister went on. This was clearly something much discussed around the Strong tea table. 'And if you ask me, they only got the King to prorogue Parliament to give themselves more time to plot and plan.'

'Which side?' asked Hippolyta, interested to hear her opinion.

'Oh, both!' Miss Ada dismissed them with a grin.

'Do you think he wants to drum up support against the Bill up here in Scotland?' Mrs. Douglas asked meekly. 'I should have thought that Admiral Gordon was against the Bill already, wouldn't you?'

'Not sure what our local Member of Parliament thinks on the matter,' said Miss Ada with a smack of her lips. 'Doesn't ever say very much on the subject. All the Commons in uproar and all he talks about is the French victory in Portugal.'

Goodness, thought Hippolyta, they are thorough devotees of the newspapers.

'It's nothing to do with his parliamentary business,' said Mrs. Kynoch at last. 'Lady Pinner has not been well. She had twins in the summer, and one died, as so often happens, of course. But she has taken a long time to recover.'

Hippolyta remembered thinking that that pretty face was too thin. Well, that might be the explanation.

'She is certainly not in the best of tempers today,' she put in.

'I gather that's a common state of affairs,' said Miss Ada. 'Her nuserymaid told me that she's a bad-tempered, sour young woman, and –'

'Ada! Gossiping with the servants!'

'She didn't speak to her husband for a whole fortnight!'

'Ada!'

'Poor lassie,' said Mrs. Kynoch again, and her eyes met Hippolyta's. 'Perhaps she needs some more stimulating society – and kindness.'

'Of course you are right,' said Hippolyta, contrite to think she had been enjoying Miss Ada's tittle tattle. Lady Pinner had been rude, but she might have had her reasons – or at least some excuse.

'Dr. Napier asked me to bring her out here for a change of air,' said Mrs. Douglas timidly.

'Well done, Mrs. Douglas,' said Mrs. Kynoch. 'You have already begun with the kindness.'

'And she'll no find a better warehouse than Strachan's this side of Edinburgh, I'd say!' said Miss Strong, loyal to Ballater. They all nodded, allowing it as the gateway to a change of subject.

'I met Mr. Worthy down by the river,' said Hippolyta after a moment's pause. 'He seems to be settling in well.'

'Well,' said Miss Ada, 'he came in the summer and the winter has not yet daunted him: if he lasts till spring he's settled in. Besides, he seems to be able to work with our brother, and our brother approves of him, for a wonder.'

'He was a lawyer in London before, I think he said?' asked Hippolyta.

'He was, and thereby appreciates the open countryside and fresh air,' said Miss Strong. 'He walks every day before work.'

'Yet the legal systems are different, are they not?' Hippolyta's father and brothers were advocates in Edinburgh, so she knew something of the matter.

'Yes indeed, but when he left London he studied in Edinburgh for a little while, before seeking a country place.' Miss Ada laughed. 'I believe truly that my brother took him on only because of his name. 'Strong and Worthy' – how fine that sounds! A few years ago he had an apprentice by the name of Weekes, but it never stuck.'

They all chuckled. Mr. Strong was a precise little man, and Hippolyta could well imagine him attending to that kind of detail.

The door of Strachan's warehouse opened and for a second they caught sight of Mr. Strachan himself, flinging it wide and eyeing the weather outside.

'It is not raining, I believe, my lady,' he was heard to say. 'Shall I keep the umbrella to be sent with the rest of the purchases?'

'No, let Clara take it,' decreed Lady Pinner, stepping into the doorway like a queen in a procession. She emerged into the grey daylight, where her lovely gown still shimmered a little, and regarded them from a distance, apparently trying to distinguish which of them she had met before. Behind her a surly-looking woman in dark brown held a furled umbrella with a pretty amber handle. Hippolyta vaguely remembered seeing the woman in the shop, but she had not seen the umbrella before, she was sure. Mr. Strachan must have some new stock after all.

'Mrs. Douglas?' Lady Pinner approached the knot of women.

'Yes, Lady Pinner?' Mrs. Douglas detached herself and stepped forward, looking a little like an early Christian martyr facing the lions.

'You asked to introduce some person to me.'

'Yes, Lady Pinner.'

'Well, get on with it!'

'Oh! Well, if I may … Mrs. Kynoch is the widow of our late minister, Mr. … eh .. Kynoch. Mrs. Napier is the wife of the physician. Miss Strong and Miss Ada Strong are the sisters of the man of law here in the village.'

'I see,' said Lady Pinner, regarding them each in turn, the wiry-haired Strong sisters, Mrs. Kynoch in her regrettable arrangement of pink gown and orange bonnet, and Hippolyta, taller than the others and closer to Lady Pinner in age. She gave a little irritable sigh. 'Lawyers, doctors and clergy: well. I should be delighted if you would all call to tea. Sometime soon, perhaps. This afternoon, in fact. I shall see you at four.'

She turned, and stalked off in the direction of Dinnet House, the surly maid stamping along behind her.

'Well!' said Miss Ada. 'I've never been summoned to tea before, not like that. I feel as if I've been arrested!'

'At least she seems determined to expand her acquaintance,' said Mrs. Kynoch charitably. 'That must be thanks to you, Mrs. Douglas, and to Dr. Napier, of course, and his good advice.'

'Best tea gowns, then, ladies!' said Miss Ada. 'Whatever you would wear to meet King William, that would be the thing.'

'Ada!'

But Miss Ada had been distracted.

'Who are they, then?' she asked.

She was looking down the green, towards the church. The others turned to see what had caught her eye. A couple of young men stood by the church door, watching the goings-on about the village, hats pushed back from their faces for a better view. Their dark clothes had them marked out as townspeople, but the cut and quality said they were labourers of some kind.

'Not the usual kind of visitor for Ballater or Pannanich,' remarked Mrs. Kynoch. 'Not even in the summer.'

'I wonder,' said Miss Ada, 'if they're the ones were down at the inn yesterday, asking where the grand people stayed when they visited.'

'The grand people? At the inn, usually, or at Pannanich,' said Mrs. Douglas.

'I hope they are not thieves,' said Hippolyta.

'Surely thieves would not make themselves so obvious,' said Mrs. Kynoch, 'or draw attention to themselves asking questions like that.'

'More sickly townspeople,' said Miss Ada with satisfaction. 'Poisoned by factory fumes and coal fires, and coming here to breathe the fine air.'

'Probably,' said Mrs. Kynoch, giving them a final glance. But Hippolyta watched them a little longer. Patrick was often about at night, alone, visiting the sick. She would warn him to be careful.

After finally making her purchases in Strachan's, Hippolyta hurried home to review what she might wear to Dinnet House that afternoon. It was important, she felt, to show Lady Pinner that it was quite possible to be entertained by village society, and that they were not all teuchters in dirty smocks – though she doubted that Lady Pinner would have heard the word. Polar, one of the cats, met her in the front garden and rubbed the excess rainwater from his thick fur off on the side of her cloak by way of greeting. She bent and scratched his head, pleased at least that the cats had been able to get outside for a little while. She was delighted with the improved weather but knew it could not last: she hoped the rain would hold off at least until she reached Dinnet House that afternoon.

It seemed inclined to. She had changed into her best blue gown with the looped decoration around the hem and sleeves puffed out with caps stuffed to their utmost with down. Her cloak would squash them a little, she knew, but they would soon fluff out again. She was almost ready when she heard the front door open and close, and in a moment Patrick appeared in the bedroom, eyebrows raised at her splendour. Ishbel the maid curtseyed and left, while Hippolyta finished her own hair.

'Off somewhere grand?' asked Patrick. 'Or have you invited a duchess or two to tea?'

'We have been summoned to take tea with Lady Pinner,' Hippolyta said in mock awe, and explained what had happened. Patrick sat down on the bed and watched her in the looking glass.

'Then she took me at my word. That's very gratifying,' he remarked. 'I thought she would be more stubborn.'

'She seems to have resigned herself to a humbler way of life than she is used to,' said Hippolyta, thinking of the way each of them had been assessed in the street. 'I'm sure we'll do our best to divert her, Mrs. Kynoch out of genuine goodness and the Misses Strong out of curiosity to see how she behaves. They are avid followers of politics, the Misses Strong: I never realised.'

'Are they for or against Reform?' asked Patrick, the question of the moment.

'I'm not sure,' Hippolyta admitted. 'Perhaps against? They seemed to think there was not enough local support to stop the Bill. Dearest,' she added suddenly, hoping the time was right, 'I had some news this morning.'

'Now, that could have sounded less ominous,' said Patrick, straightening up. 'What is it?'

'I had a letter from my mother.'

'She's not coming to stay, is she?' Patrick interrupted, alarmed.

'No, no! No, it's my brother Marcus.'

'Something's the matter? Is he ill?'

Hippolyta laughed.

'No, *he's* coming to stay. He should arrive tomorrow, I believe. Will that be all right?'

'Of course: I like Marcus. Usually,' he added. 'When he is not too - fervent. Will it be all right with Mrs. Riach, do you think?'

'I hope so. I shall have a word, of course.'

'You'd better do so soon. You know she likes to have some warning of these things.'

'I know ... And Marcus can be ... well, you know when we were in Edinburgh last he was being quite ... difficult.'

'Yes, wasn't he?' Patrick reflected for a moment. 'The refusal to drink spirits. And he was becoming interested in politics, too, wasn't he? May I ask why he is coming to visit? Not that he is not most welcome, of course, but it is an unusual time of year to choose.'

'My mother mentioned something about his bringing us some small tokens for Christmas.'

'For Christmas! But surely she could have sent such trifles by the carrier?'

'I know.'

They regarded one another. Neither of them fully trusted Hippolyta's mother: Mrs. Fettes had altogether too many years commanding and controlling under her belt to be able to do anything innocently.

'Well,' said Patrick at last, 'I daresay all will be revealed at some point, and we shall discover the part we are to play – or have already played.'

Hippolyta rose and went to him, hugging him tight. Any man who could put up with her family, even at the distance of Edinburgh, must love her very dearly, almost as much as she loved him.

Dinnet House, even when it was not actually raining, was a gloomy and forbidding place on the outside. It sat, grey and cumbersome, at the end of a shortish, curling carriageway that divided a grassy sward that seemed to have been neglected, then recently scythed when it was too wet. The gravel was sullenly soggy underfoot. Hippolyta concentrated on the happier memories of the house: Major Verney in his pony trap, smiling a welcome; cosy church services in the parlour; and of course her first acquaintance with the white cats that now lived in her own house. The reflections took her safely to the front door where she rang at the bell – a new addition, she noted. The Pinners must intend a few months' stay, at least – or be very particular about their home.

Footsteps hurrying on the gravel behind her made her turn to see Mrs. Kynoch, orange bonnet bobbing, trying to catch her up before the door should be answered.

'I hope this will be beneficial for poor Lady Pinner,' Mrs. Kynoch murmured as soon as she was within range. 'This is not perhaps the most cheerful house in which to be on one's own.'

'But I thought Sir Holroyd was here, too?' Hippolyta asked quickly – she could hear footsteps crossing the hall to the door.

'He is, dear, he is,' said Mrs. Kynoch, with a meaningful look, but at that precise moment the door opened and the grumpy-looking maid whom they had seen earlier admitted them.

'Mrs. Kynoch and Mrs. Napier to see Lady Pinner,' said Mrs. Kynoch quite as if she visited the gentry every day, and the maid curtseyed. Mrs. Kynoch winked at Hippolyta, and followed her into the parlour.

The room was if anything a little overwarm, but half the warmth must have come from the excess of wax candles in every possible position: the effect of the draught as the door opened was of a sudden wave surging across a pond. The Pinners must have taken the house furnished, for Hippolyta recognised some of the furniture from earlier times. Shawls and rugs cleverly arranged brightened the colours and made the room much more in keeping with current fashions. Near the fire, Lady Pinner was arranged on a daybed, and though she made some appearance of trying to rise as they entered, Mrs. Kynoch waved her back down to her reclining position.

'I hope, Lady Pinner, that our visit is not now ill-timed,' she said. Hippolyta saw that indeed, though her face was no paler than earlier – she was beside the fire, after all – there were darker circles under her eyes.

'Not at all, madam,' said Lady Pinner, sitting a little straighter. The effort was more due, Hippolyta thought, to her pride than to good manners. 'My physician says I must have distraction, and distraction is what I shall find. Pray be seated.'

They had no sooner sat than the parlour door opened again, and the maid ushered in Mrs. Douglas and the Strong ladies, who exclaimed loudly over the arrangements that had been made in the room.

'I see you all know the house well,' said Lady Pinner stiffly. 'Perhaps you can tell me a little of the owner? We have not met him.'

'It belongs to a lady, I believe, still,' said Hippolyta a little too quickly. 'She was left it by her uncle, a very pleasant man, who lived here for some years.'

'It can be made warm, at any rate,' said Lady Pinner, apparently oblivious to any awkwardness. 'Sir Holroyd would not hear of staying at the inn or at a hotel. He must have privacy and peace for his work, you know.'

'Of course,' said Miss Strong. 'He'll be very busy, I should think, even though Parliament is prorogued.'

Lady Pinner turned a bored expression on her guest.

'He is endlessly busy,' she said. 'There is not a moment of his day when there are not papers to read, and letters to write, and speeches to make.'

'Is he to make speeches in Aberdeenshire, then?' asked Miss Ada. 'For it seems to me that in terms of reform, our member of parliament might well benefit from a little encouragement.'

Lady Pinner's head swivelled to face the next sister.

'I have very little idea of Sir Holroyd's plans,' she stated.

The parlour door opened once again, and the maid entered, bearing a large tea tray. She arranged the tea on a central table, low enough for Lady Pinner to reach from her daybed, then came forward and presented Lady Pinner with a small glass of milky liquid, which her Ladyship drank obediently, and two small tablets, which she also took. The maid curtseyed and departed.

Lady Pinner made preparations for pouring the tea.

'Is there much business for a man of law in this little village?' she asked the Strongs, then softened the question a little by adding, 'It seems a peaceable, quiet place.'

'There's plenty to keep our brother out of mischief,' said Miss Ada with satisfaction. 'Rents and tacks, wills and inventories, bonds and sasines. Oh, aye, he's happy enough. And he's taken on a man in the nature of being his apprentice, though he's a bittie on the old side to be cried as such.'

'Ada!' cried Miss Strong. 'Lady Pinner will find all that most tedious!'

'Not at all,' Lady Pinner drawled politely. 'Mrs. Kynoch, you have stayed here in the village even after your husband's death, and presumably then you would have had to leave the house you lived in. Did you have no family to take you in, that you have remained here?'

'None, Lady Pinner, and besides,' said Mrs. Kynoch with a smile, 'I am very attached to the place. I am privileged to run a small school in my cottage for such girls in the village who wish to learn.'

'Who wish to learn what?'

'Anything I can teach them, Lady Pinner.'

'Singular.'

'Mrs. Kynoch is capable of teaching not only needlework and cookery, Lady Pinner,' Hippolyta could not resist defending her friend. 'Her pupils learn painting, French and German, accounting and music, and some have gone on to be governesses themselves. In good households.'

'Really?' Lady Pinner eyed Mrs. Kynoch a little doubtfully. 'How very commendable. For girls? And you have many pupils?'

'It varies, my lady. At present I have ten, which is really as many as my little cottage can accommodate.'

'And girls are eager to learn?'

'As much as boys, if not more so!' Mrs. Kynoch laughed.

'And their fathers are willing to let them?'

'Ah, well, sometimes indeed the mothers need them, to look after the younger ones, you know, and to help about the house. But they come when they can.'

'How very curious.' Lady Pinner considered her for a long moment, as if trying to judge whether or not she was truthful. 'And you, Mrs. Napier. Your husband – he is the physician I have met, is he not?'

'He is, Lady Pinner.'

'Well, I find I have some trust in him, though I scarcely know him. He says you are come here from Edinburgh, is that correct?'

'It is indeed.'

'And your father, what is his station?'

'He is an advocate, Lady Pinner. A barrister, in England.'

'I understand they have some considerable standing in Edinburgh.'

'It has been known, Lady Pinner.'

'What brought you here, then?'

Hippolyta smiled.

'My husband studied medicine in Edinburgh, and we met there.'

'And you followed him here? Good gracious.'

Hippolyta had to ask something that had occurred to her when she entered the parlour, with all its memories.

'Dr. Napier and I met in the Episcopal Chapel in Edinburgh, and we worship here in what is sometimes called the English Church. We used, in fact, to worship in this very room, as we have as yet no chapel in the vicinity. If you are a member of the Church of England, Lady Pinner, would you consider allowing us to worship here again? You'll find it a very practical and pretty place to celebrate Communion, and much more convenient than our own parlour, where we are constrained to accommodate the visiting clergyman at present.'

'You keep a clergyman in your parlour?' She regarded Hippolyta with open disbelief. Hippolyta blushed.

'No! Not at all. The clergyman visits once a week in the summer, once a fortnight in the winter, and if the roads are particularly bad we are reduced to once a month. He has to travel some distance, depending on where he is coming from. But the congregation is growing, and not just with summer guests, Lady Pinner, if only we had a little more room ...' She tailed off, suddenly aware of the company around her: two wives of ministers, and the Strongs, stalwart members of the Established Church. She subsided, though still eyed Lady Pinner with hope.

'I attend a Congregational church in London,' she said at last. 'Here I have already found the Kirk most welcoming. I regret, Mrs. Napier, that I am unlikely to host English services in my parlour.'

'Thank you, Lady Pinner,' said Hippolyta, humbly. She felt Mrs. Kynoch put out a hand to her, and took it, squeezing it briefly.

'My lady!' There came a sudden clatter at the door, and a moment of confusion. A man entered the room, tall and, for his age, thought Hippolyta, recovering, quite handsome. His hair was bright white and swept back from a high forehead, and his face was rosy though well sculpted. A broad chest and a narrow waist tapered down to fashionable trousers of a superb cut. Hippolyta experienced a moment's confusion: the face looked as if it should exude kindness and cheerfulness, but almost against its nature it was stern and hostile, sharp blue eyes darting about to take in the unexpected presence of guests in his wife's parlour. For very obviously, this was Sir Holroyd Pinner, master of this house and honourable member of His Majesty's Opposition in the House of Commons. Hippolyta did not know whether to curtsey, salute, or faint on the spot.

Chapter Three

'Ladies,' said Sir Holroyd abruptly, and Hippolyta was shocked to see his handsome features marred by his teeth. They were so jumbled in his mouth they looked as if they were leaving in a panic. She had to concentrate not to stare at them, and to listen to their host whose voice, at least, was authoritative. 'I was unaware that Lady Pinner was entertaining.'

'May I present Sir Holroyd Pinner?' murmured Lady Pinner, not looking at him. 'Mrs. Kynoch, Mrs. Napier, and the Misses Strong. Oh, and Mrs. Douglas.'

'Delighted to make your acquaintance.' He bowed generally to the room, but Hippolyta was sure he had noted each of them and fixed them to their names. 'I shall not intrude upon your cosy chatter,' he went on, and the Misses Strong found it hard to mask their disappointment: Miss Ada had fixed the parliamentarian with a piercing stare since he entered the room.

'Was there something you wanted, Sir Holroyd?' Lady Pinner asked.

'I wondered if you knew where the child is at present.'

'Susanna has taken her outside to the garden for a little air, I believe.'

'Very good. I hoped that might be the case: the weather has lifted a little.'

'Indeed.'

Sir Holroyd glanced about, and noticed Ada Strong's intelligent interest pinning him like an insect on a board.

'Perhaps I might stay for one cup, if I may?'

'I'm sure you may,' said Lady Pinner, and rang for another cup and saucer. The maid sent to fetch it blinked when she saw Sir Holroyd sitting amongst the ladies.

'I hope Miss Pinner is thriving in this healthy climate?' Mrs. Kynoch asked.

'I believe she is, madam,' said Sir Holroyd, and Hippolyta had to look away from the teeth again. 'The air here is as beneficial as I had been led to believe, thought the weather is … well, it is December, after all. What can one expect?'

'It is fortunate that you have been able to venture so far from London to accompany Lady Pinner,' said Miss Strong. 'You must find life very busy there at present.'

'Well, of course, the fight to oppose the Reform Bill takes up every minute of the day when I am there.' He smiled, assuming their support, and Hippolyta could almost hear his teeth fighting for position. 'Here at least it is all at a distance: I am sure the break will be beneficial not only for our daughter's health but also for mine.'

'You do not plan to campaign, then, and speechify, while you are here?' asked Miss Ada, with just an edge to her voice.

'Not at all,' said Sir Holroyd comfortably. 'Admiral Gordon is indeed an admirable M.P., and very strong against Reform.'

'He has not spoken much on the subject in the House, if the papers are to be relied upon,' said Miss Ada. Lady Pinner gave a short, exasperated sigh.

'I am afraid Lady Pinner is still not strong enough to cope with the cut and thrust of political conversation,' said Sir Holroyd, throwing his wife a look which Hippolyta could not interpret. 'I think I shall see if I can find our daughter and bring her in. I should be delighted to present her to you. She is a perfect infant in every way!'

He rose and left the room, and Miss Strong dealt Ada a particularly sharp nudge, though she said nothing.

There was silence for a moment, during which Hippolyta thought she could hear the humming of so many candles like a beehive in summer. Was it her imagination, or had the sky outside the room suddenly grown darker? It was hard to tell, with all the light in here.

'Oh!' said Mrs. Kynoch with sudden relief, 'there is to be an assembly, of sorts, in the inn on Friday night. I hope you will favour it with your presence. It will be a respectable occasion, with the best families in the village and any guests at the inn who are disposed to attend.'

Lady Pinner did not look immediately dismissive, and Hippolyta took up the argument.

'There is not a great deal of room for dancing, but we usually manage a few couples, with care. And the food is excellent.'

'It is always entertaining,' Miss Ada put in, 'and rarely goes on too late. It is not strenuous at all.'

'It sounds delightful,' said Lady Pinner, with muted enthusiasm. She straightened her back again, as if reminding herself of her physician's advice to find entertainment. 'I shall have to see what Sir Holroyd intends.'

'Of course. I am sure he would find it very refreshing,' said Miss Ada, clearly hoping to pin down her political prey and interrogate him at the inn, if she could not in his house.

The door opened again, sweeping another draught through the candle flames, and Sir Holroyd appeared with an infant in his arms, swathed in white wool up to the armpits against any possible chill, but with her pink arms healthily bare. A nursemaid followed, shutting the door softly behind them, and stood attendance, her gaze fondly on the child.

'Here she is!' said Sir Holroyd, sitting back in his chair and propping the child up in his lap. 'Maria Pinner, say good day to your guests!'

Maria Pinner gave a winning smile, and dribbled a good deal. She was inevitably passed around the cooing ladies, with the nursery maid appearing here and there to apply a cloth or adjust a wrapping.

'She is delightful!' said Mrs. Kynoch, handing her back at last to the maid. For a moment, both Sir Holroyd and Lady Pinner smiled. Lady Pinner's face was transformed.

'You think – ' she paused for a moment, then asked 'Do you think she looks healthy?'

'Bonny and braw,' said Mrs. Kynoch definitely. 'And a good weight, for six months.'

'That's ... that's good, then.' Suddenly Lady Pinner looked very young, and not at all sure of herself. But all the ladies nodded – though not one of them had had a child except for Mrs. Douglas, all had watched and held and dandled the children of the village and of relatives, and knew a healthy bairn when they saw one. Sir

Holroyd beamed at his daughter in deep satisfaction. The maid held her a little away from herself, on her thin hip, and smiled at little Miss Pinner.

'I'd better take her off, now, my lady, before …'

'Of course. Thank you, Susanna.'

The maid departed.

'Well, I should return to my letters, I daresay,' said Sir Holroyd, though he seemed more comfortable now than he had been since he came in.

'You have a kindly nursery maid there, I see,' said Miss Strong.

'A good girl, yes. She has been with Maria from the start, and is very attached to her.'

'Most competent,' added Lady Pinner.

'Alas, work!' This time Sir Holroyd managed to rise from his chair.

'We should be going, too,' said Mrs. Kynoch, looking about at the others. 'Lady Pinner will need her rest after all this excitement.'

'Not at all,' said Lady Pinner, though she did look tired again. She rang the bell for the maid. Mrs. Kynoch rose and the others followed.

'Pray do not rise, Lady Pinner,' she said again. 'We shall do very well with our cloaks. And do think about the assembly on Friday: it is always diverting!'

'I shall, I shall.' Lady Pinner managed a small smile again.

Sir Holroyd stood with them in the hallway while the maid helped with their cloaks. Hippolyta noticed that she had another glass of something ready, presumably her mistress' next dose of medicine. She wondered what Patrick had prescribed, besides more entertainment.

'Good day to you, ladies! It was a pleasure to meet you all!'

They flurried out through the door, tangling wide skirts, and found themselves in a darker world than the one they had left earlier. The rain had begun again, the ground was muddy, and even as they reached the end of the driveway the heavy drops of water were becoming colder and slushier.

'It will snow soon!' declared Miss Ada, waving a gloved hand at the pinkish sky.

'Thank goodness!' murmured Hippolyta.

'Oh, dreadful, dreadful!' she heard Mrs. Douglas moan beside her. She took Mrs. Douglas' arm firmly, and supported her down the slippery road back into the village.

On the green they went their separate ways, the Strongs to their house at the top of it, Mrs. Kynoch to her cottage on the other side, Mrs. Douglas like a little mouse scurrying away to the door of the manse, and Hippolyta the furthest, all the way down to the bottom corner of the green. Her cloak was heavy with sleet by the time she reached the front door, and she was much relieved to hurry inside and stand, dripping, in the stone-flagged hallway, while Ishbel the maid hauled the cloak off her shoulders. Patrick appeared at the door of his study.

'Is that snow?' he asked, tentatively touching the rapidly melting particles on her cloak as Ishbel brushed it down.

'Just about!' Hippolyta said. 'At last!'

'But it's soaking outside: it will never lie,' said Patrick, going to open the front door again to see what the afternoon promised. A thin, unpromising coat of greyish white almost floated on the wet ground, vanishing into blackness around the bushes at the gate. 'No, I fear you will be disappointed again, my dear.'

'Bother,' said Hippolyta. 'I just want some light!'

Patrick shut the door as Ishbel disappeared to drape the cloak by the kitchen fire.

'Come into the study and warm up, anyway, and tell me all about your tea engagement.'

He waved her into the well-lit room, where she took her usual place by the fire and stretched her fingers towards it to thaw.

'I cannot say that I was much taken with either Sir Holroyd or Lady Pinner,' she admitted, 'though Miss Pinner is charming. But with such parents she may quickly grow out of that.'

'Did you meet the nurserymaid? Susanna, I believe her name is?'

'Yes: she seemed quite devoted to the child. That may be the saving of her, if she does not spoil her,' said Hippolyta, sounding, to herself, very old. 'And Lady Pinner says they will attend the Kirk while they are here, and are not Anglicans at all, so that puts paid to my plan of returning our services to Dinnet House.'

'I had no idea you had such a plan, my dear,' said Patrick,

'though it would have been a good one. We are very cramped in here, particularly in the summer. I shall have to take to playing the fiddle for the hymns soon, perhaps outside the window, for there is little room for me to sit at the piano.'

Hippolyta laughed.

'Well, do not play outside in the winter, at any rate! Oh, but Lady Pinner can be very haughty. And sometimes she does not look at all well. Her maid brought her medicine twice while we were there.'

'Well, I hope it was the one I gave her, and not some silly concoction she has bought elsewhere.'

'I didn't ask.'

'I have not met Sir Holroyd – is he haughty, too?'

'He is more approachable, in a way,' said Hippolyta, considering, 'and very handsome, were it not for his teeth. They are most irregular. And he seems devoted to his daughter, and very proud of her. Lady Pinner is less so.'

'The loss of her child's twin has perhaps caused her to find the surviving child a difficult prospect,' said Patrick. 'I have heard it happen. And the opposite, a need to cling to the surviving child knowing that the other is dead.'

'Well, she has definitely gone down the first road, I should say,' said Hippolyta. 'And she seemed none too fond of her husband, either. In fact, the whole atmosphere was extremely hostile …' She tailed away, staring into the fire, reflecting.

'What is it, my dear?'

'I said that to Mrs. Kynoch, and she disagreed. Well, she said there was hostility, yes. But she said she thought the household a deeply unhappy one.'

'And it is the kind of thing about which Mrs. Kynoch is usually right, is it not?' asked Patrick, with a smile. He knew it was the kind of thing about which Hippolyta would like usually to be right, but she was a good deal younger than Mrs. Kynoch.

'It is,' said Hippolyta with a sigh. 'I suppose I should do my best to remember them in my prayers.'

Hippolyta woke in the night, convinced at first that she had overslept. The light that slanted through the edges of the shutters was odd, not quite dawn, not quite night. She wondered if some lamp had been set up on the village green, and slid out of bed to tiptoe to the window: Patrick had not been called out that night, and she had no wish to disturb a quiet night for him.

The shutter stuck a little and opened with a slight thump, and she clutched it as if that would still the sound. Then she gasped.

The world outside was white, and bathed in starlight.

For a long time she stared, her artist's eye taking in shapes and shadows, light and dark, then she breathed out, and closed the shutter gently. Holding the images tightly in her mind, she slid quietly back into bed, and painted pictures behind closed eyes until she fell asleep.

'Well, it settled, then,' said Patrick, surveying the garden with some dismay. Hippolyta shook snow from her skirts and boots as she joined him at the kitchen door: she had been digging out the hen run and the pig house. The door to Patrick's little dispensary was almost blocked with snow.

'Isn't it wonderful?' Hippolyta greeted him with a kiss. 'I'm going to paint after breakfast.'

'I hope you have enough white paint,' Patrick remarked.

'Oh, but it's not all white! It's blue and grey and cream and yellow – and lavender, even, under the trees. I can't wait!'

'It's pretty deep,' said Patrick, poking the crisp surface of the snowfall with his toe. 'I hope the mail coach makes it through.'

'Are you waiting for something important? Oh, Marcus!' Hippolyta's hand went guiltily to her mouth. She had completely forgotten her brother's intended arrival. 'Oh, no! What if he is stuck somewhere? What if the coach goes off the road? How will the driver even know where the road is? Oh, I must go down to the inn at once!'

'No, you must not,' said Patrick, taking her arm and guiding her back into the stuffy kitchen.

'Is that Mr. Fettes you're talking of?' demanded Mrs. Riach, the housekeeper. She was working at the stove with Ishbel, cooking porridge and eggs. 'I thought he was coming the day?'

'He should be, Mrs. Riach,' said Hippolyta. She glanced anxiously at the kitchen clock. 'We were just wondering if the coach will make it through the snow.'

'Ach, there's hardly snaw at all, Mrs. Napier. Yon coach'll

easy make it this distance.' She returned her attention briefly to the eggs, then said 'I've made up the bed in the spare room for Mr. Fettes, and I left the windaes open like you said. But I've shut the door. He might like his fresh air, but there's no sense in the rest of us sharing it.'

Hippolyta met Patrick's eye.

'That's very sensible, Mrs. Riach. In any case he might change his mind, in this weather.'

'He might, if he has any wit,' said Mrs. Riach, in a tone that implied that her expectations were not high.

'Where's young Wullie this morning?' asked Patrick, noticing that their serving boy and his dog were not in their usual place.

'He's away hame to fetch his winter boots. He hadna them with him.'

'Well, I hope his feet don't freeze on the way there.' It was not far to Wullie's house in the village, anyway, and knowing Wullie he would be moving at speed.

Wullie was indeed back safely, carrying his winter boots, within the hour. His cap was twice its normal size with the snow lying on it.

'I near missed my way altogether, though I've lived here all my life!' he exclaimed, though the life in question had not yet amounted to more than ten years. Hippolyta hid a smile as he knocked the snow off his shoulders and on to the kitchen floor. Ishbel tutted, and handed him a cloth to wipe it up. Tam the dog, who had accompanied him, made straight for the fireplace and began to wash. A cat or two made way for him out of consideration for their own fur.

'The food all looks perfect, Mrs. Riach,' said Hippolyta, who was in the kitchen making sure. Her brother Marcus was a hearty eater, being a young and busy man. She wondered again what there was to bring him up to Ballater at this time of year, when the roads were so bad, when the courts were open and there was business to be done, and all his friends no doubt enjoying the Edinburgh season. The tone of her mother's letter had been imperious, as usual, and empresses rarely felt the need to explain. Yet in Hippolyta's experience, Mrs. Fettes' lack of explanation sometimes concealed awkward facts: she hoped Marcus had not fallen for some girl her parents considered unsuitable. Marcus, unless he had grown out of it since she had last seen him, was a man very much a victim of his own emotions, though more usually over causes than over people. A heartbroken Marcus, snow-marooned in winter Ballater, could be hard to put up with. Still, if that were the case he could do little harm up here: if the snow grew worse and the mails were stopped, he would not even be able to send passionate letters to some sweetheart. He would just have to cool his heels and learn to do without her.

She returned to the parlour. The breakfast dishes had been cleared away, Patrick had retreated to his study to gird his loins for a visit to a patient, and the fire had made the room warm but not suffocating. Cats were arranged on several pieces of furniture: Franklin, she noted, was disposing of a piece of leftover bacon under the table. She hoped he would finish it, and not abandon the last scrap for someone to find later. She pressed one note on the piano, letting it resound just a little, but she was not musical and moved away to stare through the window. The snow was falling thick and strong, mattressing the world outside, or what she could see of it. She tried to imagine what it would be like to drive from Aberdeen on a day like this, when you could barely see where the road might lie. Would they even try? The horses would not be happy. The passengers on the roof would be turned to ice, coated in heavy flakes, the driver and the postilion too, except the postilion would be on the ground half the time digging snow away from the wheels. And inside the coach, would that be any better? Pressed up to strangers for warmth, little windows darkened by the steady fall of flakes, wondering what was happening outside.

Hypnotised by the snowfall, she stood half imagining the house was rising through the silence. Then she shook her head: there was nothing she could do at present. She lit an extra candle, pulled out her paints, and tried to capture on paper the scene she had memorised so carefully in the middle of the night.

By late morning, Patrick was back, tipping snow off his coat at the door and with an excited gleam in his eyes at having overcome the odds, reached his patient and returned. Mrs. Riach had thick broth and hot bannocks ready: one could not, at any rate, fault her cooking.

'I suppose you are determined to go and meet your brother at the inn,' he said, once he was settled at the parlour table.

'I must: he has only been here once before, and will have no idea where to go.'

'Even if he had been here a thousand times before, I am not sure he would know where to go today,' said Patrick with grim satisfaction. 'I nearly lost my way twice. Well, I'm sure I shan't be able to stop you, but I shall come with you.'

'Of course. Thank you.' She tried to assume the expression of a demure wife being protected by her valiant husband, but found they simply grinned at each other instead, happy to be spending part of the day in each other's company, facing a little challenge together.

But it was not really a little challenge. Hippolyta had been looking forward to being outside in the fresh air but the air was not fresh: it was cold and thick, and hard to breathe. They linked arms firmly, and stepped out into the muffling silence. They could not hear a footstep but their own, lightly crunching: they could not hear a voice, or the chatter of a bird, or the bark of a dog. They tunnelled through laden bushes to the gate, and emerged on to the green.

After a moment's walking in the odd grey light, she realised that there were other people about, but she could have been thrown from a coach into a town full of strangers. She recognised nobody. Size, shape, character were all lost in the grey-white haze, and if she had been told that no humans were there at all, that a troupe of performing bears were moving silently through the snow, she would have had no evidence against it.

She was dazed by the short walk down to the inn, and almost as dazed to reach it, crashing back into sound and warmth as though she had been travelling between worlds. There were already a few in the inn's hot parlour, waiting for the coach: a man expecting a letter, one of Strachan's shop boys there for a parcel, and the innkeeper himself standing by, checking his heavy watch. Patrick ordered hot punch and it came steaming and quick: there must have been a pan already prepared.

The coach was due at half past two, and was rarely late. But today the time came and went, and the hour after it came and went, and still there was no sign of the coach. Patrick, usually a patient man, twitched.

'Have you someone to go to see?' Hippolyta asked, anxious in case she was holding Patrick back. He glanced at the parlour's longcase clock.

'I should go, if I want to be back before it is properly dark.' Already the windows were black, though the innkeeper, as though signalling the coach, kept the shutters open. 'It's only a house behind the church.'

'Then go,' said Hippolyta. 'I am quite safe here, and when the coach comes Marcus and I can help each other up the hill.'

'If he's on the coach,' said Patrick, and Hippolyta made a face. Her brother was not the most reliable of men. 'And if the coach comes at all, and has not stopped in Aberdeen in despair.' He rose, and pulled on his damp coat. 'Well, if you are not returned when I go home, I shall come back here and fetch you. No sense in adventuring on your own in the dark if you don't have to.'

'I suppose not,' said Hippolyta, 'though you will be!'

'I can help Marcus carry his luggage, if he has arrived,' Patrick insisted. She smiled up at him. The candlelight made his hair spun gold, and his eyes were very blue. She sighed in delight.

'I hope we're back before you, then, and save you another expedition. What will Ballater do if its doctor catches a chill?'

They squeezed each other's hands, and Patrick departed into the night, waving at her as he passed the window.

She sat again, wishing she had brought something to do – a book to read, a sketchpad to work on, embroidery to stitch. Across the room the shop boy from Strachan's lounged, quite happy to be inactive during the working day. She slipped a little notebook and pencil from her reticule, and discreetly sketched him, legs outstretched to the fire, revelling in unaccustomed luxury. At any other time he would have been sent to wait in the stableyard, but that would have been inhuman this evening.

Someone must have been outside, though, for at long last a shout went up from the gate. Too eager, the waiters in the parlour pulled on their shawls and hats and coats and hurried out into the snow. It was hard to tell at first what on earth anyone could have shouted about: the snow was still falling, and it was almost impossible to see further down the road than the end of the inn wall. But the stablelad who had shouted cried 'Hush!' and they all stopped to listen. Under the soft muffling of the snow, they could just hear a thick padding sound and, behind it, a low rumble. Then the boy cried out again, and pointed. It was a light.

Chapter Four

The innkeeper, the stablelad and the shop boy ran forward towards the light, while the man awaiting his letter, who was rather elderly, waited under the shelter of the gateway with Hippolyta. The light neared, then lurched and wobbled, and they heard a horse neigh in brief alarm. Hippolyta could not resist, and plunged into the snowy road after the others. The snow was finer now, though still falling, and she could see them clearly, black cutouts ahead of her. She slithered quickly and caught up with them just as they met the man with the lantern, who, by its light, looked exhausted. He panted,

'Coach,' as if they had thought it was anything else. The innkeeper snatched him around the waist to support him, and the shopboy took the lantern. In his other hand, the man held the bridle of the leading horse. Hippolyta eased it out of his stiff fingers.

'No, it's the horses!' said the man.

'Now, now, lad, Mrs. Napier kens fine what she's doing,' said the innkeeper gently, and helped the man out of the way. Hippolyta was focussed on the horse, which was understandably nervous.

'Come along, now,' she told it softly. 'Not far to go to a good stable: it's well worth that last bit of effort. I'm sure you've had a dreadful day of it, haven't you? But you've done terribly well. I'm sure no other team could have done it, could they?' She eased the tired animal forwards, by force of will and blandishments, and in a moment the team caught their breath and the coach began to move again, slowly. 'See the lights up ahead? Hardly any distance at all, really. Good fellow! You're doing splendidly!'

She was aware of odd bits of digging and sweeping around her as she led the horse forward, and was thankful that the road was straight all the way to the inn's stableyard: they would only have to turn at the gate, and that was already swept and ready for them. The poor stablelad must have been out periodically all afternoon preparing it. The lumbering coach would hardly slide now, with a good flat piece of well-made road. It followed like a lifeless thing behind them, ominous and dark, and she shivered even as she prayed that Marcus was arrived safely.

The gateway loomed, and some pressure from the reins helped her steer the horses through and into the yard. The stablelad ran to unhitch the poor animals, and the innkeeper pushed the frozen postilion in through the door to the warmth and to the servants' waiting attentions, but it was a moment before anyone on the coach moved at all. Hippolyta's heart sank. Then the door opened with a kick, and a man blundered out, missing the steps and landing awkwardly on the cobbles. The lights from the inn lit him well. Dark brows and a quick, clever glance met Hippolyta with surprise, but passed on. It was not Marcus.

The man turned, and helped a woman down from the doorway after him. Hippolyta tried to see past them, but the coach was now empty. The innkeeper was attending to the couple who disappeared quickly inside the inn. Servants unloaded boxes from the back of the coach, and one clambered up on to the front of the coach with a cup of punch for the coachman, giving him enough warmth to thaw a little before he ventured off his perch. There came a groan from the top of the coach, and Hippolyta looked up in shock, jerking snow from her bonnet.

'Is someone up there?' she called. There was another groan, and two misshapen heaps, that she had mistaken for canvas-wrapped bundles of luggage, suddenly shifted. One half-stood, revealing himself to be something like human, and turned to lower himself over the side of the coach. The other, muttering what sounded like heartfelt curses, followed stiffly.

Hippolyta stood back to allow them space to descend. The first was nimble enough, but so wrapped about in layers of cloth that he could hardly bend his arms and legs. He gave up halfway, jumped, slipped on the snowy cobbles, and sat down. Before she could go to his aid, the other passenger had also reached the halfway point, lost control of his frozen fingers, and fell backwards on to the first man.

'Well, I must be grateful for one thing, sir,' said the first man, his very voice stiff. 'I thought I had lost all sense of feeling, but you seem to have restored it. Ouch,' he added, with emphasis.

'You are most welcome, sir,' said the second man politely. 'And I must return my thanks, for you very kindly broke my fall.'

They both scrambled up, apparently free of any serious injury, and bowed to each other.

'I trust we have reached our destination,' said the first man. His accent was now identifiable as English. 'Though from its appearance we could as easily be in one of the chillier levels of Hell. I must thank you for your excellent companionship on a journey I hope I may never have to repeat.'

'And you, too, sir,' said the other. 'I am heartily glad that we were able to offer one another some support. Otherwise I doubt either of us would be here to tell the tale.'

'In that you are quite correct, sir,' said the Englishman. 'And this, I suppose, is the inn. Well, I doubt I shall find any other accommodation this evening, so the inn it is.'

Hippolyta stepped forward, making both men jump.

'Marcus, good day to you,' she said to the second man, slightly cross with her brother for not noticing her. 'Sir, are you unwilling to stay at the inn?'

'Hippolyta! Mr. Elphick, this is the sister of whom I spoke. Hippolyta, may I present Jedediah Elphick, who has travelled with me from Edinburgh?'

'And from London before that,' added Mr. Elphick, bowing. 'Delighted to make your acquaintance, madam. I trust this weather is not typical for Ballater? I'm already wearing two coats and I can no longer feel my feet at all.'

Hippolyta laughed, as she was clearly meant to.

'Perhaps you should have come in the summer, Mr. Elphick: it is delightful then, if a little busier. Now, have you an objection to the inn?'

'Only to its prices, madam. I am but a poor journalist. I had secured myself accommodation in a small household somewhere in the village, but I have no idea how to find it just at present.'

'It could prove difficult,' Hippolyta agreed. 'Why not come with us? Come and have dinner and we shall sort you out, one way or another. And you can tell us all about your journey, for I am sure you will make an excellent story of it between you!'

'Sing for my supper, eh?' Mr. Elphick, as far as one could see, looked gratified at the idea. 'Would you mind enduring my company for a few more hours, then, Mr. Fettes?'

'Not at all.' Indeed, Marcus' pale face was happy.

'Then that is settled. Do you wish to leave luggage here or bring it with you?'

'I can manage mine,' said Marcus at once. 'I have only these two.' He hefted a bag and a small tin trunk.

'And I travel light too,' said Mr. Elphick. He had only the one bag. He glanced back at the coach, now empty, and at the coachman, being led carefully into the inn, clutching his fingers together as if afraid they would fall off otherwise. 'I shall be heartily glad of a fire and food, madam: would you mind if we set off straightaway?'

'My very thought,' agreed Hippolyta, and led the way out of the stableyard.

'Mr. Elphick, my dear,' Hippolyta explained. They had met Patrick halfway down the main street, but they had saved greetings and introductions until they were back in their cosy parlour. Mr. Elphick sneezed.

'Cats,' he explained, looking shame-faced. 'I'm so sorry. I love them, but something about them makes my eyes run.' His eyes were indeed watery, and widely anxious.

'Oh!' said Hippolyta, 'that's unfortunate. We have seven.'

'Seven!'

'And usually a hen,' Patrick added. 'But the rest are outside. We normally keep the cats out of the guest rooms, though.' He stepped out to ask Mrs. Riach to make up the other guest room for Mr. Elphick.

Ishbel, particularly attentive to Marcus, had already brought hot punch on their arrival and now removed their snowy coats with Wullie's help. Marcus and Mr. Elphick, quickly changed in their rooms into dry clothes, seated themselves, Marcus with some elegance in the very latest evening cut. Mr. Elphick, whose clothes were a little more serviceable, cast him an up-and-down glance of uncertainty, but distracted himself with his handkerchief. Two cats had immediately made straight for him, alert to his vulnerability and possibly intrigued by the scent of freshly dabbed eau-de-cologne. Hippolyta grabbed one of them, but missed the other. Mr. Elphick manfully allowed it to nest on his lap, and scratched its head. He was not at all what Hippolyta had expected from the word 'journalist'. In his forties, she supposed, he had a pleasant, rosy face, crinkly brown whiskers and hair, and eyes which though intelligent enough showed their owner was not yet quite at his ease. Even with several layers removed he was not a slim man, but he was certainly less bulky. Marcus, by contrast, was fair and angular, easily identifiable as Hippolyta's brother, though he was a couple of years older.

'Seven cats, Pol?' Marcus asked. 'You haven't added to the collection?'

'No, not at all. Well, we have a pig, now.'

'A pig.' Marcus groaned.

'She belonged to an old man in Glenmuick, and he died, and none of his neighbours wanted it. They're a bit funny about pigs in Glenmuick.'

'And it didn't occur to you to stock up on bacon and ham, I suppose?'

'No! She's ... well, she's in an interesting condition.'

'Oh, no: piglets! Mr. Elphick, you will no doubt have concluded very quickly that my sister is soft-hearted to the point of foolishness, and where animals are concerned she has no idea when enough is enough. And yet she persists in eating their flesh, which as every good medical man knows ...' he eyed Patrick's chair for a moment, challenging, 'is deleterious to both beast and man.'

'You're not eating meat now!' cried Hippolyta. 'What am I going to tell Mrs. Riach?'

'Oh, I shall be no trouble! Some lightly poached eggs will be perfectly good. And some cheese. I prefer the milder kinds, as you know.'

Hippolyta drew breath, but found she had no words. Mr. Elphick blinked and bravely dived in.

'I saw – forgive me, Mrs. Napier – I saw that her gift with animals brought us safely to the inn this evening, anyway,' he remarked, with a smile. Hippolyta felt herself blush.

'I like horses,' she said quickly. 'I don't like to see them worried.'

Patrick returned, smiling serenely at the guests. He seemed to manage Mrs. Riach much better than she did, Hippolyta thought a little ruefully. She never felt serene after asking the housekeeper to do something beyond the established routine. And anyway, he was not yet aware of Marcus' newfound aversion to meat.

'Dinner is almost ready,' he announced. 'Would anyone like more punch?'

'You know that spirits are not at all good for you,' said Marcus.

'In excess, perhaps,' said Patrick easily. He was used to Marcus' notions.

'I'm not at all sure that distillers of usquebaugh would agree with you, my dear sir!' said Mr. Elphick in surprise. 'Are not the Highlands of this country filled with your countrymen, coaxing medicinal spirits from barley and springwater? And it is sold everywhere as a tonic for invalids.'

'Very true,' said Patrick. 'And brandy or rum was the best way of warming you this evening, you have to admit.'

'The medical profession will have to admit its mistakes one day,' said Marcus darkly. He missed Patrick's little smile. 'There is a great deal we have still to learn.'

'There is indeed,' said Patrick. 'I should be the first to admit it. Now, tell me, have you and Mr. Elphick discussed politics yet? I am sure that would be a very interesting conversation over dinner. And here is Ishbel now to announce it.'

They all rose, and Hippolyta led the way to the dining room, glaring at Patrick. Politics over the dinner table? With a stranger, with the country in the state it was in? What was he thinking of? He met her eyes with a glint in his own, and she sighed.

But Mr. Elphick proved more than adequate to the task.

'My brother is active in support of Reform,' Hippolyta explained when Patrick once again touched on the subject, once they were seated. She was not sure whether to sound apologetic or not.

'Is he indeed?' Elphick regarded Marcus with interest. 'Have you been down to Westminster to see any of the debates?'

'No, I haven't been able to,' Marcus admitted.

'You should. See if you can get down after Christmas, when the bill goes back to the Lords. My, you'll see some sights! If you can take the discomfort, of course.'

'Do you report on Parliament?' Marcus, who had evidently taken to Elphick in the course of the journey, now looked upon him with something like awe.

'Oh, all the time! You need your strength for a job like that, though. Never mind Reform: what parliament needs more urgently is rebuilding. A busy night in the House and you can scarcely breathe, summer or winter.'

'Who have you seen speak?' Marcus dismissed the practicalities very quickly.

'Well, the Duke of Wellington, and Peel, of course. Sir Holroyd Pinner,' Elphick began, but Marcus was not going to be impressed by them, and he added quickly. 'Lord Grey – he's lost his looks, but not his grandeur. That man can talk!'

'Oh, yes, Lord Grey!' said Marcus happily. Grey was clearly one of his Whig heroes.

'Earl Spencer – everyone likes him. Brougham, the Speaker.'

'He's ferocious in the cause! He and Broughton are like a pair of savage hounds, defending their master against all attacks! Even if ...' He changed his mind, distracted by the glory of the man before him. 'Have you been to Holland House?'

'The hotbed of the Whigs? Once, yes.' Elphick was already easier, and Hippolyta silently thanked Patrick for finding a subject that would help their guest to relax, however accidentally. 'And I was there the night they stoned Apsley House, though that was not an honourable thing, in the end.'

'The Duke of Wellington's house? They stoned it?' Hippolyta asked. She had always admired the Iron Duke, though his heroic days of Waterloo had happened before she was born.

'They did, because it was not lit up to celebrate the Reform Bill passing through the Commons. But there was a good reason for his not lighting up, aside from the fact that he opposes Reform: his wife was lying dead in the house at the time, awaiting the funeral.' His rosy face was sombre. Hippolyta was appalled.

'How dreadful! The poor man!'

'He should have had the courage to come out and tell the protestors, then,' said Marcus.

'You question the Duke of Wellington's courage?' Hippolyta was even more shocked, and Marcus, who knew his argument was a little weak, subsided.

'You are not for Reform, then, madam?' Elphick asked her quickly. He helped himself as directed to some beef pudding, and passed the plate towards Marcus. Marcus shook his head in mild disgust.

'Very rich,' he muttered. He deliberated spooned more potatoes on to his plate, and set to with emphasis.

'I have no vote, Mr. Elphick!' said Hippolyta. 'It matters little whether I am for Reform or against it!'

'But you have a mind, and an opinion, and influence, no doubt,' said Elphick with a smile.

'Oh, she has all those!' agreed Patrick, following the conversation with interest. Hippolyta felt a little ashamed that she was not better informed. The papers had been tediously stuffed with Reform stories, who said this, who shouted that, for months.

'I ... I worry that Reform might only be the start,' she said at last. 'One hears so much about France, and King Louis, and then all the terrible things that happened there fifty years ago. I know King George was not well thought of by many, but King William seems very popular, and regardless, I should hate to live in a country where they chop the heads off anyone with a title. What if they should not stop there, too? Is it not alarming?'

'But the Reform Bill has been so watered down,' said Marcus, 'that it is scarcely anything any more. And some of the things it sets out to reform are so ridiculous! You've heard of Old Sarum?'

'Yes ... I think so,' said Hippolyta, not entirely sure. She made a point in her mind of finding Patrick's newspapers and rereading them properly. Marcus sighed sharply at her.

'It's a hill, in Wiltshire, just outside Salisbury. It returns two members to Parliament, despite the fact that no one lives there. Then there's Manchester – you've heard of Manchester?' he asked her with heavy irony.

'Of course I've heard of Manchester,' she snapped back.

'No Members of Parliament at all. None. A massive population, but just because the town has newly come to its populous status, it has no representation.'

'But that's just because of its history!'

'Exactly. Why should so many people have no vote just because of a twist of historical fate?'

Hippolyta sat back, frowning. She would have to consider all this, but she was not going to change her mind just because her brother told her to. Instead she changed the subject.

'The government should be doing something about the typhus, though: that's more urgent.'

'Oh, yes,' said Elphick. 'I hear it's as far as Newcastle. Do your fellow physicians take precautions, this far north?' he asked Patrick.

'It's hard to know what to do,' Patrick admitted. 'We're hoping that the cold weather will keep it contained further south. Good ventilation and clean linen seem to deter infection – and of course there are those now selling pastils to burn against it.'

'I smelled some in Aberdeen,' Hippolyta put in. 'They were vile. I'd almost rather have typhus.'

'You really wouldn't,' said her husband, with a smile. 'But I'm not sure they do much good. You would be better to open the windows.'

'Always,' said Marcus at once. 'I'm glad to see your housekeeper remembered that I like my windows open.'

'She did,' said Hippolyta mildly. Mrs. Riach had not been likely to forget it: on Marcus' previous visit, several squirrels had entered through the window, and caused considerable damage. Mrs. Riach herself, in the dining room to serve the pudding, snorted indelicately.

'By the way,' said Hippolyta, quickly, 'you mentioned Sir Holroyd Pinner, Mr. Elphick. Did you know he is staying in the village? Spa town?' she corrected herself. Mr. Elphick's kindly eyes opened wide, some of his nerves returned. He blinked rapidly.

'Is he, now? I did wonder if he had gone somewhere for Lady Pinner's health.'

'Well, he has, and it is here,' said Hippolyta, always proud of Ballater's reputation as a place to recuperate. 'I called on her only yesterday.'

'Her health is improving, then, I hope?'

'She can stay ill for a while,' said Marcus ungraciously, 'if it keeps her husband away from the Commons. He's a dangerous man against Reform.'

'He's very anxious about his wife,' said Hippolyta, reprimanding him. Even so, she was not quite sure that she was speaking the truth. Sir Holroyd had looked neither dangerous nor anxious.

Mr. Elphick was seized by an enormous yawn.

'Oh! I must apologise, Mrs. Napier! A long journey, a warm room and good food and drink: even your conversation cannot keep me awake much longer, I fear!'

'We should let you both get to bed,' said Patrick at once. 'Marcus, I'm sure you are exhausted, too.'

'I must confess I am,' said Marcus, flashing at last one of his winning smiles. 'As you said earlier, Mr. Elphick, that is not a journey I should wish to repeat any time soon.'

The two men retreated to their rooms, Mr. Elphick to a fire and a warming brick in the bed, and Marcus to an open window and a well-aired nightshirt. Hippolyta wondered if he would be frozen to the bed by morning.

Neither of them rose too early the following morning, anyway, which was a shame as the winter sun was toying with the snow outside in a way that made one's eyes water. Half-blinded, Hippolyta saw to the pig and hens, while the cats stepped delicately through the snow like unnatural snowballs, only green eyes and pink ears showing. It would only take them a few minutes to realise the hunting advantage this gave them, Hippolyta thought, and made a note to look out for fresh victims on the carpets.

The air was vigorous and she wanted more of it, so after breakfast she set out with Patrick on the first of his route, abandoning him with a squeeze of the hand when they met the Misses Strong. The ladies were picking their way along a deep path, cleared across the top of the green past their house and on to the main street. By the damp of their skirts, they had been out for a while already. Their hands were tucked deep into a pair of huge, matching fur muffs.

'My dear Mrs. Napier! What weather!' said Miss Strong. 'Did your brother arrive safely? The innkeeper said he had no idea who or what was on the top of the coach, until they had gone.'

'Yes, he was travelling outside, the silly boy,' said Hippolyta. 'But he is arrived safely and as far as I know still asleep. You were about early to find out the news!'

'Oh, she's always away down to the inn to find if any suitable young man is off the coach,' said Miss Ada with a snort of laughter. 'You're lucky your brother got away out of it.'

'Ada!' cried her sister.

'She's that desperate for a husband! Oh, but wait,' said Miss Ada, remembering she had something more out of the ordinary to report. 'You'll never guess who was in the coach last night! Though I suppose you were there: you must have seen him.'

'Who?' asked Hippolyta. She doubted that they meant Mr. Elphick. 'I saw a man and a woman leave the coach, but they were so well wrapped up I don't think I would have recognised my own parents, if it had been them.' But she remembered the dark brows, the sharp eyes, all the same.

'You saw him, then?' Miss Ada gave a little gasp of wonder. 'You saw George Broughton?'

'George Broughton?' Hippolyta frowned. Where had she heard that name before? 'You cannot mean the politician? The reformer?' The one that Marcus had described last night: one of the savage hounds fierce in the campaign for Reform.

'The very one! Michty me!' said Miss Ada. 'I cannot believe it.'

'And what is Sir Holroyd Pinner going to do about that?' asked Miss Strong primly. 'He'll not like it, you ken.'

'I cannot wait to see him!' sighed Miss Ada, and her sister dug her once again in the ribs.

'He's a married man! You cannot go swooning over him like a missish girl! What would he think?'

'Oh, aye, his wife's here and all,' Miss Ada added, rather more prosaically. 'Mind, she seems a nice enough lassie. She's fae somewhere Edinburgh direction, I think she said. Anyway, south. We've asked her to tea this afternoon. Will you no come? I think you'd like her, and you'd help her settle in and all, speaking the same language as her.'

'What, Edinburgh language?' asked Hippolyta, laughing.

'Aye, Edinbrese, that's the like of it. Come on, anyway,' said Miss Ada. 'And bring your brother. We can aye toss him to my sister, and keep her quiet.'

'Ada!' Miss Ada's ribs must be permanently black and blue, thought Hippolyta – or perhaps by now she wears padding.

'I shall be happy to come. I can't vouch for Marcus, though:

he almost certainly does not approve of tea, or exercise, or something.'

'Then we shall see you this afternoon!' said Miss Strong, and nudged her sister onwards towards their house.

It was too bright to paint and there was still no sign of either guest when she returned. She settled down and wrote to her mother, though she was not quite sure when the letter would go.

'Marcus has arrived safely, if a little late. He will insist on travelling outside, though I am sure it would have killed him had not there been another man there for their mutual shelter. The village is filling with visitors, most unusually for the winter, and they may all be here for some time with the snow this deep. We have Sir Holroyd Pinner and Lady Pinner, the Tory politician, staying at Dinnet House with their delightful baby daughter. And just arrived we have, apparently, George Broughton, the Whig reformer, and his wife. I am to meet them, or her at any rate, this afternoon. Society being small here at this time of year, no doubt the Pinners and the Broughtons must meet, which may be –' she was about to write 'entertaining', but remembered it was her mother to whom she was writing, 'distressing for both parties.'

But perhaps it was one of those professional rivalries, she reflected as she sealed the letter. Perhaps the Broughtons and the Pinners would have so much in common that they would mix very well, socially, and the winter would be entertaining in a much more pleasant way than she had anticipated. Well, she would see this afternoon.

Chapter Five

Mr. Elphick, apologising profusely for his late rising, took his bag and headed off to his appointed lodgings around midday: he was to stay in a cottage nearby, though, so they parted with the full intention of meeting again during his stay. It was only after he had left that it occurred to Hippolyta that he had not, at any time she had heard, said why he was to stay in Ballater in the first place. Winter visitors were altogether more mysterious than the summer ones – or did they just assume motives for the summer ones, and never ask them?

Nevertheless, the prospect of meeting Mr Elphick again soon made Hippolyta broach Patrick's study to dig out the last few Edinburgh and Aberdeen papers which he had bought secondhand from the innkeeper and had not yet passed on to Mrs. Kynoch. She settled down in the parlour with three or four of them, and was making her way through the last week's *Aberdeen Journal* when the door opened and Marcus made his appearance, wrapped in a banyan she had left out for him. His fine blond hair was still tousled, and he yawned ostentatiously.

'Well, I'm glad to see you at last!' said Hippolyta. 'I trust you slept well?'

'Very well, thank you. Though the room was a trifle chilly: your housekeeper had left the window very wide.'

'I'll mention to her,' said Hippolyta, tight-lipped. Maybe, she added to herself.

'Reading the papers, then, Pol? I thought the fashion news was on the third page, usually.'

'Hm,' said Hippolyta, closing the paper. Marcus was one to talk: if his trousers were a quarter inch too long for the fashion plates, he would not leave the house. 'Mr. Elphick has left, but no doubt we shall see him again soon. He is an interesting man, is he not?'

'I should have died of frostbite and boredom before Montrose if he had not been there,' Marcus agreed. 'Though he did not mention his political work until we came here. I had the impression he had written a book, perhaps? And he mentioned working in the Midlands somewhere. Is that not where Sir Holroyd Pinner has his seat?' he added, clearly not expecting her to know.

'Worcester,' said Hippolyta, who had just read it. 'That's in Worcestershire, I believe.' She had to turn away to hide her smile. Marcus blinked, and arranged himself on the sofa, pulling a cat over to keep his lap warm. Franklin was one of the most tolerant of the cat brood, and adjusted to the change philosophically, only applying her claws very gently to keep from sliding down the silky skirts of the banyan. Marcus winced, but tried not to show it.

'I have news for you, too,' said Hippolyta. 'Did you see who was in the coach last night? The inside passengers?'

'A couple, I believe,' said Marcus casually. 'Wherever we stopped, everyone was so well wrapped up we never saw each other's faces – and I think they took a private parlour each time. I thought they might be honeymooners – or maybe they were eloping?' He sat up a little, excited by the possible scandal.

'Not at all: no honeymooners but an old married couple. Well, not so old: I do not believe that either of them has passed their fiftieth year, by all I have read.' She tried very hard not to emphasise the last phrase. 'Mr. and Mrs. Broughton, they were – Mr. and Mrs. George Broughton.'

'The politician?' Marcus asked. He looked shocked – really, she thought, he had gone quite pale with excitement. She wondered if he had been overdoing his political activities and that their mother had sent him away for a rest cure.

'The politician, and his wife,' she replied. 'They are staying at the inn.'

'Really?' Marcus stroked the cat absently. 'Really? Good heavens. And to think … to think they were in the same coach, after all …'

'Anyway,' said Hippolyta, watching him thoughtfully, 'I have been invited to meet them, or at least her, at tea at the Strongs this afternoon. You have been invited too if you care to come – think of it! A real live Whig politician!'

'Oh ... I am not sure I should be ready in time,' said Marcus. 'I am not even dressed yet.'

'Well, I realised that,' said Hippolyta. 'I did not expect you to go out in a banyan – besides, the snow would ruin the silk. But I shall not be leaving for an hour yet: you have plenty of time.'

'Only an hour! Good heavens, no! To meet Mr. George Broughton? Or even Mrs. George Broughton? My good buff trousers are not even brushed. It will have to be another time! I doubt that they have plans to journey further than Ballater – or if they do, they will have to wait for better weather. No doubt we are all here till the spring,' he said, with satisfaction, wriggling deeper into the sofa. Hippolyta devoutly hoped he was wrong.

Mrs. Broughton might be the wife of a leading member of the Whig government, but Hippolyta, rather to her own regret, was not going to risk her best blue dress in the snow in her honour. Instead she smartened up her soft brown gown with a pretty ivory shawl and added her brown silk bonnet with the ivory lining, making sure she had her hands to her hood in case the snow started and she needed to protect the bonnet. The cold air, she knew, would put some colour in her cheeks: she hoped not too much. Abandoning Marcus to the sofa, a pot of tea, Franklin the cat and the Aberdeen papers (he seemed to know the Edinburgh ones by heart), she took up her reticule and set out.

The diggers, whomsoever they may be, had completed the path around the green now, and all she had to do to keep her feet fairly dry was to follow it up to the top of the green, then walk a few paces to the Strongs' front door. It was answered immediately: Miss Ada had been standing just inside.

'Oh! Mrs. Napier. She is not yet come. Will she jilt us, even at the altar?'

'You have been reading too many novels, I fear, Miss Ada!' said Hippolyta.

'Aye, well, when you've read everything else. Go on in to the fire, Mrs. Napier. Lizzie will take your cloak.'

Hippolyta surrendered her cloak to the maid, and went on into the Strongs' familiar parlour with its old-fashioned furniture. Miss Strong was already at the tea table, adjusting plates, and Mr.

Strong, their brother, was by the fire, reading yet another paper. He rose, old bones creaking, at Hippolyta's entrance, and showed her to the other fireside armchair.

'Delighted to see you, Mrs. Napier. I hear your brother is in town?'

'He is just arrived, Mr. Strong, and too lazy to be up in time to receive Miss Strong's invitation, I'm sorry to say. He sends his apologies.'

'Ah, young men always need more sleep than old fellows like myself, Mrs. Napier. No doubt we shall see him soon enough. I'm glad to hear he reached us unscathed, for it was an unchancy day to be travelling.'

'It certainly was. They were all very fortunate. I believe the driver and postilion are not yet well enough to make the return journey: my husband was called to see them this morning, to make sure they are all right.' The matter was general gossip, she knew, so she had no qualms over mentioning Patrick's involvement.

'Aye, aye. Perhaps in these modern times we believe the weather cannot affect us any more, with our coaches and our steam ships. It behoves us to remember that nature is still a very powerful force, altogether.'

Hippolyta was about to agree when they heard Miss Ada snatch open the front door again, and cry,

'Mrs. Broughton! Welcome, welcome. Come on inside and warm yourself!'

There was the usual scuffle of cloaks and gloves and umbrellas, and the parlour door opened to reveal Mrs. Broughton.

She had indeed not reached her fiftieth year, but was probably above her fortieth. Dressed practically, in a gown not much better than Hippolyta's own, and sporting a pair of sensible thick leather boots on her feet, she was smallish of stature but stout, in a way that implied less fat and more strength. She reminded Hippolyta straightaway of earthenware, and made her feel, by contrast, like a rather overdone porcelain ornament. Her face was squarish, handsome rather than pretty, bright and full of intelligence and goodwill. Hippolyta warmed to her immediately.

'May I present our good friend, Mrs. Napier, and my brother, Alexander Strong?'

'Delighted!' Mrs. Broughton paid the civilities the attention they deserved, but did not dwell on them. She sat where she was put, in Mr. Strong's chair by the fire, and the Strongs clustered about comfortably. 'It is more than good of you to welcome a stranger to your home so soon after our arrival.'

'But of course we knew your name long before your arrival,' said Miss Strong, 'so you are almost not a stranger to us. It is good of you, rather, to spare your time to visit. Though I am afraid you will find society in Ballater in the winter time a little restricted: you might easily tire of us quite quickly.'

'I am sure not,' said Mrs. Broughton warmly. 'And if it is a little quiet, I am sure we shall benefit from the rest.'

'Ah, yes, you have been busy lately, in London, I believe?' said Miss Ada. 'Mr. Broughton is one of the leading advocates of Reform, is he not?'

'He is,' Mrs. Broughton acknowledged, 'and he needs a rest. I was heartily glad when the King prorogued Parliament: I trust it will not sit again till after Christmas.'

'I fear you will be disappointed,' said Hippolyta. 'I read this very day that the members are to be summoned back on the sixth – in only a few days' time!'

Mrs. Broughton's face fell.

'And he will go, no doubt! Alas,' she repeated, 'he is much in need of a rest. I wonder how long I can pretend I never heard you say that?' Her face took on a mischievous expression.

'Is he able to join you this afternoon?' asked Miss Strong.

'He does hope to join us shortly,' Mrs. Broughton assured her. 'He is working on the papers for a legal case, and just wanted to finish one document before he would come out.'

'He is a barrister, is he not?' asked Mr. Strong. 'I am a man of law myself, though I practise as a notary and solicitor, of course.'

'How interesting! I'm sure he will be delighted to meet you and compare notes. Though I should also be grateful if you could interest him in some other pursuit, such as golf, or geology: I'm afraid that for the last two years he has talked of almost nothing but law and Reform, and I should be glad of the variety!'

'Are you not so interested in the politics yourself, then, Mrs. Broughton?' asked Miss Ada slyly.

'Oh, I am – who could not be? But to the exclusion of all else … well, even a bishop does not talk of God all the time.'

'Oh, are you Anglican, Mrs. Broughton?'

'Yes, of course, Mrs. Napier. But I understand there is no Episcopal chapel here.'

'No, but if the weather permits the clergyman to ride through from Banchory this Sunday, there will be Communion in our house – the doctor's house on the green, anyone could direct you, I believe. And you would be most welcome.'

'Thank you: I believe we shall be happy to attend. Though it will be a devout and brave clergyman indeed who rides here from Banchory, if the snow remains this severe!' she added. 'Oh! Here is Mr. Broughton now.'

She had seen him pass the window, and waved. A hand could be seen waving back, and in a second he was through the front door and into the parlour.

'Miss Strong, how very good of you! Miss Ada – ah, and Mr. Strong! Good day to you, sir. Mrs. Napier? – delighted to meet you. My dear, I am glad to see you have arrived safely! What snow, eh?'

He was full of energy, however much he needed a rest, thought Hippolyta. Like his wife, he was not particularly tall, but you felt his presence in the room at once. The same sharp gaze that had met Hippolyta's in the inn's stableyard last night regarded her again.

'We have met before, I think – ah! The lady who helped with the horses last night! To say we are much obliged would not do justice to our feelings at arriving safely. When we left Aberdeen I was torn between relief at being on our way, and terror that we should never see civilisation again – but here we are, and the inn is everything that one could wish for. We are very content, are we not, my dear?'

'Definitely,' said Mrs. Broughton, smiling at her husband.

'And I understand there is even to be an assembly tomorrow night? Can that be correct?'

'Oh, aye, yes,' said Miss Ada at once. 'And a bonny affair it will be, no doubt.'

'It's respectable, then?' asked Mrs. Broughton. 'Will you be going?'

'Unless the snow rises above the roof, aye, we'll be there!' said Miss Ada. 'And no doubt Mrs. Napier and her lovely husband

and her equally handsome brother and all! And the Strachans that keep the best warehouse this side of Aberdeen, and I daresay a couple of the guests from Pannanich Wells, if they can get down the road, and the minister and his wife …'

'Oh, very respectable, then!' laughed Mrs. Broughton. 'Well, no doubt we shall be there, too. I only meant that if it was to be for – for labourers and such, they might not want us intruding on them.'

'Och, no, it's no like that. You'd be more than welcome!'

'It sounds as if you have a lively village here, then,' said Mr. Broughton.

'Aye, we keep ourselves entertained, one way and the other,' Miss Ada nodded, her eyebrows suggestively high. The Broughtons both laughed.

'Ada!' snapped her sister. 'Shall we have tea?'

They moved to the tea table, and Lizzie the maid brought in the tea and hot tea bread, and plenty of butter. Everyone ate with enthusiasm: both the Broughtons ate quickly and incisively, as if any delay might result in the food being taken away. There was little conversation, despite Miss Ada's best attempts to encourage it, until they had eaten their fill. Mr. Broughton sat back from the table with a sigh, and Miss Strong poured everyone another cup of tea.

'Mrs. Broughton says you are busy on a court case,' said Mr. Strong. 'I should have enjoyed the part of an advocate myself, but my mind was never quick enough, I believe. You know, of course, that Scots law and English law are rather different?'

'I do indeed, and admire the Scots system,' said Broughton diplomatically. 'I had for a little while a Scottish clerk, who told me much about it – a basis in Roman law, I believe? He has left me to return to Scotland, so little did he enjoy the comparison with the English system.'

'Aye, aye, Roman law, indeed. I daresay both are fine systems, but it's what you're used to in the end. Now, tell me, Mr. Broughton, do you still find the lawcourts satisfying, or do you prefer the other battlefield of Parliament?'

Mr. Broughton smiled, nodding.

'You have the apt word there, "battlefield",' he said 'The trumpet of that kind of war has always called me. I enjoy both: I am most fortunate. Each gives value to the other, and each inspires my activities in the other. I could give up neither, now.'

'Alas!' murmured his wife, with a grin. 'I wish he could give up both tomorrow, and we could go and live in Brighton and walk along the seafront each day and talk of nothing but what to have for tea.'

'You would hate it in a week,' said Mr. Broughton fondly. 'You enjoy it just as much as I do. More, sometimes.'

'Well ... sometimes I think it would be a fine thing to stand up in Parliament and see how I should manage,' Mrs. Broughton admitted. 'I think I could speechify as well as any man there.'

'And better than many,' said her husband loyally, then unhelpfully added, 'Some of the members are truly terrible speakers.'

'I feel the same,' said Miss Ada. 'Oh, to stand up on a platform and tell people why they should vote for me! I'd have them queuing to elect me! They'd carry me on their shoulders to the door of the House of Commons!'

'Aye, in the recess, and lock you in,' her sister put in.

'Now that would be real reform,' said Miss Ada, nothing daunted.

'That would be a step too far even for Lord Grey!' laughed Mr. Broughton. 'No, let us get proper representation for the population first, and not tempt fate with anything so radical. You'll be saying next that women should be able to vote!'

'And why not?' demanded Miss Ada. 'Have I no a mind as good as the next man's?'

'Well ...' said Miss Strong thoughtfully.

'Ada dear,' said Mr. Strong, 'don't inflict your daft ideas on our new friends. Where would it all end? You'll be saying next that Mrs. Napier's cats should have a vote.'

'You couldn't rely on them to vote fairly,' said Hippolyta. 'They would support anyone who gave them fish and the occasional piece of liver, whoever it might be.'

'But it's an open ballot,' Mr. Broughton pointed out. 'At least you would know how they voted, and then you would know who had bribed them.'

'I'm not sure it would help. They are quite the experts at looking innocent.'

None of the company could really have asked more of the conversation that afternoon: Mr. Strong had his law, Miss Ada had her politics, and the rest of them had great good humour and the beginnings of an entertaining acquaintance. When it was time to leave, Mr. Broughton declared he had enjoyed himself so much he could barely remember where it was they were staying.

'That's because they were polite enough to let you win all the arguments,' his wife remarked. 'With better acquaintance they might be less accommodating.'

'You can't miss the inn,' said Hippolyta, 'but I'll be happy to walk back down with you. I love being out in the snow.'

'That would be most kind of you, Mrs. Napier, if you're sure.'

'Of course: I live halfway down the hill myself.'

Lizzie the maid was summoned to return cloaks and gloves, and the visitors assembled their outfits in the cramped hallway with Miss Ada and Miss Strong trying to help and only hindering. At last they were ready to venture outside.

Dusk had only been deterred by the glaring snow reflecting light from any windows or lamps along the main street, but the shadows of the eaves and side lanes were deep and black. Broughton took his wife's arm, and waved Hippolyta a little ahead to guide them. She led them on to the main street, and turned down the hill. A couple, similarly with a female figure accompanying them, were climbing in the opposite direction, and Hippolyta blinked, wondering for a second if she were seeing a reflection in something. Then she realised that all the approaching figures were taller than the Broughtons, and the lone female was smaller than she herself. There was something familiar about them, though, and as she squinted through the darkness she recognised the Pinners, with Lady Pinner's sulky maid, Clara, in attendance. Hm, she thought. This might be interesting.

She must have hesitated slightly, for the Broughtons caught up with her just as the Pinners came within range of recognising her, too. Now she deliberately halted.

'Is something the matter, Mrs. Napier?' asked Mr. Broughton. Then he looked past her.

'Mrs. Napier, is that you?' asked Sir Holroyd, approaching with more purpose. Then he looked past her.

'Broughton.'

'Sir Holroyd.'

The air, already cold, chilled by several degrees.

'Mrs. Broughton, I take it?'

Mrs. Broughton curtseyed, in silence. Lady Pinner did not look at either of them.

'Clara, will you take my arm? I wish to walk on a little way. Clara?'

Clara jumped as if she had been daydreaming. She stepped back and allowed Lady Pinner to lean on her, and they walked on, past the Broughtons and Hippolyta, as if they did not exist. At the corner of the green, opposite Strachan's warehouse, they stopped and waited. Hippolyta's face flushed with anger and embarrassment, though she was sure the slight had not been directed particularly at her. Mrs. Broughton, straightened again now, stood firmly by her husband.

'What brings you here, Sir Holroyd?' asked Broughton.

'Lady Pinner's health required rest some distance from – from everything,' said Sir Holroyd. 'May I ask in return what brings you here?'

'As you say, the search for peace and quiet.' The words were commonplace, but the tone was dangerous.

'Then perhaps it is best if we avoid each other? It is a small village, I know, but I am sure we can each keep to ourselves.' Sir Holroyd's voice had an equally alarming bite to it.

'That seems an admirable plan. The business of Parliament, I am sure, would disrupt any peace and quiet we might otherwise be afforded.'

'Exactly. Shall we bid each other good evening, then, Mr. Broughton?'

'Good evening, Sir Holroyd.'

'Good evening, Mr. Broughton. Mrs. Broughton,' Sir Holroyd touched his hat in her direction, but the curtsey she made in return was only a trifle. Sir Holroyd carried on up the street, and rejoined his wife and the maid. Hippolyta found she was holding her breath, and let it out in a puff of steam.

'I must apologise, Mrs. Napier,' said Mrs. Broughton sincerely. 'We have inadvertently placed you in an awkward position. I had no idea you were acquainted with the Pinners. As you perhaps are aware, Sir Holroyd and my husband have crossed swords many times in the Commons, mostly on the subject of Reform.'

'The man is dead against it,' said Broughton, the words ripping out of his mouth. 'He will not see reason.'

'My dear,' said Mrs. Broughton, gently.

'No matter,' said Hippolyta. 'I made their acquaintance only yesterday, I must admit. As you say, this is a small place, and those of us who live here must get along as best we can. I'm sure when people realise that you and the Pinners ... well, you will be invited to different things, of course. There is no need for any unpleasantness.' She was about to walk on a few steps, as if the matter could be left behind, when her attention was caught by a movement in the shadows on the other side of the narrow street. Down a laneway she thought she saw someone, and indeed, as they moved on down the street and she glanced back, she saw two figures detach themselves from the darkness at the end of the lane, and cross a side road towards the church.

Mrs. Broughton looked back to see what she was watching.

'Do you know those men?' she asked Hippolyta.

'I don't know: they look vaguely familiar,' Hippolyta replied. The men's dark clothing had meant that the shades around the church had swallowed them up quickly, disconcertingly fast, as if they had simply vanished.

'Hm. I don't know them myself,' said Mrs. Broughton, down to earth, 'but I'd say they were up to mischief by the way they move. I shouldn't be too surprised if some household is missing something by tomorrow morning.'

'Oh, things like that rarely happen in Ballater!' said Hippolyta lightly. 'Besides, this is hardly the weather for it. No one will leave their windows open on a night like this.' Except for my peculiar brother Marcus, she thought, but did not say. She glanced back once more at the dark church. She thought she could see movement. What were they doing?

But just as she was wondering how to find out, she caught sight of a familiar figure picking its way down the main street, carrying a basket. Mrs. Riach, the housekeeper, was stepping about three inches at a time, clutching her skirts back so that she could see her own feet. There was a shout from somewhere near the church. Mrs. Riach jerked upright in surprise, head spinning to track the noise. Her feet shot out forwards from beneath her, her basket flew into the air, and with a tremendous cry she landed hard on her back on the roadway.

Chapter Six

Mrs. Riach was not proving to be a good patient.

She had given Hippolyta quite a shock at first, for when Hippolyta raced over to her, skidding through the snow, Mrs. Riach was uncharacteristically silent and seemed not to be breathing. Her eyes were staring hard straight past Hippolyta, and it took a few endless moments of patting her hands and rubbing her face – trying not to be too violent, of course – to bring her to her senses. That, however, did not much improve matters: Mrs. Riach set up a kind of curdled groaning, from somewhere deep within her unfashionable bosom, and refused to communicate at all.

She was lying on an increasingly slushy heap of snow and Hippolyta was worried about her taking a chill, but before she could rearrange shawls or ease her out of the damp, Patrick appeared. It was the advantage of being married to the local doctor that in general quite a number of people knew where he was at any given time, and he had been summoned by passersby to see to his injured housekeeper.

'What happened?' he asked Hippolyta, struggling to make himself heard through the groans.

'She slipped and fell on her back.'

'I hope she has not broken it. Was she winded?'

'She did not speak for a moment, or even breathe, I believe.'

'I don't want to move her back or neck too much until I can examine it properly, and it's more than my life is worth to do that here. We need a board.'

The passersby had of course lingered, despite the cold, to see if anything interesting might happen, so it was not long before a few boards appeared. Patrick rejected the most splintery and the one that seemed to have been part of a long-gone hen house, and laid a blanket, again mysteriously apparent from a nearby cottage, across two of the better ones. Then he and Hippolyta, under his instructions, slid Mrs. Riach on to the makeshift bed. The groaning rose to a minor shriek, then subsided into the groans again.

'You'll want a hand, there,' said a bored carter, lacking business in the snow. He summoned his colleague with a jerk of his head, and between them they lifted and carried the double board with its droning burden back to the house on the green. They deposited Mrs. Riach in her room, which luckily was downstairs, and when they had gone Hippolyta stripped off the woman's outer layers as delicately as she could, glad she did not have to go further than her shift. For Mrs. Riach fashion had not moved on much since Napoleon had left Elba, so there was little in the way of corsetry or bulk, for which Hippolyta was duly grateful.

'Where does it hurt, Mrs. Riach?' Patrick asked, blending the authority of a master with the command of a physician. Mrs. Riach left off groaning at his tone, and eyed him balefully.

'My back, where would you think?'

'No pain in your head? Your arms? Your legs?'

'No!'

'Can you feel this?' He placed a hand across the nearest ankle. Mrs. Riach snatched her leg back as if he had bitten it.

'Dinna do that!' she snapped. 'It's no decent!'

Hippolyta looked away, trying not to laugh.

'I need to make sure you haven't broken your back, Mrs. Riach,' said Patrick. Hippolyta marvelled at his patience. 'Can you feel this?' This time he laid his hand across her stockinged toes, on the other foot. She nodded. 'And this?' He squeezed the fingertips of her right hand. She nodded again. 'And this?' The other hand provoked the same reaction. 'Can you wiggle your fingers and toes? Just a little?'

'Awww,' she moaned, but she wiggled her fingers and toes for all she was worth, clearly alarmed at the thought of what he might try to touch next. The wiggling was accompanied by a selection of heartfelt mutterings, which Hippolyta chose to misunderstand.

Patrick rolled Mrs. Riach over carefully on the narrow bed, ignoring the grunts and moans, and used his delicate fingers to test her spine, bump by bump. Once again the groaning swelled to a cry of pain as he pressed not far above her waist, and then just above her hips, but Patrick looked relieved.

'Just bruising,' he said. 'Painful enough, and she will need to lie still and rest for a couple of days, but there is nothing broken or out of place.'

'Thank goodness for that,' said Hippolyta dutifully, though the fleeting prospect of having to look for a new housekeeper had not been entirely unwelcome.

'I'll get Ishbel to bring you some hot poultices for the bruising,' Patrick told Mrs. Riach, 'and some sweet tea for the shock. My dear, can you pull the bedclothes up and keep her warm?'

'Of course.'

Since then, Mrs. Riach had managed to keep Ishbel on her toes almost every minute of the day. She had acquired a bell from somewhere – Hippolyta suspected Wullie, for whom Mrs. Riach had an unexpected soft spot – and used it to summon Ishbel for fresh poultices, more tea, and any food that might be available, citing, apparently, Dr. Napier's instructions that she be looked after. The Napier household, never more than tentatively organised at the best of times, tumbled into confusion, with breakfast late and dinner early on Friday. The early dinner was not entirely a bad thing, as Patrick and Hippolyta wanted to prepare for the assembly at the inn, but Hippolyta hoped she would not be starving by bed time. Marcus, too, after some close interrogation of Hippolyta, was dissatisfied: only Mrs. Riach, he said, knew how to cook eggs exactly the way he liked them. He seemed to feel that Mrs. Riach was avoiding the task on purpose. The fact that Patrick was dancing attendance on his housekeeper, and that Hippolyta herself had helped nurse her, was, according to Marcus, only what every employer should do for their servants. When Hippolyta argued that not every employer would be in a position to give a medical opinion on an injured housekeeper, Marcus brought in remarks about modern slavery which Hippolyta told him smartly were not appropriate, though she began to wonder when she saw Ishbel hurrying to attend to Mrs. Riach.

'Are you coming to the assembly?' she asked Marcus after dinner.

'I suppose there is little else to do,' said Marcus, languidly. 'Will Sir Holroyd Pinner be there?'

'I don't imagine he will be,' said Patrick. Hippolyta had told him of the confrontation between Mr. Broughton and Sir Holroyd. 'He will know, surely, that the Broughtons are staying at the inn and are very likely to be there.'

'Of course: the Broughtons,' said Marcus, with a little frown. 'I'll see if I have something appropriate to wear.' He vanished upstairs.

'Sometimes I have difficulty fathoming your brother,' Patrick confessed. 'He admires Mr. Broughton but does not seem to want to meet him, and abhors Sir Holroyd but seems to want to go to the assembly if he will be there. He wants us to treat our servants with care and devotion, yet complains when Mrs. Riach is unable to cook his eggs for him.'

'He's young,' said Hippolyta.

'Older than you.'

'In years, yes,' she agreed with a laugh, 'but not really. He has great ideals one minute, but if they intrude on his enjoyment of fashion or entertainment they are forgotten the next. Parliamentary Reform is the only idea I have yet seen him support for more than two days in a row – yet even then, as you say, he seems reluctant to meet the Broughtons.'

'Have you any idea yet why he is here?'

Hippolyta shrugged.

'I have not asked him directly. I suppose we shall find out in due course. I managed to post the letter to Mother today to tell her he had arrived safely: perhaps she will explain by her next.'

'Come,' Patrick stood up and put out a hand to her. 'My feet are itching to dance, and they are specifying a dance with you. Let us go and dress, and make the most of the evening.'

The inn's winter assemblies were not grand affairs, but more an opportunity for those who were bored indoors to have something to go to now and again on a dark night, to have a news with their friends and a dance to the music of a few moderately talented local fiddlers. The largest room was cleared and the carpet lifted, and a simple supper was laid out in a side parlour, just where Hippolyta had waited for news of the coach the other night. The inn was a complicated place, built on to and extended over the years, so it was possible not to meet everyone who was at the assembly, but those who danced and ate could not avoid being seen. Marcus, Hippolyta noticed, did not immediately head for either the supper table or the dance floor.

'I thought I should see if there are any card games going,' he muttered in explanation.

'I thought you did not approve of gambling!' Hippolyta was surprised.

'Well ... there is no need for me to gamble, I suppose. I could just watch.'

'Sounds like a tedious way to spend an evening,' said his sister, and followed her husband into the dancing room.

Scottish country dancing was the rule of the evening: no complicated quadrilles here. Already the first dance was in train. George Broughton was dancing with Miss Strong and Mr. Strong, frail and wizened as he was, had stocky Mrs. Broughton by the hand and a look of surprise on his face, as if the owner of a pony and trap had just been handed the reins of a coach and four. Patrick and Hippolyta were quickly beckoned to fit into the circle, and in a moment they were pacing and whirling with the rest. As they rotated, Hippolyta noticed the journalist, Jedediah Elphick, watching the dance with amusement. When it ended, and the Napiers, dizzy, went to join the Broughtons and the Strongs, Elphick stepped around the side of the room to join them.

'Mr. Elphick! Do you not dance?' asked Hippolyta.

'The dancing is fairly strange to me,' he admitted, 'and I am not ready with my feet to learn something new quickly. Later, perhaps, I might attempt something simple, if any lady is charitable enough to risk the venture.'

'Oh, may I present Mr. Elphick?' Hippolyta turned to the Strongs and the Broughtons. 'He is a journalist from London.'

'Oh, yes?' said Mr. Strong, returning Elphick's bow with a little hesitation. Mrs. Broughton turned to look at the newcomer, and her strong face flickered with some odd emotion.

'Mrs. Broughton.' Mr. Elphick bowed.

'Mr. Elphick.' She swallowed, and cleared her throat. 'What a surprise to see you again. Look, my dear,' she tugged at her husband's elbow, 'Mr. Elphick is here.'

There was a moment when Broughton did not move. Mr. Elphick, by contrast, seemed to shrink into his own collar, an effect

Hippolyta had seen many times in her youth when one of her brothers had come up before the awful judgments of her mother. His eyes had grown huge, and his hands had disappeared behind his back as if they felt they might be safer there.

'Elphick?' Broughton turned at last. 'What brings you up here? Is there not enough news in London?' His tone was not welcoming.

'I – I came here for a rest while Parliament was prorogued,' said Elphick.

'Parliament has been recalled,' said Mrs. Broughton. 'You had better be off back home.' Was she hostile, too? Or had that been some kind of warning? Hippolyta was not sure.

'But while such luminaries of the Westminster circle are here, surely the news is here too?' asked Elphick, smiling, though his smile could not be called confident.

'Perhaps we came here for a rest, too,' said Broughton. 'To a place we believed we would be unbothered by idiotic gutter scribblers and ignorant historiographers.'

'My dear,' said Mrs. Broughton softly, one hand on Broughton's arm. He glanced at the hand as though it were some harmless insect, then seemed to take her meaning. He met her eye.

'But this is an assembly, and an assembly of charming strangers with whom I hope to become better acquainted,' he said, turning his back on Elphick. Mrs. Broughton, with a kind of helpless shrug, turned after him. The little journalist shuddered slightly. His face was quite pink. Hippolyta put out a hand, but he moved away a little, and bowed to her.

'You must excuse me,' he said. 'There is a card game I intended to join.' He moved away stiffly.

Hippolyta sighed and looked at Patrick. Were none of her new acquaintances to be friendly with each other? The winter social activities looked likely to be fraught with anxieties and confusion.

The next dance was called, and Patrick led Hippolyta back out on to the floor. He leaned close and she felt his breath on her throat as he spoke.

'What a tremendous black eye your friend Broughton has! Did he say how he contracted it?'

'A black eye?' Hippolyta thought. Of course: she had noticed some colouring, but Broughton's gaze was so intense that when he looked at her she saw only his eyes. 'Well, if you told me that Mr. Elphick had given it to him, after that little conversation I should not be surprised.'

They stood back from each other to take their positions as the music started, and smiled. These visitors passed through Ballater, and left again. Sometimes they brought their problems with them, but how could that affect Ballater? No doubt as soon as they had recovered from their journey here, the Broughtons and Mr. Elphick would be away back down to the newly recalled Parliament – and perhaps Sir Holroyd would go, too. Perhaps Lady Pinner would stay for a little, and perhaps Sir Holroyd's absence would allow her to enjoy her stay better. Perhaps the winter would not be as bad as she was anticipating.

They were sharing a set with several of the children of the village old enough to dance, and Hippolyta's back soon ached from the effort of reaching down to her partners. The dance finished, and she and Patrick exchanged a look before returning to stand with the Strongs and the Broughtons. Elphick was nowhere to be seen, and Mrs. Kynoch, the Strachans and the minister Mr. Douglas and his wife were deep in conversation on the other side of the room: they would doubtless meet properly at supper.

'I believe the King is ultimately on our side,' Broughton was saying to Miss Ada. 'He is by no means like his late brother: he is an economical, practical man, much given to home and hearth.'

'Aye, there was nothing much to the coronation, I heard tell,' said Miss Ada, not entirely impressed. Hippolyta was considering whether pomp was a good thing or not when there was a hush across the room, and everyone turned, bewildered, towards the door.

If pomp had been required, it had arrived. Sir Holroyd and Lady Pinner stood in the doorway, he in the blackest of black coats, she in a gown of gold and white with some kind of headpiece in a rich violet velvet. Hippolyta gasped at the audacity of it, in such ordinary surroundings: she looked like a queen who had strayed off the route to a coronation, and not such a humble one as King William's. But her face did not match: haughty she certainly looked, but happy or healthy she did not. Indeed Mrs. Kynoch must have thought the same, for she stepped smartly to Lady Pinner's side, drawing her over kindly to where the Strachans were standing, and found her a chair. The maid Clara hovered behind her.

Sir Holroyd hardly seemed to notice his wife's departure. He stared about the room as if seeking a particular servant from a busy servants' hall. Then he saw the Broughtons. His eyebrows shot up his handsome brow, and he opened his mouth slightly as if drawing in a breath past those terrible teeth. Then he spun on his heel, and left the room.

The fiddlers, nudging each other in delighted horror, began to play for the next dance. Patrick whispered to Hippolyta:

'Would you mind if I asked Mrs. Broughton to step out with me? She seems a little distressed.'

'Of course; go on.' Hippolyta half-hoped that Mr. Broughton would reciprocate and ask her to dance, but after staring at the doorway for a moment he turned back and deliberately resumed his conversation with Miss Ada. Hippolyta did not enjoy dancing with Mr. Strong, who made her feel like a carthorse by comparison with his wizened form, so before he could feel obliged to ask her she murmured something about looking for Marcus. She strolled over to the door, smiling at acquaintances as she went. Mrs. Strachan, elegant and fashionable, seemed to be meeting with Lady Pinner's approval, and Mrs. Kynoch had fetched a glass of something for her, too. Hippolyta would be surplus to requirements there, she felt. She carried on to the doorway, and slipped out into the hall.

She was not an enthusiast for card games, not when there was dancing or eating to be done, and had never ventured into any of the card rooms during an assembly before. She wandered a little vaguely for a while, doubling back on herself and chatting here and there to those she met. Behind her she could hear the music stop, and start again. She wondered with whom Patrick was dancing this dance. He loved it so much it would have been unfair to expect him to sit out, just because she was not there. She smiled, turned a corner, and caught sight of Marcus.

He was behaving oddly, even for Marcus. He was halfway up a flight of stairs, in semidarkness. Leaning against the wall, motionless, he stared down through the banisters at an open doorway across the passage. From the room, because of the angle of the stairs and the shadows, he would have been invisible. He was clearly eavesdropping.

He had not noticed Hippolyta, focussed as he was on the room. Hippolyta wondered what on earth it could be that had attracted his attention so completely. From the room he could hear only one distinctive voice. It was that of Sir Holroyd Pinner.

In a second or two, the scene had changed. Shadows came to the doorway, and Sir Holroyd came out into the passage, talking back into the room. A second later, Jedediah Elphick appeared beside him.

'I suppose so,' Sir Holroyd was saying. 'Though I had hoped for a respite from such matters, up here. Tomorrow?'

'Very good, Sir Holroyd, of course. At your service, sir, at your service.' Elphick was smiling broadly, though his eyes were blinking nervously still.

'Now, I feel the need of a breath of air, if you will excuse me.'

'The very thing, sir, the very thing,' Elphick agreed enthusiastically, and followed Sir Holroyd towards the stableyard door. Sir Holroyd did not look as if that had been quite what he had had in mind, but he carried on, and in a moment the pair had disappeared.

What on earth Marcus could have found interesting in that little encounter was beyond Hippolyta. Yet he had still been eavesdropping, a habit of which Hippolyta did not approve – not in other people, anyway.

As soon as Elphick and Sir Holroyd had gone, she strode to the foot of the stairs.

'Marcus! What on earth do you think you are doing?'

Marcus leapt, and his fair face flushed scarlet.

'Nothing!'

'You were listening to their conversation, weren't you?'

'No! Whose conversation? I wasn't paying any attention. My eyes were tired and I – I found this quiet place to stand where the light was not bright and I could rest them.'

'Oh, what rubbish!'

'It's not rubbish! How could you possibly think that those two were talking about anything that could interest me?'

'Mr. Elphick seemed to be arranging a meeting with Sir Holroyd.'

'Sir Holroyd? That's not Sir Holroyd Pinner, is it?'

'Of course it is. Didn't you know? He's staying in town –

well, in Dinnet House. Tell me, Marcus, did Mr. Elphick say anything to you about why he was visiting Ballater?'

'I don't think so … What was that?'

At first Hippolyta thought he was trying to distract her. Then she heard it, too: shouting, coming from outside the hotel. She darted into the room vacated by Elphick and Sir Holroyd. The window was open, no doubt to let out the hot air of some hard-fought card game. Hippolyta hurried over, and Marcus caught her up. They listened hard. Outside, in the trodden snow, Sir Holroyd was now shouting.

'I had no idea you were going to be here!'

'We're staying in the inn: did you want us to keep to our room for the duration of the assembly?'

'Had you said where you were staying …'

'No doubt you might have anticipated it, had you given the matter sufficient thought. Or did you think deliberately to provoke us? Where are you staying, then: some laird's mansion nearby?'

'That's always the issue, isn't it? Jealousy! You're just not grand enough or titled enough for your Whig masters, are you? You'd better get Grey to elevate you to the Peerage: you'll need more Whig peers if you're ever going to get your wicked bill past the House of Lords anyway!'

'Well, at least my masters, as you call them, value me for my talents. What do your Tories value you for? How much did you pay for your seat? All you have to your credit – ha! – is that your grandfather was a banker. Making money from other people's money!'

'Better than making it from other people's misery, as you do!'

'I serve at the Bar and do my duty!'

'Is that what you call it? Clever words to condemn poor souls. Why not reform the law courts, instead of mangling the ancient constituencies to suit your modern fashions?'

How heated two grown men could be over such matters! Hippolyta was shocked at their fervour. Why did they not direct such energy into doing, instead of arguing?

She was aware of other figures out there in the stableyard, but it was difficult to see who lingered at the edge of the lamplight. There was at least one woman, she thought – perhaps Mrs. Broughton? But others could be watching from other windows, just as she and Marcus were doing. The two combatants seemed oblivious to all of them, as if they existed alone in their bubble of light in the snow.

Her mind had wandered for a moment, and when she focussed again the quarrelling men seemed to have reverted once more to their respective status in their parties.

'How it must cut into your time, having to work for a living!' Sir Holroyd taunted Broughton with mock sympathy.

'At least I am capable of living within my means. I did not have to marry money,' Broughton snapped back. Hippolyta nodded to herself. No wonder Lady Pinner looked so miserable, if she was just a moneybox. She was glad she had been able to marry for love.

'Maybe you didn't marry for money, but what did you marry?' asked Sir Holroyd, and his voice had taken on a sly, cunning tone, as if he thought he had found the supreme weapon.

'What?'

Broughton's word came back like a slow blade.

'Well, your wife ... you know her reputation.' Sir Holroyd was smiling. Hippolyta felt like yelling at him to stop. Broughton's face was ice white in the snow, his eyes black as coal. He said nothing, but stared at Sir Holroyd. Abruptly Sir Holroyd must have recognised the danger. He paled, the smile frozen on his face. Broughton was as tense as a lashed sapling, ready to break. At last he spoke.

'I will kill you for that, Pinner,' he said, low and clear. 'I will kill you.'

There was a gasp from somewhere in the shadows. Neither man paid it any attention.

'No, no,' whispered Sir Holroyd. 'No, I'm sorry. I didn't mean ...'

'Come here,' said Broughton, and for a second it almost seemed that Sir Holroyd would obey. He leaned towards Broughton, nearly toppling, hands pleading.

'No,' he whispered again. 'No – let us find another way.'

'Another way? Another way to kill you?'

'Maybe, maybe!' Sir Holroyd smiled, his terrible teeth eager to be off, away, somewhere safe. His voice was shaky. 'What do you say to a duel?'

This time Hippolyta gasped. Surely duels were something from history? Sir Holroyd might as well have challenged Broughton to a joust.

'A duel?' Broughton considered, still tensed. 'What are your terms?'

'One pistol each. No seconds. Monday morning, in the woods up to the top of the town. Behind Dinnet House – everyone knows where it is.'

Broughton nodded thoughtfully.

'You have your own pistols, of course?' he asked.

'I do. And you?'

'I never travel without them, not these days. Your terms are good,' he said, 'but why wait till Monday?'

'What say you, then?'

'Dawn tomorrow, whenever dawn is in this northern clime. One pistol, no seconds. But you would do well to inform the minister that his services may be required. I shall be shooting to kill.'

Chapter Seven

Their illicit arrangement made, the two men shook hands and parted company. Sir Holroyd passed close by the window, and Hippolyta could clearly see that he was shaking. Well he might, she thought: Mr. Broughton's expression as he turned his head to see him go was full of cold fury. Whatever Mrs. Broughton's reputation – and Hippolyta wondered about that, too – the mention of it had made him very angry indeed. Yet what had Sir Holroyd been doing? The two men clearly knew each other quite well, but Sir Holroyd seemed deliberately to provoke Broughton. Was he hoping to deflate Broughton's wrath? Had he wanted a duel? But who would want a duel?

Neither she nor Marcus had spoken since the men outside had parted. The only sound was the fire, humming in the fireplace, and from outside the invisible rearrangement of the witnesses to the challenge, moving quietly back into the inn from their shadows. Hippolyta and Marcus turned now and left the little room, still in silence, and went back to the dancing room. Hippolyta wondered how many people in the end had overheard the challenge in the snowy stableyard: it could not have been her imagination that the whole room seemed subdued.

The innkeeper, sensing that something had gone amiss with his assembly, had a quick word with his servants, nodded to the band and announced that supper would be served after the next dance. Only about half of the couples took to the floor. The rest, stunned by the rumours, murmured on the side lines, eyebrows raised, shaking their heads.

Even the supper was not quite up to the usual standard. The mail coach had made it through the snow that day but not everyone who had been supposed to send supplies on it had managed to reach it in time, so the inn lacked a few of the fresh goods they had been expecting. But the food did cheer the mood a little: people's voices rose again in good humour, as if they were trying their best to forget what had happened, the unwarranted intrusion into their evening. Sir Holroyd and Mr. Broughton were nowhere to be seen. Lady Pinner, a pool of gold and white, sat quietly with Mrs. Strachan in the dancing room, while Mrs. Kynoch brought her delicacies on a small plate. Mrs. Broughton acted as if nothing had happened, and carried on her lively conversation with the Strongs. Hippolyta and Marcus found Patrick talking to the fiddlers about music, and simply stood in silence beside him, unable to think of anything to say.

It was only on the way home, holding Patrick's arm, that she described what they had seen and heard. Marcus was recovered enough to put in a few additions of his own. Patrick was solemn.

'We should tell Dod Durris, the sheriff's man. I don't know what their habits are in London, but duelling is against the law.'

'But Mr. Durris is in Banchory,' Hippolyta objected. 'Surely we could not get a message to him and have him back before dawn? Not in this snow. It is already gone midnight, I believe.'

'Is he any use?' Marcus asked, then stopped as they both turned to glare at him. 'I mean, the sheriff's men in some of these little places ... Has he his wits about him, at all?'

'Mr. Durris is an excellent officer,' said Patrick. 'We have worked together before. You'll see for yourself, probably, if this duel goes ahead. I can't believe Broughton could be so foolish, though.'

'Oh, Patrick, if you had seen him! He was furious with Sir Holroyd. I believe he would have shot him then and there if he had had a pistol.'

'Then and there, perhaps,' said Patrick sensibly, 'but perhaps not in the cold light of a Deeside winter dawn. Perhaps they will see sense in the morning, both of them.' He considered for a moment. 'Perhaps I should make sure I am awake and ready if called, though.'

'What if they do shoot each other? What if Mr. Broughton really does kill Sir Holroyd?'

'Then he'll be charged with murder,' said Marcus flatly.

'One pistol each,' said Hippolyta. 'That's only one shot each, isn't it? And they'll aim wide. Won't they?'

'It is one shot, yes, usually. And many do aim wide, just so that honour is satisfied.' Patrick sighed. 'And this was over their political views?'

'And mocking each other's class. But chiefly about Mrs. Broughton and her reputation.' Hippolyta turned suddenly to Patrick. 'My dearest, I hope that you will never challenge anyone over my reputation!'

'My dearest,' said Patrick with a smile, 'I trust you will never give me cause to! Unless, of course, it is your reputation for wishing to involve yourself in the affairs of others. That reputation I should defend to the death.'

'Don't joke about it, Patrick!' Hippolyta shuddered. 'A man may die tomorrow, and another be charged with murder, and for no good reason – just because one man provoked the temper of another.'

Not for the first time, Hippolyta wondered how Patrick could sleep apparently peacefully when such an event was imminent, after such an evening. Yet there he was, breathing levelly, unconscious even when she took a candle and lit it and peered at his contented expression. She sighed. It was probably part of being a physician, she told herself: he had to be rested and ready when required, and could not waste the night in pondering what had happened, or what might happen. Nevertheless, it could be most provoking.

She took the candle carefully over to the window, and opened a shutter, holding the candle behind it so that she would be able to see. Outside snow was beginning to fall again, gently repairing the damage that the villagers had inflicted on its perfect white cloak. The carefully dug path around the green was already vanishing. But there was a pinkish light in the sky, and dawn was not far away. She longed to paint in the snow, and surely now would be a good time to try, when the light was just easing up, and when she might find some shelter in the woods. She had an image in her mind of what she wanted to paint, with sun and snow and bare trees: she could take some sketches and work it into a full painting when she came home. Setting the candle down she dressed as quickly as she could, lacing on her thickest petticoats. Then she tiptoed downstairs, collected her sketchbook and paints, and began the serious business of wrapping up against the cold. Now that she was out of the bedchamber, she found herself humming the tune that had conjured up her painting.

'O, the rising of the sun and the running of the deer!'

Praying for a visitation of deer, she picked up her bag with gloved hands, drew her hood firmly over her bunched up hair, and slipped out into the snow.

The cold plucked at her face, making her gasp at first. She had thought to bring a small lantern with her, for the dawn was still a little way away, but already many windows were lit and people were up and about at least in their own homes: dawn came late in a Scottish winter. And there were people on the street, too, other shadowy shapes with little lanterns dotting about, making her expedition feel much more respectable and, accordingly, rather less exciting. Still, the fresh snow made for easy walking at present, and she had soon left the centre of the village and skirted the enclosing walls of Dinnet House and its garden: behind it, in darkness, was the weighty crag of Craigendarroch, and at its foot the woods where she hoped she might see deer to paint. Or a duel, came a little voice in her head, but she denied that one. There had been no lights on at the front of Dinnet House, and she had seen no shape like Mr. Broughton's making its way up from the inn, so she told herself that both men had been much too sensible to venture out on a chilly morning to offer threat to each other's lives. It would be ridiculous, and she would not accept such a thing.

Nevertheless she had a strong feeling, as she pressed back her heavy skirts to squeeze between the birch trees, that she was not alone in the woodland. Perhaps some gamekeeper was already about, and she made sure that her lantern was visible, so that she should not be mistaken for a rabbit and shot. She stopped for a moment to listen, but there was a gentle breeze carrying the fresh snow amongst the trees, and it would have been almost impossible to catch the sound of another person's footsteps, particularly if they were deliberately quiet. She found the place she wanted to sit, and faced the point where she hoped the dawn light would most effectively fall through the trees. The snow was easing now, and she had hopes – rather over-optimistic ones - that there might be the least hint of a clear sunrise. She opened her painting box, unfolded her stool, and settled down, determined to move quickly before the cold made her fingers useless.

She had sketched for a moment or two when she definitely heard a footstep, somewhere off to her left. Concentrating on what she was doing, she finished a shape on the paper before looking up. Her heart sank. Two figures, one tall, one shorter, were approaching one another boldly just a little down the hill from where she sat. Each carried a lantern, larger than hers, and they set them down on the ground as if they were prepared for some conversation. Voices drifted up to her on the cold air: she could not quite hear the words, but she was sure that it was indeed Sir Holroyd and Mr. Broughton. But perhaps they had come to apologise to each other, to tell each other that it was all off and they could go home quietly?

But no: the conversation seemed brisk and businesslike. Broughton waved in one direction, to Hippolyta's left, and Sir Holroyd in the other, and there was some further discussion before they each took their lanterns and paced away from one another. For just a moment Hippolyta considered her own safety here: if they aimed at each other, she would be safe enough, but what if they aimed off? She shifted her stool slightly so that she was more protected by one of the thicker trees, and continued to watch, her heart thumping.

Each man paused and looked about, then hung their lanterns on trees near them. With some hesitation and a glance at the other, each then removed his hat, and hung it near a lantern. Hippolyta suppressed an urge to giggle. Then each seemed to spend some moments fiddling with something from their pockets: by a glint in the lantern light she guessed that they were readying their pistols. Suddenly sober again, she wondered: should she run and fetch someone? But whom would she fetch, that either of them would listen to? There was nowhere nearer than Dinnet House, full of Sir Holroyd's family and servants: she doubted that anything they said would sway his purpose.

The dawn light was spreading and the snowfall had eased even more. The tree trunks, black against the light, blended to golden where the lantern light painted them. She caught a glimpse, she thought, of two figures, one to the left of Sir Holroyd and one to the right of Broughton: they must have agreed on seconds after all.

Both figures seemed to have the same sense of self-preservation she herself had felt, and were pressed against reasonably broad trees.

A soft cry drew her attention back to Mr. Broughton. He was ready now, standing facing Sir Holroyd. Sir Holroyd waved, made some final adjustment, and nodded. He too took his stand. Each turned slightly so that his body was sideways to his opponent, though each face, pale blotches in the dawn light, focussed directly on the other. Each now raised his pistol, with what looked like unutterable calm. Each was steady.

'Three!' called Broughton, and Sir Holroyd, voice firm, joined in.

'Two! One!'

The shots echoed. Hippolyta's pulse raced. But neither man moved – neither had been hit!

Then Mr. Broughton sagged slowly to his knees, and fell hard on the snowy ground.

There was a cry, a woman's voice, and some kind of movement amongst the trees. Hippolyta paid it no attention. She ran forward, and reached Broughton at the same moment as Sir Holroyd. Sir Holroyd's face was green-white in the lantern light. Hippolyta snatched down Broughton's lantern and set it beside her own, the better to see.

'Mr. Broughton! Mr. Broughton!'

The man had fallen half on his back, his legs curled beneath him. His skin was white, eyes half-open, mouth sagging. No wound was visible. Hippolyta felt across his chest, well-padded with coat and cloak. In a moment she found it: a ragged hole, already damp around the edges.

'Have you a handkerchief?' she snapped at Sir Holroyd. Already her fingers were fumbling to undo the muffler that Broughton was wearing, to use it as a pad to stop the bleeding. Lucky for him, she thought in some corner of her mind: a countryman would never wear such a thing, but now it might save his life. She glanced up. Sir Holroyd was still standing motionless beside her, his pistol dangling in his right hand. His alarming teeth were chattering. Hippolyta suddenly found she was furious with him, with both of them. But Sir Holroyd, who had started the whole thing, who had not had the good sense to back out, and who had finally shot his opponent, was now being utterly useless. She nudged him hard with her elbow somewhere around the knee. 'Sir Holroyd! Come on, sir! If you cannot be of assistance here, at the very least go for help!'

'What? What help?' He looked as if he might faint. Hippolyta glared at him, trying to keep pressure on Mr. Broughton's chest at the same time. She could see no sign of life in the unconscious man. 'What have I done?'

'Sir Holroyd, if I could reach to slap your face I would!' she exclaimed, quite beyond patience. 'Go at once to the house on the green and fetch my husband. Dr. Napier, remember? Go now!' She gave him another shove with her free hand, and at last he staggered back, staring around him as if trying to remember where the village was. His hands flailed to save his balance, and the pistol lurched upwards. Hippolyta tried to ward it off, and managed instead to grab it, pointing the dangerous end towards the ground as she held the middle of the gun awkwardly. 'Here, give me that, you silly man! And go!'

Hands still flapping about him like a damaged bird, Sir Holroyd at last slithered off down the hill towards the village. The trail of his anxious panting could be heard distantly as he vanished into the trees. She tucked the pistol under her skirts – her bag and box were still where she had left them when she ran down the hill to help – and turned her attention back to Mr. Broughton. He did not seem to be breathing. She drew in a deep sigh, her breath wobbling slightly, frightened and angry, then squealed as a hand landed on her shoulder.

'Mrs. Napier! What on earth is going on? Did I hear shots?'

She spun on her heels, boots catching on the rough ground to tip her over so she sat hard beside Mr. Broughton. Leaning over behind her, hands now on his knees, was the journalist, Jedediah Elphick. His greenish hat tipped down over brown eyes full of anxious concern, and the sharp scent of his eau-de-cologne nipped at the fresh air.

'Mr. Elphick! Oh, a man of sense at last!'

'But what has happened?'

'Two foolish men had a duel, and Mr. Broughton has been shot. I have sent Sir Holroyd for help, but I have no idea if he knows where he is going or indeed where he is. He was in a state of some shock.'

'A duel? Good Lord! What on earth were they fighting over?'

'I don't know,' Hippolyta was looking over Mr. Broughton again, praying wordlessly as she spoke aloud. 'Some stupid reason. How could they be so foolish? Look at poor Mr. Broughton – though he was as foolish as Sir Holroyd.'

'And Sir Holroyd has gone? And taken his gun?'

'Yes, yes, I believe so. But what foolishness!'

'These things happen,' said Mr. Elphick, now philosophically soothing.

'Not in sensible society, surely!' she shot back. 'Oh, I wonder if Sir Holroyd will find and bring someone?'

'So he was the one who shot Broughton?'

'Of course he was. How many men do you think there were wandering around the hillside with pistols at this time of the morning?'

'Just clarifying things,' said Elphick. 'It's just – well,' he paused, glancing about him, then looked down at her with an assessing gaze. She met his eyes, frowning, and he nodded as if ready to accept she could take any further distress. 'I came up this way for a walk this morning – and I admit I was taking a look at Dinnet House, isn't it? Thinking that I might see if I could have an interview with Sir Holroyd later – and I had no intention of venturing into this wilderness. But I saw a couple of men – or lads, maybe, they looked young enough – coming up the road behind me, and I have to say … Well, let's say that I've worked in some of the darker districts of London, and there's a feeling that creeps up my spine sometimes and when it does I know it's time to make for the wider, safer streets. And that's the feeling they gave me. I headed up here, though heaven knows I'm not a natural woodsman. I was glad to see you, for I was wondering if I was leaving civilisation altogether.'

'Two young men? In dark coats?'

He paused, then nodded, glancing down at his own black coat. He, too, wore a muffler. It looked warm.

'That's right. Now I come to think of it, town clothes, aren't they?'

'You don't see so much in the way of dark clothing in the country, certainly, not amongst that class.' Hippolyta frowned again, considering. It was not like Ballater, she thought. That kind of person rarely troubled the village, even in the summer when the visitors came. The pair must be the same ones she had seen, near the church just before Mrs. Riach had her fall. And hadn't Miss Ada remarked on some similar men about the village? It was time the village constable had a word with them. They had certainly looked shiftless when she saw them.

Mr. Elphick leaned over further to study Mr. Broughton's face.

'I'm sorry,' he said, 'but I think the man may well be beyond help.'

'I fear so, too,' Hippolyta admitted. 'But I cannot let go yet, can I?'

'Would you prefer I went to see if your husband has been summoned, or I stayed here with you, Mrs. Napier?'

It was a good question: she had no qualms about waiting alone with Mr. Broughton, dead or alive, but the thought that there might be a couple of dubious young men wandering about at this end of the village made it a different matter.

'I hope that at least Sir Holroyd will run into someone who can get some sense out of him and send help. I think I'd rather you stayed here for now, if that's all right, Mr. Elphick. I should be very much obliged to you.'

'Then of course I shall stay.' He looked about him, as if hoping for a comfortable armchair nearby, then settled against a tree. Hippolyta tried to keep the pressure steady on Mr. Broughton's chest, though she could feel no movement at all beneath her hands. Now that her anger and fear were subsiding, she was beginning to feel chilly, and she was sure there was no heat coming up from the body, either. It was not looking hopeful.

Nearly an hour passed and the sky was liquid, like water used for washing white paint from brushes. Hippolyta was considering her abandoned drawing and hoping it was not ruined, when at last they heard voices below and with delighted relief she recognised Patrick, calling out to her from the woodland edges.

'Up here!' she called back. 'We're up here!'

Patrick was not alone. With him came a tall man in a dark brown coat, glasses perched on his nose. It was the sheriff's man, Dod Durris.

'Mr. Durris!'

'Mrs. Napier.' He bowed, steadying his feet on the slippery ground. 'What on earth have you here?'

'Hippolyta, dearest,' Patrick looked down at her hands in dismay. 'Have you been here all this time?'

She too looked at her hands. Her gloves had been stone-coloured: now they were dark, sticky red. She swallowed hard, gathering her thoughts.

'I fear it was a lost cause,' she said, rising to allow him some space. There was a rattle at her feet, and Durris ducked forward.

'Excuse me,' he said, and backed away, holding the pistol Hippolyta had concealed in her skirts. 'Whose might this be?' His intelligent brown eyes pinned her suddenly, as if suspecting her of highway robbery. She sighed: Mr. Durris often found her in difficult situations.

'It belongs to Sir Holroyd Pinner,' she said distinctly. 'And that one there,' she added, pointing to the edge of a carved wooden butt just visible under Mr. Broughton's wide-flung arm, 'belongs, I suppose, to Mr. Broughton.'

'And Mr. Broughton,' said Patrick, kneeling in the snow, 'is dead.' He had peeled back layers of clothing, matted and damp, from the man's chest, to show a smallish hole, not quite regular, just under the centre of Broughton's ribcage. Pale skin and dark hairs surrounded its ominous blackness: Hippolyta looked away quickly, feeling she had intruded on an intimacy. 'There is no pulse, and he is chilling fast.'

'Well, well, well,' murmured Mr. Elphick, and took off his odd hat, spoiling the effect of respect briefly by wiping his brow with the back of his glove.

'Can I deduce from that,' said Durris, turning his gaze from Hippolyta to the details of the scene about him, 'that the rumoured duel did in fact take place?'

'It did,' said Hippolyta. She could feel her wrath rising again, particularly now that Mr. Broughton was indeed dead. 'The stupid fools came and shot at each other, and now look what has happened!'

'Hippolyta, please don't tell me you witnessed this?' said Patrick. 'And even more, please don't tell me you came here to see it?'

'Of course not, dearest!' She swallowed again, hoping she had sounded convincing. 'I came up here to paint the trees in the dawn – I was hoping for deer, really. I had quite forgotten that this was to be where they were, if they were foolish enough to come. Look, you can see where I set up my drawing board and stool.' She pointed up the hill, thankful for the circumstantial evidence in her favour. Patrick might have been persuaded, but he was not comforted.

'You could have been killed. You know duellers often aim wide. What if one of them had hit you?'

'Well, when I realised what was happening I hid behind a tree, of course,' said Hippolyta.

'When you realised what was happening?' Durris queried. 'You did not attempt to stop them?'

'No!' cried Patrick and Hippolyta together. 'It would have been far too dangerous to interrupt,' said Patrick, while Hippolyta defended herself with, 'I was so shocked I could scarcely believe they were going to go through with it.'

'Yet they did ...' Durris again turned to examine the area. He drew out his tiny notebook, and began to make those minute points and lines that Hippolyta so longed to understand. She had never seen inside the notebook, only tried to make out from his hand movements what he could possibly be writing or drawing. It was very frustrating. 'Did they have seconds?'

'Well, they weren't going to,' said Hippolyta, and started as Durris' gaze fell on her again. 'I happened to hear the challenge – it was last night, at the assembly in the inn.'

'So I heard: I did not realise it was an event open to the general public.'

'They were in the stableyard, just outside the windows,' said Hippolyta tartly. 'It was my impression that a good number of people heard it all. My brother, for one: he was with me.'

'Indeed?' Durris made a very small point, and Hippolyta wondered if she had brought Marcus under some kind of suspicion. But it seemed unlikely: what could he have done?

'Anyway, I heard them both quite clearly. One pistol, no seconds, that was what they said.'

Durris sighed, and nodded slowly to himself.

'It sounds like a serious matter,' he murmured, which to

Hippolyta seemed like nonsense. How could any duel not be a serious matter? She was about to question him on the matter when they were interrupted by a shout from the trees below.

'Constable? Constable, you must arrest me at once. I have killed a man!'

Chapter Eight

Dod Durris, who was not a constable, nevertheless turned at the sound and waited calmly where he stood until the man thus addressing him had climbed to their level, panting a little. Clouds of steam wreathed his face. Patrick made the necessary intervention.

'This is Dod Durris, the sheriff's man. Durris, this is Sir Holroyd Pinner, M.P.'

'Indeed?' Durris was politely curious. They bowed to each other, and Hippolyta could see on Sir Holroyd's already strained face that puzzlement as to where precisely to peg Durris socially. Was he talking to a servant or an equal? Even his bow was equivocal. Then he turned to look down at Broughton on the ground, and put up a hand to remove his hat. It was only then that he seemed to remember it was not there, and his fingers made a little fan of helplessness in the air.

'Poor Broughton! This is more than dreadful. This - I did not mean – of course I did not mean that this should happen.' The hand now gestured downwards, apologetic.

'You mean you challenged him to a duel, but did not wish to kill him?' Durris asked, without emphasis.

'Well, of course I didn't wish to kill him! I wanted ...' But it was not clear, for the moment, what Sir Holroyd had wanted. He seemed genuinely perplexed. 'I aimed off,' he added, sadly.

'This is your pistol?' Durris showed him flat on his hand the one he had picked up from under Hippolyta's skirts. Sir Holroyd nodded, putting out long fingers for it.

'I'll keep it for the moment, sir, if I may,' said Durris, and lowered it with great care into his coat pocket. 'Tell me more about the arrangements for this duel. When did you offer the challenge to

Mr. Broughton?'

'Last night, at the inn.'

'Over what concern?'

Sir Holroyd's teeth seemed to shuffle awkwardly.

'I'd rather not say.'

Durris nodded, and Sir Holroyd looked relieved, until Durris made a tiny shape in his little notebook. It seemed to unnerve Sir Holroyd again.

'And what were your arrangements?'

'To meet here at dawn, single pistol, no seconds.'

'No seconds? Why was that?'

'It was not the subject of any discussion, but I believe we didn't want to draw anyone else into the business. I cannot even remember which of us suggested it, but if it was Broughton, I agreed readily enough. The matter was personal.'

'And single pistol?'

'It reduced the chances of a fatality,' said Sir Holroyd, with some of his old confidence.

'Only by half,' Durris observed, looking down again at Broughton. 'Are you sure you brought only the one?'

'Certainly, sir! I am a man of my word!'

'Then where is the pair to this one?'

'At home – that is, at Dinnet House, where we are staying.'

'Dinnet House, indeed.' Durris glanced at Hippolyta. She met his eye: it seemed that Dinnet House was to involve itself in another unpleasantness. Patrick stood up and came to her side: while Durris had been speaking, Patrick had tidied the clothing over Mr. Broughton's chest, and now the two carters who had helpfully carried Mrs. Riach home after her fall appeared with a hurdle. Patrick directed them as they arranged Broughton ready to lift him, his arms stiffened just enough in the cold, or perhaps just with the thickness of his coat, to make folding them across his chest a difficulty. Over the corpse Patrick laid a blanket he had brought with him, giving the dead man some privacy. To the east the sun slid out from the pearly clouds and sent a red-gold ray through the woods, just as Hippolyta had wanted it for her painting. She gave a small sigh of delight and frustration, and turned back just in time to see the ray glance on the great rose of blood, still bright, that had spread under Broughton's body. Now she could believe that he was dead.

The men stood, bare-headed, as the carters slithered silently down the hill sideways with the corpse. Then Durris turned away from both corpse and Sir Holroyd, and said,

'And you, sir, what is your part in this?'

Hippolyta jumped: she had almost forgotten that the journalist, Jedediah Elphick, was still there. Again, Patrick made the introductions, as Elphick slipped forward into the circle. They all moved a little away from the bloodstain.

'I arrived late on the scene,' said Elphick, eager to help, 'so I didn't see what happened. When I got here – I heard shots, see – the lady was already kneeling down trying to help the dead man – I believe he was already dead when I arrived - and Sir Holroyd here had already gone.' Elphick was nervous, Hippolyta noted: his round brown eyes darted about, just as they had before he had relaxed at their house. His sparse hair must have left his bare head chilly. She hoped that Durris would understand the journalist was just shy, and not take his nervous manner as a sign of guilt.

'You're from London, you say?'

'That's right.'

'Did you by chance know the gentleman who died?'

'I'm a parliamentary reporter, Mr. Durris. I know all their faces – including you, Sir Holroyd, of course.'

'So Mr. Broughton was a parliamentarian too? George Broughton?'

'The very man. It is as if Westminster has come to Ballater, Mr. Durris!'

The thought gave Elphick confidence, but Durris did not look impressed.

'Had you seen anything of him since your arrival in Ballater, Mr. Elphick?'

'Hardly at all. He was staying at the inn, I believe, and that's a bit pricy for the likes of me!'

'Then did you know about the duel?'

'I'd heard a rumour, but it wasn't anything definite. I didn't know where it was meant to be, or anything, and to be honest I wasn't much concerned about it. See, these things are all planned, but they don't often come off in the end.'

'Then what were you doing up in the woods just after dawn?'

'Ah,' said Elphick, 'now that's a thing that might interest you.' More settled now, he recited again what he had told Hippolyta, about being followed by the dubious-looking young men. 'I'm not saying they were following me,' he added, 'but they were heading in the same direction, and I didn't like the look of them at all. That's why I ducked in here.'

'Hm,' said Durris.

'It's true,' said Hippolyta quickly. 'I believe I've seen the same young men twice in the village yesterday. Miss Ada Strong saw them, too. They look like town men – you know, dark clothes and their skin has an indoor look, a bit grey.'

'Interesting,' said Durris, regarding her thoughtfully. 'I wonder where they are staying? Well, you'll do me the honour of not writing anything about this matter as yet, Mr. Elphick,' said Durris, with surprising firmness. Elphick blinked.

'Of course. But let me know when I can, eh?'

Durris nodded, and turned back to face the place where Broughton had fallen.

'Mrs. Napier,' he said, 'is that where Broughton was standing to shoot? Or did he move before he fell?'

'He didn't move at all,' said Hippolyta definitely. 'The two shots rang out, and there was a moment when nothing happened, and then – then he just crumpled.' Despite herself, her voice quivered. Patrick slipped her hand into the crook of his arm, squeezing it hard.

'And where was Sir Holroyd?'

'I was over here,' said Sir Holroyd immediately, about to stride towards the other end of the small clearing. Durris put out a hand to stop him.

'One moment, please. Over there, you say?' He considered the ground between them and where Sir Holroyd had indicated, then looked down at Sir Holroyd's boots.

'When I first saw them,' Hippolyta put in, 'they were standing just there, both of them. They had a discussion, which I couldn't hear, then Sir Holroyd walked over there and Mr. Broughton came to this point. And they hung up their lanterns – and their hats –'

'Really,' Sir Holroyd interrupted, in a slightly shaky voice, 'if I had had any idea that our every move was being observed …'

'Village life,' said Patrick quickly.

'And then they seemed to be preparing their pistols.'

'Of course.' Durris looked around at head height. Sir Holroyd had left behind both his hat and his lantern, still where he had hung them, a good indication of where he had stood to shoot. Hippolyta had used Mr. Broughton's lantern, but his hat was still hooked on a branch. Durris looked again at the ground between the firing points. Hippolyta tried to see what he could be looking at: there was nothing that she could see that went against her own account of what had happened.

'Mr. Broughton began to count down from three, and Sir Holroyd joined in, and then they fired.'

Durris picked up Broughton's gun from the ground, and studied it for a moment. He slid it into the opposite pocket from Sir Holroyd's pistol. His coat pockets swelled heavily.

'I wonder where Mr. Broughton's shot went, then?' he asked, half to himself. 'Dr. Napier, will you walk with me over yonder?'

Patrick gave Hippolyta's hand another little squeeze, and let go. As they walked away, her quick ears caught Durris asking,

'The wound was right for a pistol shot, would you say?'

She did not hear her husband's reply, as Mr. Elphick stepped a little closer to her.

'What's his story, then? He's a funny bloke.' He nodded at Durris.

'He's the sheriff's man. He's very good at his job.'

'I daresay,' Elphick nodded, considering Durris intently.

'He seems competent enough.' Sir Holroyd appeared to agree with Hippolyta. 'But I can't understand why we must have all this standing about here in the cold. Isn't it enough that I have admitted my – my crime? A man is dead and another killed him: what could be more straightforward?'

Durris and Patrick were studying something on a tree trunk, two or three yards from where Sir Holroyd had stood. Durris put a finger up to poke some fresh damage, pale and spiky, to the wood.

'It looks as if Mr. Broughton aimed wide, anyway,' said Hippolyta grimly.

'I did too!' Sir Holroyd was quick to defend himself. 'I aimed wide! But pistols are never very accurate, you know. All kinds of things happen with pistols. They're really very dangerous.'

'Are they indeed?' asked Hippolyta, still watching her

husband and Durris. They were circling the tree, now, and Patrick pointed out something of interest to Durris, who bent and peered at it more closely. Then they began to cast around a little further, like dogs trying to pinpoint a trail.

'Oh, yes, a pistol can be very dangerous,' Sir Holroyd went on, apparently unaware of any irony. 'I knew a man had his hand blown off when his pistol misfired. But then friends of mine attended a duel when of four pistols, not one fired! How foolish they all looked, standing there on the Heath and nothing at all happened! So you see, they are very unpredictable. Very unpredictable.'

Durris' notebook must be almost full, Hippolyta thought, only half listening to Sir Holroyd's chatter. Patrick and the sheriff's man must at last have been contented with what they had found, and to her relief they began to walk slowly back towards the others, looking about them as they went. When they rejoined Hippolyta and the two Londoners, Durris removed his glasses thoughtfully, as if he had seen all there was to see. He wiped them on his spotless handkerchief. Hippolyta noted that it was an elderly piece of cloth, but had been of rather good quality. She even thought that she caught sight of a 'D' embroidered in the corner, but she might have imagined it.

'Now, Sir Holroyd,' he said, replacing his glasses with delicacy. 'You are quite sure you and Mr. Broughton brought no seconds with you?'

'Quite sure: we agreed on that straightaway.'

'And you asked no one else to come along?'

'Of course not.'

'Can you think of anyone Mr. Broughton might have brought with him?'

'Why should he? If we agreed on no seconds, he would have brought no one. He knew how to behave,' he added, with another dubious look at Durris, as if wondering if Durris would know how to behave.

'Who else knew about the duel? Was there anyone who might have come to witness it without your invitation?'

'Of course not!' said Sir Holroyd again, then seemed to consider. 'Well, I don't suppose we were over-careful who heard us quarrel. There may have been someone, some servant at the inn, who heard what we had arranged. If you are looking for a reliable witness, perhaps ...' He may have caught the edge of Hippolyta's glare, for he did not pursue that line any further. 'I cannot think why anyone would concern themselves with our private matters. We know no one in this village, and nor did the Broughtons, I believe.'

'You don't think,' said Patrick diffidently, 'that perhaps Lady Pinner might have followed you? She must have been very concerned for your safety in the circumstances.'

'Lady Pinner? I don't believe she knew anything about it,' said Sir Holroyd. Hippolyta privately doubted that: rumours had flown at the assembly. 'And in any case ... no, I am sure she would not have followed me. She – she would not be well enough to wander the woods at this time of the morning. Surely, as her physician, it is not something you would recommend to her.'

'Of course not. But sometimes our anxieties take us to odd places, at odd times.' Patrick met Hippolyta's eye with a little smile.

'Not Lady Pinner's, I assure you,' Sir Holroyd said, and his tone was one of unexpected sorrow.

'Sir Holroyd,' said Durris, as if it had only just occurred to him, 'you are no doubt cold and tired. Please go home – back to Dinnet House – and I shall call later to question you further in comfort. But I pray you do not speak to anyone about what has occurred.'

'I may go home?'

'To Dinnet House, yes.'

'Without a guard? Not to custody?'

'Not as yet, no,' said Durris, his face bland.

'Thank you, sir, thank you!' Sir Holroyd bowed, and turned even as he straightened. In a moment he was stumbling back down the hill towards the house that could be seen through the bare trees. The duel had been arranged almost on his doorstep.

'Think he thought you'd have him chained up in a cell by now,' said Mr. Elphick with an uncertain smile, watching him go.

'Now, Mr. Elphick,' said Durris, turning to him. Elphick's nervous eyes flared wide again, and he pursed his lips in preparation for interrogation. 'You told me about these young men that appeared to be following you from the village. Did you hear them speak at all?'

'Only a little.'

'Did you have an impression of their origins?'

'Their origins? Oh, you mean what accents did they have? Well, not Londoners, anyway. Scotch, I thought at the time. Though as to whether they were local or from elsewhere in North Britain I wouldn't like to say.'

Durris nodded, but made no note.

'Did they follow you into the wood?'

'I don't rightly know, to be honest. Sometimes it's better not to look back, when you're nervous about what might be behind you. Shows them you're worried, and that means you're weak.'

'But you didn't hear anything, or have the sense that there were people there?'

'Well,' Elphick considered, 'yes, there was that. I certainly didn't think I was alone, which is what I would have expected. And then, of course, I heard the shots.'

'Yes, the shots …' Durris considered, glancing back at the tree in which he and Patrick had taken so much interest. They were again standing only a few feet from where Broughton's body had lain: it would have been hopeless now to trace their criss-cross movements in the beaten snow, but the rose of blood, somewhat darkened, was still shocking. Broughton's hat hung from the tree where he had hooked it. Durris stepped across and lifted it, granting it a quick examination: it was a warm, wide-brimmed beaver, as far as Hippolyta could see, low-crowned and silk-lined. Durris absently brushed fragments of bark off the fur, and turned his attention again to the tree trunks around it. Then he returned to Elphick. 'Where were you when you heard them?'

'Oh! Now, I'm not sure I could tell you exactly. I'm not a native woodsman, you know, Mr. Durris!'

'Then let's see if we can find your footprints,' said Durris. 'The snow is not thick under the trees, but there is in places enough to trace some movements. Let me see your boot soles?'

Elphick balanced himself awkwardly, first facing Durris and trying to turn his foot up in front of his other knee, then turning and raising his sole for inspection as if he were a horse being shoed. Durris thanked him solemnly, then began to search around where Elphick had been standing. Almost at once he found a trail, and moved off, a little stiff-legged, followed by Patrick. Both of them were careful not to step where any footprints might be. Elphick drew back to Hippolyta.

'Extraordinary! He's liked a hound on the trail, is he not? Do all the constables in the countryside pursue their quarry like this?'

'Sheriff's man. It's a fairly simple procedure to follow some footprints in the snow, Mr. Elphick!' Hippolyta laughed. 'Shall we follow? He will want you to be able to show him where you were when you heard the shots.' She set off, treading in her husband's footprints, encouraging Mr. Elphick to follow her.

They were almost at the edge of the woodland, in clear view of the road that led between Dinnet House and the village, when Elphick finally called out,

'It must have been about here, Mr. Durris!'

'You were some distance away, then,' said Durris, examining Elphick's prints. Hippolyta had caught up with them, and saw the steady line of bootprints heading up between the trees. 'How far behind you were the men you saw?'

'Oh,' said Elphick, looking towards the road and squinting as if trying to see his memories. 'I should say they were about … there? There were two of them, and one was a bit ahead of the other.'

'About a hundred yards away?' suggested Patrick.

'No, a bit less. Say fifty or sixty?'

'Fifty or sixty yards,' repeated Durris, and made a note. Elphick looked nervously at the little book.

'About that,' he qualified.

'Fifty or sixty yards away,' said Durris again. He adjusted his glasses.

'Yes, well, I wasn't measuring it exactly!'

'Tell me,' said Durris thoughtfully. 'You say you're not a woodsman, Mr. Elphick. Two men are some distance behind you on a road, and you are alarmed enough that you consider entering the woods to avoid them. Just as you reach the trees, you hear shots ahead. Did you not think to hesitate, even a little? If nothing else, you might think of poachers, of gamekeepers, of innocent men who might yet accidentally shoot you when you enter an unfamiliar woodland with no awareness of what might be happening there. But your footprints are straight and confident –

you head on into the woods, and risk the shots rather than the men behind you?'

'I – well, yes. I did. I mean, I don't suppose I reasoned it out at the time. I'm not much used to hearing shots, either, to tell you the truth, Mr. Durris. And the men – well, as I said, they – there was something about them. I did not like the look of them at all.'

'You mustn't have,' agreed Durris peaceably. 'I shall have to look into these strangers in the village, if they are causing such alarm.'

'I really think you'd better,' said Elphick, nodding hard. Durris considered him. Elphick's eyes were round with nerves.

'Well, Mr. Elphick,' said Durris at last, 'I think you had better repair to your lodging for now. You've had an eventful morning. And I'll just remind you that I do not want anything written about this just yet.'

'Oh, yes, yes. I quite agree,' said Elphick quickly, as though they had discussed it in detail. He bowed, and scurried off at speed, making even better progress once he reached the road. His boots, Hippolyta noticed, were very large.

'He seems anxious,' Durris remarked, watching him go.

'He's like that, though,' said Hippolyta. 'He was very nervous when he first arrived and met us, though he had travelled from Edinburgh with my brother. He's shy, I think.'

'I think so,' agreed Durris, and Hippolyta felt relieved.

'Well,' said Patrick, 'do you want me to take a closer look at the body? As I said, entrance wound and exit wound, and it looks just like a pistol shot – though I would perhaps have expected all his thick winter clothing to slow down a shot from as far off as that, so that there was no exit wound.'

'The carters have taken Mr. Broughton to the kirk for now,' Durris said. 'I wanted to see Mrs. Broughton before she was confronted with her husband's body, though no doubt she has already received the bad news.'

'You don't think she was somewhere in the woods, do you?' asked Hippolyta suddenly. 'Watching? Only I'm sure there were others here. And I've just remembered. I thought I heard a woman cry out, just as Mr. Broughton fell.'

'Did you indeed?' Patrick asked. He and Durris looked at one another.

'There was a woman there, we thought,' said Durris, knowing it was easier to tell Hippolyta straightaway than to try to conceal evidence from her and have her dig for it herself. 'There were prints from small boots, in two places, maybe three.'

'Are some of them mine, though?'

'Apart from yours.' Durris gave her one of his rare smiles. 'We knew where you were watching from, and how you ran down to see to Broughton. But the snow is patchy under the trees, and the other bootprints are a bit here and there. We'll have to see if Mrs. Broughton has a pair of wet boots this morning.'

'We?' asked Hippolyta, hoping she was right.

'Well, you apparently know the Broughtons a little, and as you know I prefer to have a woman with me when I am interviewing a woman,' said Durris, 'and a physician is always handy, too, if you can spare me the time, Dr. Napier?'

'Of course,' said Patrick, with a grin. 'You know we are at your service in these matters.'

'But what is this matter?' Hippolyta asked. 'There was a duel, and Sir Holroyd shot Mr. Broughton, and he died. I saw it, and Sir Holroyd admits it. Why are you concerned with anyone else being there? Or are you wondering,' she added dangerously, 'like Sir Holroyd, if I am a reliable witness?'

'Best not to answer that, my friend,' said Patrick. 'By the way, Durris, you seem to be walking very carefully. Are you in pain or discomfort?'

Durris' mouth twitched sideways.

'I'm walking carefully,' he said, stopping and reaching into his pocket, 'because I have an undischarged pistol in my pocket.'

'But –' said Hippolyta, for a moment not realising what he had said. Then it dawned on her. 'Wait a minute – do you mean Sir Holroyd's pistol?'

'I do,' he said, drawing it out with extreme caution. 'Look: it has misfired.' He held it out, pointing it carefully downwards and avoiding the least contact with the trigger. He eased back the firing pin, and waving them back he used a stick to poke out the charge, as gently as if it were a newborn baby.

'But then … But …' The picture of the duel unfolded again in her mind, and she found herself searching it, looking for the flaw.

'But then if Sir Holroyd's pistol misfired, who killed Mr.

Broughton?' asked Patrick quietly.

Chapter Nine

'So it is true, then.'

Mrs. Broughton's voice, usually low, squeaked a little. She held her head high, as if she did not wish to look daunted by their news, but her eyes were devastated.

'I'm afraid so, ma'am,' said Durris. They were in a small parlour on the inn's ground floor, overlooking the grey-brown flow of the Dee. Mrs. Broughton stood by the window: she turned away and watched the river, perhaps examining the bare trees, snow-laden, on the opposite bank. It was a bleak enough view this pearl-grey morning for anyone. The cold light outlined her face, her eyebrows and lashes as dark as the tree branches, her pallor snow-white.

'Will you be so good as to sit, for a moment, ma'am?' Durris asked politely. 'They are bringing hot brandy. It will be a remedy for the shock.'

Even as he finished speaking the door opened and a maid entered with a tray. Patrick took up the poker and began to heat it for the brandy, turning it in the blazing hearth, and the maid curtseyed and left. Mrs. Broughton, still as a painting, at last moved as if something had snapped, and sat abruptly on a stool between the window and the fireplace. Hippolyta went to sit by her, taking her hand. Mrs. Broughton looked at her in surprise, then gave a little smile, squeezing her fingers in gratitude.

'How did you hear the news?' Durris asked.

'I thought something was amiss, for I woke to find him away from our room. I went downstairs for a breath of air, and adjourned to the stables – I like horses, and find them soothing. There was a charming little pony there, though he is a trifle bad-tempered.' Hippolyta and Patrick exchanged guilty glances: the pony was theirs. 'The stable lad was gossiping with another boy. They said there had been a duel and that a man had been killed. Of course I listened, and then the boy said that Sir Holroyd had come down to the village to fetch the doctor – you, I suppose, Dr. Napier,' she added, watching absently as he dipped the poker into the jug of brandy. 'So of course, if Sir Holroyd lived …'

'You knew Mr. Broughton was to fight a duel, then?' asked Durris.

'Oh!' Mrs. Broughton's smile was painful to see. 'There are always fights! As recently as last week in Edinburgh – he has such a temper, unfortunately!'

'These are brought about by his political opinions and activities?'

'Not entirely. You know he is – was a barrister? He was often involved in sensational cases, you know, and if someone disagreed with the verdict or thought he had not spoken up well enough to attack or defend, well, people would even stop him in the streets to challenge him and he never had the sense to let it go easily.'

'But a duel is a little different, is it not?'

She cast Durris a look, as though it were a more perceptive question than she had expected.

'Who did you say you were again? Forgive me.'

'Durris, ma'am, the sheriff's man.'

'Oh.' She straightened a little, and considered. 'Yes, there have been a few duels, though they were always called by other people. He was far too hot-headed to wait for some appointed time to make polite gestures with a pistol!'

'Yet he had pistols with him.'

'Yes, but they are not duelling pistols. They were just for defence on the journey. He was quite a good shot, really, and he told me he always shot wide – of course, by the time any duel came around he had calmed down anyway.'

'Do you have his other pistol?'

'His other pistol?'

'He and Sir Holroyd agreed on one pistol each this morning,' Durris explained.

'Really? Who was his second? He knows almost no one here – oh, was it you, Dr. Napier?'

'They also agreed not to have seconds,' said Durris, before

A MURDEROUS GAME

Patrick could answer. 'Dr. Napier was not present.'

'Well, that is strange. What if there had been some disagreement? It could have been very dangerous ... oh.' Her face, which had developed a little more colour, paled again. Hippolyta opened her mouth to explain that there had been no disagreement, but she caught Durris' eye and closed it sharply again before she could give anything away.

'May I see the other pistol, ma'am? And the room you shared, if I may.' He had already ascertained from the innkeeper that the Broughtons had economically taken only the one room. Mrs. Broughton looked surprised.

'But of course ... I suppose. It's just up the stairs.' She rose to her feet.

'You don't have to be present if you don't want to,' said Durris, but she shook her head briskly.

'Of course I'll come. It feels rude not to.'

She led the way along the passage and opened a door, leading them inside. Patrick, with foresight, took the hot brandy with them, and Hippolyta and Durris followed. The room was a generous one, with not only a bed – still unmade – but also a table and hard chair and a couple of armchairs. The Broughtons' trunks were lined against the wall, all closed, but the desk was layered with papers, festooned with the tapes that had been used to tie them. Nesting amongst them was a long, flat wooden box, scuffed from travel, and closed. Durris spotted it straightaway and went to open it. It was unlocked. From her place by the door, Hippolyta could see that it contained one pistol, with a carved wooden butt. The carving was more functional than decorative, designed to give a better grip in the hand, but there was some engraving on the metalwork, and Durris murmured 'G.B.' as he pointed the initials out to Patrick. He lifted the gun out of its shaped holder, making sure he did not touch the trigger, and sniffed it delicately. Then he felt in his coat pocket and brought out the pistol that had been found under Broughton's dead arm. As far as Hippolyta could see, they matched perfectly. Mrs. Broughton cleared her throat.

'Did he – did he fire his?'

'He fired wide, Mrs. Broughton,' said Durris, turning to meet her eye. She nodded, pleased that he had done no wrong, pleased that he had not lied to her.

'Did you go any further than the stable yard this morning?' he asked.

'No – yes, a little. I walked along just to where the bridge must have been, to look at the river. I like watching it: it's peaceful.' The bridge had been almost beside the inn, so she had not been far – by her own admission, at least.

'Is that what brought you and Mr. Broughton here at this time of year?' Hippolyta asked, curious. 'Were you looking for peace and quiet?'

Mrs. Broughton smiled at her, friendly.

'I believe so, yes. London has been very busy – alarmingly so – over the last little while. When Parliament was prorogued, I told him it was a sign and he should be away, taking his chance to rest. He wanted to stay and plot, but heavens! He needed to get away, and I certainly did.'

'And you were not the only ones, clearly,' said Hippolyta.

'The Pinners? I should have preferred that they were not here – even before wh-what has happened. Anyone, from either party, would have served as a reminder of the House.'

'Do you know what they quarrelled about, Mrs. Broughton?' Durris asked. She did not reply straightaway, taking a moment to sit firmly on one of the armchairs. She sighed.

'I imagine it was a matter once again of social standing.'

'Social standing? In what way?'

She smiled.

'Many thought that my husband was not of a sufficient standing in society to represent his party. The Whig hierarchy, you see – they are almost all well born, gentlemen or the sons of aristocrats. They look down their Roman noses at the likes of us, you know! But they need my husband: they need his powers of oratory, his arguments, his wit. And the ones who recognise that try to help him fit in, find him posts in Government that will pay him so that he can drop some of his legal work and afford to be in the Commons – most of them, you know, have no need of employment for their wealth.'

'So there was friction within the Whigs? But Sir Holroyd is a Tory, is he not?'

'He is, and he is against Reform, and he is not quite good enough to march with the grandest Whigs – he is only a baronet, and his grandfather was only a banker - but he is high-headed enough to look down on us with more venom than those above him. As is so often the way, I believe.' She smiled again, sadly.

'But would Sir Holroyd have any other reason to want your husband dead, Mrs. Broughton?' Durris asked.

'To want him dead? But surely it was an accident?'

'There was certainly a malfunction of Sir Holroyd's pistol,' Durris conceded, obscurely.

'Then it was indeed an accident. Sir Holroyd and my husband disliked each other intensely, and would have done, I believe, had they both been of the same political persuasion. They simply disliked each other, as people. They could not meet but exchange hostile words, and they could not seem to avoid meeting. If I had not arranged this journey myself, almost at random, I would have been prepared to believe that George had come to Ballater chiefly to quarrel with Sir Holroyd – or that Sir Holroyd had seen to the encounter himself.'

Durris used the pause that followed this statement to extract his notebook, and make in it what seemed to Hippolyta to be several tiny circles.

'Did they know each other well, then?'

'I know my husband followed every word written about Sir Holroyd in *The Times* – his mutterings and cursings have accompanied many a breakfast table during our marriage. And from anything I ever heard Sir Holroyd say, he followed my husband's speeches with the attention of a passionate admirer. But no, they were not well acquainted, personally.'

'This next may seem an odd question, Mrs. Broughton, but I should be obliged if you could answer it for me. Was there anyone who would have desired, or who would have benefitted from, your husband's death?'

'Benefitted – do you mean financially?' She was frowning, but not with displeasure.

'In any way.'

'Financially not at all. We have not been blessed with children, and his fortune is little enough that it would not excite any nephew or cousin. Politically, perhaps, for he has been a force to be reckoned with amongst the Reformers. Yet there are others in the party: my husband's death would by no means sway the vote or stop the campaign in its tracks. If he had been a peer, then perhaps – the numbers in the Upper House are much riskier than in the Commons.'

'Then from some violent personal enmity, perhaps? Apart from Sir Holroyd?'

'Apart from Sir Holroyd I cannot imagine,' she said firmly. 'He could annoy people, I know that, and as I have said people challenged his actions as a barrister. But I can think of no one who detested him the way Sir Holroyd did. Had my husband been murdered, I believe I should direct the magistrates to have Sir Holroyd arrested at once.'

They each studied her, but she seemed undaunted by their gaze. She sipped her brandy.

'Why do you ask?'

'If it is proved that Sir Holroyd fired the shot that killed Mr. Broughton, you know he is likely to be charged with murder,' said Durris. Hippolyta was impressed by the way he skirted around the truth, then reprimanded herself silently for thinking she could learn from it.

'Of course. Poor Lady Pinner. Or perhaps not.'

'Perhaps not? Do you know the lady?'

'We have met once or twice. With another woman, perhaps, we could have sympathised with each other over our husbands' foolishness, but I found her difficult to speak to. Of course, she too considers herself rather above us, but it was not that, I think: it is always hard to penetrate such great and self-absorbed unhappiness, isn't it?'

'You think she is unhappy in her marriage?' Hippolyta asked, trying to sound discreet and concerned, rather than just nosy.

'Of course! It's as plain as can be. She is completely miserable, and he is not much better, is he? At least I can say that: at least I can say that George and I were completely happy together – or as happy as two intelligent people with minds of their own can ever be. I think you know what I mean, don't you?' she smiled at Hippolyta, who smiled back, only to see that tears were suddenly streaming down Mrs. Broughton's broad face.

'Oh, my dear Mrs. Broughton!' Hippolyta threw her arms around the woman, and held her close as Mrs. Broughton sobbed into her shoulder. The storm was brief, though violent: in a few moments Mrs. Broughton straightened away from Hippolyta and began to rummage in her reticule for a handkerchief.

'I must apologise, Mrs. Napier.'

'Not at all. You are being so brave!'

Mrs. Broughton's sniff was mingled with a smile.

'Not much choice, eh? Best to get on with – with whatever might happen. Oh, my poor George!' Another sob threatened to overwhelm her, but she swallowed hard and brought her breathing under control. She took a sip of the brandy, now only lukewarm, and shuddered. 'Strong!' she murmured.

They all fell silent for a moment, allowing her to recover a little, and became aware of footsteps on the wooden boards of the passage outside. No one spoke as the steps came closer, and paused. There was a knock at the door. Mrs. Broughton cleared her throat.

'Come in!' she called, pushing strength into her voice. The door opened, and Jedediah Elphick stood in the doorway.

'Mr. Elphick!' said Hippolyta in surprise.

'Mrs. Broughton!' said Mr. Elphick, barely glancing at Hippolyta. 'You have heard the news, then? The dreadful news?'

'Oh, Mr. Elphick,' said Mrs. Broughton, in a voice that was half-pleased, half, Hippolyta thought, oddly resigned. She put out a hand to the newcomer. 'My poor, poor George, Mr. Elphick!'

'Whatever I can do, Mrs. Broughton,' said Mr. Elphick, and for a moment it looked as if he were about to sag to his knees in front of her. Instead he took her hand, and pressed it to his lips with some fervour. 'Whatever I can do to be of service to you at this dark hour, Mrs. Broughton, you have only to ask it!'

'Good gracious, Mr. Elphick,' said Mrs. Broughton, and her voice trembled a little again. 'You are very kind – more than kind – but I cannot think of anything … This is the sheriff's man, Mr. Durris.'

'We have met, ma'am,' put in Durris.

'Have you? Oh, splendid. Mr. Elphick, Mr. Durris has asked me if anyone would benefit from poor George's death, or would have desired it at all. Of course we have talked of Sir Holroyd, but can you think of anyone else? Any other person who might, *for whatever reason*,' and she placed some emphasis on these words, 'have wanted my husband dead?'

Jedediah Elphick, releasing her hand after what seemed a lengthy spell, turned and surveyed the others in the room. His brown eyes blinked rapidly, as if he were taking in their presence for the first time.

'Why would you want to know such a thing? Sir Holroyd shot him, surely? You're not thinking that someone might have put him up to it? I can't see Sir Holroyd fighting a duel for anyone but Sir Holroyd, can you?'

'It's an interesting idea,' said Durris unexpectedly. 'I may have to consider that.'

Elphick's uncertain eyes widened in alarm.

'Oh, look, dear Mrs. Napier, gentlemen,' said Mrs. Broughton, rising with some effort from her seat, 'please. If you have no more questions for me just now, I should like very much to be left alone for a little, to prepare myself to go to my husband – my husband's body. I may go to him, may I not, Mr. Durris? Where is he?'

'He's in the kirk,' said Durris. 'If you will, I shall find the local woman who helps with such matters, and send her to show you the way. She will do all that you require her to do.'

'That would be most kind, Mr. Durris.' She pulled herself up straight. 'I shall wait for her here, if you will let me be at peace for now.'

They left her there, standing firm in the middle of the chamber, straight and strong with eyes as bleak as the snowy woods outside the window.

'You seem well acquainted with Mrs. Broughton,' Durris remarked when they reached the inn's hallway on the floor below. Elphick seemed to be leaving the building with them. He made a little grimace, and ushered the Napiers out through the narrow doorway ahead of him.

'I've known Elinor Broughton for many years,' he said.

Durris waited until they were all outside and in the roadway, so that he could speak without having to raise his voice.

'Presumably you knew Mr. Broughton well, then, too.'

'Not so well as all that,' said Elphick. 'I was acquainted with Mrs. Broughton before they were married, but then, well, social circles change. Of course, I see her sometimes in Parliament.'

'Women are allowed in?' Hippolyta asked, who had not

considered such a thing before.

'They're allowed in a little box thing at the top, where they can see what's going on,' Elphick explained. 'But, well, I've told you about the heat and the stench and the noise, and some of them were fainting and suchlike, so the Speaker turned a blind eye to a few of them sitting down near him, as long as they were quiet. It's supposed to be wives seeing how wonderfully their husbands address the chamber, but often it's the society ladies, you know, Holland House and such: the ones that organised the political soirées and house parties. They're the powerful ones, half the time, even if they're not speaking in the House. Not that Elinor Broughton has any aspirations that way – you need money for that. She goes because she's interested. She's bright, that one, you know.'

'Indeed, that is my impression of her,' agreed Durris. 'You'll know, in any case, if she was genuinely attached to her husband.'

Elphick blew out thoughtfully through pursed lips.

'I suppose so,' he said at last, as if he were not really sure. 'I certainly hadn't heard any scandal – you do, in my line of work – but I never did. No, she's a good woman, a grand woman. You have any questions about her, you come to me.'

'I'll be sure to do that, Mr. Elphick,' said Durris, his expression neutral. 'Thank you for the offer.'

Elphick tipped his hat and trotted off up the main street, keeping carefully to the cleared paths when he could. The street was growing busy now as they headed towards it again, though many were not so much occupied that they could not afford time to stop and point out the sheriff's man to their friends, and murmur theories as to his purpose in town. Hippolyta was sure she made out several times the muttered words 'duel' and 'Sir Holroyd' and 'dead!'.

'I believe,' said Hippolyta, 'that Mr. Elphick was an old admirer of Mrs. Broughton, and that his ardours have not yet cooled.'

'Oh, Hippolyta!' said Patrick, laughing. 'How can you establish such a thing based on so short an observation?'

'I think Mrs. Napier is right,' said Durris, and Hippolyta nudged Patrick in the ribs.

'See? Mr. Durris agrees with me!'

'Well, you are both far too perceptive for me, then.'

'Look at the way he kissed her hand! And then went on holding it!'

'Absent-minded, perhaps,' said Patrick, deliberately provocative.

'Anyway, if he really has had a long acquaintance with her, I may well ask him again about Mrs. Broughton,' Durris went on, ignoring them politely, 'but I'm not sure he should be treated as a reliable, unbiased witness.'

'Not at all!' Hippolyta agreed.

'Where are you bound now?' Patrick asked him.

'I shall fetch Martha Considine and send her to Mrs. Broughton as I promised,' said Durris. 'Then I thought I should go to see the Pinners next. There was definitely a woman in the woods this morning, and though I think it still could be Mrs. Broughton, I should like very much to speak to Lady Pinner.'

'I cannot imagine her having the energy to walk all the way up the hill,' said Hippolyta.

'Sir Holroyd said that you are her physician?' Durris asked Patrick.

'That's right – only while she is here, of course.'

'Would she be fit to walk up the hill?'

'She would not be wise to on a cold winter's morning, but physically I believe she would be able to and in finer weather I should be recommending it. She gave birth to twins in the summer, and it was a difficult time for her. One child died. Yet I think physically she is recovered, and she has walked into the village mostly unaided. She is suffering from ennui, more than anything else.'

'Mrs. Broughton mentioned that she was unhappy.'

'Angry, too, I should say,' said Hippolyta. 'She never seems satisfied. I don't mean that she is one of these grand ladies that complains about every detail, but there is something deeper than that – perhaps, yes, indeed it is unhappiness. But really thorough unhappiness, if you know what I mean.'

Durris pondered.

'I shall be interested to see her.'

'Will you join us for breakfast, when you have dispatched Martha Considine?' asked Patrick.

'I should be very pleased to,' said Durris, and looked it. 'I cannot say I ate well before I came out here.'

'Then we shall see you shortly.' Patrick and Hippolyta turned away, and made for the house on the green.

'I have no idea even what time of day it is – and I have had no breakfast!' exclaimed Hippolyta, who was fond of her food.

'Then you are no worse off than I am,' said Patrick, 'for Mrs. Riach was shouting at Ishbel this morning and Ishbel was so put out by it that I had no breakfast either.'

'Nor Marcus?' Marcus' dietary habits could be strange, but he rarely went without his breakfast. Patrick shrugged.

'I have not seen Marcus today. I did leave the house quite early, though, at Sir Holroyd's summons.'

Ishbel, her apron crooked and a look of flushed frustration on her thin face, managed to spare a moment to open the door to them and help at least Hippolyta with her cloak before there came a yell from the servants' quarters.

'Ye lazy wee limmer! Fae's ma tea?'

Ishbel's shoulders winced.

'She has my heart scalded, Mrs. Napier!' she announced in an urgent whisper. 'She's been gollaring all the day long!'

'Then let her lie for a bit, Ishbel,' Patrick advised. 'Maybe she'll be more grateful when you do attend her.'

'More grateful, sir? More turk and cankert, more like! I'm chittering at the thought of going near the door!'

'Nevertheless leave her for a good quarter of an hour, Ishbel. You're exhausted, and she needs some peace.'

'Indeed, Ishbel, you need some rest,' Hippolyta agreed. 'Oh! Where is my painting box? I must have left it up in the woods!'

'You're not going back up there on your own today, my dearest,' said Patrick firmly. 'If you will wait till later, I could fetch it for you.'

'But if it snows again – and it will,' she added, looking briefly into his study and at the dim light at the window, 'then my things will be ruined. I must go now!'

'Then take Marcus with you, will you?' asked Patrick.

Ishbel was turning wearily away, but at that she looked back.

'Mr. Fettes is not in, sir,' she said.

'He's gone out? Did he say where?'

'No, ma'am. I did not see him. I went to take him his hot water this morning, but his bed had not been slept in.'

Chapter Ten

'Not slept in? Then where was he last night?'

Hippolyta's memory began to play tricks on her. Marcus had walked home with them from the assembly, had he not? Had he slipped away before they left? Before they arrived? She remembered standing in the semidarkness with him, listening while a challenge was offered and accepted. Where had he gone then?

But Patrick was being more practical.

'Well, we returned from the assembly around ten, and he was with us then,' he said definitely. 'He must have gone out again afterwards, for some reason. Dearest, will you come up with me to his room, and let us see if he has left us a note at all?'

'Of course.' His good sense settled her. 'Though knowing Marcus, he will not: he'll have flown off to do something and not given us a second thought!'

Indeed there was no note in Marcus' room. The window was half-closed, a concession to the cold weather, and Marcus' evening breeches and waistcoat were strewn across the chair like the detritus after a flood. His dancing slippers, which he had carried home through the snow, were more neatly set aside on the floor nearby, and his silk hose was tucked into them for, she remembered, he had been quite certain he would not wear his best silk hose in his boots, even for the short walk home.

'Well, he has changed his clothes,' said Patrick, 'but for what? I do not know what he brought with him.'

'His boots were not in the hallway,' said Hippolyta suddenly. She had only half-noticed their absence when they were downstairs. 'And I cannot see his new woollen hose – the thick ones he bought specially, he said, to come up here.'

'Then we can assume he dressed sensibly to go outside again, for some reason.'

'Marcus is not ... He's not really used to being out of doors, very much.'

'I'm sure wherever he went there was some kind of shelter. He would not simply head into the hills, would he?'

'Heavens, no!' Hippolyta laughed through her worry. 'I cannot see that happening! Even in his warmest hose.'

'Who else does he know in Ballater?'

'No one, much.'

'No young lady?'

'Patrick!'

'Well, you know what I mean,' said Patrick easily, taking her hand. 'He's a young man, and unmarried. Perhaps he met someone at the assembly who took his fancy?'

'I don't believe I even saw him dance.'

'You don't need to dance to take someone's fancy.'

They smiled into each other's eyes.

'Is there a note? Is he all right?'

Ishbel's voice at the chamber door interrupted them. She put her head anxiously into the room.

'No, no note, Ishbel, but he's taken warm clothes. I'm sure he'll be all right, when he remembers to tell us where he has gone.'

'It gave me an awful shock, ma'am! The bed all neat like that, and him not here!'

'I'm sure he'll be back soon, and making just as much of a mess of his room as always,' said Hippolyta, finding reassurance in reassuring Ishbel. 'Now, is there any chance of breakfast? For we have invited Mr. Durris to join us.'

'Mr. Durris is in the village? Is something the matter, ma'am?'

'Oh, have you not heard? There was a death this morning in the woods – one of the visitors at the inn.'

'Oh!' said Ishbel, interested but no longer concerned. 'A visitor, eh? I'll away and see if there's any mackerel in the pantry. Mr. Durris is partial to a piece of fish, I hear.' With a last anxious glance around the room, as if she would spot a clue to Marcus' whereabouts, she left and they heard her clatter down the stairs.

'Ah, well, I expect Durris will be here shortly,' said Patrick. 'Let us go and see if at least the parlour fire is lit.'

A MURDEROUS GAME

Ishbel, when untroubled by Mrs. Riach, turned out to have a knack for bread and had practised it the previous afternoon, when the oven was good and hot. Two kinds appeared on the breakfast table, which, with the jam they had made in the summer and some thinnish butter, almost made up for the lack of any other kind of food that even a physician and a sheriff's officer might expect on their breakfast table. There were eggs, but they were rather more intensively cooked than convention dictated. There was no fish, nor ham, and the coffee was of an unusual consistency, which reminded Hippolyta of childhood trips to Leith to see the boats, and the sailors slapping tar on their ropes and boards.

'And yet no doubt we'll survive,' was Durris' politely philosophical reaction when they apologised for the provisions. Hippolyta, tasting the coffee again, was privately not sure but appreciated the sentiment. 'And the bread is excellent.'

'Durris, if you wouldn't mind and you have the time, would you be so kind as to escort my wife to fetch back her painting equipment from this morning?' Patrick asked. 'I don't want her to go on her own, but you know she will if I cannot help her at once. She has no patience.'

'I can hear you, you know!' said Hippolyta. 'And I don't need an escort.'

'I want to take another look at the site after I have spoken to the Pinners,' said Durris diplomatically. 'If you will again accompany me – for I should like to speak to Lady Pinner without her husband's presence – then I can help you with it afterwards, if that would be suitable for you?'

'Yes, thank you,' said Hippolyta, 'unless it snows. Then I shall abandon you and the Pinners and run to fetch it straightaway. You have been warned.'

'Very well,' sighed Patrick. 'In the absence of your brother, that is the best I can expect, I suppose!'

'Has Mr. Fettes left?' asked Durris, surprised. 'He did not stay long – and in this weather?'

'No, he has not left. He has simply … um.' What had Marcus simply done? Vanished? 'He has simply gone away. He must have left last night, but his luggage is still here.'

'Last night? That's … that's curious. He was at the assembly with you, was he?'

'Oh, yes! And he came home with us. And his dancing slippers are upstairs, and some of his other evening wear, but his boots and cape have gone.'

Durris considered, using his knife deftly to rearrange a piece of jam on his last fragment of bread.

'Did he know about the duel?'

'Yes, he was there with me when we overheard the arrangements. But surely you can't think that Marcus would run away just because there was to be a duel in the village? He's odd, I'll admit, but he has never been the nervous type.' Hippolyta was vaguely aware of Patrick's toe pressing hers under the table, but she was concentrating on Durris and Marcus.

'Was he acquainted with the Pinners? Or with the Broughtons?'

'I am sure he was not acquainted with the Pinners, except that he knew Sir Holroyd's name. My brother, I must tell you, Mr. Durris, is in the party for Reform and is a great enthusiast.'

'I see.'

'As to the Broughtons, he travelled up with them on the same coach – as did Mr. Elphick – but they were unaware of each other, I believe. Marcus and Mr. Elphick travelled on the outside, and that is how Mr. Elphick came to stay here on his first night in Ballater.'

'Did he, now? I may want to know more about that later,' said Durris, and to Hippolyta's alarm the little notebook made its appearance at her breakfast table. 'But the Broughtons travelled inside, presumably?'

'Yes: we were there at the inn to meet Marcus, but we never saw more than a couple of shapes leaving the inside of the coach.' Except for Mr. Broughton's remarkable eyes, she thought to herself, but Marcus would not have seen those. 'It was the night of the dreadful snow, and the coach was late. Everyone hurried off as quickly as they could. Mr. Elphick was not sure how to reach his lodgings, and so we took him in.'

'Of course.' Durris looked across at Patrick, and they exchanged a small grin. Hippolyta was forever taking in waifs and strays, sometimes quite surprising ones. 'Broughton was for Reform, of course, but you think your brother had not met him?'

'He certainly never mentioned it.'

'Not even at the assembly?'

Hippolyta considered, looking to Patrick, too.

'I don't believe so. Marcus went off to look for a card game, which surprised me. The Broughtons were in the dancing room when we arrived, and the Pinners came a good deal later. I don't think Marcus danced at all.' This time she and Patrick smiled at each other. 'It did strike me as odd, for Marcus is quite partial to dancing and likes to think he cuts an elegant figure at it. And he generally does not approve of cards and gambling, but he said he was going to watch.'

'Some do, I suppose.' Durris made another tiny shape in his notebook. 'And you and he heard the arrangements for the duel at the same time?'

'That's right – and I believe half a dozen other people were there listening, too, though I could not tell you who or where. There was simply the sense that there were others there.'

'And was Mrs. Broughton correct? Did they quarrel about social standing?'

Hippolyta considered.

'In part, yes, I believe so. Certainly something of that was mentioned, and was very much as Mrs. Broughton said. But ... but there was more to it than that, too.' She hesitated, not sure if she wanted to go on.

'You'd better tell him, my dearest,' said Patrick quietly.

'I know.' She bit her lip, then spoke. 'Mr. Broughton accused Sir Holroyd of having married for money.'

'Hardly a crime, though it might explain Lady Pinner's unhappiness,' Durris remarked.

'And then Sir Holroyd made some reference to Mrs. Broughton's reputation.'

'What did he say, exactly?'

Hippolyta thought back, picturing the half-lit scene in the stableyard – only last night! – and the faces, so intense.

'He just asked Broughton what he had married, and said that they knew Mrs. Broughton's reputation. Nothing more than that.'

'Oh, well ...'

'But there must have been something to it,' Hippolyta went on, determined now to say all, 'because that was when Mr.

Broughton said he would kill Sir Holroyd.'

'He threatened to kill Sir Holroyd? Not the other way around?'

'Definitely not. His face … you should have seen his face, Mr. Durris. His eyes alone could have killed. I have never seen a man so angry.'

'Shouting? Punching?'

'Oh, no: much worse than that. Quiet.'

'I understand.' Durris looked at both of them, and she saw that he did.

'And I could see that Sir Holroyd was scared – up to then he seemed to be doing his best to provoke Mr. Broughton, but then he realised he had gone too far. And that was when he suggested the duel – almost, I thought, as a distraction. Like dangling a ball of wool in front of a cat to keep it from pouncing on a bird – and about as reliable.'

'But Broughton went for the duel, nevertheless?'

'Yes: I was almost surprised. But the whole thing was so shocking, I was just relieved that it had not come to blows then and there, for I feared for the worst if it had.'

Sir Holroyd Pinner looked drained, but stood when they entered the drawing room. He looked very surprised to see Hippolyta accompanying the sheriff's man still, and Hippolyta quickly explained.

'Mr. Durris has been kind enough to offer to assist me in the recovery of my painting materials up on the hill,' she said, 'and as he was to come here first, I wondered if I might call on Lady Pinner? I am sure this whole business is something she will find very distressing. I hoped that a visit from someone she might perhaps call a friend would be a comfort to her.'

Sir Holroyd gave her a bewildered look.

'I daresay,' he said after a moment. Hippolyta wondered if he had considered his wife's feelings at all, either this morning or when he issued his stupid challenge the previous night. Or the daughter of whom he seemed so fond – what would have become of her, without a father? Hippolyta found she was still very angry with Sir Holroyd. 'Ah, she is, I suppose, in some kind of parlour she has arranged for herself upstairs – you know the house?'

'A little.'

'Then it's one of the back rooms on the first floor. Hold on, I'll ring for the maid to take you.'

The sullen maid, Clara, appeared at the door in response to this summons, and admitted that her ladyship would probably be prepared to receive Mrs. Napier. Turning in the doorway like a yett on a rusty hinge, she led Hippolyta across the hall to the dark stairs and up to the galleried landing above, then, as Sir Holroyd had said, off to the back of the house. There she opened a door, and ushered Hippolyta inside.

'Oh, how pretty!' she said at once.

The windows, two of them, looked out at the hill with its snow-covered spiky trees, and at the wintry garden, all under a pinkish sky that hinted at more snow to come. Indoors, there was a cheerful fire in the hearth, and curtains in warm floral patterns at the windows. A shelf contained the requisites for a baby's comfort, fresh cloths, a bottle of Godfrey's Cordial and a set of coral beads for teething. The rug was a Turkey red and more splashes of colour cheered the blank white walls. In the middle of the floor, the nurserymaid – was it Susanna? – played with the baby on a blanket, and Lady Pinner knelt beside them smiling at both. She pushed herself to her feet in surprise when she heard Hippolyta's exclamation.

'Mrs. Napier!'

'I beg your pardon, Lady Pinner, for my intrusion into your very lovely parlour! I had thought that you might benefit from some cheerful company today, with all that has happened, but I see that I should have realised that all is arranged.'

'Nevertheless it was a kind thought,' said Lady Pinner, rather to Hippolyta's surprise. 'I beg you will sit down and have a cup of tea with us – as you see, we are a little less formal here than we are in the drawing room. I hope you do not mind being en famille with us.'

'Not at all – it is very kind of you to admit me to this happy circle.'

Indeed even Clara looked happier and more relaxed today. She took Hippolyta's cloak and bonnet, and before even the tea arrived Hippolyta too was on her knees beside the baby – almost, she thought, as charming as an animal. It was probably an observation she should not make out loud, though.

'She's a lovely baby,' said Susanna, tickling the little girl's palms and drawing out a great giggle for her pains. 'Sleeps well and feeds well, and always fair-tempered.'

'Have you nursed many babies?' Hippolyta asked her, out of interest. She looked maybe Hippolyta's own age, around twenty, and Hippolyta had had very little contact with children at all. Her nieces and nephews were not particularly close.

'Oh, yes, ma'am. I've been a nursery maid from when I was twelve,' the girl announced proudly. There was clearly a freedom in this room that did not, as Lady Pinner had indicated, extend to the formal drawing room.

'She came well-recommended,' said Lady Pinner, 'and she has proved herself invaluable.' The girl blushed with pleasure, though Lady Pinner was not much older than either of them. 'And to be prepared to travel all this way with us, at this time of year!'

'It's an adventure, isn't it, my lady?' said Susanna with a sweet smile. 'I ain't never been further north than St. John's Wood before, ma'am.'

'Goodness, then, you have come a long way!' said Hippolyta. 'That shows a remarkable sense of purpose.'

Susanna blinked, smile frozen, and Hippolyta wondered if her accent was difficult for the maid to understand. There was something in the girl's expression that reminded her of her surly colleague, Clara, and Hippolyta wondered if servants took on each other's traits. She would have to watch Ishbel, she thought. She found that she had been staring at Susanna, and gave her a reassuring grin, reaching out to tickle the baby's toes.

Clara cleared her throat pointedly.

'My lady is growing tired, Susanna. Time for baby's nap, don't you think?'

Susanna glanced at Lady Pinner, who nodded, reluctantly. Susanna gathered up the little girl and her blanket, and curtseyed, though her focus was still very much on the baby. She left the room, and Lady Pinner, with Clara's help, rose from the floor and settled in a low chair.

'Would you prefer me to go, too, my lady?' asked Hippolyta. She did not think that Lady Pinner looked particularly weary, though there were still dark circles under her eyes.

'No, no, at least sit and finish your tea, Mrs. Napier,' said Lady Pinner. Hippolyta sat at her gesture, and obediently sipped. Clara murmured something and left the room, and Lady Pinner watched her go, and the moment she had left, turned to Hippolyta.

'Tell me, do you know what happened this morning? Sir Holroyd has told me nothing!'

'Oh!' Hippolyta was taken aback. 'Well ... how much do you already know?'

'I know there was to be a duel. That terrible man Broughton threatened Sir Holroyd, and challenged him, and Sir Holroyd is too honourable to refuse. Did – did a duel in fact take place?'

'It did,' said Hippolyta, interested by her description of events. 'There was a duel up on the hill there. In fact, you may have been able to hear the shots from here,' she added, then thought that was probably an insensitive thing to say. 'Um, of course, Sir Holroyd is uninjured.'

'I know that. I have seen him, briefly. But he seemed very agitated. Did that man really shoot at him?'

'No, Mr. Broughton aimed wide. But –' Hippolyta was not sure whether Mr. Durris would want her to publicise the proof of Sir Holroyd's innocence, even to his wife. It seemed likely that he would want the matter still to look as Sir Holroyd thought it was. 'But Mr. Broughton died,' she finished.

'He is dead, then?' asked Lady Pinner. 'Mr. Broughton is dead?'

'Yes, he is. I saw him myself.'

Lady Pinner glanced at her.

'Goodness,' she said, absently.

'Of course,' Hippolyta went on, trying to be gentle, though she was determined that Lady Pinner should realise the gravity of the situation, 'Sir Holroyd is upset at what has happened. You do know that to kill a man in a duel is considered to be murder, don't you?'

'Murder ...'

'Yes, murder. And he knows that: he is distraught, but he has confessed all to the sheriff's man. The sheriff's man – Mr. Durris – is here, downstairs, just now.'

'He is?' Lady Pinner turned huge eyes on her. 'But it cannot be murder! How can it be murder, when Mr. Broughton challenged him? Sir Holroyd only … how can it be murder? Mr. Broughton was a horrible, angry man! He drove Sir Holroyd to it! How can that be murder?'

'It's the law, that's the thing,' said Hippolyta, apologetically soft as if she were somehow responsible for the law's peculiarities. 'But sometimes –' She was about to say that often the charges were reduced in the case of duels, but she hesitated, unwilling to cause false hope, and in that moment Lady Pinner sprang from her seat.

'You say the sheriff's man is downstairs this minute? Then I shall have to tell him precisely that he may not arrest Sir Holroyd, for murder or anything else. I shall not stand for it. I shall not have it. It will not happen!'

And like a sudden gust of wind she flung open the door of her refuge, and stormed out on to the landing. Hippolyta could do nothing but follow.

She would not have imagined that the lethargic Lady Pinner could move so fast. She herself had hardly emerged on to the landing when Lady Pinner was already halfway down the stairs. Hippolyta ran to catch up, half fearful for Mr. Durris, half simply determined not to miss whatever might happened next.

She caught up with Lady Pinner at the bottom of the stairs, and close enough that the hems of their wide skirts were brushing together, she followed her to the drawing room door. It was ajar, and Hippolyta expected Lady Pinner to push her way inside. But the woman hesitated, a hand just brushing the wooden panel. The voices that came from within, Durris' and Sir Holroyd's, were subdued, not particularly emotional, yet Lady Pinner seemed almost afraid. For a moment it seemed she might still go inside, but she half-turned, seemed at last to realise that Hippolyta was behind her, and squeezed past back into the body of the hall. She sat on one of the hard hall chairs, her hands gripping the edges of the seat, her gaze on the floor. Hippolyta crouched beside her.

'What's the matter?' she asked 'Aren't you feeling well? Do you want me to call for Clara?'

Lady Pinner shivered.

'No, it's all right. It's not that. I'll be perfectly well in a moment. It's just … yes, I'm not feeling well, that's it.'

But whether that were true or not, whatever Lady Pinner might

A MURDEROUS GAME

have wished to avoid by not entering the drawing room, the door suddenly opened wide and Sir Holroyd strode out, followed closely by Mr. Durris. Sir Holroyd was red-faced, his mouth open to display the teeth, while Durris had a closed, tight look about his face. It seemed the interview was not going well.

'I shall show you, of course.' Sir Holroyd tossed the words behind him as he marched across the hall.

'I should be much obliged, sir,' said Durris, still in steady pursuit.

'Though how it could possibly be relevant – oh, Lady Pinner,' he said, suddenly noticing his wife. 'Are you quite well?' He almost came to a standstill.

'Quite well, I thank you, sir,' she replied in a flat voice.

'Very good, very good. In here, Durris: this is my business room.'

He opened to door to a room at the back of the hall, one which had been laid out as a business room for some years: Durris and Hippolyta were both quite familiar with it. The two men disappeared inside, and Hippolyta, almost without noticing that she had done it, scurried after them to the doorway, standing in view, but not drawing attention to herself.

The business room was much as it had been the last time she had seen it, except that there were many more papers and books there. Yet it was orderly and there was clear space on the desk to work. Sir Holroyd circled the desk, which faced the door, and sat in the solid chair behind it, leaning forward immediately to open one of the drawers with a key from the fob in his pocket. He drew out a largish, flat box, very similar to the one that Mrs. Broughton had shown them earlier, but better made and more decorative. He opened it and turned it to show Mr. Durris, all in one movement – but then almost dropped the whole thing.

'Where has it gone?' he exclaimed, snatching the box back. 'Where is my other pistol?' He laid the box flat on the desk, where Hippolyta could see it clearly. The box was lined with fine tawny crushed velvet – Hippolyta immediately thought of evening gowns – and contained, scooped into it, spaces for a powder flask and a ramrod. Sir Holroyd fingered the places, baffled, as if the pistol and accoutrements had somehow become invisible to him.

'Did you take the pistol ready loaded to the duel site?' Durris asked.

'I confess I did,' said Sir Holroyd. 'Not a very safe thing to do, I admit, but I wanted to make sure I had the light and the time to do the job properly. I have – I have had misfires before now, if you can believe it.' Clearly Durris had not yet told him that his pistol had misfired again.

'So someone stealing – or shall we say borrowing? – the second pistol would have been able to take the ramrod and the powder flask too?'

'It would make perfect sense,' Sir Holroyd admitted. 'Or rather, it would make perfect sense if I could think of any reason why someone should want to steal a pistol. Who would do it? How did they open the box? And what are they planning to do with i?'

'The opening of the box is the simplest to answer,' said Durris. He pointed to the lock, which, though Sir Holroyd's key still dangled from it, was clearly out of place. 'This has been worked with a knife, I believe. As to who would do it, I cannot tell you. And as to what they are planning to do with it – I fear that perhaps it is already done.'

Chapter Eleven

'Lady Pinner seemed entirely dry,' said Hippolyta. The snowflakes were falling through the bare tree branches, and making her dizzy, but she marched on up the hill in Durris' wake. 'I mean, her clothes and shoes were dry. But she would have had time to change, I should think.'

'But the maids would know if she had, presumably,' said Durris over his shoulder.

'No doubt,' said Hippolyta. 'But they both seem very attached to her – the nursery maid, Susannah, is a sweet girl and I think would be loyal to any employer who was kindly to her, and the other maid, Clara, is a bit like a guard dog.'

'Fierce?'

'I think so, yes. She must be good at her work – giving Lady Pinner her medicine, and so on – for she is certainly not the kind of person you would like to have in your company for either entertainment or ornament. Yet I have the impression she is Lady Pinner's own appointment, not Sir Holroyd's.'

'Why did Lady Pinner appear in the hall like that? She looked as if she had seen a ghost.'

'She was all ready to attack you, I think, for threatening to arrest Sir Holroyd. Then she stopped at the drawing room door, and all the energy seemed to drain out of her. Do you think it's that house?'

'I thought you said – or someone said – that they were not happy in their marriage. Why should she rush to defend him?'

Hippolyta was as mystified as Durris, and could think of no answer. They reached the site of the duel, and slowed, allowing the steam of their breath to gather around them. Broad snowflakes spattered the dark red blotch where Mr. Broughton had fallen: soon they would cover it completely. They crossed the fading traces of Sir Holroyd's bootprints where he had walked back to Broughton's body, and followed Hippolyta's own slithering path back up the hill to where her painting stuff had been abandoned. Hippolyta brushed the snowflakes off her work, and sighed. It was indeed spoiled, colours sliding off the page in an ugly mixture. She began to pack everything away into the box, while Durris looked about him for any final traces that might soon vanish under the snow. He seemed particularly focussed on a clump of birch trees on the far side of the duelling ground, not far from the centre point of it but a little to Sir Holroyd's end of the ground. Hippolyta, by contrast, standing straight at last with her box and stool, caught sight of something further away, closer to the point from which Sir Holroyd must have fired.

'What's that?' she asked, pointing with her stool's legs. Durris turned and frowned in the right direction, but it was clear he could not quite see what she was pointing at. She steadied herself with her burden and led the way quickly along, slightly downhill but not all the way to the firing point. Durris caught up with her almost at once, and eased the heavy painting box from her grasp, politely taking the weight himself. Less encumbered, Hippolyta strode ahead again and reached a tangle of autumn brambles wound about with purple-brown leaves.

'It would have been a good place to hide from the duellers,' she said, 'and look!'

Behind the brambles were footprints, small ones – smaller than Hippolyta's own long, narrow feet - and the snow had been swept back and forth, too.

'Skirts,' she said in satisfaction.

'Or a cloak,' said Durris. 'But I think you are right: skirts. The sweep is broad, in all directions. The trail of a cloak would narrow as the wearer turned.'

So it would, thought Hippolyta, making a mental note to remember that.

'So she probably crouched – though Lady Pinner does wear her skirts quite long. It must be the new fashion.' She gave a little sigh. Long skirts would suit her, too.

'You think it was Lady Pinner?' Durris met her eye, asking her for her reasoning.

'Well, whoever it was must have known about the duel in advance. If you were coming up the hill and wanted to hide here, you would need to get here before Mr. Broughton and Sir Holroyd, or they would see you.'

'If you were coming up the hill, yes. But what if you were coming down the hill?'

'From where?' asked Hippolyta, incredulous. 'You would have to be mad to be further up the hill, or coming over the hill, in weather like this!'

'What about coming round the hill, though?' said Durris, acknowledging her point. 'If someone had climbed it further around, perhaps ... No, that seems unlikely,' he told himself. 'Towards the village it would be much harder to climb. That side is very steep.' He looked the other way, and shrugged. 'Very well, it seems likely that someone was already here before the duel started, for whatever reason – and knowing about the duel in advance certainly seems the most likely. I can think of no other sane reason for an assignation here at dawn in the snow.'

Hippolyta smiled, pleased that he agreed with her.

'But could Lady Pinner – or whoever was here – have fired the shot from here?'

Durris considered, and stepped carefully into the place where the footprints were, angling his head to try to see through the trees the spot where Broughton had been standing.

'It would have been a difficult shot, or a very lucky one,' he said, still considering. 'Both the trees and the difference in height make it awkward. Tell me, did you see him drop his arm after he fired? Before he fell?'

Hippolyta summoned up the memory again, thinking hard.

'No,' she said, certain. 'He stood motionless, and his arm was still up.'

'Then I don't know how anyone standing here could have shot him as he was shot. His gun arm would be in the way, particularly from up here.'

'Oh, of course!' Hippolyta was cross with herself for not thinking of that. 'So perhaps you favour the clump of trees over there?' She pointed to the spot he had been studying earlier, and remembered that he and Patrick had paid it some attention on their previous visit. Durris gave a brief nod.

'I think so: the angle is much better, and we found footprints there, too. Could whoever was up here have moved position? Presumably before the duellists arrived?'

'Before I arrived, too,' said Hippolyta. 'I think I should probably have noticed someone hiding here. But perhaps not: the brambles are quite thick. If they arrived after I had sat down, and came up that far side of the clump, when I was concentrating on my painting, I might not have noticed them. Are we talking of two different people watching this duel? Or even three?'

'That's one question I should like to find the answer to,' agreed Durris. He brushed snow off his shoulders, and then wiped his glasses. 'But the snow now is growing heavier. I think if we wish to be considered sane ourselves, we had better return to the village.'

Much as she was relishing the fresh air and the puzzle, Hippolyta had to agree: it was hard even to make out the edge of the woods, and they needed to find the road soon or they might struggle to see it at all, and end in a ditch.

Though the streets were again quiet, muffled by the snow, it was something of a relief to reach the houses. Durris offered to carry her paints all the way home.

'Not at all, Mr. Durris: I'm sure you have something urgent to be getting on with,' she said. Urgent for her, just now, she thought, was drying out her stockings by a warm parlour fire, and sorting out her damp paints. And, she hoped, having a stern word with Marcus about disappearing in the middle of the night. She felt a little guilty that for the last hour or so she had forgotten all about him. But then, he was a grown-up man: he could, probably, look after himself.

'I do need to have a word with the village constable,' Durris admitted, and at her insistence handed over the painting box. Hippolyta bade him goodbye for now, sure they would meet again soon, and followed the traces of one of the paths cut across the top of the green, the fresh snow easy underfoot. She was already in a little snow world of her own when a loud rap startled her, making her slither. A window shot up in the house beside her.

'Mrs. Napier!'

It was Ada Strong.

'What on earth are you doing out in all that? You'll catch your death! Come on in to the fire! The tea is stewing. Time for a fly cup!'

The window slammed shut again, and before Hippolyta could think of an excuse the front door snapped open, and she was hurried inside.

She had never yet come across a time of day in the Strong household when the tea was not stewing, and the fire was not cosy. She was quickly divested of her cloak and bonnet, the maid flicking the snow back out on to the street before it could melt and soak the floor, and found herself in the familiar armchair by the hearth. It had clearly just been vacated by Mr. Worthy – she could smell traces of his pomade - who, with his employer Mr. Strong, had joined the Misses Strong for a morning recreation by the tea table. Mr. Worthy settled down at the table itself, and was so comfortable there that he helped himself to a fruit tart and disposed of it rapidly. The movement of his jaws caused the deep lines from his nostrils to the corners of his mouth to curl and wriggle, and his chin, nose and eyebrows fought to be noticed. His hands were long, with very prominent reddened knuckles, and Hippolyta wondered if his joints were arthritic, particularly in this cold weather. She had, as yet, little idea of his character beyond his interest in geography and poetic language: he had not been in the village long, and though friendly he seemed reserved, as if his personality were making up for his appearance. Beside wizened little Mr. Strong he was certainly an oddity to behold.

'I am glad to see you so recovered,' Hippolyta said to him with a smile.

'Recovered?'

'You were indisposed last night, were you not?' she asked, remembering that he had been too ill to attend the assembly. She had a sudden image in her mind of him dancing, waving those long fingers, and was quite glad she had not had to see it.

'Oh, yes, I am much better, thank you! I had one of my headaches,' he explained, 'and the thought of vibrant music and energetic terpsichory was quite abhorrent to me. But an early retirement and a perambulation in the fresh snow this morning and I am very much better, I thank you.'

'And of course he missed all the drama!' said Miss Ada, with glee. 'Did you hear the gossip, Mrs. Napier? You must have heard it last night, for it was the talk of the assembly.' But Miss Ada could not resist telling her anyway. 'Sir Holroyd Pinner challenged Mr. Broughton to a duel, and Mr. Broughton accepted! Did ever you hear anything so exciting?'

'Ada!' said her sister in disapproval.

'I thought it very shocking,' said Hippolyta, sounding prim even to herself. 'I mean, it's such a silly thing to do, to risk your life in such a pointless way.'

'Oh, they'll aim wide,' said Miss Ada with satisfaction. 'I'd go and see it myself, if I could find out where it was to be.'

'Oh!' said Hippolyta, feeling a little stupid. 'But haven't you heard the news this morning?'

'Is it called off?' Miss Strong asked at once, with a triumphant glance at her sister. 'I knew they would see sense!'

'They are not young men, after all,' said Mr. Strong comfortably. His feathery wrinkles, pink in the warmth of the fire, flitted across his face as he spoke. 'When the heat of the moment is past they will not wish to do anything so foolish. Sir Holroyd has a young family, and Mr. Broughton seems a man of sense. I quite agree with you, Mrs. Napier: it is a daft thing to contemplate.'

'Oh, be quiet, Sandy, I want to hear the news!' snapped Miss Ada. 'Mrs. Napier, have mercy and tell me what has happened – or has not happened!'

'There was indeed a duel this morning,' Hippolyta began.

'Oh, michty me!' cried Miss Strong.

'And I missed it!' lamented Miss Ada.

'And it ended tragically,' said Hippolyta firmly, before any more nonsense could be spoken. Mr. Worthy's jaw dropped. The Misses Strong gasped.

'Who?' demanded Miss Ada. 'Who died?'

'Mr. Broughton, I'm afraid.' Her fingers abruptly remembered the pressure she had applied to his chest, the rough feel of the torn cloth even through her gloves.

'Oh, no!'

'Poor Mrs. Broughton! Is anyone with her?' asked Miss Strong, concerned for their new friend.

'I think Mrs. Kynoch knows. And Mr. Durris arranged for Martha to go and help her with the body.'

'Is that what Mr. Durris was doing here? I thought I saw him,' said Miss Ada, 'but with the snow, I wondered. He'll have arrested Sir Holroyd, then.'

'Sir Holroyd claims he aimed wide,' said Hippolyta, intent on not giving away the whole story yet. Miss Ada would have it spread the length of the three parishes by supper time, snow or no snow.

'It's a gey unchancy thing, a pistol,' said Mr. Strong solemnly.

'Who were the seconds?' asked Mr. Worthy.

'They had no seconds. Sir Holroyd said something about not wanting to involve anyone else.'

Mr. Worthy's face twisted thoughtfully.

'But it's always a wise choice to have a second,' he said, 'who could at least act as a legal witness, if necessary, should proceedings be pursued. For of course, to kill a man in a duel is still murder.'

'Indeed,' agreed his colleague. 'I wonder will Sir Holroyd have need of a man of law to attend him? Have you seen the good baronet, Mrs. Napier?'

'I have: I don't think lawyers were mentioned at this stage. He is still very much upset.'

'Of course, a gentleman would be.'

'I should think anyone would be, Sandy!' Miss Strong reproved him. 'And his poor wife, too! And the wee bairnikie – such a shame, for all the connexion.'

Hippolyta cleared her throat.

'I believe Mr. Durris is looking for anyone who might have seen anything useful this morning. Perhaps someone may have seen Sir Holroyd or Mr. Broughton setting out for the duel or seen them on the hill – up behind Dinnet House, it was.'

'Out in that snow this morning? I have more sense, Mrs. Napier!' said Miss Ada cheerfully.

'We haven't stirred all morning,' her sister agreed. 'That's why we hadn't heard the dreadful news. Och, poor Mrs. Broughton! We'll have to go to her now – well, when the snow stops, anyway,' she added, casting a glance at the window. Outside it was almost dark with snowfall. Hippolyta hoped that Patrick was somewhere warm, preferably at home. And Marcus – where was Marcus?

She pulled herself back to the matter at hand.

'Mr. Worthy, I think you said you were out for a walk this morning in the snow?'

He grinned in surprise.

'I believe I did mention it, Mrs. Napier: most gentlewomanly of you to pay attention to my little ramblings! Yes, yes, I did permit myself the pleasure of a peregrination this morning, just after dawn – which of course is not so early at present anyway. I walked in the direction of Tullich kirkyard, taking due precautions to remain on the road, or what I could perceive of it, at all times, for my own safety. Then I made the discovery that even the road was embraced to a great depth in an accretion of snowy precipitation, and I was constrained to admit defeat and return to the centre of habitation.'

'Well,' said Hippolyta, realising she had been staring at him, 'the wrong direction altogether, then.'

'I fear so.'

'Have you – I suppose in your London practice, Mr. Worthy, you had some experience of duels and their consequences? I imagine they might be more common in the kind of fashionable society there than they are here.'

'I have been involved at the latter end of one or two such occurrences, Mrs. Napier. But only by way of issuing letters and dealing with testamentary issues. I was a humble solicitor, Mrs. Napier, and though I did at one stage in my somewhat ill-starred career in that noble city have aspirations to work towards the Bar, in the course of exercising my abilities for a short period in Lincoln's Inn with several barristers of some repute, I found I did not take much pleasure or satisfaction from the labours therein. There was indeed considerably too much excitement and hurry, and a grave necessity for every detail to be found to be black, or white, and I regret to say that most matters are in my perception a shade of grey, light or dark as it may be, and sometimes even in a state of mutation or transfiguration from one shade to another. I found that such perception was a severe disadvantage in the Courts, and so I chose to return to a more sedentary way of existence, and in due course to eschew the advances and alarums of the city altogether and to retreat to a place that was – and still is – in every way more suited to my temperament.' He finished with a beaming smile. Hippolyta realised she was staring again, and took a hurried sip of tea.

'Thank you, Mr. Worthy,' she said. 'Most interesting. My father and brothers are all men of law, as you may know, and I like to hear of it.'

'In Edinburgh?'

'That's right, yes.'

'Ah! A charming city. I should perhaps have liked to practise there, once, but by the time the opportunity arose I had already developed my abhorrence of cities in all their forms. Alas! For I am sure I should have benefitted from the very great instances of cultural events and spectacles that occur there so frequently.'

'Hm, yes. But I think I too prefer Ballater, Mr. Worthy: perhaps I am not very cultivated.'

'Not at all, Mrs. Napier! Not at all!'

Not cultivated at all! thought Hippolyta, smiling to herself. Well, perhaps not. But she still had a painting box to take home.

'The snow has eased, I believe,' she said, rising, 'and I should not trespass on your time and your kindness any longer, Miss Strong. May I have my cloak and bonnet?'

The maid was summoned, and in the midst of Hippolyta wrapping herself up again the Misses Strong decided they had better go and see if Mrs. Broughton was receiving visitors at the inn. The little hallway became a flurry of cloaks and bonnets and umbrellas and walking sticks, and Hippolyta was heartily relieved to pop out through the front door with her painting box like a cork from a bottle, and wave goodbye to her friends. It was only a step down the hill to her house, and she flopped in through the front door, not as cold as she had been before visiting the Strongs, but still eager to dry her stockings properly and have a little time on her own to straighten her paints, well before dinner time.

But it was not to be. The parlour fire was not lit, and several of the white cats expressed their displeasure over the matter as she came in, bleating plaintively. She knocked at Patrick's study, but there was no answer, and when she peeped inside the study was empty and the fire there, too, was cold. By contrast there appeared to be some heat in the servants' quarters: she could hear shouting coming from that direction. Followed intently by the cats, she went to the kitchens.

In the main kitchen, Ishbel was attempting to make bread, though her face was flushed and unhappy. She seemed to have been crying. Tam, the dog that belong to the serving boy, sat beside the table with his ears flat, and under the table Hippolyta could just see the stockinged feet of the serving boy himself, Wullie. The cats went straight to the fireplace and arranged themselves cooperatively on Mrs. Riach's ancient armchair there, which fortunately for them was otherwise vacant. The shouting continued.

'What has happened now, Ishbel?' Hippolyta asked.

'It's Mrs. Riach,' said Ishbel, 'of course.'

'Something new?' The shouting indicated a high level of dissatisfaction, though Hippolyta was finding it difficult to make out particular words – except for one or two that she had discovered were quite expressive in the local dialect, though not for use by ladies.

'She persuaded Wullie here –' Ishbel made a sharp movement, and by the yelp from under the table Hippolyta realised she had kicked the boy, 'to fetch her some brandy.'

'She said it was for the pain!' cried Wullie, shuffling himself further from Ishbel's end of the table.

'She's drunk the half of the bottle, and now she's worse than ever. She battered me with the candlestick,' said Ishbel, pulling down the collar of her gown to show a reddened bruise on her collarbone, 'when I tried to take the rest of the bottle from her, and she threw her Bible at me when I left the room. That's no right,' she added darkly, 'besides that it's got sharp corners.'

'Do you want me to have a word with her now, or wait until she has sobered up?'

'Madam, you'd be best no going near the auld besom till she's out of it,' said Ishbel frankly. 'I wouldn't like to say that she wouldn't throw something at you and all, though I think she's run out of the heavy stuff. Mind, she can throw a grand punch when she's crossed, so no, I'd no go in at all.'

'Wullie,' said Hippolyta, 'come out from under there, please.' Wullie made a meal of emerging, brushing down his coat with slow reluctance. 'Wullie, however much she asks you, or however much she gives you, you must never bring Mrs. Riach any brandy again. Or any other strong drink, all right?'

'I will not, ma'am. She clouted me and all with the bottle because she said it wasna full enough.' Indeed, his cheekbone was red and hot.

'Go and put some snow on that, Wullie. And take Tam outside for five minutes: he looks as if he is in pain. Then come and light the parlour fire.' Tam hurried out through the kitchen door. 'Have you heard any word from Dr. Napier?' she asked. 'Or from Mr. Fettes?'

'There's been no word from Mr. Fettes, ma'am,' said Ishbel, an extra little flush passing across her face. 'But Dr. Napier is in his dispensary. He said he could light his own fire in there and be cosy, and he would be in to dinner.'

'And will you manage dinner on time?'

Ishbel sighed.

'Well, see, it's like this, ma'am, with it being Saturday and laundry soaking day and all. You can have dinner on time, but it might not be what you're used to. Or you can have all the things you usually have, but it might well be a wee bittie late. Oh, and ma'am, there's a letter came for you on the hall table – I dinna ken if you seen it.'

'A letter?' Perhaps it was word from Marcus. Not wanting to disturb Patrick at his work, she suggested that dinner should be a little later than usual, and went to see what the letter might be.

It was instantly recognisable as her mother's handwriting: the mail coaches must be coming through from Edinburgh with some success now. She undid her boots luxuriously in the parlour, and waited while Tam lit the fire and bowed. Alone at last, with a sigh she propped her feet, still in their damp stockings, on the other end of the sofa, nearest the fire, and settled down to read the letter. Her mother's writing was as spiky as her moods, but the letter was if anything sharper than usual.

'My dear Hippolyta,' it began. 'My thanks for your letter announcing Marcus' safe arrival with you. You say the Broughtons are also staying in Ballater at present. I know that Ballater is a small and insignificant village, but you will do your utmost to ensure that Marcus and Mr. Broughton do not meet. Marcus has disgraced himself in Edinburgh, and must not be allowed the opportunity to do so again, in however obscure a place. It must not be allowed to happen.'

Chapter Twelve

Hippolyta sat up and quickly scanned the rest of her mother's letter, but to no avail. Her mother was the kind of woman who expected unquestioning obedience from her children, therefore she clearly saw no need for further explanation here: the orders had been issued, and Hippolyta, like a good little girl, was simply expected to do as instructed. Well, it was possible that she might have, had she had the information in time. But now Mr. Broughton was dead, and Marcus was missing: had they met before all that?

The Broughtons had arrived on the same coach as Marcus, yet Marcus claimed never to have seen them. Was he … Hippolyta scrambled in her mind for some explanation. Was he hiding from them? Secretly following them? But why on earth would he do such a thing? And what had he done in Edinburgh to disgrace himself? Aside from the puzzle over the Broughtons, Hippolyta silently and sardonically thanked her mother. It would have been good to know the real reason behind Marcus' visit, instead of simply being used as some kind of exile, like Tomi for Ovid. Her mother would never learn, she thought, that her children were grown up and on the whole preferred not to be manipulated without their knowledge or consent.

She badly wanted to talk to Patrick, but that would have to wait until dinner time. Patrick needed to concentrate when he was in his dispensary, or he might make a mistake in his mixtures of medicines. Should she go instead and talk to Mrs. Broughton? Mrs. Broughton might well know what had happened between her husband and Marcus in Edinburgh: she struck Hippolyta as the kind of woman who was well acquainted with her husband's business. But on the other hand, she had just been bereaved in a truly shocking fashion. It would be wrong to go and ask her awkward questions, questions which might indeed put Mrs. Broughton and Hippolyta at odds with each other. Or would they? Even if Marcus had done something to offend Mr. Broughton, had not Mrs. Broughton talked of befriending Lady Pinner even though their husbands were enemies? Or perhaps that was only talk, easy in the abstract, not so when the sister of her husband's enemy was there in front of her.

And what on earth could Marcus have done, anyway? Was she wrong to assume her mother meant they had had a quarrel, just because Broughton was quarrelsome? But what could they have quarrelled about? What was Marcus likely to be worked up about? There had been any number of things since he had been a schoolboy: harsh treatment of carters' horses, slavery, consumption of spirits, doctors prescribing expensive drugs … each, though worthy, had been the craze of a few months then flashed back occasionally in his conversations like a swirl of true colour in a blend of paint. His sisters teased him endlessly, in part because it was so easy to make Marcus' pale cheeks flare in spirited argument. But with Mr. Broughton? Surely they could not have come to blows over the consumption of spirits. And it would not be like Marcus to offer any insult to any man's wife, whatever her character. She thought back to Broughton's fight with Sir Holroyd. Class would hardly be an issue, either: if anything, apart from their age, Broughton and Marcus were about on a level. Then what? Marcus' chief delight at present seemed to be the Reform cause, and if anyone else was fierce in that it was George Broughton. Over what could they have quarrelled? If indeed it had been a quarrel: really, her mother had been infuriatingly unspecific.

She tapped the letter on her knee, her mind dancing from thought to thought. Then she rose and made herself dry and put away her paints in their box, and clean her brushes, keeping her hands busy while she tried to think what to do. She could not intrude on Mrs. Broughton, not at this time. But where was Marcus?

It was time to dress for dinner, and she went upstairs where Patrick soon joined her.

'I met Durris after he saw you back to the village,' Patrick said. 'He told me about the Pinners. I've asked him to come to supper: I know you won't mind.'

'Not at all,' Hippolyta agreed. She could not tell Mr. Durris about her mother's letter, though. Could she tell Patrick? She wanted to, but what if he then thought she should tell Mr. Durris? What would Mr. Durris think of Marcus then? She sat down on the bed in a heap of petticoats, and tried to think.

'What's the matter, my dear?' Patrick asked, seeing her in the mirror as he washed his face.

'Oh …' She knew she would have to tell him. 'My mother sent a letter about Marcus.'

'About Marcus? Has he gone home?'

'No, no: well, if he has I think he would have arrived after this was sent, anyway. And why would he have gone in the middle of the night? And how? And what about his things?'

'Dearest,' said Patrick, bringing her back to what she had been saying.

'Oh! Well, it's very odd, to be honest. She says I am not to let him meet Mr. Broughton because Marcus has done something to disgrace himself in Edinburgh and that seems to be why he was sent up here, out of the way.'

Patrick sighed.

'It would be kindly of your mother not to regard Ballater as the last outpost of civilisation,' he said mildly.

'I know, I know.' She resolved not to show him the actual letter. It took a good deal to make Patrick cross, but her mother seemed determined to make progress towards it on every occasion. 'But what am I to do? Marcus is disappeared –'

'He's not back yet?'

'There's no sign of him, and no word,' said Hippolyta. 'At least …' She seized her shawl, and darted across the landing to the guest room. It was just as they had found it earlier. She returned, crestfallen. 'No, no sign of him, wretched boy. So I cannot ask him what has happened, and of course I cannot ask Mr. Broughton. And what if … what if it were something serious? Patrick, what if it were Marcus who fired that shot this morning? What if he killed Mr. Broughton?'

'My dear,' said Patrick, abandoning his shaving to take her in his arms, 'I very much doubt that Marcus could kill anyone.'

'Do you think?'

'I should be very surprised.'

Hippolyta reflected for a moment. She was not entirely sure that on Marcus' behalf she should be pleased with Patrick's analysis. It made it sound very much as if Marcus was a soft weakling. She shook herself, seeing sense.

'Maybe you're right. But he does go into such a passion about some things: Reform, for instance. He has been very energetic over that.'

'But isn't Broughton for Reform, too?'

'Exactly. It makes no sense.'

Patrick pondered, returning to his shaving bowl.

'I suppose there are degrees of reform. I know there are many who think the present Bill does not remotely go far enough, saying it has been watered down to try to get it through. Perhaps that was the nub of their quarrel, for I have read that some of the discussions have become very heated. Some, of course, are even talking about revolution.'

'Goodness …' Hippolyta grew more anxious. Where on earth was Marcus? Was he capable of stirring up revolution? If Patrick thought he could not even kill one man, surely he could not foment rebellion. She now hoped Patrick was right in his assessment of Marcus' character. 'Do you think I should go and see Mrs. Broughton?'

'Mrs. Broughton? Of course not! The poor woman lost her husband this morning! I don't think it would be a good idea.'

'No, of course not. You're quite right. I should not intrude on her distress, of course. I had already decided that, but then – I'm very worried about Marcus.' Hippolyta pulled her gown on over her head, and Patrick helped her to fasten it: it was useful to have a dextrous husband, she thought, when your maid was frantic over making the dinner. 'Patrick, Mrs. Riach got hold of some brandy today, and struck both Ishbel and Wullie.'

'Badly?'

'She gave them nasty bruises. She hit Wullie with the bottle, and Ishbel with a candlestick, and then threw a Bible at her.'

'How on earth did she get hold of the brandy?'

'She made Wullie bring it to her, for the pain, she said. He's been warned not to fall for that one again.'

Patrick frowned.

'The trouble,' he said, 'is that in a small place like this we should never be rid of her. If we did ask her to leave, she would still be living in the village.'

'I know. I've thought of that. I wish I had my mother's skills with exile.'

Patrick smiled absently.

'In a way it's easier to keep her, but to try to keep her ... I don't know. Sober, anyway.'

'Yes. And she is a very good cook, when she's able.'

'And Ishbel is not, really.'

'That's because Mrs. Riach won't teach her. She gives her all the rough jobs to do, all the vegetable chopping and throwing out the peelings, and fetching and carrying, and doesn't actually tell her or show her how to do things. Ishbel was making bread again this afternoon, and it looked as if it might turn out quite well.'

'Could you teach Ishbel? A little, anyway?'

Hippolyta wondered. She knew something of cooking, and an aunt had sent her a new edition of Elizabeth Cleland's *New and Easy Method of Cookery* for a wedding present. Perhaps it was time for her to learn more, even if it were just for helping to fill in when Mrs. Riach was incapacitated, or any of the other emergencies that seemed to afflict their household – hens in the study, pigs in the kitchen, dead frogs on the hall floor, that kind of thing.

The dinner bell rang, a little haphazardly, and they went downstairs, puzzling over households and brothers, and what to do about them.

Dinner was beef, which was overdone, and a cabbage pudding, which had burst and had to be served with a soup ladle. The food was brought in by Wullie, who had an individual method of transferring food to the table and was accompanied at all stages by his dog, who was keen to be involved. Still, the dinner was edible enough and there were no guests to shock: Hippolyta noted that Ishbel had optimistically laid a place for Marcus, but it remained empty. Marcus ... what if he had made contact with Mr. Broughton? He had been acting very strangely at the assembly, she remembered, watching Sir Holroyd, and he had not danced at all despite being dressed in the latest fashion which she would have expected him to want to show off. Where had he been for most of the evening? He had said he was going to watch a card game. Then Broughton had left the dancing room, too: Marcus had been with her during and after the quarrel between Broughton and Sir Holroyd, but before that he could have spoken to Broughton. Or, since he had clearly left their house not long after they had returned home, he could have gone to speak to Broughton at the inn that night – or hidden somewhere to follow him the next morning. Oh, thought Hippolyta, whatever he was up to it could be nothing good, surely. Silly, silly boy. Where on earth was he?

'My dear, the salt, please?'

Hippolyta jumped. Patrick was grinning at her.

'Salt?' She passed it to him, wondering how often he had asked for it.

'You were miles away! You're not much company this evening. I should be better talking to the cats.'

'I'm worried about Marcus,' she said, then put out a hand to his. 'Sorry, my dear. And the cats are very good company, you know.'

Substantial intervals between courses meant that they had only just finished dinner when Durris arrived for supper.

'Would you prefer me to leave and return later?' he asked politely, but the snow was still falling full and steady and Patrick hauled him into the hall and the warmth.

'You can as easily wait here as back at the inn,' he said. 'You are friend enough to be welcome at any time.'

Durris' face went a little blank, and Hippolyta thought that he was taken aback by the compliment. Did he have other friends? He never even mentioned family, that Hippolyta could remember.

'You are very kind,' he said, and sounded as if he were actually grateful for the sentiment. 'And the inn is in a mournful state, so I am particularly grateful.'

'Mrs. Broughton?' said Patrick, with a glance at Hippolyta.

'She is not roaming the corridors howling with grief, if that is what you mean,' said Durris unexpectedly. 'She is very restrained, in fact, and considerate of others' feelings. But the innkeeper offered to give her a room for Mr. Broughton's body, and its arrival seems to have sent everyone into a gloom. Mrs. Kynoch is sitting with her, and Martha has helped with the laying out, but the three of them are the most sensible people in the place. The maids are gushing tears.'

'Had they conceived such an affection for Mr. Broughton in such a short time?' Hippolyta asked in surprise. 'I liked the man, I admit, but not to the extent of weeping constantly.'

'It's just the way girls act when a few of them come together,' said Patrick. 'One cries and the others must compete, even if they are unaware of it.'

'There is a good deal of sympathy for Mrs. Broughton,' Durris added. 'Whether there was affection for Mr. Broughton or not, there seems to be for her. There is,' he said, staring into the parlour fire, 'a grace to her that commands respect and admiration, particularly in her grief.'

There was a long silence. Patrick, unseen by Durris, raised his eyebrows at Hippolyta, who shook her head crossly. She cleared her throat.

'Well, do you think in her grace she might be willing to see me? I need to ask her – about something.'

'About what?' asked Durris.

'I gather, from a letter from my mother, that Mr. Broughton and my brother Marcus were acquainted in Edinburgh. I want to know if Marcus went to see Mr. Broughton at the inn after the assembly, or said anything to him about where he might have gone. Marcus, I mean.'

'He's still missing?'

'He is. No sign and no word.'

Durris was concerned.

'In this snow, too … I should think that in the circumstances she might indeed be prepared to receive you. That is, I should think she would be pleased to see you as a visitor, anyway, but if she knew you were worried about your brother I don't think she would consider any questions inappropriate.'

'Then I should go at once,' said Hippolyta, jumping up. 'If I wait until Ishbel serves supper it could be midnight before I can go, and that really would be a little odd.'

'My dear, could you not wait until the morning, at least?'

'But what if Marcus is outside somewhere? What if he is in trouble of some kind?'

'Trouble?' Durris queried. Hippolyta could almost see his ears pricking at the word. She had to be careful.

'I mean what if he has fallen somewhere, or become lost, or Heavens! been attacked by those men who have been lurking around the village? Have you found out anything more about them? They could have hidden him anywhere in this weather!'

'My dear!' said Patrick. 'It's hardly Mr. Durris' fault if your brother has lost himself.'

'But the men!'

'It's true,' said Durris, 'that I have not yet been able to find out more about them. The constable had caught sight of them once, but had a notion they were visiting for some funeral – I think it was the dark clothing that confused him. I have had no reports of them today after Mr. Elphick's sighting of them this morning. And to be honest, I wonder about that. By his account, they were walking up that road very early in the morning: I think perhaps they have just been passing through, and are now on their way to the north.'

'But what is up that road?' demanded Hippolyta. 'Braemar? There is nothing there. They barely even understand English!'

'Perhaps they were indeed returning to visit family, perhaps even for a funeral,' suggested Durris. 'The constable might have misunderstood something he heard.'

'And anyway, that does not explain anything about Marcus. I must go and speak with Mrs. Broughton,' she insisted. 'She is the only one who might know something of what he was doing last night.'

Durris and Patrick took their turn to exchange looks.

'I believe Mrs. Broughton will be happy to help,' said Durris.

Patrick sighed.

'Then we shall go down to the inn – but after supper, all right? Poor Ishbel has been working hard to feed us this evening: I don't think it would be a good idea to leave the house just when she is about to feed us again.'

Hippolyta opened her mouth to respond, but before she could, the parlour door opened. It was Ishbel.

'Ma'am, I'm awful sorry but the supper will be late. The snow's got down the lum and the kitchen fire went out, and the room was that hot that I didna notice at first, so there's bread and jam and nothing else, not even hot water.'

Hippolyta's eyes widened.

'How long is it likely to be?' she asked.

'Och, a good hour at least,' said Ishbel, warily.

'See, Patrick?' Hippolyta spun round. 'It was meant to be. Now we can go and see Mrs. Broughton at once, and come back here for supper.'

Patrick had already admitted defeat.

'Will you come, Durris, or would you prefer to rest here by the fire? There are books aplenty, or the newspaper.'

'I'll come,' said Durris. 'If she has anything useful to say regarding Mr. Broughton's movements, it might help with my own investigation.'

Hippolyta tried to hide her dismay. If Mrs. Broughton knew that Marcus and Mr. Broughton had met, either last night or this morning, it might add to Durris' suspicion of Marcus. And would that be a well-founded suspicion, or not?

But she needed to move quickly or Patrick might change his mind. She darted into the hall and wrapped herself quickly in shawls and her cloak, and was already tying her bonnet strings when the men emerged to pull their own coats and boots back on. She lit a lantern, and they headed out once again into the snow.

The inn was as usual warm and welcoming, but Durris was right: Mr. Broughton's corpse had brought with it a melancholy air. The maids who took their coats had red noses and bleary eyes, and showed them in to the dead room with reverence. Mrs. Broughton and Mrs. Kynoch, startled, half-rose as they entered.

'Mr. Durris!' exclaimed the widow. 'It is good of you to come to pay your respects. And Mrs. Napier, and Dr. Napier.' She made a small curtsey in the direction of each of them. Mrs. Kynoch, knowing that the three of them had conspired to investigate deaths in the past, looked more concerned as she bade them good evening. However, each of them went to make the correct salutation to the dead man as he lay, sheet to his chin, in the centre of the room. Hippolyta gazed down at the face she had last seen in the snow on the hillside. Then, she could almost have believed he would come back to life with a bright and ferocious argument. Now, she knew he was dead: all that wit and fury had gone. She offered up a silent prayer for his widow and his colleagues, and went to sit with the other ladies.

'Is it coincidence that you have all returned together?' asked Mrs. Broughton, who was far from slow herself. 'Or have you come to ask me more questions, Mr. Durris, with my husband even in the room?' But her slight smile showed she did not reproach him. 'If I can help, I shall. Yet I am not sure yet that I quite understand why so many questions must be asked, if the matter is as straightforward as you portrayed.'

'To begin with, Mrs. Broughton,' said Durris, with a little bow, 'Mrs. Napier has something she would like to ask you.'

'Mrs. Napier! Are you turned detective, too?'

'Oh, goodness, no!' Hippolyta managed to look alarmed at the thought, though indeed it pleased her very well. 'My question is more of a personal nature – that is, personal to me. I don't know if at the assembly last night you happened to meet my brother, Marcus Fettes?'

Mrs. Broughton frowned.

'I'm not sure ... there were so many new people ...'

'He looks not unlike me, poor boy,' Hippolyta went on. 'He's tall, with blond hair, brushed forward and a little full at the front.'

'I don't think so,' said Mrs. Broughton.

'Does the name mean anything to you? Marcus Fettes? You might have met him even in Edinburgh. Or someone of his description might have called to see Mr. Broughton last night, after the ball?'

'None of this sounds remotely familiar, I'm afraid, Mrs. Napier,' said Mrs. Broughton. 'What does your brother say on the matter?'

'My brother, who arrived from Edinburgh on the same coach as you – but outside – was staying with us, but he has disappeared,' Hippolyta explained briefly.

'Disappeared!' Both Mrs. Broughton and Mrs. Kynoch exclaimed together.

'I'm afraid so.' Hippolyta shrugged, as though slightly ashamed of this social faux-pas. 'Did you by any chance notice him on the coach?'

Mrs. Broughton made a face.

'I'm astonished that anyone survived travelling outside on that journey! He must be a strong young man. But no: at each stop I'm afraid we hurried from coach to inn and from inn to coach: we had a private parlour each time, for my husband did not wish to be recognised, and we paid no attention to the poor unfortunates outside. Even had we wished to see them it would have been difficult in the snow.'

'That's what I thought,' Hippolyta agreed. 'Mr. Elphick was also outside, you know.'

'Mr. Elphick! Was he?' The expression on Mrs. Broughton's face was a curious one: it was not, by any means, altogether pleased.

'Then, you see, my mother has written from Edinburgh insisting that I do not allow Mr. Broughton and my brother to meet, for apparently ...' here she did hesitate, but Mrs. Kynoch was a good friend and Hippolyta respected Mrs. Broughton's discretion, 'apparently my brother disgraced himself in some way in Edinburgh in connexion with Mr. Broughton. My mother has not yet been more specific.'

'Well, there were no duels in Edinburgh, of that I am fairly sure,' said Mrs. Broughton, immediately jumping to the same conclusion as Hippolyta had. 'I know there was at least one fight, for someone dealt George a very fine black eye – in fact, it has not quite faded, poor man!' She turned her gaze to the corpse, a little fond smile on her face. 'It will not fade now ... But I heard no names of anyone he fought with. Duels I would know about, but fights would just happen, you know?'

'Are you from Edinburgh yourself, Mrs. Broughton? I think you mentioned relatives or connexions there,' Patrick put in suddenly. Mrs. Broughton smiled.

'I have relatives there, yes, though I am not from there myself. We certainly saw a good deal of them when we were there.' That appeared, from her face, to have been a mixed blessing. 'Well, Mrs. Napier, I hope you find your brother safe and well, but I'm afraid I cannot help you. No one, as far as I know, called to see my husband after the assembly, and I have no recollection of your brother by either name or appearance. I am sorry.'

'He would be mightily offended that you did not remember his appearance, at least!' said Hippolyta, trying to lighten the mood a little for her own sake. 'He is vain of his looks.'

'That is true,' murmured Patrick, a little too sincerely.

'Perhaps I am over-sensitive,' said Mrs. Broughton, 'but I

cannot help feeling that your enquiry after your brother has perhaps another layer to it. Again, you are trying to find out who my husband saw or who might have been connected with him last night, otherwise why would you have accompanied Mrs. Napier, Mr. Durris?'

Durris gave that little bow again, clearly pleased with her intelligence.

'I'm afraid that your husband's death was not as straightforward as might at first have appeared, Mrs. Broughton. I mentioned that Sir Holroyd's pistol suffered an accident. In fact, it misfired altogether, but a shot from somewhere else was the one that killed Mr. Broughton.'

'He was - murdered?'

'He was.'

Chapter Thirteen

'He was what?'

None of them had noticed the dead room door opening. Patrick and Durris, still on their feet, spun round. The ladies turned their heads. In the doorway stood Mr. Elphick. His jaw had dropped, his anxious eyes wide.

'George Broughton was murdered?'

'Please keep your voice lower, Mr. Elphick,' said Durris calmly, 'and remember your agreement to publish nothing as yet. News, as you will no doubt know, travels with great speed in a village, and I should like not to imperil the investigation too early with rumour and gossip.'

'My dear Mrs. Broughton.' Mr. Elphick ignored Durris entirely, and slid to his knees in front of her with surprising fluidity. 'How can you bear it?'

'My husband is dead, Mr. Elphick,' said Mrs. Broughton with some dignity. 'I think the worst has happened. How he died is – almost – secondary.'

'But for someone to show such hatred – to someone you loved so dearly …'

'My dear Mr. Elphick!' Mrs. Kynoch could not help interrupting at last. 'I hardly think that is appropriate!'

Mr. Elphick blushed hard, and sat back on his heels.

'Madam, you are quite right. I must apologise, Mrs. Broughton. I was overcome by the news I had just heard. Murdered! It is at the very least a most dreadful shock.'

'That much is true,' said Mrs. Broughton, 'though from Mr. Durris' questions, gentle though they were, I had begun to suspect that something untoward had happened, beyond the duel itself. I believe I said to you earlier, Mr. Durris, that if you were to seek a murderer for my husband Sir Holroyd would be at the top of my list. I take it that you do not suspect him?'

'Sir Holroyd had only the one pistol with him, and it definitely misfired: the charge was still in the barrel when I examined the weapon,' said Durris. 'The pair of the pistol is missing. Though it is just possible that Sir Holroyd fired with both pistols simultaneously and flung the other pistol away to hide it, we have not been able to discover it, and we have a witness to the duel – at least one so far – and from their account it seems unlikely. It is more likely that another of the witnesses was a murderer. There is evidence of several other people being in the woods at the same time.'

'Good heavens.' Mrs. Broughton's voice shook a little. 'Perhaps I should have gone along. It must have been a popular event.'

'Do you know who the others were?' Mrs. Kynoch asked, putting out a hand to Mrs. Broughton's. She cast a glance at Hippolyta, meeting her eye briefly: she knew the strength of Hippolyta's curiosity and clearly had not ruled her out as one of the witnesses. Hippolyta, though, was again thinking back to her memories of the duel. She would not have seen him flinging it to one side, for she was already running down to see to Mr. Broughton. Could Sir Holroyd have used a second pistol? Wouldn't she have noticed? In her memory he had his right arm, the one further away from her, raised. Surely she would have seen it if he had his left arm raised, too? And how could he have foreseen that a pistol would misfire, leaving him looking innocent?

'We have some idea of the other witnesses, Mrs. Kynoch,' Durris was saying. 'Though perhaps not of all of them: it was a busy morning in the woods above Dinnet House,' he added wryly.

'I believe the challenge was also overheard by quite a number of people,' said Mrs. Kynoch. 'That would have drawn attention to the event, no doubt.'

'Oh! My husband completely lacked discretion about that kind of thing,' said Mrs. Broughton, again looking over to the corpse as if she expected argument. 'He was quite capable of punching someone in the middle of the Meadows at midday, or accepting a challenge outside the doors of Parliament itself.'

'This time it was in the stableyard here,' said Durris. 'Again, we know positively of a couple of witnesses, and we know there were others.'

'And one of those witnesses was my brother Marcus,' Hippolyta put in.

'He told you that? Then perhaps … but no, I cannot say that,' said Mrs. Broughton firmly.

'My brother is not your husband's killer, I am sure of it!' cried Hippolyta. 'Whatever might have happened between them in Edinburgh, I am convinced Marcus could not have killed anyone!'

'Yet someone clearly did, someone who was in Ballater and presumably had known my husband before.' Mrs. Broughton deliberately kept her gaze on Mr. Durris. 'That limits the field somewhat, does it not?'

The silence that followed was unnerving, to say the least. Then Mr. Elphick coughed, and pushed himself up from his kneeling position to return to stand at the doorway, clearly embarrassed.

'Well,' he said, 'this is all very mysterious, there's no doubt about that.'

'Mrs. Napier,' said Mrs. Kynoch suddenly, 'Mrs. Broughton belongs to your church. Do you know what the arrangements are for tomorrow? Will she be able to see a pastor?'

'Oh!' Hippolyta had almost forgotten that the following day would be Sunday. 'Well, we do not entirely know. Mrs. Broughton, I should explain: there is no Episcopal chapel in Ballater, and so we are dependent upon clergy travelling here to take services. And in weather like this, it is often very difficult for them. But if he arrives tomorrow – I think it will be Mr. Whittling – I shall direct him here, of course. In fact, perhaps if he manages to arrive it would be better to see if the innkeeper can spare us a room for the service. Do you think so, my dear? It would be more central for those travelling, and Mr. Whittling will be stabling his horse here anyway so we could catch him before he goes elsewhere.'

'That makes sense to me,' said Patrick at once. 'I shall go and ask the innkeeper – and see if we can borrow his pianoforte, too.'

'That would be very comforting, even if I cannot attend myself,' said Mrs. Broughton gracefully. 'To know that there were prayers in the same building would be a very great solace.'

'Then we shall do our best,' said Hippolyta, beginning to think of the various arrangements that would have to be made. 'If Mr. Whittling cannot arrive, we shall read Morning Prayer in any case.'

The innkeeper, whose business was not particularly brisk at present, readily agreed to allow a parlour to be made available for anyone who could travel to the Episcopal service. A thin morning sunlight allowed Patrick and Hippolyta to carry a few books down to the inn without harm. Hippolyta wondered if it might be possible to have the services in the inn more often: each week they had to rearrange their parlour for the purpose, and the strain of keeping the cats from invading the more solemn moments kept her on tenterhooks throughout.

The usual time for the service was almost upon them, and Patrick had even turned to Morning Prayer in the prayerbook, when a greyish blond young man rushed in through the door, waving his case in front of him.

'Made it!' he cried.

'Mr. Whittling! Allow me to fetch you a glass of brandy before you begin!' said Hippolyta in alarm. The young man looked exhausted, if triumphant.

'That would certainly not go amiss, Mrs. Napier,' he said in his peculiar Oxford tones. 'I had to leave my horse behind and came here mostly walking on the tops of hedges, I believe – it was hard to distinguish!'

Hippolyta called for the brandy, which came hot. Mr. Whittling gulped it down gratefully, then turned his attention to donning his surplice and arranging the communion equipment on the table they had set out for the purpose. Hippolyta watched him anxiously, hoping he was not overdoing it. Too many young clergy came north to attend to the needs of the Episcopal Church only to wear themselves out in the harsher climes that they were not used to, and have to retire south again to recuperate their health.

A few families had gathered for the service, but no one from far outside the village. To Hippolyta's surprise the maid Clara, Lady Pinner's attendant, was amongst them, as sour-faced as ever. She must not be a dissenter like her mistress. The Pinners themselves were certainly not in evidence. Mr. Worthy, trailing a scent of pomade, came in just in time, face pink from a brisk walk.

After they had sung the first hymn, to Patrick's accompaniment, Hippolyta heard the door of the parlour open and shut quietly. When she had the chance to look round, she saw Mr. Elphick perched on a seat at the very back of the room, fumbling through the prayers as if he had known them once. She wondered if he were there to try to impress Mrs. Broughton, then reprimanded herself for such a thought – and in church, too! In any case, Mrs. Broughton, attendant on her husband's body, was not at the service, but the parlour was the nearest to the dead room and Hippolyta had noticed when she fetched the brandy that the dead room door was ajar, no doubt so that she could hear the service from her post.

Mr. Whittling, in no rush now he was warm and dry, gave the final blessing and processed, insofar as he could in such a small room, to the door to greet the congregation on their way out. Patrick played the pianoforte softly and Hippolyta collected the books, as was their usual habit. The congregation was in no hurry, either: in the winter after church they usually took a glass of negus or something similarly warming against their journey home, and exchanged gossip. Hippolyta busied herself with the books, trying to listen to several conversations at once in case she heard anything useful concerning the duel, but no one seemed yet even to know that Sir Holroyd was probably innocent. There were whispers, and discreet pointings at Clara, who tilted her chin towards the door and joined the queue to greet the pastor and leave. Hippolyta slipped out past the queue, smiling at the pastor, and went to tap gently on the door of the dead room. Mrs. Broughton must have been waiting, for she opened the half-closed door wide immediately.

'Thank you for allowing me to hear that, Mrs. Napier. The singing is quite exceptional for a small church, and you are lucky to have such an accomplished pianist to help.'

'Oh, that is Patrick,' said Hippolyta, affecting not to be too proud of him. 'He does enjoy it. Shall I ask Mr. Whittling to step in when everyone has gone?'

'Yes, please do.' Her attention was already more on the pastor than on Hippolyta, and she watched as he spoke to various worshippers. 'He is very young, is he not?'

'I think it takes someone young to have the energy ... and

besides, they often begin their career here and then return to England, sadly. For us, that is.'

'Who is that man to whom he is speaking at present?' Mrs. Broughton asked suddenly. 'Does he live locally?'

'That is Mr. Worthy. He is a kind of apprentice to the local man of law – to Mr. Strong, you know.'

'He's a lawyer? Yes, that makes sense. I am sure I have met him before, and the name – Worthy. It is not so common, is it? I think … Frederick Worthy? Would that be it?'

At that point Mr. Worthy and the clergyman ended their cheerful conversation, and Mr. Worthy walked down the passage to leave the inn. Mrs. Broughton put out a hand.

'Frederick Worthy?' she said on a question, but she seemed more certain now. Mr. Worthy stopped at once.

'Mrs. Broughton!' he said, and bowed low. 'Oh! Of course! Madam, I understand I must offer you my deepest condolences. Mr. Broughton – well, he was instrumental in introducing me into the intricacies of the English legal system and the mysteries of the Inns of Court, for which I shall always be most grateful. Most grateful.' He bowed again, almost backing into Clara the nursemaid who was passing behind him. She let out a small yelp, and hurried on her way, glaring back at him.

'Your words are kind,' said Mrs. Broughton. 'I hope I shall see you at the funeral, when it is arranged. The people of Ballater have done everything in their power to make me feel at home, but to have someone from his own world there, someone who worked with him, would be very good.'

'Of course I shall do my best,' said Mr. Worthy at once.

'Now, if you will excuse me,' she went on, 'I must just speak to the clergyman here.'

'Ah, Mr. Whittling?' said Hippolyta quickly. 'Mrs. Broughton, may I present Mr. Whittling? Mr. Whittling, Mrs. Broughton has but very recently lost her husband …'

Mr. Whittling, with an appropriately solemn smile, bowed and took over, guiding the widow back into the dead room to discuss arrangements. Mr. Worthy watched them go.

'A very fine woman,' he pronounced. 'I only met her a couple of times, when I was assisting Mr. Broughton with a very tragic case. It was one of those cases which in the end made me sure I no longer wished to aspire to the Bar, to be frank, Mrs. Napier. Nevertheless, Mr. Broughton was most hospitable: I was at supper at his home on two occasions, and very well treated. And then to see him rise in Parliament! But he was always a splendid orator. He would have been a marvel on the stage, too.'

'Too?'

'Well, Mrs. Broughton was an actress, didn't you know?'

'An actress?' Hippolyta just about managed to express her surprise quietly. 'I had no idea! She seems so respectable!' Yet in her mind she could hear Sir Holroyd's voice in the stableyard. 'Maybe you didn't marry for money, but what did you marry?'

'I daresay she is, now,' said Mr. Worthy, his tone also low. 'And I should judge they were very happy together. It is a tragedy, certainly, for her and for the law. And for the Reform cause.'

'Are you, too, a supporter of reform, Mr. Worthy?' Hippolyta's mind was bouncing again from one thing to another.

'Oh, yes, Mrs. Napier! Of course I am. Any man of sense must be, I believe.'

Gracious, thought Hippolyta, there are more Reformers around me than I ever dreamed. I really must read the papers more.

'Well, I suppose I should finish tidying up,' she said at last, not sure where her thoughts were. Mr. Worthy bowed again, and smiled.

'And I must go and join the Strongs, if they are back from their service at the kirk. They always make sure I have a fine dinner on a Sunday. It is very pleasant indeed!'

He trotted off, and Hippolyta watched him for a moment. Behind her she could hear faintly murmured prayers coming from the dead room, and Mrs. Broughton's decisive Amen at the end. Patrick had finished playing, and she returned to the parlour to see him gathering up his music. She stacked the books in their basket, ready to take home for next Sunday.

'All well?' he asked, smiling across at her.

'Yes, I think so,' she replied, then after a moment added, 'I was puzzling over Mr. Broughton.'

'It is a puzzle, certainly,' Patrick agreed. He pulled on his coat and came to join her, lifting the basket of books. 'What in particular has you wondering?'

'Well, it's odd,' she said, fastening her own cloak. 'For a man who had just arrived in the village, Mr. Broughton seems to have had more connexions here than he was expecting.'

'I think it's time we had a long conversation with Mr. Durris,' said Patrick. 'Shall we see if the kirk is out yet?'

They caught Durris as he was replacing his tall hat outside the centrical kirk, just where the minister, stamping a hole in the snow with his chilled feet, was bidding farewell to his parishioners – not so many, perhaps, as usual, for the spread of the three parishes was wide and the terrain was not easy, even in good weather.

'Shall we retire to our parlour fireside, and share some information?' asked Patrick.

'That is an invitation it would be difficult to resist,' Durris admitted, and followed them around the green where the paths were easier, and home. The parlour fire, again, was not lit, but it was laid, and it took Patrick only a moment to set it going. He went to fetch the brandy from the dining room, and Hippolyta ventured to the kitchens to see if there was any hot water. Surprisingly, there was plenty, though Ishbel and Wullie were not yet back from church. She poured a pot of it, took some glasses on a tray, and returned to the parlour where Patrick busied himself with the poker, mulling the brandy at the fire. The cats followed her, and assembled around them, keen to be part of the discussion: Polar, who had an affection for him, settled against Durris' leg on the sofa, and Franklin selected Patrick. Hippolyta divided her attention between the rest, quite glad at least that the hen who ventured indoors had not yet found the parlour.

'Have you further information, then?' asked Durris. 'Did you see Mrs. Broughton this morning? How was she?'

'We did, and she seemed as she was last night: sad, but sensible,' said Hippolyta. 'And we saw Mr. Elphick, and one of the Pinners' maids, Clara. I don't believe that anyone else involved was there.'

'The Pinners were at the kirk,' said Durris, 'but of course their nursery maid was not: she will have been at home with the bairn.'

'And how did they seem?'

Durris considered.

'In her case, cold and proud and very stiff. In his ... I should have said he seemed contrite.'

'You have not yet told him that the pistol had jammed?' asked Hippolyta in surprise.

'Not quite yet,' said Durris, who did not seem to be contrite. 'Soon, though: I want to tell him before any rumours reach him.'

'Do you really think he might have fired both pistols and cast one aside?'

'No,' said Durris, 'I don't. He could not possibly know that one would misfire – I don't see how he could fix it to do so without risking serious injury to himself. And from how you described the scene I should have thought you would have noticed.'

'They both stood sort of sideways,' said Hippolyta, wriggling her shoulders. She stood up and held out her right arm, making a straight line from her hand back to her left shoulder. 'Like this. If he had tried to bring up his left hand, too, it would have been very awkward looking, particularly from the side I was watching from. I'm sure he did not do anything of the sort.'

'So unless he took the pistol, and did not use it – and I don't think he did, either – then someone else stole his pistol and took it away, and quite possibly used it to kill Broughton. But who could have done that?'

'Surely,' said Patrick, 'as Mrs. Broughton said last night, it has to be someone who knew him before he came here. And that is indeed a small field: there is Mr. Elphick and the Pinners.'

'I'm not sure he really knew Lady Pinner,' Hippolyta objected.

'No, perhaps not, if she is so aloof,' said Patrick.

'But she would certainly have known of him, and who he was, and what he was to her husband,' said Durris. 'She might have wanted to kill him on her husband's behalf, with or without his knowledge.'

'But she seems so delicate and gently-born,' said Patrick.

'My dear,' said Hippolyta, 'I am sure I have occasionally wanted to kill people on your behalf! Particularly one or two of your patients!'

'Yes, but my dear, you are very much more robust than Lady Pinner. In a good way,' he added quickly. She scowled at him nevertheless. 'Her wrists are very thin: I wonder if she could manage a pistol without injury.'

'Well,' said Durris, who had brought out his notebook and was making his ominous little marks in it again. 'The Pinners, and Mr. Elphick. He seems to me to have a strong motive.'

'Jealousy,' said Hippolyta deliciously. 'He loves Mrs. Broughton, and always has: Mr. Broughton snatched her from his affections, and he has taken his revenge.'

'I really must see what novels you have been reading, my dear,' said Patrick mildly.

'Nevertheless it is a motive which bears consideration,' said Durris seriously. 'Mrs. Broughton is undoubtedly the kind of woman who would inspire that degree of admiration and, perhaps, devotion.'

Hippolyta looked at him for a moment.

'Did you know she was an actress?' she said at last. She told herself that he needed to know for the sake of the investigation.

'An actress?' Durris was suitably startled. 'Who told you that?'

'Mr. Worthy: I don't know that you have met him. He is a kind of apprentice to Mr. Strong, the man of law, but he used to live in London and for a time worked with Mr. Broughton.'

'Did he indeed?' said Durris sharply. 'Then we have another to add to our list. How did you discover this?'

'Mr. Worthy was at our service this morning, and saw Mrs. Broughton as he was leaving. He had only met her once or twice, but he recognised her. In London he worked, he has told me before, at Lincoln's Inn, and assisted in some court cases which, apparently, put him off court work and city life, and he retreated first to Edinburgh and then to here. He said he owed a debt of gratitude to Mr. Broughton, and spoke warmly of Mrs. Broughton, too,' Hippolyta summed up.

'But he told you she had been an actress.'

'That's right. And wouldn't that explain Sir Holroyd's taunt? About knowing what Mr. Broughton had married?'

'And you said that that was the point at which Mr. Broughton grew particularly angry with Sir Holroyd, didn't you?'

'Yes. That precise point.'

Durris fell silent for a moment, considering. The cat Polar received a good deal of absent head-scratching, and purred loudly.

'Do you think,' he said eventually, 'that Mrs. Broughton

might have gone up on to the hill with the intention, perhaps, of taking her own revenge on Sir Holroyd, but killed her husband instead?'

'I'd say it was more likely that she killed her husband in order to run off with Mr. Elphick,' said Patrick surprisingly, 'but I don't think that that is very likely, either. The light was quite good, good enough for Hippolyta to distinguish one man from the other easily, and neither was her husband. And since his death Mrs. Broughton has shown nothing but a very natural affection for Mr. Broughton. If you told me that Mr. Elphick killed Broughton, I'd be much more inclined to believe it.'

'I agree,' said Hippolyta, solemn, in case Durris would think she was simply backing her husband without a mind of her own. 'If you told me that Mrs. Broughton had killed someone, if she had had good reason to do it, I could think of few women of my acquaintance more competent to keep her head and face the task. And if she was an actress, all the more reason why she should be able to present a sorrowful appearance afterwards. But I can't believe she killed her husband. They seemed genuinely attached.'

'Hm,' said Durris, but he looked pleased. 'So we think she is less likely. What about Mr. Worthy? You say he spoke warmly of Broughton.'

'He did: of course, if he had killed him he would want to hide the fact.'

'He bears more investigation, then. What kind of a man is he?'

'Serious, but amiable,' said Patrick, with a look at Hippolyta.

'He likes landscapes and long words,' added Hippolyta. 'A decent man, I think all would say.'

Durris made another tiny note.

'Thank you. And of course Mr. Elphick is still a possibility, too. I have my doubts as to when he entered the woods, from the evidence of his footprints. Sir Holroyd is likely in terms of motive, but in terms of opportunity he seems a poor candidate – unless, of course, he had someone do the job for him.'

They looked around at each other.

'That would explain the missing pistol, wouldn't it?' said Hippolyta, excited. 'How easy to pretend there had been a theft, and give the pistol to someone to carry out the deed!'

'Well, but who?' asked Patrick. 'I have not even seen a

manservant up at Dinnet House. And no man could ask a maidservant to shoot someone for him, could he?'

'I think some more questions need to be asked,' said Durris, 'at Dinnet House.'

Chapter Fourteen

It had been kind of Durris, Hippolyta decided as she lay awake again that night, not to list Marcus amongst the suspects who had known Broughton, in whatever way, before he came to Ballater. She was convinced that it was not absent-mindedness, or the possibility that he had dismissed Marcus as innocent. What had her brother done in Edinburgh? Had he done something in Ballater, too? And where was he?

The snow continued to fall. Weary, she slipped downstairs to the parlour, stared out at the blanched garden for a moment or two, then lit a candle and surveyed the bookshelves. Elizabeth Cleland's *New and Easy Method of Cookery* jumped out at her and she took it down, leafing through pages she had previously all but ignored. But now … what could she teach Ishbel to make? A pupton of pigeons? Oyster sausages? Pigs' petty-toes? Oh, no: she could not think of cutting off the feet of her lovely pig. But the pigeons … with forced meat, and sweetbreads, and mushrooms. That sounded like a warming dish for a cold day, and not too complicated, if they could obtain a few pigeons. Mushrooms would be buried under the snow, but she knew that there were some dried ones in the pantry for she had seen Mrs. Riach arranging the strings. Stirrings of hunger twitched her stomach, but she did her best to ignore them. She read on to the section on fruit tarts and custards. She had never had much of an appetite for the sweeter things on the table, and she could look at them more impersonally. She wondered, though, if Ishbel could be trusted to make a custard. It was a useful basis for many things. The more she read, the more she realised that their diet had grown a little stale, even for the winter season – though the real trial came in the spring when the supplies dried and salted for winter were running short. Perhaps Mrs. Riach's incapacity was a blessing in disguise, and she and Ishbel could refresh their kitchen. She wondered if they could start in the morning.

Then she remembered that the morning would be taken up with Mr. Broughton's funeral.

'It's such a rush, I know,' said Mrs. Broughton briskly, greeting them as they arrived at the dead room at ten. 'I am sorry to cause any inconvenience. But Mr. Whittling could not promise to be back in Ballater for a fortnight, and so he stayed overnight to carry out the service today – well, he said he would only be able to do it if the ground was soft enough, of course, but someone went to the churchyard today – somewhere called Tullich? Is that right?'

'You'll have passed it on your way here, though you certainly won't have seen it in the snow,' said Hippolyta helpfully. 'It's a pretty spot, though, around the old ruined Tullich kirk.'

'Near the river, he said.'

'Yes, near the river.'

'And the ground was soft, so there was a great hurry to have a coffin made and a mortcloth borrowed and – and – oh! Everything is happening so quickly!' Her eyes were bright with tears and her voice was breathless, but she was focussed on all she had to do. She might well, though, thought Hippolyta, collapse afterwards.

Old Martha had watched through the night with her, and stayed, half-dozing, in the corner. Mr. Whittling had gone to see the minister to make whatever arrangements were required for burying an Episcopalian in a parish kirkyard. At some point Mrs. Broughton had changed into smart black mourning clothes that suited her well.

'A cousin died just after we arrived in Edinburgh,' she explained when Hippolyta tentatively admired them. 'I had them made there, little knowing … But I am glad I can look smart for him. It would have been more important in London, of course, but he did like me to look like the wife of a successful man. And I was proud of him, too. Mrs. Napier, I know I said yesterday that it mattered less how he had died than that he was dead, but I should like to find out who killed him, and why. I find that to know someone hated my husband hurts me very much.'

'Mr. Durris will do his very best,' said Hippolyta, putting out a hand to Mrs. Broughton's arm. 'He is a good man, and a wise one.'

'That was my impression. Thank you for confirming it.'

And for you, thought Hippolyta to herself, he will I believe make an extra effort. Then she reprimanded herself sharply. She doubted that Mr. Durris ever put in any less than his full energies, whosoever was hurt or bereaved.

She and Patrick paid their respects once more to the body, now lying in an open coffin, and sat near Mrs. Broughton. The inn's staff had brought in extra chairs, and also set aside the parlour in which the Episcopalians had held their service yesterday for the funeral meats. When a few more people had arrived, the Napiers would go and take something as custom required, but for the moment they had no wish to leave Mrs. Broughton almost alone.

The Strongs were the next to appear, the sisters wide in shiny black like a couple of lumps of coal on a shovel, and Mr. Strong wizened to a thread after them. Along with them came Mr. Worthy, looking humble.

'May I present my colleague, Frederick Worthy?' said Mr. Strong in a dead room voice.

'We have met, Mr. Strong. Mr. Worthy, thank you so much for coming this morning.'

'Mrs. Broughton, I could not allow myself to be absent from such a tribute, sorrowful though it must necessarily be, to a man who was the guiding star of the Old Bailey and then of the parliamentary stage! I had thought when I retreated here to my rustic fastness that all momentous events of the metropolitan world would pass me by, to be read of only in the papers, but here the most notable tragedy of our time has happened in this very town. I am wretched, madam, torn between honour and grief, amazement and devastation.'

'You are too kind, Mr. Worthy,' said Mrs. Broughton, slightly perplexed. 'Please, do help yourself to refreshment next door.' Mr. Worthy bowed low, hair shining in the lamps, and followed the Strongs into the next parlour. Mrs. Broughton sank into a chair with a sigh.

'A gentle soul,' she said, 'but very much attached to the English language, as if to a large dog that needs constant exercise.'

Hippolyta laughed, then cleared her throat.

'I'm sorry,' she said. 'I'm afraid …'

'George liked a joke,' said Mrs. Broughton. She sighed. 'And he liked his work, and good red wine, and a pork chop done with parsley and butter, and a waistcoat with a bit of crimson in it, to cut a dash. And he liked to win, in arguments or in court or in Parliament. Why did we not have children? Who is going to remember all these things with me now?'

'Perhaps you should write a memoir of him,' suggested Hippolyta. 'I am sure the public would be interested, or you could make it just for private circulation.'

'Publish him abroad …' Mrs. Broughton evidently found this a novelty. Her intelligent brows knitted as she considered it. 'You know, I think he would like that? "The Memoir of a Reformer", do you think? Perhaps you are right.'

'It seems to me that you would do it splendidly,' said Patrick warmly.

'I'm sure I should,' said Mrs. Broughton with a twinkle in her eye. 'No one better. Ah, Mr. Whittling.' She rose, at the same time switching her face to that of the sombre widow, with the swiftness of a turned page. Hippolyta blinked. An actress, of course, and perhaps a rather good one. But which part was she playing, and which was the real Elinor Broughton? Or was neither on display?

Mrs. Broughton moved away to discuss matters with the clergyman, and the Napiers went to avail themselves of funeral meats next door.

'Mr. Worthy,' said Miss Ada, the moment they had gone in, 'says that Mrs. Broughton was an actress before she married! The scandal!'

'Ada!' Her sister whacked her in the ribs, as usual.

'And perhaps not so much of a scandal,' said Patrick reasonably. 'After all, he is not a peer or heir to some mighty fortune, that she might have been said to be after him for his money. Nor is he a clergyman or similar. It seems to me that she worked on the stage, as many of her class work, and met a man she loved, and they married. Would you not agree, Mr. Strong? Or is there an objection to lawyers marrying actresses, too?'

'Eyebrows might be raised in Edinburgh,' said Mr. Strong precisely, 'but perhaps not in London. A different world, you see, Dr. Napier.'

'It canna have done him much good amongst the Whig grandees, though!' said Miss Ada in delight.

'Miss Ada, I thought you liked him? And I am sure you like her,' said Hippolyta, as close to reproach as she could come to her elders.

'Oh, I do, I do. I find them both mightily entertaining. But you canna help but wonder how she went down in Holland House with Lady Grey and the rest of them. Michty me!'

'I'm not sure it's material, though, Ada,' said her brother. 'If someone had been blackmailing him over the matter, then that might be a different thing. But it seems to have been open knowledge, from what Mr. Worthy here tells us.'

'Open knowledge, yes, Mr. Strong, indeed,' Mr. Worthy confirmed. 'But it was not something one discussed, you know? And certainly never in front of Mr. Broughton. That was completely understood.'

'It was only the mention of that that caused the duel, I believe,' said Hippolyta, keen to contribute to the gossip. She ignored Patrick's pressure on her hand. After all, how many other people had heard, too?

'Aye, and look what came of that!' Miss Strong lamented. 'A man lying dead before his time! And another like to be hanged for it!'

'Sister,' said Miss Ada, 'if you carry on like that you can hardly blame me for being over dramatic, can you?'

'Och, away with you, Ada!' Miss Strong complained. 'It's a tragedy, and that's the beginning and end of it.'

Mrs. Kynoch arrived, with the Strachans. The shopkeeper was a striking man with jet black whiskers and an unctuous attitude in his warehouse, which seemed to need a reversal in his private life to a sharpness of manner that his whiskers only emphasised. His wife was lovely, throwing Mrs. Kynoch's short figure and eccentric dress into marked relief. Mrs. Kynoch today was mercifully in black.

'It is indeed an awful tragedy,' Mrs. Kynoch agreed with Miss Strong's declaration, then angled her peculiar bonnet towards the dead room. 'She's doing very well, do you no think? It's clear she feels her loss, but she's very sensible.'

'Did you know she was an actress?' hissed Miss Ada

delightedly.

'Aye, she told me as much last night,' said Mrs. Kynoch, gently deflating Miss Ada. 'She said she didn't want me helping her under any misapprehensions, which I thought kind of her in the circumstances.'

'I don't suppose you said you minded at all, did you, Mrs. Kynoch?' asked Hippolyta with a smile. The older woman was the epitome of sensible kindness and goodwill.

'Who knows what she may have done in her day,' said Mrs. Kynoch. 'but at present she's a grieving widow, and in a state of shock. I ken Mr. Durris has all his questions to ask, but sometimes I wish he would just wait a whiley until people are more ready for him. I suppose that's the point.' She sighed. 'Well, I'll just have a bannock here and then go back. I'm not sure Mr. Whittling's conversation is awful sustaining, Mrs. Napier, however well-intentioned he might be.' She smiled, though, to take any sting out of her criticism, and Hippolyta, struck with guilt, swallowed down her own bannock and hurried back. She found Mr. Whittling well away on some discourse of heaven and hell and the consequences of anger, and Mrs. Broughton with a fixed humble smile on her face, eyes half-closed as if turned towards a strong wind.

'Mr. Whittling!' Hippolyta interrupted firmly. 'I wonder if we might discuss the possibility of a chapel building in Ballater? Taking Communion in one's own parlour is all very convenient on a Sunday morning, but it is hardly suitable as a long term solution, and all this galloping about and walking along the tops of hedges is not good for your health, or for that of any of the other clergy who do their best to serve us.'

The subject was enough to distract Mr. Whittling and turn his energy towards plans for building churches the length of Deeside, if he were blessed with a long career in the area. Hippolyta was happy enough to allow him to talk while she interjected one or two questions, and watched Mrs. Broughton greet her various guests, her husband's mourners, almost strangers to her for the most part. She wondered what family or friend she might have chosen to be there with her at this sad time, to comfort her. The thought of losing Patrick amongst a community she did not know, however kind they might be, made tears surge in her eyes, and she had to blink. When her sight was straight again, she saw that Mr. Elphick had arrived.

Mrs. Broughton seemed to be directing him in the customs of a Scottish funeral, for he blushed and rolled his uncertain eyes, pursing his lips awkwardly, then scuttled off to the next room. In a moment he was back with a glass in one hand and a bannock in the other, spraying crumbs around the dead room in his confusion. Mrs. Broughton took pity on him and gestured to him to sit beside her, then talked gently to him while Mr. Elphick brought his bannock under control. Hippolyta, still only half-listening to the clergyman, tried to catch what they were saying.

'Do you think what that sheriff's fellow said is true?' Elphick was asking quietly.

'I can't see why he wouldn't tell the truth,' said Mrs. Broughton reasonably. 'I believe I trust him.'

'Well, I'm not sure I do,' Elphick murmured back. 'I mean, they don't exactly have the Bow Street Runners up here, do they? What does he know about murders? They probably haven't had a duel since Elizabeth was on the throne. Look, you know me: remember when I used to report on the cases around the Old Bailey? Before I went all grand and moved to Parliament!' He chuckled at himself, clearly expecting her to join in, but she did not and he squirmed a little, still not sure of himself.

'Reporting on a court case and investigating a crime are not the same thing at all, Mr. Elphick,' said Mrs. Broughton. 'Let the sheriff's man do his job. He knows the law up here and he knows his district, no doubt, and you don't know either.'

'He don't know I saw the crime,' said Elphick, almost inaudible.

'You saw -!'

'Hush! Hush,' said Elphick, patting her hand. 'I was there. I told him I only arrived later, but no: I was there. That's what a reporter does, see?'

'Then what did you see?'

'Well,' Elphick sat back a little to tell his tale, just as he had for his anecdotes of parliament in the Napiers' house that first night. Then he remembered the circumstances, and sat forward again. Hippolyta made sure Mr. Whittling was still talking happily, then concentrated on Mr. Elphick. 'I'd overheard the arrangements, as it were, so I was here at dawn. I saw your husband arrive, and Sir Holroyd, and discuss what they were doing, then march off and get ready. Then they turned, and fired. There was a dreadful moment of stillness, then your husband just dropped to the ground.'

Mrs. Broughton gasped, but very softly.

'My poor George!' she murmured. 'Then you are convinced that Sir Holroyd really did kill him?'

'It looked very much like it, from where I was standing,' said Elphick. 'But if this sheriff's man is really right, and Sir Holroyd's gun jammed, or whatever, well: I'll tell you, I saw someone else up there, too. Someone I was not expecting to see in this neck of the woods, I can tell you. Most surprised, I was.'

'Well, tell me, man!' Mrs. Broughton's patience was at last tried.

'Mrs. Broughton,' came a new voice. 'Good day to you.'

'Mr. Durris!' Mrs. Broughton jumped up and Hippolyta glanced quickly round to see Mr. Elphick with a look of disgust on his face. He paused for a moment in his chair, fists on his knees, and watched Mrs. Broughton greeting Durris. Then he rose, and stalked off to the other room.

'Are you all right?' Patrick was suddenly beside her. 'You look a little dazed.'

'Oh, Mr. Whittling was just telling me his plans for the expansion of the church on Deeside,' said Hippolyta. 'Weren't you?'

'And further afield,' said Whittling eagerly. 'You must not forget that, madam: there is no end to my dreams of furthering God's kingdom!'

'Indeed no! I pray you will be granted the energy to continue!' Hippolyta wondered what she had missed: would Whittling's enthusiasm drive him the whole way across Scotland, scattering Episcopal churches in his wake? No: his health would undoubtedly fail him before that, unfortunately.

'Well, as to that, you must excuse me, Mrs. Napier. I must eat something, for straight after the funeral I must go on to Tarland for a baptism, if I can reach it. That is why I begged Mrs. Broughton to be kind enough to start early.' He disappeared, still talking, to find himself some sustinence.

'Patrick, I overheard something just now –'

'Dr. Napier, I'm glad to see you,' said Miss Strong, 'for I wanted to talk to you about my left shoulder.'

'Well, now is hardly the time ...' Patrick began, used to fending off such gambits.

'Oh, of course it's not! No, I just wanted to ask you before I should come to see you about it – what if I were to bathe it in tobacco water?'

'I'm not quite sure how you imagine that would help,' said Patrick hesitantly. He sighed. 'What do you think is wrong with it?'

Hippolyta gave him a little smile, and slipped away from the conversation. Mr. Durris was talking with Mrs. Broughton still, and Mrs. Kynoch was deep in some consultation with the Strachans. The minister and his wife appeared, civil even to those not of their flock. The little room was crowded now, and Hippolyta gathered her wide skirts together to squeeze through the press of people to the door. She would have liked another bannock, not particularly relishing the heavy, moist teacake that was now being served, but she remembered that Mr. Whittling had gone into the parlour where the food was, and she was not sure she could take much more of him just at the moment. She remained in the passage, enjoying a moment of comparative peace, and as she leaned against the wall she closed her eyes.

'Mrs. Napier!' She opened them at once, to find Mr. Elphick in front of her. 'Are you quite well? You aren't going to faint or anything, are you?'

She laughed.

'No, I don't believe so, Mr. Elphick! I was enjoying the cooler air out here, though.'

'I had thought to see your brother here. I hope he is quite well, too!'

'Well, Mr. Elphick, I really have no idea, and I find it very worrying,' she admitted. 'He has disappeared, without telling us where he was going. I wish he would send some message – preferably an apology!' she finished, trying to sound light-hearted about it, as if by not taking it too seriously she would find in the end that it was indeed not a serious situation. Mr. Elphick, though, frowned.

'In this weather? I hope he has taken warm clothing with him.'

'He has, I believe. Otherwise I should be even more concerned.'

'I hope he is soon restored to you.' Hippolyta noticed that Mr. Elphick made more effort to speak without a strong London accent to her than he had been doing when he was speaking to Mrs. Broughton. Perhaps he thought she would not understand him.

'Mr. Elphick,' she could not resist saying, 'when you were on the hill on Saturday morning – you know, just after the duel.'

'Yes, of course.'

'Did you see anyone else up there? Apart from Mr. Broughton and me, of course.'

'I didn't see Sir Holroyd, if that's what you mean,' said Elphick, his eyes innocent. Did he think she had overheard him just now? 'He must have gone down another way, maybe closer to his own house.'

'Yes, very probably. Anyone else?'

'Who are you thinking of? Those town lads that followed me?'

'Maybe.' She let him think for a moment. 'You know that Mr. Durris believes that Mr. Broughton was murdered, and not by Sir Holroyd. I – I'm very much alarmed that there might have been a murderer prowling around up on the hillside there, when I was there virtually on my own!' She let a little tremor enter her voice. 'It is a favourite painting spot of mine, you see, and I have always felt safe there. I should be so pleased to know that any person with, you know, criminal intent, had been safely arrested!'

'Well, I for one don't feel secure while they are still wandering around,' said Mr. Elphick, his face bland. 'Why doesn't that sheriff's man get them locked up? They're clearly up to no good.'

'I must ask him,' said Hippolyta. It was true that the men had not been mentioned in their discussion with Durris yesterday – nor had anyone mentioned seeing them since Mr. Elphick had seen them heading north on Saturday morning. Perhaps it was true that they had left the village.

Mr. Whittling emerged from the parlour, wiping his mouth with his handkerchief.

'Time for the kisting, I believe!' he said solemnly. It was true: the carpenter who had made the coffin was ready now with the lid, and he followed the clergyman into the crowded dead room. Mr. Elphick and Hippolyta stood at the door, heads bowed, as he did his work.

The coffin, now sealed, was covered with the borrowed mortcloth from the parish kirk. Mrs. Broughton had hurriedly asked some of her new acquaintance to be bearers, though the job would have to be shared amongst several more for the difficult walk through the deep snow to Tullich kirkyard. Patrick, Durris, Mr. Worthy and Mr. Elphick at least began the journey, bearing the coffin at hip height out of the parlour and into the hall of the inn, where the innkeeper and staff stood respectfully to watch their erstwhile guest leave. Only a short prayer had been said in the dead room: by contrast with the established church's ceremonies, the Episcopal clergyman would accompany the coffin to the grave. Hippolyta hoped it had not filled up with snow, and instantly began to picture all kinds of accidents that might occur if it had. The men gathered outside the inn's front door, and the women stood just inside, watching Broughton's departure. Hippolyta glanced around. Mrs. Broughton's face was bleak and drawn, as if all joy had been drained away.

The bearers paused to readjust the weight, then hefted the coffin on to their shoulders, steadying it with their hands. Hippolyta hoped that Patrick's gloves were warm enough. They exchanged a word or two between them, then shuffled their feet as if about to find their pace for the first step. Then there came a shout.

'I'm sorry! I'm so sorry!'

The bearers jerked to a halt. The women craned to see where the shout had come from. Hippolyta, strategically, left the narrow doorway with its restricted view, and darted to the window.

There in the street was Sir Holroyd Pinner, his handsome face scarlet and wet with tears, clutching the wall of the house opposite and pointing at the coffin.

'Let me mourn him too! I'm sorry! I'm so sorry!'

Chapter Fifteen

Mrs. Broughton let out a cry, and the women inside the inn gasped. Durris glanced across at Patrick on the other side of the coffin, and looked around. The constable, an elderly man, was not far away.

'Morrisson, will you escort Sir Holroyd back to Dinnet House?'

'Me?' said the constable in surprise. He looked over at Sir Holroyd. 'Me take on a high heidyin like yon?' He was aghast.

'Then come here, man,' said Durris quickly, 'and you, too.' He pointed to one of Morrisson's fellow gawkers. 'You two can take the first turn bearing the coffin to Tullich, if you can't walk a distressed man to his home. Dr. Napier, will you assist me?'

'I'll bear him! I'll bear him!' cried Sir Holroyd, getting in the way. 'My fault put him here – it's only right I'd take the weight!' There was confusion as Durris tried to hand over his share of the weight to Morrisson while fending off Sir Holroyd's attempts to seize it. Mr. Elphick's greenish hat, presumably his only one, was knocked askew and Mr. Worthy, who was not one of the first team of bearers, quickly offered him his own respectable black one with a narrower brim. He rescued Elphick's hat from the snow and tipped it on to his own head, while Patrick tried to avoid tripping over him. Hippolyta could not resist hurrying outside, as if an animal were misbehaving.

'Sir Holroyd! Sir Holroyd, please come over here!' she cried, reaching out a hand to guide him. 'There'll be an accident if you're not careful.' She snatched at his arm, and eased him away from the unseemly crowd at the coffin's head, though he would not look round at her. His gaze was caught on the coffin and its bearers. 'Please, Sir Holroyd, leave it be. Leave it be.' She made her voice soothing and soft, though her grip was firm. Free from his immediate attentions, Durris and Patrick each managed the transfer of their quarter of the coffin to the constable and his crony, and unconsciously shook their shoulders after the weight. The bearers set off, and Sir Holroyd emitted a heart-rending groan.

'It's my fault. My fault.' He turned a pleading face to Hippolyta. 'You know, you were there. It was all my fault.' She blinked and nearly coughed at the smell of brandy that hit her on his breath, and turned to Patrick as he came to her.

'He's drunk, I'm afraid,' she explained.

'I feared as much,' said Durris. 'We'll get him home.'

'No!' said Sir Holroyd, surging forward again in the straggling wake of the funeral procession. The men of the village might have gathered to escort George Broughton to his unforeseen resting place, but they were not going to relinquish too quickly the vision of a senior member of Parliament accusing himself of murder in the middle of the street. Durris waved the lingerers on, at the same time blocking Sir Holroyd's path. Sir Holroyd gripped Durris' coat, staring over his shoulder in desperation.

'Come, Sir Holroyd,' Hippolyta used her horse-taming voice again, and Sir Holroyd fell back from Durris, loosening his grip hopelessly. 'You are not very well, Sir Holroyd: it is time to go home.' She took him again by the arm, both hands wrapped around his elbow, and guided him gently towards the main street in the trampled snow. She realised he had come out without a thick coat or gloves: he would be freezing, even if he did not realise it yet. She cast a glance back towards the funeral procession as Patrick and Durris gathered round her and Sir Holroyd for support: the two old men were already staggering a little at the head of the coffin, but someone would soon exchange with them. There were plenty in the procession, plenty to take their turns.

Nevertheless the village seemed to be full of women, not expected to go to the interment, who could afford the time to stand in the cold and discuss their slow passing up towards the high end of the village. Hippolyta felt very conspicuous with her hands grasping Sir Holroyd's arm and the two men following closely. It seemed a very long walk.

At last they reached the short curling drive of Dinnet House, and at the door rang the bell. It echoed inside for a moment or two before at last they heard footsteps within, and Clara opened the door. Judging by her expression she was expecting something distasteful, but her surprise at seeing her master thus returned home seemed genuine. They were all ushered quickly inside, presumably in case anyone should see what was happening: Hippolyta hoped she would not hear about the spectacle Sir Holroyd had made of himself in the village.

'Sir Holroyd has had a trying experience,' said Patrick diplomatically. 'Is there a fire lit somewhere?' The house was warm, certainly.

'In the drawing room, sir,' said Clara, ushering them in that direction.

'Some tea, then,' said Patrick, with all his medical authority, and Clara raised her eyebrows and disappeared, while the three of them between them manoeuvred Sir Holroyd through the narrow drawing room door. Hippolyta led Sir Holroyd over to the sofa and encouraged him to sit. Sir Holroyd's knees bent abruptly and he bounced as he landed, his face shocked. He began to shiver.

'Here's a rug,' said Patrick, retrieving one of them from the back of a chair. Hippolyta tucked it around Sir Holroyd, and rubbed his hands. He looked as if he might be sick. He leaned forward suddenly and clutched his head, moaning.

'What have I done?' he cried. 'What have I done?'

'You've become inebriated and interrupted a funeral,' said Durris, stern, 'but it seems to me that you have not killed anyone. Not George Broughton, anyway,' he added carefully.

Sir Holroyd lifted his head, his eyes suddenly much more focussed.

'What did you say?'

'I said it seems likely that you did not kill George Broughton.'

'But …'

'You had only the one pistol with you throughout the duel?'

'I swear it. Only one pistol, the one I used to shoot past him. To shoot him!'

'The one I showed you after the duel, when you came back to meet us at the duel site?'

'That's it.'

'Then if that is true, you did not shoot him. Your pistol misfired: I removed the charge myself.'

Sir Holroyd stared at him, mystified, his teeth agitating in his open mouth.

'But,' he said at last, 'it went bang.'

'Well ...'

'And Broughton is dead. He was shot. Wasn't he? I saw the wound in his chest. It was a gunshot, surely!'

'It was. Broughton is dead. There was a bang. But it did not come from your gun, and you did not kill him.'

Sir Holroyd swallowed deep and noisily. Tears welled in his eyes. He shot to his feet.

'Are you telling me the truth? I did not kill him?'

'You did not kill him.'

Sir Holroyd seized Durris' right hand and pumped it up and down as if his life depended upon it.

'Thank you, sir! Oh, thank you, sir! Oh, sir, you are most welcome in this house at any time! You'll stay to dinner? And you, Mrs. Napier? Dr. Napier? You will stay, won't you? I shan't take no for an answer, you know! Oh, the relief! The relief! Clara!'

The maid had just entered the room with a tea tray, and looked at her master in shock.

'Are you quite well, sir?'

'Yes, yes, Clara! All is well! All is very well, and these delightful people are all to dine with us today. Yes?'

'I'll see to it, sir,' said Clara, her surly face twisted in confusion. 'Shall I tell my lady?'

'Oh, of course! Tell her the good news, Clara! Tell her I am not to be arrested for murder!' He turned back, beaming, to the others as Clara hurried from the room. 'Even she must be pleased, surely? If nothing else, it cannot be good for one's social standing to be the widow of a man hanged for murder. And Lady Pinner is very enthusiastic about social standing – particularly her own,' he added sadly.

'Is she?' Hippolyta thought she would take advantage of Sir Holroyd's new confidential mood. The brandy would wear off soon enough, she knew. 'She seemed to me quite condescending to the circle in Ballater.'

'Oh, she can seem kindly enough. But what she would love is to be the centre of a great political salon, you know, like Holland House? But for the Tories, of course,' he added quickly. 'Alas, I am not sure that we are quite the couple to host such things.'

'It would be a fascinating thing to do,' Hippolyta said, toying with the idea. 'I can see the attraction for her.'

'But she takes no interest in politics, that is the problem,' Sir Holroyd admitted. 'She would like the social part, but not the aims. Alas! But then she is very young. And now she is not so well, either ...'

'She will regain her strength,' said Patrick, 'and sooner rather than later. As you say, she is young.'

'But in all other respects,' said Sir Holroyd, 'the damage is already done, I fear.'

Hippolyta frowned. She was about to ask what he meant, when there came a crash in the hallway. They heard a sharp scream.

'What was that?' Sir Holroyd took three long steps to the door, followed by his guests. For the second time that day, Hippolyta found herself stuck at the back of a crowd in a doorway, unable to see what was going on. She scowled, and ducked down, making a mushroom of her skirts, squinting between the legs of the men in front of her.

Lady Pinner was on the bottom step of the stairs, her hands to her pale face. Beyond her, Hippolyta could just see Clara, who must have been coming back from the kitchen quarters. On the floor between the drawing room door and the foot of the stairs was a heap of broken china.

'What happened here?' Sir Holroyd had regained something of his usual authority.

'It fell,' said Lady Pinner, pointing to the china.

'Where was it before?' Hippolyta asked, quickly standing to avoid looking ridiculous. The men turned to look at her, surprised. 'May I see?' she asked sweetly. She pushed through to the hall. 'What a shame: it looks as if it was pretty.'

'It was up there,' Lady Pinner pointed upwards, and Hippolyta moved further into the hall to look up and back to the landing above the drawing room door. There was a solid-looking ledge there, and she vaguely remembered there had been a vase there in the time of the previous occupants at Dinnet House. 'How could it have fallen?'

'Someone must have nudged it,' said Durris, also now looking up.

'But who?' Lady Pinner demanded, a little crossly. 'I see Clara was in the kitchens, and Susanna and the baby are in the nursery – I have just left them. And I see you are back, Sir Holroyd, and also not upstairs.'

'Have you no other servants here?' Hippolyta asked in surprise. Though she had only seen Susanna and Clara, she had assumed there would be others behind the scenes.

'No cook,' said Lady Pinner, impatiently, 'only a woman from the village who helps in the mornings.'

'Goodness,' Hippolyta could not help saying. What was this apparently grand household doing here with only two servants and a daily help?

'Anyway, that is irrelevant,' said Sir Holroyd quickly. 'The vase must simply have wobbled on its ledge. Perhaps you trod on a loose floorboard as you crossed the landing, Lady Pinner?'

'I am sure I did not, Sir Holroyd,' she said firmly. 'I was nowhere near the ledge.'

'Well, it is one of life's mysteries,' said Patrick, with a smile intended to defuse the sudden hostility.

'These people are staying to dinner, Lady Pinner,' Sir Holroyd accepted the opportunity to change the subject.

'Oh really? Why?' She regarded them without much sign of hospitality.

'Well, Lady Pinner, they have brought me some wonderful news! My pistol misfired: I did not kill George Broughton!'

'You did not?' Lady Pinner's eyes widened abruptly, and she sagged back against the banister beside her. Hippolyta darted to her side.

'It is a shock, I know, Lady Pinner, but such a good one!'

Clara was there too, though Hippolyta had not even seen her move.

'My lady, perhaps a little rest before changing for dinner?' She shot Hippolyta a look that Hippolyta had most often seen on the face of one of her more territorial cats to an intruder. Hippolyta backed off, and glanced at Patrick.

'We should change, too,' she said, 'if you are in earnest, Sir Holroyd.'

'Of course, Mrs. Napier. We shall expect all of you back here in …two hours?'

'We shall look forward to it, Sir Holroyd,' said Durris with a bow.

'And we'll get that mess cleared up,' said Sir Holroyd heartily, nodding to the heap of china fragments. 'Silly thing.'

But when Hippolyta glanced back at him, he was frowning up at the ledge. There was more than puzzlement on his face, too: in fact, she was sure Sir Holroyd was frightened.

Two hours was more than was necessary for changing into dinner clothes, as far as Hippolyta was concerned, and Patrick had time to go and see a patient in the village. She armed herself with Elizabeth Cleland's book, and made for the kitchen. Mrs. Riach, as she had expected, was still in her bed. Ishbel and Wullie were engaged in laundry, and were both very pink from the steam when she popped her head into the laundry room.

'It's a fine job on a cold day,' Ishbel remarked, when Hippolyta shot her a sympathetic look.

'But my chilblains are singing to me,' Wullie added, holding up reddened fingers.

'We're going to Dinnet House for dinner,' Hippolyta told them, 'so that's one thing you won't have to do. And Ishbel, I have an interesting book here: we could perhaps go through it some time and I'll help you make some of the dishes in it. Your bread-baking is excellent, so I think you are more than capable of making some other things, too. Do you think we could get hold of pigeons this week?'

Ishbel considered.

'Aye, I reckon so,' she said. 'Though I canna thole plucking the things.'

'I dinna mind that,' said Wullie helpfully.

'We'll do that tomorrow, then. Has Mrs. Riach improved at all?'

'She's still in her bed,' said Ishbel sourly. 'I juked in the door to see was she living, and she gave me her cludgie to empty. She seemed peaceable, so I gave her her breakfast,' she added, as if Mrs. Riach's diet now depended on her good behaviour. Hippolyta nodded with understanding.

'No sign of my brother, I suppose?' she asked, having made

herself leave the question to last, as if it might charm him back into the house.

'No, ma'am. Neither sign nor word.'

'Wretched man.' Hippolyta smiled, trying to look unconcerned. 'Well, I must go and change, I suppose.'

There was no point in trying to train Ishbel as both lady's maid and cook at the same time, particularly when she was doing the laundry anyway. Hippolyta was perfectly capable of dressing her own hair for every day, and with a little concentration could manage an evening arrangement, too, particularly in the winter when one could not be expected to have to wrestle with fresh flowers. She divided her hair carefully in four, tied the back half in a simple bun, and draped the front quarters artistically over each ear to meet it. Then she added pins to decorate it, and was pleased enough with her efforts. After all, there was no sense in trying to compete with Lady Pinner, who had both money for the latest fashions and Clara's no doubt skilful attendance. Then she removed her wrapper and began to assemble her collection of petticoats over her shift and corset, finishing with the gown she had worn to the assembly on Friday night. It was the best she currently had, and she was pleased with it, and she was no grand lady in the London season to have to wear a different gown every night. For a moment the thought made her wistful, and then she wondered where on earth in their little cottage she might store them all if she had to.

Her slippers in her reticule and her boots on her feet, she felt about ready to face the evening, and the appreciative look on Patrick's face when he came home to find her sitting waiting was reward enough for any society belle.

Durris appeared at the door to collect them on his way, just as they were donning their cloaks.

'Snowing again,' he remarked, knocking more flakes off his hat as he waited.

'It's not far,' said Patrick cheerfully, and gave Hippolyta his arm.

Indeed they were not long on the road, for the dug tracks were still fairly clear and they were able, mostly, to keep their feet dry. Hippolyta felt a little nervous as they once again rang at the door bell. Would Sir Holroyd's cheerful mood have persisted? What had he been afraid of? Would he and Lady Pinner be civil enough to each other for a pleasant meal, or had they condemned themselves to an evening of awkward silences and frantic attempts at cheerfulness?

Clara opened the door to them again, glowering.

'Good evening,' she said, quite as if she meant the very opposite, and gestured them to enter. She led them to the drawing room, and fed them in through the narrow doorway like meat into a mincer. Sir Holroyd and Lady Pinner were already waiting for them, and rose politely when they came in.

'A pleasure, a pleasure!' said Sir Holroyd, whose mood clearly had not yet passed. 'Mrs. Napier, will you take some negus against the cold? Come closer to the fire, I beg you.'

'Thank you, Sir Holroyd. Lady Pinner, good evening.' Hippolyta curtseyed, and Lady Pinner favoured her with a slight smile.

'It is very pleasant to have company for dinner,' she remarked. 'And I was delighted when Sir Holroyd explained why he had invited all of you. Such excellent news.' She did indeed look quite pleased at her husband's exoneration, yet there seemed still to be some reservation in her eyes. Had she looked forward to being rid of him? Hippolyta wondered. Yet the shame would have been difficult for anyone to bear, let alone someone of such delicacy and breeding as Lady Pinner.

Both the Pinners were on their best behaviour, to Hippolyta's relief, though Durris had to field perhaps too many questions about his family and background which he answered with as much discretion as ever – no one was any the wiser by the time the cloth was removed and the table laid with puddings, pancakes and rice pots. Comparisons of London and Edinburgh were made, and in addition Glasgow featured in the conversation: it transpired that the Pinners had come north from Sir Holroyd's estates in the Midlands, and travelled to Glasgow, then Perth, then circuitously to Aberdeen and Deeside, dodging the worst of the weather on the way. In all the questions Sir Holroyd asked, and all the statements he made, the politician could be seen, testing what the mood was in each place and how the people were likely to behave if the vote went one way or the other.

'The trouble is,' he said at last with an absent smile, 'that the Reform party makes the whole business sound very sensible and reasonable, with their changes in constituencies and representation. I'm not an old stick-in-the-mud: I appreciate that it makes no sense for great populations to have no member of parliament of their own. But I fear what might happen if that door is once opened even a chink. We've seen violence and rioting already: surely revolution will follow! And I would do nothing to endanger the King.'

'Yet sometimes,' said Patrick, 'when there is pressure on a sluice gate it is important to ease it open slightly, to let some of the water spill out, or the sluice gate will be destroyed completely and the place will flood.'

'I know ...' Sir Holroyd looked less sure than he had done in the past. Hippolyta watched her husband with interest: he had never been known to press his political views before. Marcus would love to be here, she was sure. Where was he? 'The thing is, my own estates are suffering. For years I've done my best to look after the poor there – my father set up a village school, and I've made sure that the parish is augmented with extra money for anyone in need. If someone is injured in my employ they will have a pension and a roof over their heads – I'm not made of money, but I do my best. There are factories near us now, and many from the estates go to work in them, but if they come home no longer able to work they are still helped – oh! Some of the injuries they suffer in those places! But they will go, for most of them are young and think they are invincible ... Yet they threaten – well, that's another story. But what more can I do?'

'Another apple pancake, Mrs. Napier?' asked Lady Pinner. 'The apples from the orchard here are very fine, I have found.'

The gentlemen allowed the conversation to be turned gently back to London politics, and the coverage in the newspapers.

'You'll have met Mr. Elphick before, then?' asked Durris casually.

'Oh, now and again, yes. He's a great hanger-on of the Whig cause, too. I believe he only came to report on Parliament in the last year or two, since the business began. Before that I think he reported more generally. Yet you find that some reporters become addicted to the House as to laudanum: they lament the conditions, complain of the long hours and criticise mumblers and mutterers, but they are still there when the doors open and are thrown out with the rest of us at the end of the evening.'

'Have you visited Parliament, Lady Pinner?' asked Hippolyta. 'I gather that there is a gallery for ladies.'

'Oh! That place!' Lady Pinner was clearly not impressed. 'I have been once. The debate was not very exciting, and the gallery is completely airless. I felt like a prisoner on a gallows.'

'The buildings are not in a fit state, certainly,' agreed Sir Holroyd. 'The whole place stinks by half past five in the afternoon. If we sit on till the early hours, smelling salts are essential.'

Lady Pinner glanced around the table. Everyone had finished their puddings. She nodded to Clara, who again was the only servant in evidence.

'Mrs. Napier, shall we go to the drawing room?'

The ladies rose and the gentlemen stood as they departed. Hippolyta hoped that the men would not be long in joining them: she did not fancy a quiet conversation only with Lady Pinner. Though perhaps, if she could find out if Lady Pinner had really been at the duel …

'Quickly,' said Lady Pinner, stopping as they crossed the hall. 'Come this way.'

To Hippolyta's astonishment, Lady Pinner gathered her skirts close and tiptoed back towards the door to the kitchens, just beyond the dining room. Hippolyta had been in the passage to the kitchens before: it was lined with various cupboards and presses, both freestanding and built in. Lady Pinner made for one of the latter, a few yards down the passage on the right hand side. She opened the door, and slipped inside, gesturing Hippolyta to follow her.

'I must know,' she whispered, by way of explanation. 'Something is troubling him, and he won't say. But I think he'll say to your husband and Mr. Durris. I think that's why he bade you all stay to dinner. Now,' she pressed a finger to her lips for silence, before Hippolyta could reply.

Through the wall between the cupboard and the dining room she could hear Durris, his back to them, asking something. Then she heard Sir Holroyd clear his throat, and push his chair back a little. There was a pause, probably while something was done with the brandy decanter.

'The thing is,' said Sir Holroyd, 'now that the matter of the duel is settled – or rather, now that the matter of the duel is no longer settled – I feel I should tell you. I fear, very much, that my life is in danger.'

Chapter Sixteen

'I don't want Lady Pinner to be made alarmed by this,' Sir Holroyd went on, his voice hovering between his usual authority and a tremor of urgency. In the dark of the press, angled on to the candles in the servants' passage, Hippolyta could still see Lady Pinner's rueful smile twist her pretty mouth. Sir Holroyd carried on, evidently encouraged by Durris and Patrick. 'She has no idea of the severity of my situation. On my own estates in the Midlands: well, I hope the loyalty of my household staff will protect what is there, but I am told that attacks are planned on my very home, and that, if I venture there again, my life will be most completely under threat. A noose was pushed through an open window. Crude drawings of the most explicit kind – skulls, knives, chopping blocks – have been left about the place for me to find. In the summer matters came, I hope, to a head – it was dreadful at the time, and I hope that it will never be worse. I found myself going from house to cottage to hovel, begging the inhabitants not to harm me or mine. I made speeches, reminded them of what I had done, what my father had done – even my grandfather. I addressed them from my own front door step, talked with their leaders, tried to explain …They simply will not listen. The blood of revolution is boiling in their veins, and I fear they will not stop, they really will not stop until they have brought France's filthy guillotine here and felled anyone who stands in their way.'

He paused, the practised orator, though as far as could be told through the wall his speech had been truly heartfelt. He was not only alarmed, he was hurt. There was silence in the dining room for a long moment, in which Hippolyta was sure she heard Lady Pinner murmur, in surprise,

'The summer …'

'But surely,' came Patrick's voice, soothing as usual, 'you are safe here? Ballater is very far from the Midlands.'

'Not so far, perhaps, when you make a mistake as I have done. I chose to come here, as I said, by way of Glasgow. I wanted to see for myself how one of the great manufacturing cities is holding itself in these troublous times. The member for the Clyde Burghs is of course a Whig, so I did not trouble him, but there are Tory sympathisers there and I spoke with them. And thinking myself safe, I made a public speech or two. I had no idea how some of the connexions between the revolutionary populations of different places could communicate so quickly. I am sure I saw, in the crowd, some of my own old tenants from my estates, and many of their new Glaswegian friends. There is no loyalty left, no discipline: they take jobs in the factories, and then abandon them to take up their revolutionary cause. And I was naif: I had thought that nothing I had done in one place would affect the other. But there was uproar, and I was pelted with – well, a variety of things it might be best not to mention at the dinner table. All I can say is that the people of Glasgow do not lack imagination when it comes to expressing their opinions.'

'They are noted for it,' said Durris, with dry clarity. 'Well, that was Glasgow, and before that was your estate in the Midlands of England. What of Ballater, sir?'

'I fear,' said Sir Holroyd, 'that the trouble has followed me even to this peaceful place. Our maid Clara has noted two or three men of a menacing appearance about the place: she might be a very unprepossessing girl, but she does not lack wit, and she has been very loyal to us through this business. We keep the doors locked. I have pared down our staff, as Mrs. Napier noticed earlier, Dr. Napier, to the bare essentials, not wanting us inadvertently to nourish a viper in our bosom. My very bodyservant – I found him reading a Reformist tract! I have come to this quiet and simple place for peace and safety, only to find that murder treads here, too, and the threat to my person – and to my wife and my daughter, the thought of which I cannot bear – has simply followed us on our journey. We are safe nowhere, and I have brought this upon us. Yet what else could I have done?'

'If by a threat following you,' said Durris, 'you mean the two or three men in town clothes who have been seen about the village in recent days, we have some reason to believe that they have moved on to the north.'

'Are you sure?' Sir Holroyd, full of sudden hope, sounded ready to trust him, but Durris would not allow it.

'No, I am not sure. No sightings of them have been reported to me since Saturday morning.'

'Last Saturday morning? The day before yesterday? The time of the duel?'

'Yes, indeed, or perhaps a little later. The account we have has not yet been verified. They were apparently seen then on the road heading north. Past the gate of your house here.'

'The gate of the house ... did they truly go past?'

'I don't know,' said Durris honestly. 'I have not investigated fully. They had done no reported harm in the village, having only caused a little alarm, and I had my mind on more urgent matters.'

'Of course, of course.' Sir Holroyd subsided a little, knowing the guilt he still bore even if he had not actually killed Broughton. He, after all, had suggested the duel. Then he cleared his throat again. 'Could they ... for whatever reason, could they have shot George Broughton?'

'It is possible. But no one has reported seeing any of them with a gun, and I cannot see, if they are indeed for Reform as you say, what their motive might have been.'

'He would not have been extreme enough for them, no doubt,' said Sir Holroyd gloomily.

'But would that be a reason to remove him?' asked Patrick.

'There is also the question of your own missing pistol, Sir Holroyd,' Durris went on. 'You said there was no sign of a break-in, so if they used it how did they steal it, and if they did not steal it, who did?'

'I've heard enough,' Lady Pinner made Hippolyta jump. She herself was engrossed in the conversation in the dining room. Lady Pinner, though, pushed past her into the passageway. 'Come, we had better go back to the drawing room, before they realise we are not there.'

Reluctantly, Hippolyta followed her hostess back across the hall where tea was waiting for them beside the fire. Her skirts were crumpled, and she did her best to fluff them out: Lady Pinner's skirts seemed perfect. Nevertheless, Lady Pinner herself seemed disturbed, and thoughtful. She poured tea, and handed a cup absently to Hippolyta, but stared into the fire. Hippolyta took up the embroidery she had brought with her, appreciating the sea of candles that lit the room again. The colours of the threads danced and slithered on the silk.

'Mrs. Napier,' said Lady Pinner at last, just when Hippolyta had settled into a meandering dream of her own, 'do you love your husband?'

'Oh, yes,' said Hippolyta, not in the least bothered by such a personal question. 'Very much. We are only married two and a half years.' She smiled. Lady Pinner nodded, her expression serious. The fire cast shadows across her fair face.

'We, too, about the same length of time. And I love my husband, too – truly, I do. Or I did ...'

'And does he love you?' asked Hippolyta quietly, remembering that it had been said to be a match for money.

'I believe he did. I'm sure he did, but then I thought I had somehow lost his favour ... and now I wonder. Though I had thought he no longer cared for me, now I wonder if I have been wrong.'

'People can be very confusing,' said Hippolyta encouragingly. Lady Pinner looked at her vaguely, then took in what she had said.

'Yes, can't they?'

This time Hippolyta was patient, waiting to let Lady Pinner speak. It was not easy for her, but she concentrated on the stitched curve of a leaf border, and at last her patience was rewarded.

'Last summer, Mrs. Napier, as you may know – well, as you will know, I was brought to bed of my daughter, Maria. At the same time ... at the same time, I gave birth to her twin, a little boy. He was christened Francis. He was born dead.'

'I am sorry,' whispered Hippolyta.

'It was, I am led to believe, a hard birth. It certainly seemed so to me. I could not have imagined ... but perhaps I should not say to you, who are not yet a mother.'

'Well ...' Hippolyta did not want to stop her speaking, but at the same time she had no wish to be frightened. Childbirth was dangerous enough, without allowing panic to accompany it. She preferred not to think about it.

'I am told, too, that my life was for some days in extreme

danger, that my husband was sent for, that it was feared that at any moment I should abandon my daughter to be an orphan, and follow my son into the next world. My husband was sent for. He did not come.'

'Where were you?'

'In Leamington. It is a healthy town in the Midlands, where I was to receive the best of medical care. My husband was on his estates, not a day's ride away. He did not come.'

'But ... but last summer ...'

'I know. I have just found out why. He never told me – he never said what he had been doing, or that he had been in such danger. He was protecting me from the knowledge of that threat, while all the time I thought him neglectful of me in my hour of need.'

'My dear Lady Pinner,' breathed Hippolyta, realising at last the cause of the pain in this household.

'He should have told me!' cried Lady Pinner, then, as if she were trying to learn a new way of thinking, she said steadily, 'I should have trusted him. I should have trusted him.'

'But now you know,' said Hippolyta, trying to sound encouraging.

'Yes, now I know,' repeated Lady Pinner. 'But I am in such a habit of resenting him – can I learn not to? I truly believe that somewhere inside me, I do still love him. I want him back, and I would do anything to protect him. I truly would.'

'You even went to witness the duel, in case he was hurt,' said Hippolyta, taking the chance. Again she kept her eyes down on her stitching.

'I did,' admitted Lady Pinner softly. 'I could not let him go off like that, with no second – no friend. That man could not be trusted to aim wide, like a gentleman. If anything happened ... I needed to be there.'

'Did you go alone?'

'No. I thought that one person would be much less obvious than two, but I did tell Clara where I was going, in case – in case of accidents, and she insisted on coming with me. After all, if Mr. Broughton had fired wide – well, he might have caught me instead. At that point I am not sure that I should have cared very much, but now ... Now I am pleased that he missed both of us. I have things I need to say to my husband, and things I need to hear from him, and neither of those would benefit from either of us being dead.' She gave a little, ironic smile, but there was more life in her than Hippolyta had seen before. She thought that perhaps there was some hope for the Pinners now, for their happiness: it could be, though, that Patrick would no longer be needed as a doctor in the house. There was a pause as the ubiquitous Clara herself came in to see if more tea was required for the gentlemen coming.

'Look,' said Hippolyta, keen to help, 'if I may I shall tell Mr. Durris all of this. I'm almost convinced that someone from Mr. Broughton's past is the key to this,' she added, her mind tossing between Mrs. Broughton and Elphick, 'and that there is no threat to Sir Holroyd here, but Mr. Durris has some experience in these things and will certainly find out the truth, if you will but let me tell him what you have told me.'

'Of course,' said Lady Pinner, growing in energy once more. 'If you can do that for me, Mrs. Napier, then I can do my part and speak with my husband.'

The return of the gentlemen prevented any further confidences, but during the general conversation which followed, Hippolyta was pleased to see Lady Pinner paying some little attentions to her husband which she had not seen her do before. Sir Holroyd was not unobservant: he watched his wife with some puzzlement, and a growing, slightly distrustful, pleasure. Hippolyta felt they should not linger.

Nevertheless the company was easier now, and it was an hour or so before Durris began to make his excuses, explaining that he had a good deal of work the following day. Patrick concurred, and the visitors gathered themselves up and took their leave, happy to find that the snow had once more eased, though it lay thick on the driveway, and did its best to enhance the appearance of Dinnet House itself, which was no bad thing. The sky was clear and full of stars. They said their farewells quickly, not wanting to let the cold in, and arm in arm set off towards the gateway and the road beyond.

'That's a frost, I reckon,' said Patrick as they went. 'It must have set in almost as soon as we went indoors.'

'It's bitter,' Durris agreed. Hippolyta could feel her face pinched by the cold, her eyes already watering. The fresh snow had crisped over to a depth of two or three inches, so that when one stepped into what looked like a cushion of flakes, there was a half-second of thinking the cushion was hard, then almost a snap beneath one's boot before feet sank, betrayed, deep into the older snow below. It was worse out on the road, where the trodden tracks must have frozen before the fresh snow could cover them properly. Underfoot was treacherous.

'Oh!' said Patrick, suddenly stopping. He let go of Hippolyta's arm, and half-turned – then flailed his hands in the air and fell suddenly. 'Oh!'

'What's the matter?' Hippolyta was on her knees beside him.

'Oh, my stupid ankle!' Patrick cried. 'Ow! How foolish of me!' He had propped himself with a bare hand in the snow, but now snatched it clear, rubbing it.

'Patrick, where are your gloves?'

'That's just it: I cannot imagine how I came out without them. I had just noticed and was about to go back for them when – well, I turned badly.'

'You cannot sit there all night,' said Durris. 'Do you think you will be able to walk?'

He put his free hand out – the other held their lantern - as did Hippolyta, and between them they helped Patrick to rise to his one good foot. He tried tentatively to set the other foot to the ground, uneven as it was. He yelped.

'No, I don't think so,' he said, trying to sound reasonable about it.

'Have you broken it?' asked Hippolyta. If he had ... well, it would make life very awkward for a long while, particularly in this weather.

'I don't know until I can look at it properly,' he said, a little impatiently.

'But did you feel anything? Sometimes you say people can feel their bones –'

'I don't know!' Patrick snapped, with uncharacteristic temper. Durris did not look at either of them.

'Come on,' he said, 'I'll help you home. Mrs. Napier ...'

'I'll go back and fetch his gloves,' said Hippolyta, now a little cross herself.

'Hippolyta, you can't go back on your own,' said Patrick.

'I don't think you're really in a position to stop me,' she said, turned carefully on the snow – it would spoil her exit completely if she were to fall, too – and marched back up the hill towards Dinnet House. Durris still held the lantern, but the starlight was crisp and bright. She hoped Patrick would call after her. He did not.

'Why didn't he remember his silly gloves anyway?' she muttered to herself when she was out of hearing. 'Always absent-minded. He needs a nursery maid, not a wife. It's not as if it isn't cold outside. Why didn't he realise when he came out of the front door?' Because, she realised, he had his hand tucked under her arm to make sure she did not slip and fall. 'Well, who said I needed looking after? He was the one who fell over!'

Grumbling fuelled her steps all the way back to Dinnet House, and she rang the bell sharply. There was a longer wait than usual before Clara opened the door, only a chink at first, looking more surly even than usual.

'My husband left his gloves behind. Might I fetch them?' Hippolyta asked sweetly.

'Oh,' said Clara. 'Wait a minute, ma'am.' She left Hippolyta standing on the doorstep. Inside, the hall was darkened, and she could see that the lights had been extinguished in the parlour: the household had evidently gone to bed already. Behind her, too, it grew darker: the sky was clouding over again, and the stars dulled rapidly. Snow began to fall with a silent, steady stealth. Hippolyta sighed. She hoped it would make the road less slippery, but it would do her gown skirts no good at all.

Clara returned, holding Patrick's gloves in one hand and a lantern in the other. She had donned a bonnet and cape.

'My lady said as I should go with you down to the village and not let you walk on your own,' she announced, lighting the lantern.

'I'm sure that's not necessary,' said Hippolyta, not relishing Clara's company, however well meant.

'My lady said I should,' said Clara, slapping her lips shut. There was the end to any argument, it seemed. Hippolyta tucked Patrick's gloves into her reticule on top of her embroidery, and led the way without further comment down the driveway. The snow grew thicker.

'Watch underfoot,' she said, 'for there was a frost earlier, and some of the snow is slippery.'

'Yes, ma'am,' was Clara's only reply. She walked by Hippolyta's side, holding the lantern to show them both their path. The snow fell more densely still, and Hippolyta peered ahead – even if they caught up with Patrick and Mr. Durris, it would be almost impossible to see them now.

Their pace necessarily slow, they had to stop every now and again to bat gathered flakes from their cloaks where it was weighing them down. Hippolyta helped Clara to dislodge snow from her hood, which had folded heavily around her neck, and Clara cleared Hippolyta's shoulders a couple of times, attending to her with the deft gestures of a practised lady's maid. Hippolyta was pleased that the road to the village was fairly obvious, even in the dark and snow: it was the kind of night when it would be easy to miss one's way and end up dead in a snowdrift. She shivered at the thought, and stared harder into the darkness beyond the lantern's pool of dotted light, anxious to find some distinguishing feature in the night. There was very little to help them. Even the question of whether they were walking gently uphill or downhill was now a mystery.

At last the lantern's light caught a wall on their right, only appearing a foot or two above the top of the snow.

'The Strachans' garden wall!' cried Hippolyta. 'There, we are at the edge of the village at last. I shall be safe from here, if you wish to return home, Clara.'

'I'm not sure I should leave you, ma'am,' said Clara dubiously.

'If you stay out much longer you might not get home at all. If you wish, though, you can come on with me and stay the night at our house, which might be safer.'

'No! No, ma'am, I cannot leave my lady without attendance.'

'Then go back from here, and take the lantern,' said Hippolyta firmly. 'There is no sense in your walking me down the street which I know better than you do, is there?' She smiled gratefully, though. 'Thank you very much for coming with me.'

'Not at all, ma'am,' said Clara, expressionless. She nodded, by way of some kind of curtsey. 'I wish you safe home, ma'am.'

'Thank you, and the same to you. Walk carefully!' Hippolyta watched as Clara turned away, and in a very short time, it seemed, the lantern light almost winked out and Clara was gone.

She turned, a hand on the Strachans' garden wall for support, and steadied herself to find her bearings. It should not be difficult, surely, even without a lantern. She knew exactly where she was. The Strachans' fine new house was on the north west edge of the village, more part of the village than Dinnet House, as if Mr. Strachan could not quite let go of his business even in his grand home. There would be a little space between the corner of the wall and the next house, one of a row of cottages that formed a side street off the main street – she would be crossing that lane, and then there would be a straight run of buildings, houses and shops, all the way down to the green. Then what would be better – crossing the main street and following the houses along the top of the green, where the Strongs lived, then crossing another side street before she could reach the guiding line of the garden walls that would take her to her own front gate, or crossing the green in a wild diagonal line straight to her front door, or trying the other side of the green, with gaps on either side of the church and still the main street to cross at the bottom of the green? Which way would Patrick and Mr. Durris have gone? Would she come upon them? Surely they could not have been moving too quickly, in the snow and with Patrick's ankle. She hoped they would not go so slowly they would take a chill, particularly Patrick with his bare hands. How could he have forgotten his gloves?

She sighed sharply. She would take a chill herself soon if she did not make up her mind and move. The top end of the green seemed the easiest of the paths to take, but she would start on the kirk side of the street until she reached the green. Taking a deep breath, she lifted her hand from the corner of the Strachans' garden wall, and stepped out into the spattering darkness.

The blow to the side of her head was sharp and hard. The snow, green against yellow, took a sudden lurch upwards, and she felt the soft ground leap up to meet her as her world spun. But the snow seemed warm, and she felt herself nestle into it, as full darkness descended.

Chapter Seventeen

Hippolyta was cosy and warm, but a hand was shaking her shoulder violently. She was not impressed. Patrick? why would Patrick be rousing her so importunately? And why would he be calling her 'Mrs. Napier?' Could it be Ishbel? Maybe the house was on fire! But it was so hard to open her eyes.

She felt herself being hauled upright into a sitting position, nevertheless. Surely that could not be Ishbel: she would not have the strength. Unless it was Ishbel and Wullie between them – she hoped suddenly that her shift was decent, for the servants to be seeing her sitting up in bed. Then she noticed that her feet were terribly cold, too cold for indoors, surely? And too cold for a house on fire. She dragged her eyelids open with all the force of her will, and found herself staring at a lantern, on the ground, in the snow. She appeared to be sitting beside it.

'What?' she asked. It sounded groggy, but she felt it covered everything. She closed her eyes again, not wanting to waste the effort now she had apparently seen all there was to see.

'Mrs. Napier,' said a voice that was familiar enough, but certainly neither Ishbel nor Wullie. It sounded like a man. The minister? She had been somewhere near the kirk. Or Mr. Strachan? Or maybe Sir Holroyd ... Somebody? There had been someone around, certainly.

'Mrs. Napier, wake up!'

Oh, for goodness' sake, she thought. What did they want now? She strained to open her eyes again. The lantern was still there, and so was the snow. Then she saw a hand wave in front of her face, and tried to turn her attention to the person waving it. A whitish blob loomed out of the darkness, and subsided again, coming and going like the pendulum in a clock. It was strangely fascinating and she stared at it, forgetting her aching eyes and head. Then the blob developed dark patches, which turned, gradually, into eyes. Odd, she thought, and stared harder. It was a face, she discovered, and as she realised that it seemed to slow its motion and hover in the air in front of her.

'Mr. Durris,' she said at last, finding a name in her head, 'what are you doing?'

'Trying to waken you, Mrs. Napier. Can you stand?'

'No, no, it's Patrick that has hurt his ankle,' she said indistinctly. Why would her tongue not wrap tidily around the words? 'I can stand. Of course I can stand.' She pushed down with one hand, slithered, and had the unpleasant feeling of her arm sag under her. 'Or maybe not,' she corrected herself. 'Where am I?'

'You're in the main street,' said Durris, business-like now as he took both her wrists and tugged her to her feet. His arm was quick to catch her as she wobbled again. 'Dr. Napier was worried about you, you took so long, and begged me to come and find you. And here you are, and who knows what might have happened if he had not insisted. But we'll soon have you home now. That's right, stepping forward … It's not so slippery now the snow has fallen more. Not far …'

Goodness, she thought, she had never heard Mr. Durris speak so much all together in all their acquaintance. Maybe it was not Mr. Durris at all. Could she be mistaken? Nothing seemed terribly clear. Yet surely this was her own front gate, and that was her door, and there was Ishbel, opening it, drawing her hurriedly, anxiously, inside where there was a fire in the parlour that seemed an inferno to one who had been out in the snow for - how long? How long had she been away? She had no idea. But it was Mr. Durris that followed her in, and it was her own dearest Patrick that sat with his poor darling foot up on the sofa and bandages and ice over it, and she sagged forward and knelt by him and felt his warm arms surround her tight and safe and definitely home.

It was a little while again before she heard distant voices above her head.

'Quite a blow …'

'Nothing that I saw that could have cause it – and just under her bonnet … unfortunate …'

'Thugs?'

'In this weather? I'd have thought ...'

'Hippolyta, dearest, are you awake again? Best to keep that way, if you can, for now. You have a concussion.' She felt Patrick's delicate fingers probe lightly at the side of her head, just behind her right ear, and pain jabbed at her. She sat up straight and found that she was still propped against the sofa, held up mostly by her corset and by one of Patrick's arms still about her. She was enveloped in a nest of rugs, inexpertly tucked around her. There was a bowl of reddish water on Patrick's lap, and a bloodstained cloth in his other hand.

'Patrick! Are you hurt? Is your ankle –' She struggled to free herself from the rugs.

'Dearest, my ankle is not bleeding at all: it is a bad sprain, I believe. You, on the other hand, have been properly in the wars. What happened? Can you remember?'

She tried to turn as if she could look at her own head, and instead dislodged a fold of blanket and saw a sodden, bloody mess at her right shoulder, where the lace bodice edging of her gown had sat crisp earlier. The movement sent another spear of pain through her head, and she turned back to face forwards more carefully. Mr. Durris sat at the table, his notebook at the ready, gazing at her in some concern.

'Thank you for looking for me, Mr. Durris,' she said. 'I am extremely grateful. But I think my gown is ruined.'

'Here, Ishbel has warmed you some brandy,' he said, and leaned down with a glass.

'If you can manage it,' Patrick added. 'Take it slowly.'

She tried a small sip, and felt it burn round her mouth. She shuddered, and felt her head again. She closed one eye, which made her feel a little better.

'Can you remember anything?' Durris asked.

'Um. Where did you leave me? I – I sort of remember you hurting your ankle,' she said, half-over her shoulder at Patrick.

'You went back to Dinnet House to fetch my gloves. They are in your reticule, so you must have been there.'

'Dinnet House ...' She pictured at once the house as they usually saw it, dark and glum. Then she remembered the snow, and the starlight. 'Yes, I went there and I got your gloves ... from

Clara, that's right. That's the maid, isn't it?'

'Yes, good. And then did you start for home? The snow would have started not long after.'

'Snow ...'

'And you had no lantern.'

'No, Clara had the lantern. Oh!' A piece of memory slipped into place almost with a clunk. 'Lady Pinner told Clara to come with me, that's right. Because the snow was really thick, and we could scarcely see. But then ... I sent her back. Oh, I remember! We reached the Strachans' garden wall, and I knew where I was so I sent her back. I did ask her if she wanted to come and stay the night but she said she needed to go back to Dinnet House, so she took the lantern and went. And I ... um, I tried to work out the best way home from there, and then I crossed the road to the end of the main street ... Then I'm a bit blank.'

'You weren't much further down the hill than that,' said Durris. 'And you don't remember anyone else around?'

'Good heavens, Mr. Durris, I could barely see Clara! I watched her go – I could see the lantern for a little, but only for a little. I remember ... I had a feeling that someone else was around, but as to who it might have been, I have no hope of remembering. I very much doubt I had any idea at the time.'

'Well, that fits,' said Patrick. He set aside the cloth and basin. 'It looks as if you were hit from behind.'

'I was hit?'

'We think so,' said Durris seriously. She felt her mouth drop open, and closed it firmly. 'There was nothing nearby that you could have hit yourself on like that if you had just slipped and fallen. I'm afraid we believe you were attacked.'

'But why? Why me?'

'Well, that is the question.' Durris and Patrick met each other's eye over her head.

'What?' she demanded.

'We wondered if perhaps you had seen something that morning at the duel. Something you were, perhaps, keeping to yourself?'

'No!' She reflected, though, for a moment. 'No, I don't think so.'

Durris gave a little smile, which irritated her.

'Something, then, that you might have seen and not considered significant?'

'Well, if I didn't consider it significant then I'm not likely to remember it now, am I?' she asked, crossly.

'You might. The other option, of course, is Sir Holroyd's revolutionaries.' Again, he and Patrick met each other's gaze. It was a habit she found intensely annoying.

'Explain,' she commanded, though a hazy, unlikely memory was beginning to surface of standing in a press earlier that evening.

'Sir Holroyd confided –' there was the least stress on the word '- in us this evening that he believes the two or three strangers who have been roaming the town, that so alarmed Mr. Elphick, are in fact Reform supporters from Glasgow – or perhaps from near his home in the Midlands – who have pursued him here for the purpose of threatening him. He fears that his life is in danger.'

'You seem less than convinced,' said Hippolyta. She tried to turn to see Patrick's face, too, but her head hurt too much. And she was surprisingly comfortable just where she was. Durris looked less easy.

'I think,' he said at last, 'that I had expected more of intelligence in him. He was sincere enough, I believe – and you thought so too, did you not, Dr. Napier? But his reasoning did not seem that sound, and I was not entirely convinced in the end that he had the right of the matter. He seemed to me to have acted in panic.'

'He has nearly destroyed his marriage in the course of the business,' said Hippolyta. 'He should confide more in his wife.' She told them quickly of her conversation with Lady Pinner.

'So she at least was one of the witnesses to the duel!' said Durris with satisfaction. 'I must have a word with her.'

'I'm not sure that she would say anything to her husband's detriment,' said Hippolyta. 'Because she has now realised what happened last summer, and what Sir Holroyd's fears are, I think she intends to try to make up with Sir Holroyd and recover their marriage. She would not endanger him with a charge of murder now. I'm not saying,' she added with judicious niceness, 'that she is has any more wit than he has, but together they might make some use of themselves, and at least be happy.'

'And her health would benefit from her mind being under less strain,' said Patrick, echoing Hippolyta's thoughts earlier. 'His, too.'

'Well, that is all very well,' said Durris the bachelor, 'but I need to discover whether or not these thugs are truly out to attack Sir Holroyd, whether they attacked you, Mrs. Napier, and why, and whether indeed they are still in the village at all. We do not even know yet where they have been staying – I doubt town dwellers would be sleeping rough, particularly in this weather, but if we can have people look into their byres and steadings we might find out where they have been and whether they are still around.'

'Not tonight, though,' said Hippolyta drowsily. Her right eye was closing again, and her left was eager to follow.

'Is she still looking confused?' Patrick asked Durris, unable to see Hippolyta's face for himself. Durris bent down from his chair and gazed into Hippolyta's face. She struggled to keep both eyes open.

'She looks exhausted,' he said.

'Well, I think we had best retire for the night,' said Patrick. 'There is a spare bed upstairs if you want to use it. I think the fire is even lit, for Ishbel is always hopeful of Marcus' return.' He squeezed Hippolyta's shoulders, acknowledging that she, too, was anxiously awaiting her brother. Durris hesitated, weighing up some unseen factors behind his glasses. He folded away his notebook slowly.

'Then yes,' he said, 'if it will not inconvenience you in any way. I admit that the thought of facing the snow once again tonight, and waiting at the door of the inn for admittance at this hour, is not appealing.'

'What is this hour?' Hippolyta finally asked. 'How long was I out there?'

'You were missing for two hours,' said Patrick. 'My dear, you are very, very lucky to be alive.'

Hippolyta woke in the morning with stiff limbs and an aching head, but aching only, she noted optimistically to Patrick, on the one side. He brought her some headache powders from his dispensary and she took them gratefully with her morning tea, and after a few gentle callisthenic stretches she had seen described in a newspaper, she could face feeding the hens and the pig, even helping Wullie to dig the worst of the snow off henhouse and piggery. Wullie then retreated to scrub out the privy, which he said was almost a pleasure when the cold air kept the smells down – Wullie always relished the nastiest jobs about the place – and went to discuss pigeons and breakfast for Mr. Durris with Ishbel. She was attempting, with cold water, to scrub stove blacking off her hands and arms.

'Oh, Mrs. Napier!' she said in dismay, 'I went in to Mr. Fettes' room this morning and my heart leapt for I thought he was safe returned to you! And then I saw Mr. Durris instead.'

'Well, never mind, Ishbel,' said Hippolyta. 'Mr. Durris will need breakfast too. Did you bake bread yesterday?'

'Aye, ma'am.'

'And we have eggs. Was there ham?'

'There's still a great lump of it in the pantry, ma'am, from last week.'

'And there's plenty of jam, isn't there?'

'No so much as there might be, ma'am, but there's plenty for breakfast.'

'Really? What has happened to it?'

'That I dinna ken, ma'am. I thought maybe Wullie had taken some to Mrs. Riach, but he says no, and the boy's no a liar, ma'am, whatever else he might be.'

No, it was true: Wullie knew very well that his ears turned red if he tried to tell a lie, and had long ago decided it was not worth it.

'Well, we have breakfast, then. No doubt Mr. Durris will be up shortly.'

'Och, he's up and out already, ma'am, but he said he would see you both at breakfast nonetheless.'

'Oh! Very well.'

Indeed there was already an air of achievement about the party as they assembled for breakfast: Hippolyta had sorted out the linen washed the previous day, Patrick, hirpling badly with the aid of his grandfather's old walking stick, had already mixed up the medicines he thought he would need for his morning and afternoon calls (though how he was to make them it was hard to tell), and Mr. Durris had discovered where Sir Holroyd's revolutionaries had been staying.

'There's an empty cottage down the back of the kirk – not

facing it, further down that way near the old howff. The man that was in it, apparently, has gone to live with his daughter in Glengairn for the winter, and according to the neighbours these fellows, three of them, said they were some kind of cousin from Paisley direction. The neighbours say they have been living quietly enough, but not keeping regular hours, and since they supposed the men must be there for the good of their health it seemed strange that they should be out late, but there was nothing, they said, to complain about and the men were civil enough when they met them.'

'They saw no sign of a gun amongst them, then?' asked Patrick.

'None at all. Though if they were wise, of course, they would have kept it hidden.'

'And have they gone north?' Hippolyta asked, irresistibly putting her fingers to the lump on her head. The cut was bandaged and she felt thoroughly self-conscious about it, though she had tried to arrange her hair lower to cover it.

'They have not.' Durris looked at them both significantly. 'But they were not in when I called just now.'

'Late out and early up, too?'

'It appears so.'

'Did they hear them in the house last night?' asked Patrick again.

'They could not be sure. They have a youngster themselves who I think makes enough noise for three households: I saw a large bottle of Godfrey's Cordial on the shelf, but I don't think they've been using it much. The child looked content, but the parents were very wabbit.'

'I should think they don't use it too much,' said Patrick. 'It's full of opium.'

'Goodness!' said Hippolyta, trying to remember where she had seen another bottle recently. It was a common enough purchase: she had certainly noticed it on the shelves at Strachan's warehouse. She gathered her thoughts back to the matter at hand. 'So if we discover that the thugs – Sir Holroyd's revolutionaries, I do like that! – if we discover that they attacked me, for whatever reason, does that mean that they also murdered poor Mr. Broughton?

'Because he was not fierce enough for Reform? That's what Sir Holroyd suggested.'

'Or they tried to kill Sir Holroyd, and got the wrong man? If they had not seen his face,' Hippolyta wondered.

'Apparently they saw him speak in Glasgow, or their fellow Reformers did. The two men did not look very much alike. I should be surprised, even in the dawn light which was, after all, clear enough for them to shoot at each other, that one could be mistaken for the other.'

'Then is Sir Holroyd wrong about them coming to threaten him?'

'Heavens,' said Patrick, 'this is a guddle!'

Durris pressed his lips together in a kind of wry smile, and tapped his notebook thoughtfully. He managed to keep it well away from any crumbs or splashes of tea, Hippolyta noticed.

'We know that Lady Pinner was there with her maid. We know that Broughton and Sir Holroyd were there. We know, Mrs. Napier, that you were there. Who else?'

'Oh! Mr. Elphick, he was there.' Hippolyta suddenly remembered.

'Yes, later, you said, after Sir Holroyd left.'

'Not according to what Mr. Elphick told Mrs. Broughton. He said to her that he had seen the whole thing!'

'When did she tell you this?' asked Durris, surprised. Hippolyta was a little abashed.

'I – ah – I overheard them at the funeral. Yesterday morning, it was.'

'Of course it was. You're sure?'

'Quite sure. He said he was sure at first that Sir Holroyd had shot Mr. Broughton, for there was no evidence that anything else had happened, but if you were to be believed about the jammed pistol, then he had seen someone else on the hillside, someone he had not expected to see there.'

'Well, who?'

'I don't know. They were interrupted just at that point.'

'So he never told Mrs. Broughton who it was he had seen?' Durris pursed his lips. 'I wonder who interrupted them.'

'Well, Mr. Durris, actually, it was you.' She grinned.

'Was it?' He rolled his eyes. 'That is most unfortunate.' He considered for a moment. 'I wonder who it was that Elphick saw? And I wonder if he would tell me? I wish he had told Mrs. Broughton, for there is a good chance she would have passed the information on.'

'That would be useful,' said Hippolyta brightly.

'But I'm not sure Elphick would speak to me. He has, after all, lied to me so far. I knew from his footprints he had not heard the gunshots when he was at the edge of the wood: he must have been farther in or farther back. And I wonder, too, if he was really heading for the woods to escape Sir Holroyd's revolutionaries: no one else I have spoken to saw them heading north that morning.'

'But they could still have been there, shooting Mr. Broughton. But ... oh, then why would Mr. Elphick tell Mrs. Broughton he had not expected to see them in the woods? No doubt he would have told her and you straightaway and had them arrested!'

'Hm, I think you are right. But was he talking of Lady Pinner? He could not have been expecting her there, could he?'

'Oh.' Hippolyta was slightly disappointed. In her mind's eye, the wood was populated that morning with all kinds of suspicious and unexpected characters. But if it were really so few ... 'But what about Mr. Elphick himself? Surely that is our answer? He was in the woods, he lied about his time of arrival, and he was jealous of Mr. Broughton because he loves Mrs. Broughton! There, the mystery is solved!'

She could see that her reasoning was not being totally rejected by Patrick and Mr. Durris: their faces were thoughtful, working through the idea bit by bit.

'Maybe, indeed ...' Durris was just saying, when the risp at the front door was rattled vigorously, and a voice called out,

'Dr. Napier! Are you within?'

Ishbel could be heard galloping along the passage, and the door was opened with a thump. In a moment, a man from the village, a squarewright by trade, was shown into the parlour. He was too full of news to be abashed at interrupting their breakfast.

'Dr. Napier, sir, and oh! Mr. Durris, too! That is grand, indeed. It's outside, sir, on the green.'

'What is? Has someone had an accident?' Patrick demanded, pulling himself to his one good foot.

'Patrick, be careful!' cried Hippolyta.

'Aye, sir! And I dinna think it looks too good, but if you'll just come quick!'

'I can't come quick,' said Patrick, 'but I'll come as quick as I can.' He arranged his grandfather's sturdy stick and made it to the front door, where Hippolyta and Durris helped him to hop as fast as possible out through the front gate. On the green outside, a small crowd had gathered, blinking in the bright white sunshine. A heap of snow in the midst of them seemed to have been excavated, and there was something that had been under it, dark and damp.

'I ken by his hat,' said one man excitedly, '''at's yon journalist that wrote for the papers, ken? He's biding wi' Agnes Boag.'

'Aye, that's the loon,' agreed Agnes Boag herself, nodding solemnly down at the form in the snow. 'Though fit wye he come to be here I dinna ken, for I gived him breakfast wi' my ain hand not an hour since, and here he is up till his oxters in snaw.'

'Mr. Elphick!' breathed Hippolyta. 'Surely not?'

She and Durris helped Patrick manoeuvre himself on to his knees beside the still form, and he reached in under the distinctive hat to find a pulse. By the look on his face, Hippolyta knew there was none. Durris waved the crowd back a little.

'Who found him?' he asked generally.

'Och, it was me,' said a small man, desolate. There was snow down the front of his coat and breeches. 'Did I no trip over him? An' me hurrying over till the manse to ask the minister would he cry me and Flora Pringle the next three Sundays.'

'Och, have you asked her to marry you at last?' demanded Agnes Boag, wrapping her shawl tight around her in delight.

'Well, I dinna ken if I should, now,' said the small man miserably. 'I dinna think tripping over a corpse on the way to the minister is a good sign, div you?'

'Well, man, it canna get much worse,' said the squarewright. 'And there's me marrit three times. Will I never learn?'

'Oh!' said Patrick in surprise, and they all turned back as if on the one string. 'Look!'

He had turned the corpse a little, making sure that there was no sign of life, and the hat had slipped away. Under it, to everyone's surprise, was not the rosy face of the journalist Jedediah Elphick, but instead the strong features of Mr. Worthy, the lawyer.

Chapter Eighteen

'Mr. Worthy? Oh, no!' cried Hippolyta. 'Poor man!'

'Can you tell how he died?' asked Durris, more softly. He leaned over to see more clearly, his hands on his knees beside Patrick.

'He was always going out for walks and fresh air,' said Hippolyta. 'Could he have slipped and fallen, and not been able to get home?'

'Where does he live?' asked Durris, over his shoulder.

'He lodges next door to Mrs. Kynoch. Over the other side of the green.'

'Then he was not far from home,' said Durris, 'though in the snow last night that would have made little difference.' He poked at the heap of snow that had been pushed from Worthy's body: it looked deep enough. Hippolyta wondered if Worthy could have been about as she had been trying to get home. She knew she had sensed someone nearby.

'Look,' said Patrick, angling the hat slightly. Durris and Hippolyta peered over, and the others who had been standing closest by and heard him also tried to see. Patrick's fingers touched lightly around the hairline behind Worthy's white ear. There was a wound on the side of Mr. Worthy's head, the blood dark and clotted, marking his clean collar and making a trail down it and his pale neck to the ground behind him.

'Well, he fell from the blow and stayed down, by the looks of it,' said Durris. He glanced up at Hippolyta. 'It would have been quick, at least. He may have known nothing about it, and the cold would have helped. Look familiar, Mrs. Napier?'

She winced.

'I suppose so,' she admitted, and shivered. 'I was lucky,

wasn't I?'

'Was you hit an' all?' Agnes Boag asked suddenly, studying Hippolyta's new hair arrangement with interest. 'Michty, is it them loons staying down by the howff? Are we to be safe in our beds?'

'In your beds, likely yes, madam,' said Durris, straightening. 'Out after dark, perhaps not, for the moment. You would be wise to be cautious. Does Mr. – Worthy, did you say? Did he have family in Ballater?'

'No,' said a few people, shaking their heads.

'He bided wi' auld Mrs. Comyn,' said Agnes Boag helpfully. 'But he wasna kin to her. He worked for Mr. Strong, the man o' law, so he paid her a good price for bed and board. No' that I'm no' saying it was fair, an' all.' Landladies presumably had to stick together.

'I'll have to find out when he was last seen,' Durris murmured, half to himself. 'And the Strongs: someone will have to tell them, too.'

'Would you like me to do that?' Hippolyta asked quickly, forgetting her sore head.

'You know them quite well, I believe?'

'Quite well, yes.'

'Then by all means, if Dr. Napier does not need you at home.'

'Patrick? Dearest, can you manage without me if I pop up to see the Strongs?'

Patrick grimaced.

'If you could both help me home first, it would be useful!'

'Of course! And I shall fetch you more cold cloths for your ankle!'

'I'm not sure it needs them, after sitting out here in the snow,' said Patrick, pushing himself upright with the help of Hippolyta's arm and his stick. 'I don't think I'll be going to see many patients this morning, anyway,' he added to her, though his disappointment was clear. 'I'm sorry, my dear: coming out here has made me realise that I really must rest this, at least for today.'

'Of course. Wullie can run and tell your patients.'

'And perhaps if any of them is fit to come and see me here … I could use my study, of course.'

'Well, why not? As long as Ishbel doesn't have to cook for them! Oh!' she remembered. 'I must be home in time to help with the pigeons, or she won't know what to do with them.'

'Pigeons?' Patrick's eyes lit up. 'She's going to cook pigeons for dinner?'

'If she can get them, yes.'

'Well, there's something to look forward to!' They were at the front door. 'Here, then, take your bonnet and cloak and go and break the bad news to the Strongs, and be back in good time! Though it feels heartless to leave that poor man's corpse and talk straightaway of a fine dinner tonight.'

'That's true: I wonder if he had any family elsewhere to mourn him? He seemed a rootless man.'

The Strongs, though clearly upset, were inclined to agree with this assessment.

'He never mentioned anyone,' said Mr. Strong sadly.

'No, he did,' said Miss Ada. 'He talked of a brother in Edinburgh.'

'Then we had better try to find him. Worthy is not a common name, surely.'

'It isn't, but the brother died when he was sixteen,' said Miss Ada. 'I doubt there's no one left to mourn the poor man at all, at all.'

'When did you last see him?' asked Hippolyta, her suspicions confirmed. Poor Mr. Worthy.

'When we finished business yesterday afternoon,' said Mr. Strong. 'It would have been around five: we worked a little later than usual, partly because the funeral delayed us in the morning, and partly because Mrs. Broughton had asked us to take a look at Mr. Broughton's will, and we did not want to detain her over the business.'

'He didn't join you for dinner?' Hippolyta wondered what was in the will, but knew better than to ask a lawyer.

'No! He preferred his landlady's cooking, would you believe?' said Miss Ada. 'Here for his tea, but away for his dinner. And us dying for a bit of company!'

'Ada!' snapped her sister.

'Aye, well. Maybe not dying, exactly.'

'And Mrs. Comyn has the reputation of cooking well,' said Miss Strong, as if defending Mr. Worthy's choice. 'Look how many she has asking to stay with her in the summer, and it's all for the cooking.'

'Aye, there's not much else to be had in that wee house,' said Miss Ada. 'Has anybody tellt her her lodger's dead on the green?'

'Ada!'

'Mr. Durris was seeing the body back to his lodging, and he'll talk with Mrs. Comyn,' Hippolyta explained.

'Aye, well, no doubt Mrs. Comyn'll take some consolation from seeing yon sheriff's man in her ain house,' said Miss Ada with lubricious satisfaction. 'No doubt he appreciates a good dinner an' all.' Her sister scowled at her. Hippolyta decided to pursue Mr. Worthy instead.

'So he went back to his lodgings around five, and you didn't see him after that?'

'No, we closed up the doors and shutters and settled in for the night,' said Miss Strong. 'No sense in going out in that weather after dark. Not at our age.'

'We hadn't finished our work on the will,' Mr. Strong added, 'so there was no need to hurry down to the inn with it. We had planned to finish it this morning. I was expecting him at any minute!' He sighed. 'Aye, well, just when I was growing used to having a fellow to work with!'

'But why do you think he would have been attacked?' asked Miss Ada, just a hint of glee in her eyes, though Hippolyta was fairly sure she would miss Mr. Worthy, too. If nothing else, despite her age she had still not entirely given up hope of marriage, and Mr. Worthy might have been a persuadable candidate. 'Is it those fellows that have been seen around the village? The ones in the dark clothes?'

'Why, had they said anything to him? Or he to them?'

'Not that I know of.' Miss Ada, uncertain for once, looked to her brother and sister for any information.

'I know Mr. Durris is hoping to talk to them,' said Hippolyta, 'but that's not to say it was them, of course.'

'What's wrong with your neck, Mrs. Napier?' asked Miss Ada suddenly. It was a mark of how shocked they had been by her news that Miss Ada's sharp eyes had not spotted Hippolyta's bandages till now. Hippolyta squirmed a little, embarrassed.

'I fell in the snow last night on my way home. And Patrick has sprained his ankle,' she added quickly.

'It must have been quite a fall!' said Miss Strong. 'You poor things!'

'And I had better go back to him now,' said Hippolyta. 'He cannot go out to patients today, but he hopes that any that can will come to the house instead.' She rose, and the Misses Strong bounced out of their seats at the same time.

'We should go and see Mrs. Comyn, and discuss Mr. Worthy's funeral,' said Miss Strong. 'Will you be able to contact your Episcopal minister at all?'

'Oh, I shall try, of course,' said Hippolyta. 'He will come if he can, I am sure.' Though no doubt he would lament the loss of another member of his little congregation here, when he talked so much of expanding the church on Deeside.

She had not removed her bonnet, but she adjusted it carefully so that the edge did not dig into her bruise, and left the house with both Misses Strong. The sun was still shining, and the snow was taking on a glossy look, dazzling and a little damp on the surface. All three immediately angled their bonnets to block the worst of the glare, and as they turned towards the kirk Hippolyta saw Mr. Durris emerging from the house beside Mrs. Kynoch's. The Strong sisters headed for him at once, like a couple of large hens waddling well-wrapped through the snow. Hippolyta thought she would not follow just now, but indeed go home to Patrick and to help Ishbel with the pigeons. She was about to pursue this respectable goal, when a shout from behind her made her turn round, a little more nervously than usual. To her surprise, she saw Sir Holroyd Pinner loping down the street on the snow-cleared path, slithering a little and birling other pedestrians out of his way.

'Mr. Durris!' he shouted. At the sound the Strong sisters parted abruptly, allowing Durris to be seen, framed by them on either side. They watched with their mouths open as Sir Holroyd ran towards them, and wild horses would have had a struggle stopping Hippolyta from following, too. She was with them just after Sir Holroyd reached them, and as he stopped to catch his breath she heard all he had to say.

'Mr. Durris,' he began, outrage in his handsome face, his looming teeth large. 'Last night my wife's maid was attacked in the street! What have you to say about that? You claimed this was a safe and peaceful place: if so, then the men I pointed out to you must be questioned! They must be guilty of this abomination!'

'Was it Clara?' Hippolyta asked irresistibly. 'Sir Holroyd, this is partly my fault.'

'Your fault?' He spun on her, ready to be furious in any direction.

'Yes – you see, I sent Clara home last night after she escorted me as far as the village. I made sure she had the lantern. I did ask her if she wanted to come the rest of the way and spend the night with us,' she added, in her own defence, 'but she insisted she had to go back. But I should never have let her come out with me in the first place. It was very kind of Lady Pinner to insist, but I should not have allowed it.'

Sir Holroyd stared at her.

'Is that why she was out? It wasn't clear.'

'Is she all right? Was she badly hurt?'

'She was hit on the head,' said Sir Holroyd, clearly calming a little. 'She is somewhat dazed and confused, but otherwise … well, it could have been much worse.'

'Did she see her attacker?' asked Durris, turning Sir Holroyd's attention away from Hippolyta.

'She says not. It was snowing heavily.'

'And where was she?'

'Near the edge of the village. She was stunned, but did not fall: she says she thinks she wandered a little with her lantern, not quite sure where she was, then found some distinguishing feature and made her way home. She has a very sore head.'

'And any other injuries?'

'No, but that's hardly the point. She was attacked!'

'If she was near the edge of the village still she could only just have left me,' said Hippolyta quickly to Durris. 'Do you think whoever it was attacked her then came on into the village and struck me?'

'Mrs. Napier!' Sir Holroyd spun back to her. 'Were you attacked too? Mr. Durris, this is a disgraceful state of affairs! Is no woman safe?'

'Not just women,' put in Miss Ada, eyeing Hippolyta with interest. 'My brother's apprentice Mr. Worthy has been attacked, too, Sir Holroyd. What do you think of that, then?'

'Another one! Mr. Durris, I insist that you discover the hiding place of these men, these strangers to the village, and question them immediately. And I insist on being present when you do. This affair must be ended at once, at once, do you hear? A man murdered and three people attacked! I shall remove from the village with my wife and household the minute it is safe to travel! I should have been better off on my own estates, threats or no threats!'

'Sir Holroyd,' said Durris quietly, and something about the expression on his face caused Sir Holroyd to catch his breath, and blink hard. 'Sir Holroyd, I have discovered where the men are staying, though I have not yet caught them there. I was intending to go there now to question them. That is not proof that they carried out any one or all of these attacks. I am sorry to hear that your maid Clara has been a victim of some assault, and I shall want to question her, too, to find out what she remembers of the event, but I must see if I can question the men first.' Sir Holroyd drew breath again, but Durris stopped him with one half-raised hand. 'You may if you wish accompany me to see these men, but I beg you will remain silent, and certainly refrain from any outburst or exclamation, for the duration of my interview. If you cannot remain silent I shall ask you to leave. If you will not, believe me when I say that I shall have you removed from the house.'

Sir Holroyd shut his mouth with a clack. He nodded briefly, not quite submitting to an agreement, but certainly acknowledging Durris' instructions. Hippolyta felt like cheering.

'Right,' said Durris. 'If you will come with me, I shall show you where the men have been staying.'

The two men moved away. The Misses Strong and Hippolyta stared after them, at least two of them itching to follow and see what happened next. Hippolyta glanced down at Miss Ada.

'Do you suppose,' she said, 'if we also remained silent and refrained from any outburst or exclamation, that we might just overhear what they say?'

Miss Strong's eyes widened in shock, but Miss Ada grinned.

'I can refrain if you can, Mrs. Napier,' she chuckled. 'Come on!'

'I'm not going anywhere near it!' said Miss Strong firmly.

'That's finey,' said Miss Ada. 'Away home and toast your

chilblains.' She and Hippolyta set off, not too fast, after the men. Miss Strong tottered a few steps after them.

'Ada, you are a disgrace!' she hissed.

'Aye, well, I suppose,' said Miss Ada, unconcerned. She did not look round, but Hippolyta could hear Miss Strong still faintly pursuing them.

'Ada! Come back here at once!'

'See? She canna refrain from outburst or exclamations. We're as well off without her,' Miss Ada said cheerily to Hippolyta. Ahead the men disappeared round a corner, and with a rush of skirts Miss Strong caught up with them, breathless with excitement.

'If it's the house I think it is,' she said, 'there's a laney down the side of it. If we stood there quietlike we'd not be seen and I think we'd hear most of what was happening. The doors and windows about there are no very thick.'

'Aye, she's right,' said Miss Ada, winking at Hippolyta.

'It seems sound advice,' said Hippolyta, and they reached the corner the men had taken. She peeped round, and ducked back quickly.

'It's the fourth house along: the one beside the howff. They're just standing outside now: I think they're waiting for the door to be answered.'

'Which side of it is this laney you know, then?' Miss Ada asked her sister.

'The far side,' Miss Strong sighed.

'We'll just have to walk past once they've gone inside,' said Hippolyta, 'and try not to draw attention to ourselves. It would take too long to go round the other way.'

'Try not to draw attention to ourselves?' asked Miss Ada cynically, 'when we look as if a gowf club and a couple of balls got tied up in a bolt of dress fabric?'

Hippolyta frowned, then laughed, admitting to herself that she was indeed built rather like a golf club. 'Well, maybe. But the windows are small, and if we move fast no one will notice us.' She looked carefully around the corner again. 'They're just going in now. Count to ten, and then we'll go.'

They solemnly counted to ten, then gathered themselves together and slipped down the little street – slipped being an appropriate word, as the road had not been cleared here and they missed their footing a couple of times. They steadfastly did not look at the house as they passed it: Hippolyta knew it as one of several with low windows and a small door, and just now a roof laden with snow. Regardless of the cold outside, one window was slightly open, to her delight: the room must have been smokey. The lane, as promised by Miss Strong, ran down the side of the house to the greens at the back, and was fortunately deserted. The three women swung into it, turned and arranged themselves as close as they could to the mouth of the lane, ears straining towards the open window. They had to concentrate hard to hear anything.

'... want to speak to the three of you.'

'They're in!' exclaimed Miss Strong. 'He's found them!'

'Sshh!' hissed Miss Ada and Hippolyta.

'... names, please?'

There seemed to be a pause, and Hippolyta wondered if they were considering some fakery. Then another voice came, with a Glasgow accent.

'William McTavish,' he said. His tone implied that he thought that was good enough for anyone.

'Jamesie Halloran, sir,' came the next, more conciliatory. 'We haven't made no trouble, no trouble at all, sir.'

'And you?'

'Billy Eames.'

'You're not a Scot, then, either?' Durris remarked.

'I'm from down Warwick direction.'

'I see. It's unusual to see visitors in Ballater at this time of the year. Do you mind telling me what you're doing here?'

'We're looking for work,' said McTavish quickly.

'And what is your trade?'

'We was in a weaving manufactory in Glasgow, sir,' said Halloran. 'We're skilled men, but the work ran out, see.'

'Bad luck,' said Durris, unemotionally. Hippolyta wished she could see the men he was questioning. It was so hard to tell much about them from their voices alone, when she had only previously glimpsed them and not seen them distinctly. She wondered if the house had windows at the back: it was surely only one room deep, anyway. 'And where did you think you would find a weaving manufactory up in this direction?'

'Is this no the road to Aberdeen?' asked McTavish, innocently.

'If you've been told that, you've been misdirected, I'm afraid,' said Durris. 'You need to head east. I'll set you on the right road as soon as you like.'

'Aye, well, in this weather,' said McTavish, 'we thought we might bide here a while, anyway.'

'The air's very healthy,' added the man Eames. There was a silence, as if even his friends were taken aback that he had spoken.

'Have you any acquaintance in this direction? There was some talk that you had kin up Braemar direction.'

Their denials sounded entirely natural. Hippolyta was not surprised: Braemar was even smaller than Ballater, and the chances had been slim.

'Well, you need to take care hereabouts,' said Durris. 'Three people were attacked out on the main street last night. Were you out and about yourselves?'

'Last night in that snow? Never at all.' McTavish was firm. 'I'll tell you what we did last night: we had a hen to put over the fire, and we had a bottle of whisky and that pot of tea you see there in front of you, and we sat and Jamesie here sang songs and we told stories, and a grand night of it we had, and never a bit of snow touched any one of us all night, thanks be to Heaven.'

'Well, you'll understand that as you are strangers in the village, some suspicion is likely to fall on you,' said Durris reasonably. 'Take care, as I said, when you are out and about. There are two men dead.'

'Oh, aye, we heard tell of one of them! Some high heidyin frae London, eh?' said McTavish.

'Aye, true enough, for one of them,' said Durris mildly. 'And I should ask you, for there's more to that one than meets the eye and we're looking for anyone who can help – where were you last Saturday morning? Around dawn?'

'Last Saturday? Was that the day, boys, we took a look up the road to … what was it cried … Crathie?'

'There was no work to be had in the place, whatever it was,' Jamesie Halloran confirmed with a sigh. 'And we must have asked every living man in the townland.'

'Aye, and one or two dead ones, by the look of them,'

grumbled Eames, and the other two laughed. Then McTavish cleared his throat and spat.

'Not that we want to be disrespectful to the gentleman that died, ken. And you said there was another dead?'

'That's right. And two women injured,' Durris added.

'Women?' This time even McTavish seemed shocked. 'There've been women attacked and all?'

'Yes. A maid and the wife of the local physician.' Hippolyta felt a little flutter of excitement as she heard herself identified.

'That's no good,' said Halloran. 'Who would attack a woman? Unless you'd be mad altogether,' he added thoughtfully.

'Well, somebody did!'

The women listening jumped. He had been so obediently quiet up to now that they had forgotten that Sir Holroyd was in the cottage, too. Clearly his patience had reached its limits. Hippolyta ran to the back of the cottage – not more than a few paces away – to see if she could find a view of the inside. She was in luck: there was a low window, uncurtained and open, facing back on to the green. She crouched down quickly, and peeped round the side of it. The smell of stale smoke and fresh smoke mingling made her eyes sting.

Inside she could see Durris standing with his back to the fire, holding his notebook and pencil, and turned towards Sir Holroyd. He was against one of the front windows. The three men sat on a bench in defiance of their guests, or perhaps at Durris' instruction, facing the two visitors. Sir Holroyd was still shouting, though Durris was trying to interrupt.

'What kind of savagery is this? A respectable maid cannot walk along a village street of an evening without being attacked? Two others attacked the same night, and in who knows what state of shock or injury? And a member of parliament shot and killed within shouting distance of the main road, almost in sight of a gentleman's house! If it was not the three of you with some hand in this – and do not think, Eames, that I do not have some notion of you and your family and your activities in Birmingham – then who was it? This was a quiet, decent place before you three arrived!'

'Sir Holroyd,' snapped Durris, 'kindly leave this building.'

'I will not!' said Sir Holroyd, and even in the awkward light Hippolyta could see that his face was quite pink with anger. 'I will not accept orders from a sheriff's officer!'

'Then I shall have to remove you, as I promised.'

Durris calmly replaced his notebook and pencil in his pockets, while Sir Holroyd breathed fast, clearly sure Durris would not dare. There was a quick movement which Hippolyta could not quite see, the door opened and shut, and somehow Sir Holroyd was no longer in the room. Hippolyta wished she could see him from here, too. The three men on the bench sat with jaws swinging.

'Gentlemen,' said Durris, 'I trust I shall find you here again if I think you can be of further assistance to me. For now, good day: and good luck in your search for employment.'

He bowed, and left the cottage.

Chapter Nineteen

Hippolyta slipped back into the lane again, and saw that the Misses Strong were watching intently round the corner on to the street, not moving. She came up quietly behind them. Miss Strong, who must have heard her nevertheless, put out a gloved hand to stop her. There was a long moment's wait, as they all held their breath. Then the two older women relaxed, and turned back to Hippolyta.

'They're away round the corner going back to the kirk,' said Miss Ada. 'My, did you see Mr. Durris throw Sir Holroyd out the door?'

'I saw something,' said Hippolyta honestly. 'I'm not quite sure what. One minute he was in the room, the next he wasn't.'

'Aye, yon Mr. Durris, eh?' said Miss Ada with delight. 'Sir Holroyd came out that door like a rabbit. You'd swear if he had a tail it would have been so far between his legs he'd have tripped on it.'

'Well, Mr. Durris did warn him,' said Hippolyta. 'He told him to keep quiet.'

'I'm not sure Mr. Durris learned anything in there anyway,' said Miss Strong, and she turned to lead the way back to the main street in the opposite direction from that in which Durris and Sir Holroyd had gone, the other two sides of the square.

'It's interesting that Sir Holroyd knew one of the men, though,' said Hippolyta. She had a visual memory of their faces now, with the quickness of the artist: one had been small and thin and hunched with red hair, and she had him down as Jamesie Halloran. One had been taller, with a pugnacious jaw, a misshapen nose, and hair like tow standing straight up on his head. She thought he might be Billy Eames, for he in particular had had his eye on Sir Holroyd. That meant that the last one was William McTavish, and he was dark haired with a sharp chin and lips drawn in tight over teeth that leaned back into his mouth, and a calculating look in his eye. All of them had a grey, indoor look that spoke truly of a working life in manufactories, and Halloran had coughed several times – perhaps the fluff that came from the looms was in his lungs. Life in manufactories was hard, she had heard: it might be better paid than farm work, but accidents and illness were just as rife.

'Do you think they're here after him?' asked Miss Ada. Hippolyta had forgotten that they did not know of Sir Holroyd's fears. 'He's no made himself awful popular with his stand against Reform, and him with a constituency up near Birmingham.'

'And his estates in the Midlands, too,' added Hippolyta. 'Yes, I think he feels anxious about it all.'

'Aye, so he should! See, when I'm in Parliament,' Miss Ada went on with a mischievous grin.

'Yes, when you're in Parliament there won't be one there who can understand you,' said her sister primly, 'for you'll talk Scots the whole time like a servant.'

'I will not,' said Miss Ada, drawing herself up to her full four feet. 'I shall speak entirely properly, like an English lady. Almost as grandly as Mrs. Napier here, for as we all know very well, Edinburgh is far grander than anything England can offer.'

They all laughed, even Miss Strong. In another moment they had re-emerged on the busy main street. Hippolyta found herself looking about to see if Marcus was amongst the passersby, but of course he was not – nor could she see Mr. Durris or Sir Holroyd. Perhaps Mr. Durris was telling Sir Holroyd off for his misbehaviour, or perhaps – here she felt rather more concerned – Sir Holroyd was voicing his opinions of upstart sheriff's men that put respectable members of Parliament out through doorways unexpectedly.

Miss Ada nodded along the row of houses, pointing out silently that Mrs. Comyn's shutters were closed: presumably she and Martha would be laying out Mr. Worthy's poor body. The jumble of snow where he had been found was already being trampled by small boys in some dramatic game, and Hippolyta saw Ishbel with a basket amongst the busy villagers on the green.

'Oh, pigeons!' she exclaimed.

'That's an unusual oath,' murmured Miss Ada, 'but quite effective. "Oh, pigeons!"' she repeated with relish. 'Even my sister could barely object to that.'

'Often, Ada, it is not the words you choose but the way you use them that causes me distress,' said Miss Strong warmly.

'You must excuse me,' said Hippolyta, 'I have pigeons to attend to.'

'Heavens,' said Miss Ada, grinning, 'what creatures will she adopt next?'

But Hippolyta was already hurrying after Ishbel, trying to remember the name of the recipe she had chosen.

In the kitchen, Wullie had happily taken the pigeons and was plucking them on the back doorstep. Two of the cats chased the downy feathers into the snow, perhaps hoping for some more interesting meat. Ishbel was unpacking sweetbreads at the table, while Hippolyta looked through the pantry for dried mushrooms. There was not much mushroom picking to be done in December with two feet of snow.

'Did you make the forced meat?' she asked Ishbel.

'Oh, aye, it's in the meat safe,' said Ishbel. Hippolyta found it and drew out a plate of pink, deliciously spiced minced meat, pleasantly cool. 'How long do you think the thing will take to cook?'

'There's not so much to the preparation, once the pigeons are ready,' said Hippolyta, reading through the recipe again. 'As to the baking time ... how hot is your oven?'

'It'll be hotter soon.'

Hippolyta eyed her, frowning, but Ishbel had not meant any disrespect.

'Well,' said Hippolyta, 'I think perhaps an hour? And you have gravy to make to pour over it when it's done, and we'll need ... carrots, perhaps, if you have them in store?'

'Aye, in the bucket of sand under the shelf,' said Ishbel.

'And potatoes, of course, either boiled or ...'

'I could put them in a tray over the – the thing,' said Ishbel, 'and give them a roast. If I boil them now they'll be grand.'

'I'll put the mushrooms to soak,' said Hippolyta, fairly sure she remembered her mother's cook doing something similar. Ishbel, whipping the dark peel off a heap of potatoes to reveal their creamy interiors, did seem quite competent: perhaps she would learn more than the maid would. 'Ishbel, do you know anyone in Crathie?'

'In Crathie? Well, of course I do,' said Ishbel reasonably. 'And me coming fae Braemar, mysel'. There's not so many in Crathie that you couldna nearly sit them round your own dinner table, ma'am.'

'Do you come from Braemar?' asked Hippolyta in surprise. 'I thought you were born in Ballater.'

'No, not me! I only come to Ballater when I was a quinie – maybe eight year old.'

'Then ... but you don't speak Gaelic?'

'I do, to my ain tongue,' said Ishbel, unconcerned. 'I learned Scots when I come here.'

Hippolyta, monolingual except for some schoolgirl French, was humbled. Then she remembered why she had asked.

'Would there be any work going in Crathie?'

'At this time of the year? Hardly. You dinna mean for the doctor, do you? You mean for labouring men?'

'Well, yes. Three men from a weaving manufactory in Glasgow.'

'You mean the loons that have been about the village? The fellows in black?'

'That's the ones, yes.'

'Fit wye are they looking for work in Crathie?'

'They said they'd gone there last Saturday looking for work.'

Ishbel gave a short laugh.

'I doubt that,' she said, 'for my cousin up the road tellt me the road was closed just near Ballater for the now, or it was on Saturday. Sure there wasna a body in the kirk on Sunday from that direction at all. The snaw was that deep they could have lost a Highland cow in it, and not found her till the spring.'

'Well, now, there's a thing,' said Hippolyta thoughtfully. 'I wonder does Mr. Durris know that?'

'What do I do with the forced meat, ma'am?' asked Ishbel.

'Oh, divide it in two and press one half down into the bottom of the dish – oh, did you butter the dish?'

'I did, ma'am,' said Ishbel patiently. The pale wintry butter could be seen flecking the earthenware, now Hippolyta looked. Ishbel took a great handful of the pink forced meat and landed it in the dish with a slap, sending a wave of nutmeg scent into the air. She flattened it competently, then looked expectantly at Hippolyta.

'Now the pigeons,' said Hippolyta, checking her recipe book. Wullie scrambled up from the doorstep, bearing the denuded birds in a tin tray. The cats followed with devotion. Hippolyta tweaked two nuggets of forced meat from the lump left on the table, and dropped one in front of each cat as a distraction, until they would find the innards of the pigeons where Wullie had left them. 'Lay them on the forced meat. Then the sweetbreads and the mushrooms – oh, I should drain them, I suppose.' She stepped outside the back door, and tipped them over the soakaway, where the snow had been melted back by the various liquids thrown there. She returned to the table and handed the dish to Ishbel. Wullie watched with deep interest.

'This looks grand!' he breathed.

'Keep your neb out of it, ken,' said Ishbel in fluent Scots. Hippolyta wondered if Mrs. Riach had had a hand in teaching her the local language.

'Then the rest of the forced meat goes on top,' said Hippolyta, wiping her hands on a cloth. 'And then the lid. Do you think an hour will do it?' she asked anxiously.

Ishbel regarded the oven with her head on one side.

'I'd give it the twa hours, mebbe,' she said. 'But there's mutton broth to start, and I made a pie for pudding.'

'Ishbel,' said Hippolyta, 'I'm not sure what I'm here for.'

'Well, ma'am, I've never made a – what? A pupton of pigeons afore. Mrs. Riach would no let me make the main course at all.'

'Then perhaps we can look at some other dishes, and you can teach me how to make them, too!'

'Aye, ma'am, I'd be very pleased with that!'

'And if there's any of yon thing left over,' added Wullie, 'I'd be affa pleased an' all.'

'Well, there's certainly plenty,' said Hippolyta. 'I hope you'll both be able to sample some of it!'

'Fit's going on here, then?'

The pleasant mood was gone. An ominous voice came from

the kitchen door. Hippolyta turned: Mrs. Riach, resplendent in a plaid shawl of monumental proportions, stood in the doorway, her feet bare and unflinching on the stone floor.

'I have been instructing Ishbel in the making of a pupton of pigeons, Mrs. Riach,' said Hippolyta, trying to take any responsibility from Ishbel.

'That would be my job, ma'am,' said Mrs. Riach dangerously.

'You have been ill in your bed for half a week, Mrs. Riach. Do you expect the household to starve?' Even as she said it, Hippolyta knew she had crossed a line.

'The household's feeding is what I do. No Ishbel,' said Mrs. Riach. Hippolyta had had no idea that the word 'Ishbel' could sound so much like a curse.

'You don't when you're ill. And you have not helped yourself to recover very quickly, have you, Mrs. Riach?' She could not help it: the dangerous ground seemed to be beckoning her on like witch lights on a marsh. 'I hear you have been drinking again, and causing trouble for Ishbel and Wullie, and not eating properly.'

'You've been clyping on me!' Mrs. Riach turned on Ishbel – not, Hippolyta noted, on Wullie, her favourite.

'I couldna hide such things fae Mrs. Napier!' said Ishbel. 'The shouting and the getting on you've been doing, half the village would ken fit you were doing!'

'Ishbel did quite right,' said Hippolyta firmly. 'She was concerned at the effect on the whole household.'

Mrs. Riach turned on her an expression of outraged disappointment so intense that Hippolyta felt as if she had been slapped.

'I am *black* affronted!' said Mrs. Riach, her voice dripping with low menace. 'Never did I think I should see such a thing in my ain kitchen. Never did I think any mistress of mine would take the side of the *kitchen maid* agin me.'

'But Mrs. Riach,' said Hippolyta, trying to steady her own breath, 'this is not your own kitchen, is it?'

Mrs. Riach's mouth fell open.

'Not my ain kitchen?' she said incredulously. 'Not my ain kitchen?' She cast a glance around the room, as though reassessing it rapidly. 'Right, then. That's it. I've stood enough in this house. Pigs and cats and hens in the study, and a pair of folk out all hours and guests with manners you'd never believe ... That's it, I'm aff.'

She swung the tails of her plaid like an ermine robe, and stalked out at the height of her dignity. Hippolyta, her heart beating twenty to the dozen, watched her go, torn between delight and the urge to run after her and beg her to stay.

'Oh, my,' Ishbel breathed.

'I think you and I will be learning a few more main courses, Ishbel,' said Hippolyta unsteadily. 'Um, I think I'd better go and have a word with Dr. Napier.'

There was a good deal of crashing and banging from the servants' quarters as Mrs. Riach packed to leave, her back mysteriously up to the task. Hippolyta found Patrick in the study and explained what had happened. Patrick was as ambivalent at the situation as Hippolyta herself.

'Where will she go?' Hippolyta asked.

'She has a nephew along at Tullich,' said Patrick. 'I don't know of any other kin nearby.'

'She's demanded the use of the pony and trap,' said Hippolyta. They met each other's eyes. The pony was notorious for nipping. Again, Hippolyta's feelings on the matter of the loan were mixed.

'Wullie had better go with her, then, and bring it back,' said Patrick.

'And I'd better be the one to fetch both from the inn. You know the stablelads there won't touch him if they can help it.'

'Of course: they're not stupid. How is Ishbel?'

'A little shocked, I think. But the dinner is in hand.'

'Will she do well, do you think?'

'I think she might,' said Hippolyta with a smile. 'She's more the cook than the lady's maid, anyway.'

'Then perhaps it is all for the best. Oh.' He stopped as the door risp rattled. 'That may be Ben Whitehouse for his lump. Would you mind showing him in, my dear?'

Hippolyta went and ushered in a young farmhand, and then fetched her cloak and bonnet once again. She had been so distracted by pigeons and cooks that the squeak of pain in the side of her head when she knocked it with her bonnet took her aback. Poor Clara, she thought: she should have been more firm, and insisted that the maid come back here. She sighed at her own laziness, gathered up Wullie, his dog and his boots, and set off to fetch the pony and trap.

They had acquired the pony, and the trap, when its owner had died and no one else would take on the bad-tempered animal. Hippolyta was the only one it would tolerate without nipping, so that, since they had no stable of their own and kept the beast at the inn, they often had to pay extra to compensate for offended guests and irritated stable boys. It was certainly easier on occasions such as this for Hippolyta to hold the pony's head while a stable boy harnessed it, and Wullie watched with interest. The dog was less concerned, washing the snow off its wet paws fastidiously.

'Do you think it will manage the road to Tullich?' Hippolyta asked the stable boy, 'with a load of boxes and a – a person?'

'Aye, ma'am. It hasna snowed this morn, and the road is part-cleared for the coaches, onywyes.'

'What about the other way? Up towards Crathie and Braemar?'

'Och, that's a different case altogether, ma'am. I wouldna take anything less than a garron up yon road even now, and then not wi' a trap at all.'

Yes, a sturdy Highland pony might make all the difference, but they tended to be used as pack animals, not as carriage horses. But the three weavers had said they had gone to Crathie: if they were lying, as they clearly were, what had they done instead? She would have to tell Durris. She wondered if he had spoken to Clara yet, and if so where he might have gone then. She glanced up at the inn beside her. He might, she thought, be visiting Mrs. Broughton. Just to make sure that the widow was quite well. And there was nothing to stop Hippolyta popping in for the same purpose, was there?

When the trap was ready, she handed the pony's reins to Wullie, who took them with caution. He had a large pair of Patrick's old gloves on his hands, and his clothes were thick: unless he allowed his ear too near the pony's quick teeth he should be all right. With strict instructions to him not to allow Mrs. Riach to detain him beyond dusk, and a reminder of the dinner waiting for him if he hurried back, Hippolyta sent him on his way. The dog chose to ride in the trap for the first part of the journey, keeping its paws dry.

There would certainly be time before dinner for her to make a call on Mrs. Broughton, Hippolyta reckoned, glancing up at the inn's clock. She tipped the stable boy and made her way over to the main building. There was a window open at the back, and she reckoned that the room beyond must be the parlour where she and Marcus – where was Marcus? – had stood on the night of the assembly, listening to the quarrel and the challenge out here in the yard. She looked about her. The doorway of the inn, the one that travellers would enter by when they alighted from the coach, was only a few yards away. The stables were close by. There were a couple of other small windows facing this direction. A goodly number of other people might well have been listening to that challenge, and heard when and where it was to be, and they could have passed the news on to endless other people even by the next morning. Lady Pinner had known, and she surely could not have been there in the dark, so someone who could tell her must have been. Thoughtfully, she went to stand just under the window, just below where she herself had been that night. Was there anything she had seen that might help, something she might have forgotten? Something, even, for which she had been attacked last night? She touched her head below her bonnet, and winced. Even through the dressing it was still very tender. There was no one about: the stable lad had disappeared, perhaps for his dinner. She leaned back against the wall, and closed her eyes, picturing the dark yard, the two angry men. Where had she sensed movement? What had she seen?

'Mr. Elphick, thank you for coming.'

She jumped, and opened her eyes. She knew that voice.

'Well, your note said you had something important to tell me. What's that, then? I'm a busy man, you know.' Mr. Elphick sounded nervous. She could picture his uneasy eyes widening and rolling.

'I thought you were here for a rest, Mr. Elphick?' said Durris. 'Please, take a seat. I did not think it would be a hardship for you to come to the inn, when you might also take advantage of your visit to call on your old friend, Mrs. Broughton.'

'Well ...' Elphick sounded dubious. There was the least scrape of a chair leg on the floor as he must have sat down. 'Of course we have a long acquaintance, Mrs. Broughton and me. Naturally she turns to those she knows well at a distressing time.'

'Naturally. And just as naturally you might confide in her, too.'

'Might I?' Elphick sounded confused.

'You might, for example, tell her if you had any words of comfort to offer about the circumstances of her husband's death.'

'Might I?' said Elphick again, this time wary.

'If you had such information. Say, for example, if you had been at the site of the duel on Saturday morning –'

'Well, I was, wasn't I? You saw me there yourself.'

'But you were actually there when the duel happened, weren't you? You did not just chance to be on the edge of the woods when you heard gunshots.'

'What makes you think that?'

'That's what you told Mrs. Broughton, isn't it? You said you saw the whole thing.'

'Oh, I see!' said Elphick, and there was a nastier hint to his voice than Hippolyta had previously heard there. 'Your pretty little friend Mrs. Napier – she was there, wasn't she? Listening in?'

Hippolyta's jaw dropped at his rudeness. Then she had the grace to blush. After all, what was she doing now? And it was the second time today. But she was just trying to be helpful, wasn't she?

'If she heard you, she was not the only one, Mr. Elphick. You should perhaps be more discreet in your private conversations.'

Nicely put, Mr. Durris, thought Hippolyta. And certainly discreet. But who else could have heard him? Then she remembered: he had of course been talking to Mrs. Broughton. But had Mrs. Broughton also told Mr. Durris? Had they had some intimate conversation on the matter? She found herself hoping they had not: and she had been the first to tell him, anyway, she was sure of that.

'Well, what if I was on the scene?' Mr. Elphick was asking. Hippolyta remembered that he had been familiar with theatres and the stage – and so, of course, had Mrs. Broughton. How good an actress had she been?

'I'd be very interested to know who else you saw there, Mr. Elphick,' said Durris.

There was a small movement in the room before Mr. Elphick spoke, levelly. Hippolyta wondered if he had folded his arms.

'I saw Sir Holroyd Pinner, and George Broughton, and your Mrs. Napier, no doubt nosing in on the matter.'

'Yet you saw someone else, too: someone else you had not expected, Mr. Elphick, did you not?'

'And what if I did?' He was defiant, but his voice was still a little uncertain.

'You know very well, Mr. Elphick, that George Broughton was shot dead and not, it appears, by Sir Holroyd Pinner. Someone else up there that morning had a pistol and shot him. Was it the person you saw? The unexpected person? Or perhaps, Mr. Elphick, it was you?'

'Me?' Hippolyta could not work out from the tone of one word how Mr. Elphick had reacted to that. 'Why would I kill George Broughton?'

'We have already mentioned your long friendship with Mrs. Broughton,' said Durris.

'What?' Elphick gave a laugh that did not sound fully genuine. 'You're saying I killed off George Broughton to get his widow? That's a joke. It was me turned her down years ago!'

'You turned her down?'

'Well, obviously it's not something I would normally say,' said Elphick quickly. 'Not very gentlemanly, of course. But if you're going to accuse me of – of that, of murder! – then I'll have to say it. I liked her, yes, of course, and she was a fine actress in her day, but when it came down to it she was fonder of me than I was of her, Mr. Durris. And she seemed very happy with George Broughton. She did well there, better than she would have done with me. I told her that at the time, see.'

The chair shifted again. Elphick seemed pleased with himself. Hippolyta was not impressed.

'Nevertheless,' said Durris, and Hippolyta was interested that he did not allow himself to become distracted, 'you saw someone up on the hill, and if you say you did not kill Mr. Broughton then someone else did. And I have very good reason to believe that the person in question saw you, too.'

'What?' The chair jumped this time.

'Last night, Mr. Worthy – a lawyer in the village, whom you

met at George Broughton's funeral – was killed in the middle of the village under cover of night and snow.'

'And what is that to do with me? I was in my lodging from dusk to dawn.'

'Perhaps you were, Mr. Elphick. But Mr. Worthy was wearing your green hat.'

Chapter Twenty

Mr. Elphick must have been struck silent at last. In the pause, Hippolyta heard footsteps, soft on the floorboards. Too late, she realised that Durris had stepped over to the window, perhaps to close it. She sank quickly to the ground, but she had a horrible feeling, as her wretched skirts spread out around her, that she was perfectly visible and only more ridiculous than before. In fact, at that point one of the stable lads emerged from some kitchen end of the inn and ran up to her.

'Mrs. Napier! Fit's wrang wi' ye?'

'Oh, nothing! Er, that is, I just felt a little faint, and leaned against this wall,' she said loudly and clearly, hoping that if Mr. Durris had seen her he would think her entirely innocent. However, it was unlikely now that she would hear much more: Mr. Durris would no doubt keep his voice down. She sighed, and exchanged a few words with the stable lad about the pony, then decided she might as well go home and dress for dinner. If nothing else, her feet were freezing.

She meandered back up the main street, going over what she had heard in her mind. Mr. Elphick must have been shocked when Durris told him of Mr. Worthy's death. But if someone had been killed because they were mistaken for Mr. Elphick, then it seemed to say that Mr. Elphick was not the murderer – and she had thought that fitted all the facts! It was extremely provoking. And of course, Mr. Worthy could not have been the killer, either. So who did that leave? The weavers in the cottage, McTavish, Halloran and Eames? But even if they had killed Mr. Broughton, for whatever reason or through whatever error, why on earth would they then have gone on to attack Mr. Worthy and Clara? And why attack her? Had she inadvertently seen one of them when she was observing the duel? And she had not been there to nose around, whatever Mr. Elphick might say, she thought crossly to herself. She had been concerned, that was all. Concerned that a couple of silly men might be about to make dangerous fools of themselves – which indeed they did. So there, she was justified in every way.

So intent was she on self-exoneration that she did not realise at first that she was being followed. When she did, she jumped, and spun around, feet dancing on the path slippery with compacted snow.

'Mrs. Napier,' said Mr. Durris, 'perhaps I could have a word?'

He was not smiling, but then he rarely did. She found she was a little breathless.

'You gave me a shock, Mr. Durris. I had no idea you were there.'

'Perhaps we can walk towards your house.' He did not offer his arm, but she did not mind.

'Of course, Mr. Durris. What was it you wanted to talk about?'

'Well, Mrs. Napier,' he said, 'it seems to me that when I want to speak to someone privately and question them, there is always an open window at which, by some mischance, you find yourself waiting in the snow, taken with an unaccustomed dizzy turn, or perhaps visiting the sick in some neighbouring cottage – who knows?'

'But Mr. Durris, I really did feel dizzy in the stable yard! When I realised you were in the room above me I was terribly surprised!' Which was almost the truth, she told herself. She had felt quite dizzy when she realised she was found out. And after all, she had not gone over to the window expecting to hear Mr. Durris' conversation, with Mr. Elphick or with anyone else.

'Hm,' he said. 'How long did this dizzy fit last, then, Mrs. Napier? I am ashamed that I did not catch up with you earlier to see that you were going safely home. Perhaps it is a result of your head injury.'

'Oh, yes! Perhaps it is!' cried Hippolyta, glad to find the bruise on her head might be useful for something. 'For my head is still quite sore.'

'I am sorry to hear it,' he said drily. 'I understand that walks in the fresh air are considered a very good tonic for ladies whose health is not the best. Perhaps you and the Misses Strong felt the need for a walk in the fresh air earlier today?'

'Perhaps we did.'

'But waiting outside a smokey window is not likely to help a sore head, is it?'

Hippolyta sighed, and turned on him.

'Look, Mr. Durris ... all right, I admit it. The Misses Strong and I were very anxious to hear what those men had to say for themselves. After all, the safety of the village depended upon it. But I really did not set out to eavesdrop on you and Mr. Elphick, I promise! I was in the stable yard seeing to the pony which has gone to Tullich with Mrs. Riach for she has left us and gone to live with her nephew, though whether he wants her or not is another thing, and I had the idea that I might go in and visit Mrs. Broughton before dinner to see if she was all right. Then I saw that window open and I was trying to remember – for that was the parlour Marcus and I were standing in – I was trying to remember if I had seen anyone specific that night who might have heard the arrangements for the duel. I went and stood under the window to get the right angle, and then I heard your voices. I truly did not know before then that you were there.'

Durris' face throughout this rambling explanation was stony, but now she thought she caught the least smile playing around the corner of his mouth. He removed his glasses, and wiped them carefully.

'The next time,' he said at last, 'I think I shall just invite you inside. You might as well be there, and it is disconcerting for me to be wondering where you might be hiding, listening in to the conversations.'

'Oh, Heavens, Mr. Durris, I am only trying to help!' She swung away from him, cross, then turned back. 'Will you come and join us for dinner? The kitchen maid – I suppose she might be the cook now – and I have concocted an experiment, and there will be plenty of it if it is good. Well, even if it isn't,' she added honestly. 'And there will be mutton broth. As long as we leave a little of the main course for Ishbel and Wullie, there is plenty.'

Durris drew breath apparently to object, but then shrugged.

'Oh, very well. That is to say, thank you, Mrs. Napier, I shall be delighted to join you both for dinner. But allow me on this occasion to return to the inn and change into more appropriate clothing.'

'Of course. We shall have to change, too.'

'Oh, don't promise anything, Mrs. Napier!'

Or that is what she thought he said, as he bowed and left her again to finish the walk home on her own.

The pigeons, to Hippolyta's surprise and delight, were delicious, and if the potatoes were a little burned around the edges she was sure it was only for want of some practice of timing on Ishbel's part. Ishbel had reported, on Hippolyta's enquiry, that Wullie had returned safely and the pony and trap were back at the inn, so it was with pleasure that Hippolyta saw there was plenty of the main course left, despite the enthusiastic inroads of Patrick and Mr. Durris, for both the servants to enjoy. The pie that followed, served with a thin custard (the hens were moulting and not particularly productive), proved Ishbel's capacities once again as a baker. If this meal was her bid to be cook in room of Mrs. Riach, Hippolyta would be inclined to appoint her on the spot. She would talk to Ishbel again tomorrow, she decided, as she retired alone to the parlour, leaving the gentlemen to take a glass of brandy in peace. She hoped that Durris would not clype on her to Patrick: sometimes Patrick, lovely as he was, did not fully understand the necessity for overhearing others' conversations when one was trying to be helpful.

She was glad when the men followed her within a few minutes, sure that they had had no time to discuss her perceived faults with any thoroughness, but her misgivings returned when Patrick grinned at her.

'I thought we had better not leave you long, and allow you to get up to more mischief!'

'I was not - !' she began, but Patrick waved her down, still smiling.

'My dearest, it is, I know, very difficult to stop you. But please be careful: for one thing, patients do not want a nosy wife for their physician. For another, remember you have already been attacked because you knew something dangerous to this murderer: I could not bear to lose you, particularly if you are risking your own life in this cause, or in any other.' He took her hands, and she blushed, unable to defend herself further. Durris discreetly stepped around them, and went to the fire.

'Another cold evening,' he remarked, warming his hands. 'I believe there may be another frost, rather than more snow, tonight.'

Patrick broke away and sat by the piano, beginning to toy with the black notes mysteriously. He drew out his glasses and slipped them on, squinting at the music on the stand.

'Perhaps that will keep the murderer tucked up at home,' said Hippolyta. 'I suppose you are sure now that it is not Mr. Elphick.'

'Almost sure,' said Durris. 'If we read Mr. Worthy's murder that he was killed in mistake for Elphick, it seems very unlikely that Elphick killed Broughton.'

'Was Mr. Elphick very shocked to find that Mr. Worthy had been mistaken for him?'

'Unsettled, certainly,' said Durris, patient with her as always. 'When I last saw him he was going to Mr. Worthy's lodgings to pay his respects and to recover his hat. But he was more subdued and uneasy even than usual.'

'Do you believe he has told you the whole truth now?' asked Patrick, his fingers blurring over a soft chord.

'No, I do not.' Durris sighed. 'He will not yet tell me who, if anyone, he saw at the duel. I begin to wonder if there was anyone there of any interest, or if he was simply trying to intrigue Mrs. Broughton. He claims that all the affection was on her part, but that seems unlikely to me from all I have seen of the two of them. He may have been trying to impress her or make her feel indebted to him in some way.'

'But there must have been someone there of interest,' said Hippolyta. 'So far we know of Sir Holroyd and Lady Pinner, Mr. Broughton, Mr. Elphick and me. Sir Holroyd did not shoot Mr. Broughton, it seems unlikely that Mr. Elphick did because of Mr. Worthy's death, and we don't think that Lady Pinner was capable or had any reason to do it. And I certainly did not. So there was someone else there, of interest to Mrs. Broughton at the very least as the murderer of her husband.'

'The men you spoke to this morning, perhaps?' asked Patrick.

'McTavish, Halloran and Eames?' Durris glanced at Hippolyta. 'What did you think of them, Mrs. Napier?'

Hippolyta was pleased to be asked.

'It was difficult to see their faces. I thought that McTavish was the leader of the group, but Eames is there because he knows Sir Holroyd and he must be determined, if he has travelled so far to follow him.'

'Where is he from?' asked Patrick.

'Eames is from somewhere in the Midlands, Dr. Napier. McTavish is from Glasgow, and Halloran I have down as an Irishman.'

'The Midlands, eh? I see the connexion.'

'Mr. Durris, I don't for one moment believe they were looking for work in Crathie on Saturday.' Hippolyta was eager with her information. 'Ishbel says the road was closed and no one could get through.'

'Is that so? I did wonder,' said Durris, taking out his notebook, 'but had not yet found anyone to ask. Of course, the kirk was not as full as it might have been on Sunday.'

'Exactly. That's what Ishbel said.'

'Then I wonder now why they bothered to lie? Where were they instead? If they had simply said that they sat in the cottage and stared out at the snow, I should not have been able to prove otherwise, I should think. What you may not have noticed, though,' Durris made one of his minuscule notes, 'from your viewpoint at the window, was that there were four beds made up in that cottage. The bench on which the men were so casually sitting was one of them.'

'Then there are four of them? Is that what you mean? Then where was the fourth?'

'That's a very good question,' said Durris.

'Could he be keeping some kind of watch on Sir Holroyd?' asked Patrick. 'After all, Sir Holroyd believes they are here to threaten him. Would they be taking it in turns, do you think?'

'Are they our only suspects now?' asked Hippolyta.

'Well …'

'It's just – they seemed to me very surprised when you said about two women being attacked. I thought they sounded quite sincere, did you not?'

'Perhaps they could not tell, in the heavy snow,' suggested Patrick.

'Then why attack either of us at all? Even if they feared there might be a witness to Mr. Worthy's murder, in that snow if they could not distinguish us, neither of us was likely to be able to distinguish them very convincingly. Do you not think?'

Patrick took off his glasses and tapped them thoughtfully on the back of his hand, sitting sideways on the piano stool.

'And I still cannot understand why the men, however many there might be of them, would kill Broughton rather than Sir Holroyd, since he was convinced they were here to threaten him.'

'There is still Mrs. Broughton to consider,' said Hippolyta firmly. 'The weavers, and Mrs. Broughton. I even think I remember her being in the stableyard when the challenge was laid down. Is there not anyone else? I mean, there could have been any number of people up there, in the end, but is there anyone else likely?'

There was a long, contemplative silence. Then Durris said softly,

'Mrs. Napier, where is your brother?'

She had tried very calmly to examine Marcus' case as a suspect with Patrick and Mr. Durris, but inside she had been furious. It was all, she thought later in bed, because Mr. Durris had a – a what? A respect? - for Mrs. Broughton, that was it. She had only just turned the subject to Mrs. Broughton, wondering if she could be guilty of her husband's death, and at once Mr. Durris had to spring in and spin things round so that every move that Marcus had made since he arrived in Ballater up to his disappearance had to be examined and considered. She was very cross indeed. Cross with her mother, for not telling her what precisely had happened between Marcus and Mr. Broughton in Edinburgh; cross with Marcus, for disappearing without a word – four days ago, now. Where in Heaven's name was he? – and cross with Mr. Durris for daring to line him, her brother, up with the other suspects.

So they had paced through Marcus' arrival with the Broughtons – unwittingly – and with Jedediah Elphick, his friendliness with the journalist, their dinner at the Napiers' house and the evening, pleasant enough at the time, that had followed. They had considered Marcus' late rising the next day, Ishbel's affection for him, Marcus' own awkward habits and attitudes, his sympathy for Reform, his campaigning for sobriety and justice and finer breeches. They had come to the matter of the assembly, and his undoubtedly odd behaviour there. Odd, that is, in Hippolyta's eyes: she tried to make it sound as if it was exactly the way any young man, perhaps not so inclined to dance, might spend an assembly in a country village in the winter.

'He went to look for a card game to watch: he does not play, himself, but he likes to watch. Then later I saw him on the stairs, and then just after that was when we saw the duel being organised. Mr. Elphick met the Broughtons for the first time in Ballater: they were not at all friendly together,' she remembered.

'Hm. But Marcus Fettes - what was he doing on the stairs? The assembly was held in the ground floor rooms, I think?'

'Yes, but … well, I think he had just found somewhere cool and quiet to sit, you know?'

Durris made a little mark in his notebook, and Hippolyta felt her face flush red. Should she tell him?

'He was watching Sir Holroyd, if you must know.' The words gushed out before she could stop them.

'Watching Sir Holroyd?'

'Yes. Sir Holroyd was in a small room by the stairs, trying to get away from Mr. Elphick, now I come to think of it.'

'Trying to get away from him?' Durris' question was sharp, and she had hoped that might lead him down another path, well away from Marcus.

'No, not that dramatic! I had the impression that Mr. Elphick was trying to arrange a meeting with Sir Holroyd, and Sir Holroyd was not very interested.'

'Was a meeting arranged?'

'Only something very vague – 'tomorrow', I think, was all that Sir Holroyd said. He was quite dismissive, and Mr. Elphick was trying his best to be very humble and subservient. I don't even think they had met before. They were speaking like two men who had only just made each other's acquaintance.'

Durris had paused, making spirals, for all Hippolyta could see, in his notebook.

'So, Sir Holroyd and Mr. Elphick were arranging to meet on the Saturday, at a time unspecified. And tell me again, what was Marcus doing?'

Hippolyta sighed impatiently.

'I don't know why, but Marcus was watching them.'

'And then what?'

'The two men came out of the room – that was when I saw clearly who they both were - and went away, out into the stableyard. Then I told Marcus off for eavesdropping –' she glared at the faint snort that seemed to come from both her husband and Mr. Durris. 'Well, he had no good reason to! He hardly knew either of the men, surely! And they were talking of nothing that should concern him.'

'Then what?' Durris had used his soothing voice, and she found herself resenting that, too. She was not some feeble witness or nervy suspect that needed calming.

'Then we heard noises outside and we went into the room the men had come from, and that was when we heard the argument and the arrangements for the duel.' She had thought Durris would stop his questions there, where the story, as far as she was concerned, seemed to end. But he had wanted more. She had wished Patrick would leave his piano and come and sit beside her: she had felt exposed, as if Durris were painting her portrait. She preferred to be on the other side of the canvas.

'Marcus was with me for the rest of the evening,' she told him firmly. 'He came back to the dancing room with me, though he said nothing, and he stayed with us while we had supper, and then we left together, the three of us. And we walked home here, and he said … he said that if one of the duellers shot and killed the other he would be charged with murder. That was about all – I mean, we both told Patrick what we had seen and heard, of course, and Patrick said you should be informed, but we wondered if you would reach here in time to prevent anything as early as dawn when the snow was so bad. And the snow fell again during the night, and it was only next morning, after we came back from the whole duel business, that we realised his bed had not been slept in. He is usually a late riser,' she had finished, in tone that struck her now as very mournful. Could the worst have happened? Could Marcus be dead somewhere, under the snow like Mr. Worthy? She prayed fervently that he was not, but as she had reckoned earlier, he had been away for four days now.

She turned over in the bed, seeking a fresh area of cool pillow.

It was not hard to find one: the bedroom fire, small as it had been, had long gone out. There was a lingering scent of woodsmoke in the air.

She thought back to that morning in the woods, her painting, the arrival of Broughton and Sir Holroyd, the dawn light that she had missed for her picture. Sounds: crunching feet in the snow, the beginnings of birdsong, three or four crows croaking to each other over the trees, light movements in the branches and in the brambles – perhaps Lady Pinner and Clara arranging themselves behind a few trees to see what was going to happen. Had Mrs. Broughton been there, too? The air had been clear: if Mr. Elphick had been there, as he had said, she had smelled no eau-de-cologne. Instead there was the first trace of woodsmoke coming up from the village, carried on the lightest of moving air. And she had seen smoke, too, a delicate thread, rising from somewhere off to the right of Dinnet House.

Where had that fire been?

It could not have been the kitchens, which were to the left of the building as she saw it from the hillside. Could it have been the nursery fire?

She closed her eyes tight in the darkness, picturing it.

The smoke was rising from somewhere nearer than Dinnet House itself.

She sat up suddenly. There had been something, somewhere, someone nearby, with a fire that morning, presumably awake, presumably able to leave that fire and come closer to the duel site. What was there? Who was it? Could it have been Marcus?

She glanced down at Patrick, as usual sleeping soundly. There was no point in waking him: with his ankle still tightly bound, he could barely make it up the stairs. Mr. Durris, thankfully, had returned to the inn after supper. She would just have to go on her own.

She slipped into her warmest shift and as many woollen petticoats as she could move in. Her boots and cloak were downstairs and she found them quickly, then discovered that Ishbel had put away all the lanterns. She had to go to the cupboard in the servants' passage and find one, then find a light, then at last ease the front door open and shut again and find herself standing on the frosty path, dazzled by the stars. It would be a slippery walk, but at least bright and clear. Should she wait until morning? But if the person – Marcus – was sleeping in some shelter up behind Dinnet House, she was more likely to catch him at night, wasn't she? Determined to find out what her silly brother was up to at last, she arranged the lantern and her cloak and hood, and set off.

It was a beautiful walk, whatever the success of her adventure. The stars danced above her, and cast their light over the village, making the church, the houses, the trees, sparkle like the most extravagant ballroom. She used other people's bootprints to anchor each step safely and prevent her feet from slipping, and for that she had to watch where she was going, but every now and again she would stop and stare about her, partly to watch for attack – however foolish Patrick might think she was she was not going to walk that unwarily – and partly simply to stare at the light. How on earth could one paint that?

Once she reached the shelter of the woods, the ground was softer but no easier to walk on, with branches and rocks strewn about. She wanted to walk fairly quietly, so that Marcus would be taken by surprise by her arrival, but it was difficult, and on occasion she missed her footing and let out a little involuntary gasp. The cold pinched her face so that she was sure her cheeks were like last year's apples. Eventually, though, she reached the point where she had on that awful morning set up her painting box, and stood to assess where she might have spotted that thread of smoke. She closed her eyes, pinpointed it, and opened them again, peering downhill towards a jumble of bushes between her and the dark bulk of Dinnet House. Was she mistaken? Was there, in fact, the dimmest of lights somewhere in the depths of that jumble?

She kept fixed on it as she carefully descended the hill again, making for the place as directly as she could. At one point she lost her footing entirely, but clutched at a tree and saved herself, stopping to catch her breath. So much for a quiet approach! She steadied her swinging lantern, and advanced again.

In the jumble of bushes was, to her surprise, a small hut, wooden-roofed but built of unworked stones heaped up. To the uphill side was a tiny window, hardly more than a handspan in either direction. That was where she had seen dim light, probably from a small fire inside. She could indeed smell woodsmoke. To the left, as she had approached it, was a low doorway. She held her breath, put a hand to the door, and pushed it gently.

The hut was empty except for a small closed stove and a high stool. She frowned, annoyed. She must have just missed him.

There was a sharp shove at the back of her waist, and she found herself in the hut, with the door closed behind her. She had hardly drawn breath to protest when she heard a bolt slam across. She was locked in.

Chapter Twenty-One

'Marcus!' she cried, staggering back to the door. 'Marcus, come back here this instant! Is this some kind of joke? Let me out of here at once!' She thumped hard on the wood. 'Marcus! Wait till I tell Mother!' She stopped, regretting that last sentence: it sounded a little childish. But good heavens, how childish was Marcus being? She drew breath to shout again, but then in the silence she heard footsteps, steady and focussed, heading away from the hut and down the hill. Whatever her ridiculous brother was up to, he had no intention, clearly, of letting her out just for the moment. She stepped back from the door again, glaring at it, then jiggled at it to see if the bolt would shift. It seemed oddly sound for such a humble building. She lifted the lantern and looked about her: the stove was lit, and had been for some time, to judge by the warm pink glow of the fire, and there was a little pile of firewood beside it, but she must be careful, she noted. The hut was small, and her skirts were wide. The stove certainly made the hut tolerable at the moment, but it was still quite early in the night – probably not long after midnight. The coldest spell was still to come. She would be glad of her thick cloak and hood, certainly. Was there anything else that might help? She could see no food or drink of any kind that might have been heated for internal warmth, not even a bucket of water. She gave an exasperated sigh. Did Marcus expect her to starve? She moved the high stool, and found a bundle behind it. Her hopes lifted – but she soon discovered, when she untangled the old blankets from around it, that that was in fact it – old blankets. They were not appealing. She wondered where on earth Marcus had found them, while at the same time was rather glad he had not borrowed any of her good blankets for his temporary hermitage. At least, she assumed it was temporary.

Or had Marcus gone another step down the road of campaigning, and decided to eschew not only drink and meat, but also houses?

She laughed a little to herself, hoping it was only a joke. She flicked out the blankets, and taking care to keep her cloak between her clothes and the rough wool, she wrapped the blankets around her shoulders and perched, as best she could, on the high stool.

Why was it so high? She was glad it would keep her out of the worst of the draughts, but it seemed a little precarious. Then she realised: it was perfectly obvious. There were in fact two little windows in the hut, one, that she had seen from the outside, facing up the hill, and another, almost as small, facing down the hill, with, presumably, rather a good view of Dinnet House. Sitting on the stool gave the viewer the best perspective, while not being too close to the stove. She smiled, then frowned. Marcus had not taken leave of civilisation altogether then, as she had supposed. He was watching Sir Holroyd, just as he had on the night of the assembly. But why? What did he hope to achieve by any scrutiny, let alone one that had him living rough in the woods in December? She sat more securely on the stool, staring out at the starlit bulk of Dinnet House in the valley below. There were no lights on at all that she could see: she was not surprised. All good Members of Parliament and their households would be long in their beds, no doubt. She sighed again, and wished that she was, too.

The hours passed slowly. She dared not fall completely asleep, in case she either grew too cold or tumbled into the stove. The lantern, though, dwindled and expired while her eyes were closed at one point, and she was alarmed at the dark when she opened them again. But the stars were still bright enough outside, and dawn was far away. She settled again, staring at the warm glow of the stove, then reconsidered and fed some more sticks into it. It was a simple construction, a little as if a chimney had come down to the ground to roost, but it burned comfortably. Such smoke as it produced disappeared through a thin part of the roof, not a hole, exactly, but a weak point where the stream dissipated. It must have been that that she had seen on the morning of the duel.

If Marcus had been here that morning – and someone certainly had been – then what had been his part in what had happened? Could he really have killed Mr. Broughton? She tried hard to see Marcus as a killer – and it would have taken a degree of thought in advance, would it not? He would have needed a pistol … oh! She had not thought to look amongst his things. He might well have had travelling pistols with him for his journey from Edinburgh. Would he have brought them out here? If so he must have left at least the case back at the Napiers' house. There was nothing in here of that kind. She would have to look again, when she was allowed to go home.

Well, if he had pistols, might he have taken aim at Mr. Broughton? If they had quarrelled, or whatever, in Edinburgh, could Marcus have decided to end the quarrel here? But then to attack Clara, and Mr. Worthy, and her … Mr. Worthy had said that he had worked for some time in Edinburgh. Could they have met there, and also had some quarrel? Both were men of law: there was a good chance that Edinburgh's powerful law circles would have brought them together. But there was no one nearby who could tell her the answer to that: Marcus was absent, and Mr. Worthy was dead. Poor, odd, Mr. Worthy, she thought. What could he have done to bring about his death? Oh, where was Marcus? He had a great deal of explaining to do.

She slipped back into wandering, dreamy thoughts, eyes closed, arms wrapped round herself under her layers. When dawn came, reddish and startling, she was aware of the gradual increase in the light. She opened her eyes reluctantly, wriggled her shoulders and her toes, and stretched as best she could. Outside, Dinnet House was beginning to loom out of the darkness, and to the south and west bundling clouds of grey and pearl lingered on the horizon, considering what to do about the liquid sunlight. Oblivious to their plots, lamps flickered into life in Dinnet House, first in the kitchens, down to the left, then up in the nursery to the right. Hippolyta watched, longingly, feeling the first pangs of morning hunger strike her stomach. She always had a healthy appetite in the mornings. Marcus knew that well: it was particularly cruel of him not to leave her any food.

Oh, poor Patrick! What was he going to do when he woke and found she was not there? Not that she had had any intention of concealing her night time expedition from him – not after the fact, anyway – but she had at least meant to be home around the time he would be getting up. What would he do? Where would he think she had gone? Oh, why had she not left a note? He would not be able to go out looking for her, not with his ankle still so sore. He would try to send someone, maybe poor Wullie, and he would be so worried, and doubtless, if he was worried, he would then be cross. Poor darling Patrick! She should never have left him. How could she have been so thoughtless? He would be so anxious, and he would have been quite right, for after all she had been attacked before, and now she was locked in here with no hope of a quick rescue or release. And would Ishbel remember to help him to get about, or Wullie think to run to see his patients? Who would remember to feed the hens and the pig, and the cats? Though the cats would no doubt remind people of their requirements. How would the household run if she were not there at dawn to see to it?

She considered the proposition, and after a moment's reflection realised that the household would run very well, if not better, without her help. She sighed. Only Patrick would miss her. But he really would miss her, and if she were not back by breakfast, who knew what he would do?

Oh, she thought again: breakfast. She gazed down once more at the kitchen lights in Dinnet House, and wondered what they were having to eat. Well, porridge, no doubt, in the kitchens. But Sir Holroyd might have kidneys, and beef, and toast, and eggs, and oh! all manner of delights that began to make her mouth water at the very thought of them. Drawn by the thoughts of the Pinners' breakfast table, she even tried a few shouts for help in that direction. But Dinnet House was too far away, tucked safe and muffled down in its valley. There was no chance of anyone hearing her, even if they ventured outside.

She watched it, though, picturing what was happening inside. It held her attention long enough that she did not notice those louring clouds creep up from their mountain fastness over Glen Tanar. It was only when darkness descended again, almost as if dawn had been rescinded, that she saw that it was again snowing.

The flakes were luscious and thick, even penetrating the woods here, catching on branch and fungus and dead leaf and sometimes managing all the way to the black earth beneath, speckling it splodgily. The speckles were soon joined by other splodges, and the ground was whitening fast. Well, it would be warmer now, she thought, at least: clouds and a layer of snow would keep in her precious heat here until Marcus came to let her out. But in a moment or two she could no longer see more than pinpricks of light at Dinnet House, and soon the trees in front of her were blurring and unsure. She turned away from the window, where the falling flakes were beginning to make her dizzy, and regarded the stove.

There was not much firewood left. She fed in a few more sticks, eager to be warm but wondering, at the same time, how much longer she was going to need it. Surely Marcus would come back for her soon. But if he did not … She studied the stone walls of the hut, and the wooden roof. How foolish would it be to break bits off the roof to keep herself warm? The cold would come in more easily, and the warmth go out, if there were a hole in the roof. But if she had no fire, there would be cold all around and no warmth to go out, anyway. The roof was low, and she reached up a hand to try to break off a piece or two of the rough planks from which it was made. They were surprisingly strong: perhaps the question did not arise. She turned to look at the stove again – was it burning less steadily than before? Surely not! It must be her imagination. But the light inside it grew dimmer and dimmer, and too late she realised that snow was relentlessly covering the hole in the roof, smothering the fire and spilling stray smoke into the hut itself. The fire quickly went out, so that there was not too much smoke around her, but that was undoubtedly a mixed blessing. The hut grew colder almost at once, and she clutched at her unsavoury blankets.

She was about to stoop to the stove and see if she could possibly light it again, when she heard movement outside. She caught her breath, on the point of shouting out, but something made her stop. Was it Marcus? She listened hard. Footsteps, definitely footsteps, and larger than a deer's delicate feet. There was a pause, just outside the door. Then the footsteps moved away. Again she drew breath to shout, but then she realised that the person was not leaving: they were beginning to walk around the hut.

She glanced at the little window that faced uphill, and in a moment she was crouched beneath it, huddling the tails of her cloak close. The footsteps paused again, and she was sure someone was looking in through that little window. She held her breath. Then the footsteps moved on, carrying on around the hut. She shivered, trying to judge just when the person outside might turn the corner, might be able to see in through the downhill window. She shuffled across the earth floor, gathering her skirts after her, trying to make no sound. If she could hear the footsteps in the soft snow outside, whoever it was was bound to be able to hear her if she made the least noise. She scrunched herself into the corner where the blankets had been, one leg pressed against the side of the stove. She jammed a blanket between her cloak and the hot metal, praying that the wool would not start to singe and smell. Her jaw trembled, and she gritted her teeth. She heard the footsteps turn the corner, skid a little as the ground sloped away, then pass along the front of the hut. There was silence again. Had the person reached the little window? What could they see?

She held her breath. It seemed like an age until the footsteps went on, slowly, tired, even, round the hut again until they reached the door. Then she heard the bolt begin to move.

If ever a bolt took an age to be drawn, it was this one. The tiny, oily creak seemed to last a lifetime. Hippolyta considered trying to hide in her corner, saw the pointlessness of it, and decided to face whoever was outside standing, and ready. She arranged herself in the very centre of the hut, standing as tall as she could – which was quite tall – with her hands by her sides. She tried to steady her breathing. As an afterthought, she flung the dusty blankets over the stool, and brushed off her cloak. Right, she thought, with a tilt of her chin, let's see who you are, then.

The bolt stopped moving. The door, light on its hinges, swung slowly towards her. A figure, thick white about the shoulders and hat with snow, stood before her.

'Well, now, there's a surprise,' he said flatly.

'Mr. Durris!'

He peered past her, trying to see the details of the hut in the snowy dusk.

'How long have you been here?'

'All night,' she said, trying to sound quite matter-of-fact about it.

'An unusual choice of habitation. May I come in?' He shrugged some snow off his shoulders.

'Oh, of course!' But the hut was very small. She pressed her back against the uphill wall, trying to keep out of his way. He in turn kept as close as he could to the stove, though there was still some heat coming from it. Despite their efforts, there were only a few inches between them.

'What is this place?'

'I – I don't really know,' Hippolyta admitted. 'I came here looking for Marcus, and then he locked me in.'

'Marcus Fettes locked you in?'

'Yes. When I catch him …'

'You found him, then? But what was he doing here? Why did he lock you in?'

'I don't really know.'

'It's hardly a brotherly thing to do,' said Durris.

'Ah,' said Hippolyta wrily, 'didn't you have any brothers, then?' Durris looked at her, and she backtracked rapidly, certain she had stepped too far into his personal life. 'I don't know why he locked me in, but I believe I know what he was doing here. Remember I told you he was watching Sir Holroyd Pinner at the assembly? Well, look through that little window.'

To get to the window, Durris had to squeeze between her and the stove to reach the little corner with the stool. He kept his back to her, and she looked away, feeling his elbows brush slightly against her arm as he balanced in the narrow space.

'Dinnet House,' he murmured at last. 'He was watching again. Or someone was.' He surveyed the contents of the hut again, as best he could. 'Marcus Fettes was staying here? Is this where he was all the time he was missing?'

'I suppose so. There's no food, though, nor any evidence of food.' Even she could hear the note of longing in her voice.

'It's just …' Durris began, then hesitated. He looked again through the window, and around the hut. 'It's just that I came up here looking for somewhere the fourth weaver might be. Somewhere that they might have taken it in turns to sit and watch Sir Holroyd and his household, and find out his habits and movements. And this seems ideal.' He considered again. Hippolyta looked around the hut again too. Could she have been wrong?

'But if you have been here all night,' said Durris suddenly, 'does Dr Napier know where you are?'

'Ah, not exactly …'

'Mrs. Napier.' His voice was resigned.

'Oh, all right! No, he doesn't. The thought of looking for somewhere like this struck me, and I didn't want to waken him. And his ankle was bad anyway: he would not have been able to come with me. I remembered, you see – I was trying to think what I might have seen on the morning of the duel, some reason why anyone would have attacked me –'

'I'm glad you remember that someone attacked you, Mrs. Napier.'

She ignored him.

'And I remembered seeing, or smelling, a thread of woodsmoke from this direction, so I came here.'

'Of course it would not have occurred to you to wait until morning.'

'I wanted to catch them.'

'And instead they caught you, did they not?'

She did not dignify that with an answer, either. Durris was silent for a moment, and she resisted the urge to speak, letting him carry on.

'The trouble is,' he said at last, 'if they locked you in – or if he locked you in, as you say – no doubt he or they will come back for you.'

'But that's good,' she said quickly. 'Then we can catch them! If it is them, and not Marcus.'

'We?' Durris repeated. 'You will not be catching anyone, Mrs. Napier. The trouble is, as I was going to say, someone will doubtless come back for you, and though I should like to catch them, I do not want you around when any kind of confrontation occurs. I shall take you home, first.'

'But Mr. Durris!'

'I shall hear no arguments, Mrs. Napier. Whoever comes back for you, you would only get in the way –'

'But if it's Marcus!'

'Especially, Mrs. Napier, if it's Marcus Fettes. You would be in the way, and you would be placing yourself in danger – and I cannot allow that.' He met her eyes for a second. 'And Dr. Napier would never forgive me, which would be entirely his right.'

'Then stay here, and trap them – I could bolt you in, if you like,' said Hippolyta, trying to show how useful she could be. 'I shall be perfectly fine going home alone, now that I am at liberty.'

'Mrs. Napier, have you even looked at the snow?'

She had not: she had not paid it any attention since Durris had arrived. But now that she looked outside the door of the hut, she gasped. If there was a tree eight inches from the door it could not be seen. The flakes, steady and endless, had dropped a grey-white screen in front of them, and nothing more could be seen.

'Good gracious!' she whispered, staring at its relentless fall.

'In fact, reluctant though I am to admit it,' Durris went on, 'I don't think for the moment that either of us is going anywhere.' For a moment a small, wistful expression seemed to pass over his face, and then was gone. Hippolyta wondered if there were somewhere he particularly wanted to be. Had he an assignation with Mrs. Broughton? If he had, too bad. But the moment passed. 'Take a seat, Mrs. Napier, and with your permission I shall close this door and keep in what heat there is until the way is a little clearer.'

She sat back down on the blanket-covered stool in the corner, and watched him shut the door. The hut was hardly any darker with it closed, but Durris was a big man, and the room seemed to have shrunk with him in it. Mercifully he stayed close to the door even when he turned round.

'Look, Mr. Durris,' she began, 'I don't know what Marcus was doing here, or what his interest is in Sir Holroyd Pinner, but I'm almost sure Marcus could not have killed Mr. Broughton. Not deliberately, anyway. No doubt he has been foolish, probably even more foolish than usual, but I simply cannot see him planning to kill anyone. He's just not that kind of person – daft, yes, always has been, but never destructive!'

'I'd still very much like to know what he has been doing here, Mrs. Napier. If as you say you saw smoke coming from this hut that morning, then he or someone else was here, and may have had something to do with the whole business. Though I accept that the purpose of this hut, at least as it is arranged at present, is to observe Dinnet House, and I cannot square that with anyone wishing to kill Mr. Broughton.'

Hippolyta gave a little impatient sigh, and glanced at the window, but the snow was still falling. She could only just see the faintest of lights in the direction of Dinnet House: they would have needed to keep the lamps lit in this weather, though it was now some time after dawn.

'You say he is an enthusiast for Reform?' he asked her.

'He is an enthusiast, full stop. He has always caught ideas and run with them. You know he does not drink spirits? Recently he has abandoned wine, too, but that will not last long. He does not gamble. He is training with my father to be an advocate in Edinburgh, but he is more often around the lawcourts demanding changes and insisting that such and such a trial has been misheld, or the verdict was unjust, or no account was taken of the pannel's health or sanity: it is almost a mercy to me, Mr. Durris, to find him so focussed on Reform for he has never before given his heart so wholly to such a cause: he flits from notion to notion. I don't mean to say,' she added hurriedly, 'that he is not sincere in his opinions: he is just so easily distracted, you know?'

'Mrs. Napier,' said Durris wearily, then suddenly – 'Mrs. Napier! Are your skirts on fire?'

She leapt from the stool, backing into the tiny room away from the tight corner. Was she on fire? She could smell smoke, certainly. She spun awkwardly, trying to find any sparks or smouldering, and Mr. Durris seized her arm, turning her more gently, examining her cloak and skirts with rapid care. There was nothing.

'Oh, goodness!' she breathed. 'But you're right: I can smell smoke.'

'Then where – ?'

But at that instant, the door was flung open.

'Take your hands off my sister!' came a voice, flaring with anger. Hippolyta, sensing danger, ducked, and a fist flew close to her bonnet. Mr. Durris fell to the ground, half against her skirts, senseless. She turned clumsily to the door.

'For heaven's sake, Marcus!'

And this time it certainly was him.

Chapter Twenty-Two

'Who on earth is that? And what are you doing here with him?' Marcus demanded, pale nostrils flaring.

'This is the sheriff's officer, Marcus: you've just punched a sheriff's officer. We were here looking for you,' she generalised rapidly. 'Where on earth have you been for the last four days? What have you been doing? And why, precisely – and your answer to this had better be a good one, Marcus – why did you lock me in here last night?'

'A sheriff's officer?' Marcus had the grace to look much more anxious than Hippolyta had seen for a while. 'But what on earth was he doing?'

'He thought my skirts were on fire. Can't you smell smoke? Oh, Marcus, help me lift him: I can't even kneel down to see if he is all right with the angle he's lying at. Couldn't you have hit him somewhere a little more spacious?'

But she was already on her knees as Marcus crouched to manoeuvre Durris out of her way, and Durris in any case was already coming round, one half of his face in a furious frown. The other half seemed, as far as Hippolyta could see in the half-light, to be swelling rapidly. He sat up, awkward on the cold earth floor, determinedly rubbing his injured eye.

'Give me a handful of snow, Marcus,' said Hippolyta. She handed it to Durris, who pressed it gratefully against the spreading bruise. His frown eased a little, too, and he managed to straighten himself into a proper sitting position. Hippolyta moved out of his way.

'Well,' said Durris, his teeth only slightly gritted, 'perhaps, Mrs. Napier, you could introduce me now?'

'Mr. Durris, this is my brother, Marcus Fettes. Marcus, Mr.

Durris, sheriff's officer.' Marcus blinked at the order of the introduction, but said nothing of it. Instead he bowed gracefully, even though he was on his knees.

'Mr. Durris, I must apologise. I had not … I thought …' He faded away as he met Durris' good eye.

'I see,' said Durris. 'Well, I'm afraid you'll have to manage a longer explanation than that, Mr. Fettes. Your departure and your absence has caused some confusion, to say the least.'

'Well, it wasn't my fault!' said Marcus, blushing like a schoolboy accused of some misdemeanour.

'What wasn't?' asked Hippolyta. 'Did someone snatch you from the house? Allowing you to change out of your evening clothes and slippers first, of course.'

'No, of course not! I left your house of my own free will. But I haven't been able to come back since.'

'Because you've been here in this hut?' asked Durris. The snow in his hand had all but melted. Hippolyta stepped outside to fetch another handful, and saw that the falling snow was easing. The sky was lighter by the minute.

'In this hut? What on earth do you mean?'

Durris sighed. He used the stove, now much cooler, to pull himself to his feet, steadying himself with a hand on the rough stone wall of the hut.

'This hut, Mr. Fettes. Have you been staying in this hut?'

'I don't understand –'

'Just answer, please, sir, would you?' My, thought Hippolyta, Marcus has almost driven Mr. Durris into losing his temper! She would not have thought such a thing possible – but Marcus was indeed very talented in that direction. 'Have you or have you not been staying in this hut?'

'I have not,' said Marcus precisely, 'been staying in this hut.'

'Thank you.'

'But you locked me into it last night!' cried Hippolyta.

'Am I imagining it,' said Durris, rubbing his nose, 'or is that smell of smoke growing stronger?'

'I never saw this hut before in my life until now, Pol! Talk sense, would you?'

'Then who locked me in, you silly boy?'

'I don't know! It wasn't me! What were you doing in the hut

anyway? Does Patrick know you're here?'

'Of course he does … well, nearly. He will do,' she finished weakly. 'Wait: yes. That smoke is stronger now. Where is it coming from?'

'Oh, from Dinnet House,' said Marcus. 'It's on fire.'

It was remarkable how quickly one could fly down a snow-covered hillside in an emergency, Hippolyta thought, her boots miraculously leaping from one foothold to another. Durris was well ahead of her. Marcus, she assumed, was somewhere behind, perhaps preserving the delicacy of his buff trousers. The garden gate of the demesne faced the hillside and was open: they ran for it, noting with horror that there was smoke, confusingly white in the snow, billowing from two downstairs windows. Hippolyta thought they were probably Sir Holroyd's study and the room next to it. The windows were flung wide, and from one there was a great rustling and clattering. On the snow-covered lawn, huddled together, were Lady Pinner, Susanna the nursery maid, and bundled up like a ball of wool little Maria. Clara, efficient and sedate, was by the window, catching various items that flew through it and laying them on the ground beside her.

'Oh, Mr. Durris!' cried Lady Pinner when she saw him. 'Help us, please! Help my husband!'

'It's all under control,' came a muffled voice from the study. 'The fire is nearly out. If I could just get these papers out of the way of it …'

'Are you sure you're all right, Sir Holroyd?' called Durris, running up to the window. 'Is there anyone else in the house?'

Hippolyta, further behind, saw Clara twitch suddenly. She looked across at Susanna, but Susanna's face was blank. Had one of them been hiding a young man in the house?

'The fire is in the next room, too,' Durris was shouting through the window.

A curse was heard from inside.

'The kitchen door is open. Can you help me, please, Mr. Durris?'

Durris was already running towards the kitchen door. In a moment or two, they heard a ferocious hiss from the next window. He appeared at the opening with a bucket, gesturing to Hippolyta.

'Fill that with snow, will you, Mrs. Napier? This one seems to be out – the curtains are a mess – but I'll check the other rooms.'

Hippolyta scooped snow into the bucket and handed it back to him, pleased to be helpful. Durris disappeared. Hippolyta went over to the women, whipping off her cloak to wrap around them. Lady Pinner seemed to be only in a nightgown and wrapper. She huddled into the cloak gratefully, enveloping Susanna and the baby in it, too.

'How did it start?' Hippolyta asked. 'What happened?' Oh, and where was Marcus again? she thought, but that thought was becoming familiar now. She put it to one side.

'I'd just come down with Baby,' said Susanna, at Lady Pinner's nod, 'to fetch more milk, and Sir Holroyd was just on the landing when I went past. And he went down the main stairs and I went down the back stairs, and when I reached the bottom I heard him cry out "Fire!", and I ran but he said the fire was in the study. So I went back into the hall and called out for my lady –'

'I had heard my husband's voice, but it is strange: one word makes no sense, and I was standing in my chamber wondering why he had shouted "Fire"!' said Lady Pinner, with a slight giggle. 'But when Susanna called, too, I came straight down.'

'And the master told us to get out quick, so we came out through the kitchens – for we wanted to see what was happening,' said Susanna honestly. 'And we brought Clara out on the way, of course.'

Durris appeared at the other window again, and called Hippolyta back over.

'I believe everything is out. Sir Holroyd has made a fearful guddle in his study, but it is mostly water now. This room was almost empty. You can tell the ladies it is safe to come back inside, before they freeze.'

'Of course.'

She hurried back over with the good news. Still covered by the cloak, Lady Pinner, Susanna and Miss Maria went in through the kitchen door again, and Clara, seeing them go, turned and headed after them. Sir Holroyd stuck his head out of the window, and saw her disappear, then turned his attention to the pile of damp papers on the ground in front of him.

'What a mess, what a mess!' he muttered to himself, then saw

Hippolyta. 'Mrs. Napier, would you mind very much handing me those back in again? I should be very grateful.' He smiled his most charming politician's smile. Hippolyta shrugged to herself, and decided that to move quickly might at least keep her warm for a few minutes, cloakless as she was. She handed up the papers in several bundles, excused herself, and ran for the kitchen door.

The kitchen was deserted: she followed the trail of wet footprints back along the servants' passage, past the cupboard in which she and Lady Pinner had hidden – she was not the only one eavesdropping! – and across the hall to the drawing room. There she found Clara busy lighting the fire, and her own cloak draped across the back of a sofa. Lady Pinner was in her usual chair with her child cuddled on her lap. Susanna was just leaving the room.

'Tea,' she said quietly to Hippolyta, and smiled.

At that, Durris and Sir Holroyd appeared at the door, and stood back to let her pass. They came in, Sir Holroyd striding straight to the fireplace.

'My dear,' he said, 'are you all right? And our little one?'

'We are both quite well, thank you, my dear,' said Lady Pinner, with a slightly stiff smile. 'And you?'

'Some of my papers ...well, at least it was only papers.'

'Do you know how the fire started?' asked Durris. He was standing very straight by the door, hands behind his back. He managed to look formal despite the darkening of his left eye.

'Well, it was just starting as I entered the study, I should say,' said Sir Holroyd, who appeared not to have noticed. 'The window was open, and there were flames on the curtains and in a box I had set on the window seat.'

'And the next room?'

'I didn't even know about that.'

'It seemed, however, to be the same pattern,' said Durris. 'I'm afraid it looks to me as if someone opened the windows and threw something in, something alight, at those two windows. Why those two?'

'They're the easiest to reach,' said Hippolyta. Everyone turned to look at her. 'Well, they are. The front windows, because of the way the land lies, are higher off the ground. And the kitchen windows are very high up.'

'True enough!' said Sir Holroyd, his face dark. 'That will be it, no doubt. I must find some way of locking them, clearly.'

'Both windows and shutters, Sir Holroyd, or they will simply break the windows if they try again,' said Durris, sombre. He was pale, Hippolyta thought, though a little smudged where the smoke must have brushed him. He coughed. 'I have checked the rest of the rooms, and there appears to be no other open window or evidence of fire. I'd recommend, Sir Holroyd, that you employ a manservant for the rest of your stay here. If you like ask me concerning the character of any candidate, and I shall do my best to ensure you do not … nurse a viper in your bosom.'

'But why can you not simply arrest those men? We saw them yesterday, you and I. And now they have done this!'

'Have you proof that it was them? Did you see them?'

Sir Holroyd's face grew tentatively cunning.

'Perhaps I did!' he said, but he knew it would not work.

'This was not a particularly serious or successful attack, Sir Holroyd, but next time they might manage better. Take care. Hire a manservant. Or, perhaps, go back to London.'

'They'll only follow,' said Sir Holroyd sadly. He reached out and took his wife's hand as she cradled their daughter. 'But I must do something. If you will not arrest them, Mr. Durris, I must do something to protect my wife and household.'

'I didn't like the sound of that,' said Hippolyta firmly, as she and Mr. Durris returned along the road to the village. 'It sounded to me as if he intended some particular attack on those weavers.'

'I'm not saying they might not deserve it,' said Durris, 'but I must go straightaway and speak with them. Mrs. Napier, where has your brother gone? Did I just imagine him appearing at that hut?'

'No, I don't believe so – and he did punch you, after all.' She cast a sideways glance at Mr. Durris. He was still not a healthy colour.

'That may be what is confusing me.'

'There he is! Marcus!'

The slender figure before them on the road was not moving fast and they were quickly catching up as they entered the village. Marcus turned wearily and waited for them.

'Why didn't you come and help, if you knew Dinnet House was on fire?' Hippolyta asked him at once.

'I wouldn't go near Dinnet House again if you paid me,' said Marcus, with unexpected feeling. 'Considerable sums, I mean, not just pocket money.'

'Whyever not?'

'Excuse me, Mrs. Napier, Mr. Fettes: I must go along here and see to those fellows,' said Durris. They were at the corner where Hippolyta and the Strongs had rejoined the main street the previous day. 'I am sure Mr. Fettes will see you home safely now. And Mr. Fettes, I should like a word in an hour or so, if that is quite convenient for you.' He might have added the courteous phrase, but Hippolyta sensed from his expression that Marcus had better find it convenient or there would be trouble.

'Of course: good day to you, Mr. Durris!' said Hippolyta. 'Now, Marcus, home straight away. There are a few words I should like to have with you, too, but first I must see Patrick, as soon as possible!'

Her interview with Patrick, though it began well, with his arms about her and his mouth pressed against her hair telling her how glad he was to see her safe and sound, did not continue in quite the same vein. Patrick was not at all pleased that she had once again gone out alone, at night, without even rousing him to say where she was going. When he heard that she had been locked in a hut matters did not improve. In the end Hippolyta was reduced to apologetic tears, and she offered to promise never to do such a thing again. But Patrick, calmer now that his initial relieved anger had passed, came over to where she was sitting at the parlour table and touched her cheek gently.

'Don't make any promises, my dear Hippolyta,' he said softly. 'We both know you will find it impossible to keep them. But please, do try to be more sensible. At least tell me where you are going – at least give me the chance to talk you out of it, or to rescue you if you are locked in a hut!'

She looked up at him, and met his smile with a sniff.

'I'll – I will, I will.'

'If anything were to happen to you, dearest Hippolyta, I don't know what I should do. Please remember that!'

'I will. I will.'

He held her close again then, and she breathed deeply into the front of his waistcoat, feeling her sobs ease. She knew he was right: why could she not resist trying to find things out for herself?

There was a clatter at the parlour door, and Ishbel appeared with the first of the breakfast things. Hippolyta ran upstairs to wash her face and sort out her clothing, and then rapped at Marcus' door to let him know that breakfast was ready. He appeared at speed.

'Oh!' he gasped in awe, as he saw the food laid out on the table. 'Oh, but I have missed this!' He snatched up ham, eggs, and beef, and about half a loaf of bread, smearing it with quantities of butter. 'Oh, paradise!' he cried, his mouth full. Hippolyta, who wanted to do much the same thing, was shamed into delicacy by his enthusiasm, and nibbled at her bread with restraint despite her hunger.

The risp rattled when they were half-done, and Durris appeared, shown in by Ishbel.

'Will you join us, Durris?' asked Patrick, gesturing to the food. 'There is plenty left.'

Ishbel must have seen Marcus' look of dismay for she quickly put in,

'Aye, sir, and there's more forbye. I'll be back wi' it.'

She hurried off and returned with china and cutlery, and more of everything. There was a spring in her step today, Hippolyta saw: she hovered around Marcus as much as any servant could, refreshing his coffee and finding a choice piece of beef for him. Durris, beside him, was almost family, and not to be made much of. He had to help himself from the coffee pot, and did so.

'Have you been to see the weavers?' Hippolyta asked, as soon as Ishbel had gone.

'Yes –'

'What happened your eye?' asked Patrick, suddenly noticing. 'Did they attack you?'

Durris' eyebrows gave a slight twist.

'No, they came fairly peaceably. There was indeed a fourth, a man named Green who had come up with Eames from the Midlands. Only Eames and Green were there, though, and they denied knowing where McTavish and Halloran had gone – out for a walk, was all I got. I asked them about the hut, and they denied all knowledge. I asked them about the fire, and they tried to do the same. But Green's hands were burned, and Eames had lost an eyebrow, and both of them stank of smoke. It did not take much to persuade them – and in the end to have them admit that the hut was indeed theirs, too.'

'And where are they now?' asked Hippolyta. 'For for their own safety …'

'I know, Mrs. Napier, I know. Sir Holroyd should be pleased. They are on their way to Aberdeen in a cart with the constable and two young fellows to help him.'

'Then we are safe!' said Hippolyta.

'Are we?'

Patrick and Hippolyta looked at Durris.

'Well, then, are we?' asked Hippolyta. 'You are right, of course, they were not the only suspects. But surely, if they admitted the fire …'

'They will not admit anything else,' said Durris, meeting her eye.

'What is there to admit?' asked Marcus, finally swallowing the last fragment of food from his plate. 'If it's kidnap you're accusing them of, then I'm not sure …'

'Mr. Fettes,' said Durris, returning to buttering his bread, 'perhaps you could tell me how well you and George Broughton are acquainted?'

Hippolyta gave a tiny gasp, but forced herself to stay quiet. Patrick took her hand under the table, and squeezed it lightly.

'George Broughton? The politician? Hardly at all. But he's here in town, I believe.'

'You met him in Edinburgh.'

'Well – yes, I did, as a matter of fact. How do you know that?' Marcus took a sip of coffee, then turned to face Durris. 'Has he made a complaint?'

'About what do you imagine he might have made a complaint?' Durris asked with precision.

'Well, I don't know, honestly,' said Marcus, pushing back his fair hair with the heel of his hand. 'He was just as much to blame as I was, I should say. In fact, you could really say that he started it. Yes, I think a case could easily be made of that. I was provoked, sorely provoked.'

'Marcus, you are easily the most annoying man in the world!' snapped Hippolyta, unable to keep quiet any longer. 'Why do you not simply answer the question? If you had some confrontation with Mr. Broughton, simply say so! And don't sit there trying to define 'confrontation' or argue that it was the fault of someone on the other side of the road or tell us what the weather was like: did you and Mr. Broughton have a disagreement?'

'I suppose … yes.' Marcus caught Hippolyta's eye, and left it there.

'In Edinburgh?' asked Hippolyta.

'Yes.'

'About politics?'

'Politics? No! Of course not. George Broughton is one of the greatest assets the Reform section has. He is a splendid orator and has a fine mind.'

'Then what – and keep it simple – what did you quarrel about?'

'About one of his court cases, of course.'

Hippolyta sat back, quickly rethinking several things. Durris, by contrast, leaned his wrists on the edge of the table and studied Marcus thoughtfully.

'Was this a case you witnessed?'

'No, but I heard about it. It took place in London, of course.'

'You read about it in the papers?'

'A little, at the time. But I heard more about it later from someone who had been there, and who had been most dissatisfied with the outcome.'

'Was it a murder trial?'

'Yes, it was, as a matter of fact. A woman was accused of killing her husband, and found guilty. You know how the courts hate a woman who kills her man.'

'Had Broughton failed to defend her, then?'

'No, no: Broughton rarely fails! And he rarely defends, either: he is usually brought in for the prosecution. But after she was found guilty there was a good deal of talk: the husband had mistreated the woman badly, and in any case there was considerable doubt about his manner of death. He had been drinking, of course, and could have fallen on the bottle with which she was accused of hitting him.'

'And was there a retrial?' asked Patrick.

'Never a one. She was hanged. There was nothing of her, apparently: she was a tiny thing, and he had been a great hulking villain. I could not see how Broughton could have seen her convicted, when he must have known the details of the case. I knew he was in town, so I kept an eye open for him at assemblies and such. One morning I met him in the Meadows by chance, and my anger rose, and we had words, and I punched him.'

'You gave him a black eye?' asked Patrick. 'He still had it, didn't he?' he asked Hippolyta.

'He did, yes. That was you?'

'I think we can be fairly certain that Mr. Fettes is capable of bestowing black eyes on impulse,' said Durris, somewhat bitterly. Patrick looked from Marcus to Durris and back, shock on his face. Hippolyta shrugged, embarrassed.

'And Mother knew, I take it,' she said.

'Oh, yes, Mother knew.' Marcus gave a wry smile. 'There was a town sergeant walking by, and – well, I was fined.'

'Foolish boy.' Hippolyta's tone was not fond.

'Well, then, Mr, Fettes,' said Durris, applying his napkin to his lips. 'Perhaps now you can tell us where you have been for the last four and a half days? For I understand you left here on Friday night, and no one has seen you since. Please,' he added, 'keep to the facts for now. You can add the decoration later.'

Marcus pushed his chair back and surveyed them.

'Oh, very well,' he said. 'I'll try to keep it simple. I left here on Friday night after the assembly. I had seen Sir Holroyd Pinner at the assembly and knew where he was staying. I could not believe that such an eminent man would have left London without bringing papers with him for his work, and I was sure that they would include something concerning the fight against Reform, some plans the Tories might have to stymy the Whig vote, particularly in the House of Lords where it's perilous. I thought if I were to slip in to Dinnet House, perhaps that very night or maybe in the early morning if he really did go out to fight a duel, I might find something useful for our cause. I never did, of course: his study was always locked.'

'And then where did you go?' asked Durris.

'Where did I go? Why, nowhere, man! I have been at Dinnet House for the last four days, and mightily pleased I am to have escaped at last!'

Chapter Twenty-Three

'Marcus, what have you been doing?' asked Hippolyta.

'It really wasn't me, this time!' he said. 'I went there that night – we had only just come back from the assembly, and your front door was not even locked for the night when I left. I was sure I would be back by morning. I wore my warmest clothes. What a delight it was to rid myself of them this morning!'

'Mr. Fettes, please go on,' said Durris, patiently.

'Of course. I shall be very pleased to explain it all, insofar as I can. I arrived at Dinnet House and the lights were still on, and while I was wondering what best to do I heard voices at the end of the driveway. Sir Holroyd and Lady Pinner were only just returning from the assembly, with some servant with them. I decided to try the front door before they could see me there, and to my satisfaction it was open. I moved fast, for I knew they would be at the door in a moment and no doubt some staff would be ready to meet them – surprising lack of staff in that house, though, I find – so I dashed up the stairs as quick and quiet as I could, and found an empty bedchamber towards the front of the house. I thought Sir Holroyd might have his study on that floor, for the sake of peace and quiet. I listened very carefully as the family came in and up the stairs, and worked out which rooms they had all retired to: Sir Holroyd's room, Lady Pinner's room, a nursery, I later found, and some kind of parlour, all on that floor. But the rest of the rooms were unused. When everything was quiet I tiptoed back downstairs, and found a drawing room and a dining room, and two locked doors. There was a passage to the kitchens, too, of course, but I didn't trouble with that.

'I was sure one of the locked doors must be to Sir Holroyd's study. It was most frustrating, and in the end I did venture into the kitchen quarters to see if there might be a spare set of keys. I looked about in there for a bit, but found nothing useful. I suppose I could have forced the door, but that did not seem quite right.'

'I see,' said Durris, somewhat drily. 'Very sensible of you.'

Marcus nodded, serious.

'I was checking inside a largish cupboard – the kind you can walk right into – when I heard the door of it latch behind me. It must have swung shut in the draught. Of course I could not cry out: I just had to wait till daylight and try to lever my way out when I could see the latch more clearly. I made myself comfortable in the cupboard and fell asleep.

'When I woke, I wondered if I had imagined the door shutting, for now it was ajar. It must have been just before dawn, I believe: the light was just growing a little, and I thought the servants would be about very soon. I slipped out of the cupboard and back into the main house, and tried the locked door again. But it was still locked. Again I went upstairs, but then there was some movement in one of the rooms – the nursery, I think now – and I opened a door at random and went inside. It was the stairs to the attics. I waited there, listening as people moved about the house: I think three people tiptoed down the stairs at various points. I wondered if Lady Pinner is prone to migraines, for I never heard such a quiet household!'

'Sir Holroyd creeping out, followed by Lady Pinner,' said Hippolyta, and Patrick and Durris nodded. 'And the third?'

'Clara?' said Patrick.

'Of course.'

'Is Clara the little nursery maid?' asked Marcus.

'No, she's the other maid.'

'Then she sleeps downstairs, by the kitchens,' said Marcus with authority. 'I found that out later. She's – really quite alarming looking, don't you think?'

'Go on,' said Durris. He had his notebook out now.

'Well, when everything fell silent again, I tried the door to return to the landing. And wouldn't you know, it had latched shut!'

'Another one?' asked Hippolyta dubiously.

'Another one! The landlord needs to see to the doors in that house! So there I was, trapped again. The house was silent: I don't believe anyone was within hearing distance if I had called out.

Well, I wandered around the attics for an hour or so. They are all quite abandoned: only some old trunks and dust, as far as I could see. And the windows were all very small. When I eventually tried the door again, it was open, and out I went.'

'This was still Saturday morning?' Durris confirmed.

'That would be right, yes. I could hear voices in the drawing room place, so I found the back stairs and went down towards the kitchens again. But every blessed way out of the place was either too high up, or too small, or locked. Fortunately I found some bread and cheese, and a barrel of ale, and helped myself. Then I heard someone heading back for the kitchens, so I fled back upstairs, and hid again in the attics. And that's sort of what I have been doing since Friday night,' he confessed, only a little shamefaced. 'Sometimes the door latched shut, sometimes it didn't. Once – oh! that was so close! I was out in one of the other first floor rooms, and I heard voices and thought I was on the point of being discovered, and – well, there was a moment of some confusion and I knocked a vase over the gallery. But I think they put it down to a loose floorboard, and I was safely into the attic again before they found me. So I slept in the attics a good deal, and sometimes found food to take from the kitchen. And then this morning – well, that was an extraordinary stroke of luck!'

'Marcus,' said Hippolyta with sudden concern, 'you didn't set fire to the house, did you?'

'No, of course not! But I heard the cry of "Fire!" and of course I had no wish to be trapped in the attics if they were burning. I heard Lady Pinner and the nursery maid – she's a pretty thing, don't you think? – I heard them running down the stairs, and I knew Sir Holroyd was already down there. I followed them, at a discreet distance, and when they had all run out of the kitchen and around to the gardens, I skipped out fast and made for the hill. The garden gate was opposite the kitchen door: I thought I was least likely to meet anyone there. But instead, Pol, I met you!'

Hippolyta did not, for the moment, wish to encourage him to speak more of that encounter, and besides, the other two were silent, too. Durris turned a page in his notebook, and made some more tiny marks. Marcus tried to see what they might be, and failed.

'So you were in Dinnet House all this time?' asked Patrick.

'I was, yes. And I never wish to darken its door again, thank you.'

'Understandably. But why didn't you just break out through a window? Or unlock the front door at night?'

'There was never a key left anywhere that I could find,' said Marcus. 'And I had no wish to cause any damage. That would not have been right. Taking food for my own survival – well, it was no more than they would have offered a guest, had they known I was there. In fact, it was rather less, for I'm sure they give their guests more than bread and cheese and ale. But I could not break anything, of course.' His long, pale face grew self-righteous.

'Marcus,' said Hippolyta, 'you are not only annoying, you are downright peculiar.'

'Do you really believe that you were there without the knowledge of anyone else in the house?' asked Durris suddenly.

'What?'

'I simply wondered: you seem to have been very unlucky in the matter of escape, but very lucky in the matter of food and drink. You were almost a prisoner, in fact.'

'Oh, don't be ridiculous, man! No one ever saw me!' Durris did not reply, but made another mark in his notebook. Marcus squirmed. 'Anyway, why would anyone do such a strange thing?'

'Indeed,' Durris agreed. 'Forgive me, Mr. Fettes. At times my imagination is a little wild.'

'Well, yes,' said Marcus, satisfied. But Hippolyta looked at Durris with interest. She had never known Durris' imagination to be in any way out of control. What was he thinking? Or was he just wondering if there might be witnesses to Marcus' captivity, proof that Marcus had not murdered anyone?

'Marcus, would you mind livening up the fire?' asked Patrick. 'I'd do it myself but by the time I hirpled over there it might have gone out.'

'Yes, what happened your leg?' Marcus asked, rising willingly enough.

'I slipped and fell in the snow.'

'And what about you, Pol? I see you've been in the wars, too.'

Hippolyta looked at Durris.

'I was attacked, the night before last. Someone struck me from behind in the street.'

'What?' Marcus spun round from the fire, poker in his hand. 'In Ballater?'

'Yes, indeed. But the snow was heavy, and I didn't see who did it.'

'But surely – Mr. Durris, aren't you out hunting for this attacker? Pol, how can you sit there so calmly? Patrick! What are you doing?'

'Patrick can't do much at the moment,' said Hippolyta, quickly leaping to his defence. 'And Mr. Durris has had plenty to do. Marcus, we have had two murders since you disappeared, and that maid, Clara, she was attacked too!'

'Murders!' Marcus hauled himself into the corner of the sofa, the nearest seat to the fireplace. 'Who has been murdered? Not that I am likely to know them well, but who?'

Durris nodded, and Hippolyta went on.

'The first was last Saturday morning. Mr. Broughton was shot dead.'

'Oh, you mean the duel? Oh, that is tragic.' Marcus' face fell. 'That is a true loss. You'll be arresting Sir Holroyd, then, I suppose?'

'No, we will not, Mr. Fettes. Sir Holroyd's pistol did not fire. The shot came from elsewhere.'

'In the woods? That was where they were supposed to be, wasn't it? Ah! That's why you were interested in that hut, no doubt! Now I see.'

Hippolyta could see Durris reassessing Marcus slightly: he had not previously seen much evidence of her brother's intelligence, but it was there – though sometimes remarkably well hidden.

'The hut is part of one line of enquiry, certainly,' he said. 'But we are aware of several people who were on the hillside that morning. You were slightly acquainted with Broughton, or at least with his activities in Edinburgh: were you aware of any threats to his life while he was there?'

'No,' said Marcus, after a moment's consideration. 'I don't believe I was. Indeed I had my own quarrel with him, and there may have been others who would have taken it further, but I saw no evidence of that myself, and heard no rumours.' He reflected again, but came up with nothing more. He shrugged. 'And who then was the other murder victim?'

'A man I do not believe you knew, and in any case we think he might have been killed in mistake for Mr. Elphick – remember, the journalist you travelled with?'

'Of course, but who could want to kill him?'

'He was long acquainted with Mrs. Broughton,' said Durris, before Hippolyta could continue. 'It is possible that some historic quarrel has led to these deaths.'

'Then who was it who actually died?' Marcus asked, seeing that he could be of little assistance with the Broughtons' history.

'A man named Worthy: a man of law working here in the village.'

'Frederick Worthy? A lawyer, you say?'

'Had you met him?'

'Not here, no,' said Marcus with a degree of excitement, 'but I was acquainted with him some years ago – not long – in Edinburgh. An odd looking man, prone to long words?'

'Often, yes,' said Hippolyta. She could not resist a smile at the memory of Mr. Worthy's circumambulatory conversation.

'Yes, he worked in Edinburgh for several months, perhaps even a year or two? He had come from London but that made little difference for he had originally been apprenticed in Scotland, so he knew the law. But he never really settled, I believe, and soon I heard that he had gone to look for a quieter place, somewhere outside the town. So he chose Ballater, did he?'

'He did,' said Durris. 'You had not seen him about the village?'

'I only arrived on Thursday. I did not see him at the assembly, I think?' He turned a questioning face to his sister.

'No, he was indisposed,' said Hippolyta, then added, suspiciously, 'though he seemed well enough the next day.'

Marcus gave a little humourless laugh.

'So Worthy is dead – a shame, for I liked the man. I wish I had known he was here, in fact. It's a strange coincidence, but it was Worthy, in fact, who told me the full details of that case over which I quarrelled with George Broughton.'

'It was?' asked Hippolyta.

'About the case where the woman was hanged for murdering her husband?' asked Patrick. 'But I should imagine that the outcome was not solely Broughton's fault. The judge and jury would have had something to do with it.'

He was half-smiling, but Marcus shot him a cross look.

'You never heard Broughton speak, did you? He was a splendid orator: he could persuade almost anyone of almost anything. And my informant – that is, Frederick Worthy – he certainly implied that there was something to do with witnesses, that Broughton summoned the woman's sister for the prosecution and then didn't call her, so the defence couldn't use her. I don't know the ins and outs of it: I'm not au fait with the English system. But certainly George Broughton was untroubled by any guilty feelings on the matter. When I challenged him, he said the whole thing was a game and he played to win.'

'Harsh,' said Patrick, solemnly. 'Had Worthy been to the trial?'

'Oh, yes! He had indeed. He was assistant to George Broughton at it: he said it was that case that made him leave London. He said he was not up to the pressures of the English Bar, and would try no longer to find a place there. I'm not sure that he found the Scottish one any less alarming, for as I say, he left Edinburgh quite soon.'

'And was he there when Broughton quarrelled with you?'

'No, not that I'm aware of. I haven't seen Worthy for a year or so, and I had no idea where he was. Poor Worthy!'

The room fell silent for a little, and the fire hummed. Outside the snow was falling again, and Hippolyta was pleased that this time she was no longer worried that Marcus was somewhere out under it, even if the story of his incarceration seemed an odd one. He was a silly man, certainly, but she was sure in her own heart that he had not killed Mr. Broughton. He had been quite sure that Broughton was alive until they told him otherwise.

'I suppose the thing is,' said Durris at last, 'that if Mr. Worthy worked for Mr. Broughton, there is a possibility that Mr. Worthy was the real target of the attack, and Mr. Elphick's hat was only a coincidence.'

'If Worthy was the real target,' added Patrick, 'it seems to me that the answer is in one of Broughton's law cases, and nothing to do with your weavers or Sir Holroyd.'

'What was the woman's name?' Hippolyta asked suddenly. It

took Marcus a moment to remember.

'Mary Wilson,' he said. 'That's her married name, of course, in the English fashion.'

'Oh, yes. Poor woman,' murmured Hippolyta. To think that some little woman had suffered so much at her husband's hands, and then been hanged for killing him when he had died accidentally, seemed the worst injustice. Had Mr. Broughton really thought it only a game? She hoped not: she did not want to think such a thing of anyone she had known. But if he had stood there and said that to her, particularly if the woman had been someone she had known – well, would she have shot him, given the opportunity?

'I believe,' said Durris, 'that I must go and speak with Mrs. Broughton once more. She may remember this case, or others that linked Mr. Worthy and Mr. Broughton, and see some possibilities there that will fit.' He rose from his seat at the breakfast table, and put away his notebook and pencil, then removed his glasses and cleaned them. 'Dr. Napier, I wonder if you would permit your wife to accompany me once again to visit Mrs. Broughton? I find I prefer to interview her with a woman present.'

Patrick gave Hippolyta a look in which she read all his admonitions from their earlier conversation. Then he nodded, satisfied that she would at least try to be sensible.

'Very well, yes. And anyway,' he added, pushing himself up on to his good foot and seizing his stick, 'you and I both know that if I did not give permission, and you did not ask her, she would find some way of overhearing your conversation. Better to keep her where you can see her!' He smiled, and Hippolyta was washed with guilt at his resigned understanding. She would try to be better, she really would. But first they had to find out who had killed Mr. Worthy and Mr. Broughton.

Mr. Durris had to wait until she had dressed her hair properly and laced on her boots, but it was not long until they were heading down the main street to the inn once again. Marcus had retired to his bed and Patrick was arranging his day's work with Wullie's help, and Ishbel had the dinner plans well in hand – Hippolyta would hardly be missed, anyway, she told herself. She was much more useful considering the mystery at hand.

Mrs. Broughton clearly also felt she could be more useful elsewhere: wearing a slightly less fashionable mourning gown, she was packing her trunks to leave.

'I'm not going yet,' she explained. 'I should like very much to stay until you have found my husband's murderer. Mr. Strong says he sees no reason why I cannot afford to pay for the accommodation from my husband's money until then, for I am his only beneficiary. But then I shall go at least to Edinburgh, where some of my relations are, and later perhaps return to my friends in London. My life revolved so much about his that I am spinning aimlessly now, Mr. Durris: I don't know what to do next.'

'Couldn't you still be active politically?' Hippolyta asked. 'There seem to be so many ladies these days helping in all kinds of ways.'

'Ladies with money and connexions, Mrs. Napier. Yes, intelligence is valued too, in those circles, but not on its own, sadly. But no doubt I shall find something useful to do.' She smiled, but it was not the most natural of smiles.

'You'll have heard, ma'am, of the unfortunate death of Mr. Worthy?'

'Yes, poor man! I knew him a few years ago in London. I hear that he was killed in mistake for Mr. Elphick?'

'Are you aware of any reason why anyone should have killed Mr. Elphick?' Durris asked. 'The same person, perhaps, who killed Mr. Broughton?'

'The only connexion that my husband and Mr. Elphick had was that they both knew me, I believe,' said Mrs. Broughton, without vanity. 'Or wait: I suppose you could say that Mr. Elphick wrote about both Parliament and the law courts, and my husband worked in both places. So I suppose it could be something in either world.'

'And what if Mr. Worthy were actually the intended victim?' asked Durris.

'Oh, no one would want to kill Frederick Worthy! He was such a pleasant man, though a little odd in his speech and appearance. But harmless, and very well mannered. I only met him once or twice in London, I believe, but my husband always spoke well of him and was disappointed when he decided to abandon London for Scotland. No, I cannot see anyone intending to kill Mr.

Worthy.'

'What if some case they had been involved in had gone sour?' Durris asked.

'And someone decided to take revenge? Good gracious, Mr. Durris, you should write for the theatre!'

'Do you remember a case in which your husband acted for the prosecution, a few years ago, where a woman killed her husband and was hanged for it?'

Mrs. Broughton considered. Her face was strong and closed: Hippolyta found she had no idea of the thoughts going on behind it.

'I remember something like that. A drunkard, wasn't he? And so probably was the wife. There are plenty of cases like it in the worse parts of London, and no doubt other cities, too. Overcrowding, poor conditions, and to cap it all no representation in Parliament to defend them. It's no wonder blood boils and tempers fray.'

'Tempers like your husband's, Mrs. Broughton?' asked Durris softly. She met his eye.

'My husband's temper was not as controlled as it might have been, certainly, Mr. Durris. But it is someone else at issue here. Someone else has lost control, and killed two men, and my husband never killed anyone.'

Not by his own hand, Hippolyta found herself thinking. But perhaps otherwise?

'If you want to know more about my husband's cases, Mr. Durris, you would be as well to talk to Mr. Elphick. He followed all of them, I believe, before George became a Member of Parliament. He should be able to remember one of the hundreds, if anyone can.'

They were dismissed. Hippolyta gave an apologetic glance backwards, feeling they had somehow overstepped the mark of good behaviour. Mrs. Broughton was standing watching them go, head high, shoulders back, undefeated. Hippolyta could not imagine her fading away for want of something to do. Mrs. Broughton would make her own road.

'Mr. Elphick, then,' said Durris when they left the inn again.

'Am I allowed to accompany you?'

Durris sighed.

'I suppose so. Though I shall make sure his landlady is within reach, for all our sakes.'

He did not seem in the best of moods today, Hippolyta thought, as she followed him back up the main street and around the corner by the church. Mr. Elphick had taken lodgings in a house that was usually full of paying guests in the summer time, and had been built up and out in order to accommodate them. At this time of year, though, Mr. Elphick was the only guest, and they had no trouble in securing the parlour on the ground floor for their sole use. Elphick did his best to look as if he had cosied himself into an armchair by the fire, but Durris had settled opposite him and Elphick's eyes were jumpy. Durris had left the parlour door open. Hippolyta sat by the window, avoiding the draught.

'There's a possibility,' said Durris, 'that you were not in fact the intended victim when Mr. Worthy was killed the night before last. It seems that Mr. Worthy had some connexion with Mr. Broughton.'

'Did he, indeed?' Elphick's wandering eyes calmed a little. 'What kind of a connexion was that, then?'

'Apparently for a little while they worked together in London. Tell me, Mr. Elphick, do you remember a case a few years ago where a woman was hanged for murdering her husband? Mrs. Broughton thought you might have reported on it for the newspapers.'

'A Broughton case? Well, that would be Mary Wilson, I should think. What on earth do you think that has to do with all this?'

'It seems to have aroused some strong feelings, by all accounts,' said Durris without emphasis. 'You think, then, that any connexion is unlikely?'

It would be easy, thought Hippolyta, for Mr. Elphick to insist that a connexion was probable: with Worthy dead for reasons of his own, Mr. Elphick was, to her mind at least, a strong suspect again.

'There was certainly something a bit off about it at the time,' Elphick reflected. 'Broughton was often over-confident. He liked to win, but in this case I'm not sure he did the right thing. There was some idea that the poor woman had been badly treated by the husband, - still shouldn't have murdered him, of course - but anyway, there was a strong chance that it had been an accident.'

'Did you see the trial?'

'Yes, I did, I recall. The wife was a tiny thing, just skin and bone. It's a wonder the jury believed she had the strength to do it. But Broughton told them she had, and Broughton was very convincing.'

'What about the sister?' Hippolyta asked. She was supposed to keep quiet, but the notion of that sister had been bothering her. If you thought you could defend someone in your family, and then were not allowed to: that would make for some unhappiness.

'What sister?' asked Elphick, blinking at her.

'There was a sister who was called as a witness but never appeared.'

'Oh! Her, yes! I heard about her. Never saw her, though. I tried to find her and talk to her afterwards, but she kept herself to herself. Same name as my own sister, she had, otherwise I might have forgotten all about her. She was Clara, Clara Trowell.'

Chapter Twenty-Four

'Clara Trowell – you're quite sure?' Durris had asked, making a little shape in his notebook. Elphick watched his hands anxiously.

'Oh, yes. Definitely Clara, and I'm pretty sure about the Trowell bit.'

'Very interesting. Do you remember Mr. Worthy there at all?'

The conversation, such as it was, continued, with Hippolyta gripping the seat of her chair with impatience. Clara! Could it be the same one who was maid to Lady Pinner? But it was a common enough name. Clara … Clara could certainly have attacked her in the snow, but then she had been attacked herself, apparently. She looked – well, tough, was perhaps the word. Hippolyta had no difficulty imagining Clara hitting poor Mr. Worthy hard. But surely she could not have shot Mr. Broughton? She strained to remember what Lady Pinner had told her, her fingertips numb against the wooden seat.

At last Mr. Durris finished his interminably calm interview and they left, with Mr. Elphick visibly relaxed. Out in the street, Hippolyta bounced on her toes.

'Yes, yes, Mrs. Napier. I am quite aware of Lady Pinner's maid's name.'

Really, the man was thrawn this morning. Never had she known him in such a mood.

'What are you going to do, though? I'm sure she could have killed Mr. Worthy, but what about Mr. Broughton?'

'I want to go and speak to Mrs. Broughton again.'

'Again! But she said she knew very little about the case!'

'But she might know if he had been receiving threats from a woman.'

'She might not have sent threats. She might just have been waiting to take revenge.'

Durris made a small sound which in anyone else Hippolyta would have taken for irritation, but he still managed to keep his voice down as they walked back towards the green.

'How on earth could Lady Pinner's maid have known that the Broughtons were going to be here? The Broughtons and the Pinners were not even on speaking terms!'

'Maybe it was just an unhappy coincidence. Maybe it was only when she came here that she thought of the whole thing. After all, even Mr. Broughton didn't know that Mr. Worthy was here, so it was hardly an elaborate plot, was it? It was just luck – bad luck, for Mr. Broughton and Mr. Worthy.'

'You're saying,' said Durris, reducing his voice even further, 'that Clara Trowell – if she is Clara Trowell – was capable of hitting you and knocking you unconscious, then going and finding Mr. Worthy and hitting him so hard she killed him?'

'Have you met her? She looks strong.'

'And then how, may I ask, did she manage to attack herself?'

'Ah,' said Hippolyta. 'That's a question. Maybe she only pretended she had been injured? She's doing the cooking at Dinnet House. She could have dabbed some pig's blood or suchlike on her head, and groaned a little. Mrs. Riach could have taught her a few useful expressions.'

'Well,' said Durris, not wholly convinced. 'Could she have shot Mr. Broughton? Where was she?'

'And that,' said Hippolyta, 'is a more worrying question. For Lady Pinner told me that Clara went up to watch the duel with her that morning. They hid together behind a clutch of birch trees – where you saw the footprints. But maybe they parted for some reason for the crucial moment? You'll need to ask Lady Pinner, I suppose.'

'I shall.' Durris' mouth was firm. 'And I think this time you're coming with me, Mrs. Napier. For if Lady Pinner says that Clara was with her all through the duel, then any accusation, whether she is Clara Trowell or not, will be a complete impossibility.'

'That is a complete impossibility.'

Lady Pinner, looking better than Hippolyta had seen her yet, sat regally in her chair in the drawing room. Clara had opened the front door to them and shown them in, then vanished, leaving Durris to explain their purpose with some discretion.

'You're quite sure, my lady, that she was with you the whole time?'

'Of course she was. Where else would she have been?'

Durris glanced over at Hippolyta, expressionless. Hippolyta sighed.

'Lady Pinner,' she asked, 'may I ask what Clara's surname is? Is she unmarried?'

'She is,' said Lady Pinner, a little surprised at Hippolyta's question. 'Her surname is Trowell.'

'And she's from London?' Hippolyta asked. She would have flashed a look of triumph at Durris, but the problem of the duel persisted.

'She is, yes. Sir Holroyd prefers usually to hire servants from his estates, but in this case he was determined to have Londoners to avoid any – well, undesirable elements, he said.'

'Quite so,' said Durris. Hippolyta could see that he was hesitating over whether or not to disclose Clara Trowell's background. It hardly affected her efficiency as a servant, but the notoriety, such as it was, might damage her relationship with her employer. She decided to take advantage of his hesitation.

'Would it be all right,' she said, 'if I had a word with Clara? We were both attacked on the same night, and I wondered if perhaps she had had the same impressions of her attacker as I had.'

'Well ...'

'In Ballater we do not like to be in the position of worrying about night time attacks. Everyone would like to see whoever was responsible receive a just punishment.'

'Well then,' said Lady Pinner, reassured. 'Shall I call her?'

'That would be kind.'

'I don't understand why she is of interest to you,' said Lady Pinner, after she had rung the bell. 'She has not been with us for long, of course, but she has been very attentive and reliable, despite the extra work that she had not perhaps anticipated. Not many ladies' maids have also to cook for the household. I hope that my husband will take on more staff again when we return to London.'

'It must be inconvenient, certainly,' Hippolyta was agreeing, when Clara reappeared.

'Mrs. Napier has some questions to ask you,' Lady Pinner explained, waving at Hippolyta. Impassive, Clara turned to her. It was a little like seeing her own reflection: Clara could not wear her hair so elaborately, but she too had changed the style a little to conceal the bandage towards the back of her head. It was perhaps less noticeable under her maid's cap.

'What do you remember of being attacked?' Hippolyta asked.

'Nothing much, ma'am,' said Clara. 'You sent me back when we were at the edge of the village, and I couldn't have walked many paces – ten or twenty, maybe - before I felt the thump. No doubt if the snow had not been so thick you would have seen it happen. I didn't fall, though. I staggered a bit, but I found a wall to lean on and stood there till my head stopped going round, ma'am.'

'So the person attacked you and then me, it seems,' said Hippolyta. 'They were heading into the village from the north.' She glanced around at Durris. Gratifyingly he made a mark in his notebook – but what mark? Did it just mean 'there she goes again?' 'May I see the injury?' she asked. Clara's eyes questioned a little, but her hands went to the bandage and loosened it. Underneath, it was clear that the blow had been just as real as the one to Hippolyta's own head: the skin was broken and still quite swollen and dark below the hairline. Hippolyta nodded. 'Sore, isn't it?' she said softly, meeting Clara's eyes.

'It is indeed, ma'am,' she agreed, momentarily human.

Behind her, Durris cleared his throat.

'Miss Trowell,' he said, 'can you tell me what you were doing on Saturday morning? We are still trying to find witnesses who can help us establish precisely who was on the hill behind the house.'

'At the duel, sir?'

'That's right, but if you can start a little earlier than that, please?'

'Well … I got up out of my bed and went to prepare the breakfast,' Clara started, checking to see that he was happy with this. 'I hadn't but cleaned the stove when Lady Pinner came into the kitchen all dressed and said she was for heading up the hill to see what would happen, for she said the master was to take part in a duel. So of course I said I'd go with her. Her ladyship has not been well, and I would not like to see her going out on her own.'

'Of course not,' said Hippolyta encouragingly. Clara's eyes wandered over to her mistress, and back.

'So I got our cloaks and off we went. Bitter cold, it was, too, but we were well wrapped up. I hadn't been up the hill into the country before, and nor had my lady, so we went out the garden gate and just – went up. We could see the master's footprints where he had gone ahead of us, and when we got into the trees we kept quiet so we didn't surprise him.'

'I felt my husband would have preferred me to stay clear of the danger,' Lady Pinner explained quickly. Clara looked across at her again, and away.

'Where did you conceal yourselves, Miss Trowell?' Durris asked.

'Behind some trees. We could see the master up ahead, to our left a bit. He was fiddling with a pistol. Over to the right there was that man that died, and he had a pistol too. One of them called to the other and then the pistols went off. It was a really funny smell.' She wrinkled her nose. 'Then the other man fell down. Someone came running down the hill – oh, that was you, ma'am, wasn't it?' she asked, turning to Hippolyta in mild surprise. 'My lady tugged my arm and we went back down the hill again, as fast as we could to the house.'

'So was that all you saw up there?' Durris asked. 'You saw Sir Holroyd and Mr. Broughton, and Mrs. Napier. Anyone else?'

'Oh, yes I did,' said Clara, as if it had been obvious. 'There was another man up there apart from the master and Mr. Broughton. He was off in the trees up above the master, if you see what I mean – not up a tree, but up the hill a bit.'

'Ah, yes,' said Hippolyta. No doubt that would be Mr. Elphick, sneaking around before he came down to Mr. Broughton's body after Sir Holroyd had left. But if he had been up just above Sir Holroyd, then surely he could have shot Mr. Broughton easily from there? She turned to Durris, but he was still busy with Clara.

'What did this man look like, then?'

'Well, he was young.' What age was Clara, Hippolyta wondered, that she would call Mr. Elphick young? He was surely in his forties, at least, and she would have said Clara was ten years younger. 'Quite tall and thin, and I could see under his hat he had very fair hair.'

'Very fair hair?' Hippolyta could not help repeating.

'That's right, ma'am. And he was pale to go with it.'

No one could call Mr. Elphick's hair very fair. Nor was he tall, nor thin. Now Hippolyta had no wish to meet Durris' eye at all. She swallowed hard, feeling herself redden. Clara turned curious grey eyes on her, but said nothing.

'I believe,' said Durris, 'that we might know someone of that description.' He made another little mark in his notebook, and put it and the pencil away. 'Lady Pinner, may we ask Miss Trowell to accompany us to the village for an hour or so? It would be most useful if we could make some identification of this man.'

No, no, don't, said Hippolyta to herself. I certainly don't want him identified. Frantically she tried to remember any other tall, thin, fair-haired man in the village. It could not have been Patrick, of course: he had been safe in his bed, and Clara would have recognised him anyway, as the physician attending her mistress. Was there anyone else who looked like that in the whole village?

'Mrs. Napier, are you ready to leave?' Durris was asking politely. 'Miss Trowell has gone to fetch her cloak.'

'Oh! Oh, yes, yes of course, Mr. Durris.' Hippolyta gathered her thoughts. Would Marcus still be at home? Would he be up yet? It would not do much for his dignity to be arrested in his nightgown, she thought, stifling a sudden panicky urge to giggle. She followed Durris in bidding good day to Lady Pinner, and went out to the hall, where Clara was already waiting.

They set off. Hippolyta had no wish to speak with Mr. Durris, so she dropped back to walk beside Clara. She had to find out more, particularly if it could do anything to help Marcus.

'Tell me, Clara,' she said, 'are you the same Clara Trowell whose – who was associated with a murder trial a few years ago? In London?'

Clara said nothing for a moment, concentrating on picking her way through rutted snow on the road. Then she took a deep breath.

'Yes, ma'am, I am.'

'I am sorry to hear it. The case seems to have been a dreadful one.'

Clara looked sick.

'It was, ma'am. Forgive me, but I must say it: Mary was innocent of all harm. She was the best of us, always. And that creature treated her like a whipping post. I would not just say it, ma'am, I'm telling the truth.'

'I believe you, Clara.' She did: it was what she said she had seen in the woods that Hippolyta was having trouble coming to terms with. She tried to think of something else to say, but what was there to say to someone who had lost their sister in such a terrible way? She fell silent, and they walked on in Durris' path to the village.

The green was busy with morning wanderers. Susanna, the Pinners' nurserymaid, had just emerged from Strachan's warehouse and Mrs. Kynoch had taken the baby to hold while Susanna, smiling and chatting, packed her purchases into a large basket. Sir Holroyd was in solemn conversation with the minister on the green near the church door: he noticed his wife's maid in the company of Durris, and frowned. Patrick was making slow progress with his stick across the green towards the church presumably to see his patient who lived beyond it. And to Hippolyta's horror, he was being accompanied by Marcus.

Durris cast her a warning look, and seemed about to lengthen his stride towards Marcus, But it was Clara he should have warned.

'That's him! That's the man!' she cried, as if she were telling the whole parish. She flung out her arm, pointing straight at Marcus. 'He shot Sir Holroyd!'

At that point, several things seemed to happen at once.

Almost everyone on the green froze.

Marcus and Patrick, surprised by the sudden noise, stopped and looked about. Sir Holroyd and the minister followed Clara's indication, and stared at them.

Two figures, abruptly in motion, sprang from somewhere beside the church and ran forward to Sir Holroyd and the minister. Both threw something, and there was a cry of alarm.

Something flashed past Hippolyta, and snatched at Clara's arm. Durris spun around to see what was happening behind him, trying to watch the two running figures at the same time. But Sir Holroyd had seized one of them, and the other seemed to be on the ground, injured.

'Stop!' someone shouted, and Hippolyta's gaze darted about

the green. Mrs. Kynoch was still outside Strachan's front door, holding baby Maria. But she was alone. Susanna was beside Clara, clutching her right arm in her own left one. She still clutched her basket.

Durris drew breath.

'Mr. Fettes, come over here, please,' he called. 'Perhaps if Dr. Napier could manage, too? Sir Holroyd, if you can hold that man for a moment I shall be with you shortly. Ah, here comes Constable Morrisson – with unaccustomed promptness.' Hippolyta looked across the green to where Morrisson came reluctantly and carefully through the snow to reach Sir Holroyd and the two figures. Sir Holroyd seemed to be an unusual colour, and the minister, who had also been splashed with – something, was standing back and trying to wipe down his coat, his face expressive.

'That's the man,' said Clara loudly and definitely, before Marcus and Patrick could reach them. 'That's the man I saw on the hill that morning. The morning of the duel.'

Susanna dropped Clara's arm, though she seemed tense. Her habitual smile was absent: she was focussed on Marcus and Patrick, and their slow progress across the green. Durris looked at her, and cast a glance back at Mrs. Kynoch and the baby.

'Are you Sir Holroyd's nursery maid?' he asked.

Susanna blinked, and nodded.

'I am, sir.'

'Have you seen this man before?'

'No, sir. Never in my life.'

'Where were you last Saturday morning?'

'When the duel was happening?' she asked quickly. 'I was looking after Baby, in the nursery. I didn't know nothing of all of this till afterwards.'

Durris nodded, then flexed his nostrils. Hippolyta had noticed it, too: a nasty aroma was in the air. Sir Holroyd was approaching. On closer inspection, which Hippolyta for one would have forgone happily, the stain across his clothes appeared to be the scrapings from a winter byre floor. Behind him, irresistibly following, came Constable Morrisson with his large hands firmly in the collars of, Hippolyta could now see, McTavish and Halloran. Neither of them was particularly fragrant, either.

'Is this the man who shot Broughton?' Sir Holroyd asked in wonder, taking in Marcus' pale fashionable trousers and fine boots as he helped Patrick the last few yards to where Durris and Clara were standing. 'Who is he?'

'Shot Broughton?' Marcus must have heard at last. 'Who shot Broughton?'

'You, Mr. Fettes, according to this woman here,' said Durris.

'I most certainly did not!' Marcus flushed red and white. 'I would never have shot the best orator the Reform movement has!'

'Oh, another Reformer!' sighed Sir Holroyd with mock drama. 'Will I never be rid of them?'

'Never!' cried Marcus, rising easily to the bait.

'This woman,' said Durris, interrupting without apparent effort, 'saw you on the hillside where the duel took place, during the duel on Saturday morning. Can you explain what you were doing there?'

'No, I cannot,' said Marcus firmly, 'because I was not there. I have told you –' he looked suddenly at Sir Holroyd as if he had just recognised him. 'I have told you where I was.'

'He was on the hillside,' said Clara stubbornly. 'I saw him clearly.'

There came a heavy throat-clearing from behind Sir Holroyd, and everyone turned to look. McTavish, his hands filthy, was trying to straighten up in Morrisson's grip.

'Far be it from me,' he said with ceremony, 'to interrupt the business of the gentry, but I can tell you where this gentleman was while the two of them were shooting each other.'

'What?'

It was Marcus who spun to stare at him. Durris examined McTavish's expression thoroughly. Halloran, too, was nodding.

'Where, then?' Durris asked at last.

'He was in the big house,' said McTavish, and Halloran's nodding grew more enthusiastic. 'We were watching the big house, and he was up there in a window. Near the back somewhere, over to the ... well, the end that wasna the kitchens, that's where.'

'Up in the ... Oh, yes,' said Marcus, his face clearing. 'I was in what seemed to be the nursery. Was that when the duel was happening? I was trying to find a way out.'

'Where were you?' Durris asked the two weavers. McTavish

sighed.

'You ken rightly where we were. We were in yon wee hut with the stove. It was our turn to watch the house: we'd no idea there was going to be a duel ganging ahint us.'

'And that was when you saw this man at a window in the house?'

'Oh, aye. See, Halloran says to me, he says, yon fella's trying to see up the hill what all the shots is for.'

'But,' said Hippolyta slowly, 'if you were in the nursery, Marcus, where was the baby? Where was Miss Maria?'

'I don't know. I don't know anything about babies,' said Marcus. 'Asleep? Off playing somewhere?'

'She could have been asleep,' said Clara. 'She sleeps dead well.'

Something slid into place in Hippolyta's mind.

'Godfrey's Cordial! I saw a bottle in Lady Pinner's parlour!'

'Well, yes, ma'am. It's meant for babies but sometimes ladies take it too – when they wish to take away the pain a little.'

'It helps them sleep, doesn't it?'

'It should,' said Patrick with some emphasis. 'I've heard of cases where there are as much as four grains of opium in a bottle.'

'And the other thing,' said Hippolyta, meeting Patrick's eye, 'is that if you were in the nursery, Marcus – and the baby might have been – then where, Susanna, were you?'

'Godfrey's Cordial,' said Susanna absently. 'I've a bottle of that here in my basket, if you want a look at it, Dr. Napier –'

But when her left hand came from her basket, it was holding a pistol.

'Get back, all of you, and away from us!' she ordered, her voice calm, though the hand with the pistol was wavering from right to left.

'Is that my pistol?' demanded Sir Holroyd. Constable Morrisson with admirable speed whisked his charges as far back as possible from the gun, making sure they were in front of him. Marcus gasped. Durris, Patrick, and Hippolyta froze.

'I've killed twice. I'll do it again,' said Susanna, her pretty face sombre.

'The best of us,' said Hippolyta.

'What's that?' asked Patrick.

'Clara said that Mary Wilson was "the best of us". She had more than one sister, didn't she?'

'And why not?' said Susanna, dismissing this. 'And she was the best of us. She was an innocent. That husband of hers as good as killed her, but he's dead. But George Broughton put the noose about her poor neck with his arguments and his fine talk. And he's dead and all.'

'Then it's finished, isn't it?' said Durris. 'You might as well let me take that pistol, don't you think, miss?'

'Oh, I don't think so. I'm not done yet, you know. Now they'll put a noose round my neck for Broughton and his lawyer's clerk, but I've one more to do before I give myself up. So back off, and let me go.'

'Let you go to kill again? You can't imagine we'd do that,' said Durris. Hippolyta's heart was beating like a steam engine, but Durris seemed entirely calm.

'Well, you might,' said Susanna reflectively. Then she grabbed at Hippolyta's arm, swinging the pistol around to aim at her stomach. Hippolyta gasped. 'If I said I would shoot this lady if you don't, eh?'

Durris and Patrick each took a step backwards.

'Susanna, please let my wife go,' said Patrick at once.

'That does colour things a little,' Durris admitted. 'Mrs. Napier, please stay quite calm.'

'That seems sensible,' said Hippolyta, a little breathlessly. She could feel the hard nose of the pistol pressing into her side. Was that good, or bad? A chest wound, she felt sure, would be quicker than a stomach wound: that might be a slower and more painful death. But if it was not immediate then perhaps Patrick could save her … But truly, neither prospect sounded inviting.

'Now, let us pass. I have business to finish,' said Susanna. Her face was harsh now, but for a moment she cast a glance back towards Mrs. Kynoch where she watched, horrified, with the other villagers at Strachan's door. Mrs. Kynoch was still holding baby Maria. 'I don't suppose they'll let me see her again,' she murmured, her face pretty once more. 'And I do love her so much.'

Then she prodded Hippolyta's ribs again with the pistol, and pushing her along she and Clara guided her down the hill, towards the inn.

Chapter Twenty-Five

'You'll know what room she's in, ma'am,' said Susanna in a low voice, as they approached the inn. She had concealed the pistol in her cloak.

'Who?' asked Hippolyta, though she was sure she knew.

'His wife. Mrs. Broughton.'

'You can't kill her! She had nothing to do with it, surely!'

'Please keep your voice down, Mrs. Napier,' said Susanna, 'and just tell us. Or Clara will go and ask anyway.' Hippolyta had almost forgotten Clara: she had been silent for so long, but she was there and attentive. Hippolyta hesitated, but she did not want to risk the life of some innocent hotel servant, either.

'Oh, very well. She's upstairs.'

Susanna nudged her towards the stairs, smiling confidently at a passing maid who took no further notice of them. Hippolyta breathed a small sigh of relief at that. She wondered if the folds of cloak could possibly stop Susanna's pistol from firing – wasn't there some kind of lever thing on the top that had to move for the gun to go off? Or maybe it would block the pistol somehow and make it explode. That was not a thought she relished. She led Susanna and Clara to Mrs. Broughton's room. Susanna knocked smartly on the door, and Hippolyta held her breath.

But there was no answer.

Susanna knocked again, but again there was silence. Perhaps Mrs. Broughton was simply hiding in there, not responding, but why would she? And it had the feel of an empty room.

'You've called on her, ma'am, haven't you? Where else would she be?' Susanna asked. Hippolyta could see an uneasiness in her, a conflict between the habitual servant and the person with the gun. She would have found it interesting, in another setting.

'There's a parlour downstairs that she favours, I believe,' she said, after some thought. Could she misdirect Susanna somehow? She knew there were several parlours on the ground floor. But what would happen if she did? What if someone else, someone unconnected, were in the parlour she chose? Why could she not think faster? But that nudge in her side at each step down the stairs, that kept grabbing her thoughts and twisting them away from anything useful, turning them back to the anticipation of blood and pain and death.

They were on the ground floor already. Which parlour should she choose? There was the one looking out at the stable yard, where she and Marcus had stood as the duel was arranged. There was another facing the same way. And then there was the one Mrs. Broughton favoured, the one looking out over the river. The door was ajar. Perhaps the room was empty.

But it was not. Susanna nodded to Clara who knocked and opened the door, and Hippolyta could see that someone was seated in the armchair by the window. It was Jedediah Elphick.

He leapt to his feet as they came in, turning towards them, and his eager smile melted away at once.

'Oh!' he said. 'I'm sorry: I thought …'

'Where's Mrs. Broughton?' asked Susanna, quite politely.

'I'm not sure: I'm expecting to see her here soon.' The smile returned, but now it was simply polite, and a little unsure of itself. 'I don't really know. I was just waiting. But can I help at all? Mrs. Napier?'

Hippolyta shook her head. She was almost sure she could manoeuvre the sisters out of the parlour now with no harm to Mr. Elphick, but Susanna suddenly narrowed her eyes.

'You were at the trial, weren't you?' She looked quickly to Clara for confirmation. Clara frowned and nodded.

'He was.'

'What trial?' asked Elphick, as Hippolyta's heart sank.

'Our sister's trial, of course. What was your part in it?'

'Who was your – oh! Are you Mary Wilson's sister? Clara Trowell?'

'I'm Clara,' said Clara. 'She's Susanna.'

'Yes, yes, I was at your sister's trial! A tragedy,' he added soberly.

'What was your part in it?' Susanna repeated, her voice deep with suspicion.

'He's just a reporter, a journalist,' said Hippolyta quickly. 'He thought your sister was gravely mistreated. He said so himself earlier. I heard him.'

'I did, it's true,' said Elphick, looking with bewilderment from Hippolyta to Susanna. 'I thought it was all wrong. I tried to speak to you afterwards,' he added to Clara, 'but you weren't talking to anyone.'

'You could have said something,' said Susanna with deliberation. 'You could have written down in your newspaper how it was all wrong.'

'It doesn't always work like that,' said Elphick. 'I can't always write what I want to write. And anyway, what good would it have done?'

'It might have spared her the noose,' Susanna breathed. She flicked aside her cloak, just as Hippolyta had dreaded she might. 'You should have done it, whoever you are.'

'Sister, no: we agreed.' Clara spoke up unexpectedly. 'Come on: we have to find the woman. You said it would be her.'

'Well, where is she, then?' Susanna kept her eye on Elphick, but the pistol still hard against Hippolyta.

'She's coming here, soon. The innkeeper said so: he said she'd not long gone out,' said Elphick eagerly. 'If you go out to the stableyard, chances are you'll catch her there!'

Hippolyta wondered briefly if Elphick had a plan, or was simply trying to save himself. Susanna watched him for a moment, perhaps thinking the same thing. Then she waved the pistol at Elphick.

'You go on ahead, then. And don't try to escape: I've killed already, you know.'

His cheeks flushed, Elphick stepped as if over eggshells out of the room, and towards the stableyard door of the inn. Hippolyta followed, with Susanna still close by her side. Hippolyta hoped that Elphick would not do anything stupid that might make Susanna twitchy: at the moment she could sense Susanna's tension right through the fingers gripping her arm. If only she were an animal, then Hippolyta might have been able to calm her down, talk gently to her to make her see sense – like their pony, when he was particularly tetchy.

The yard door was open. The stableyard itself was empty. They advanced in their little group to the centre of it, and stopped.

'She'll be coming in that way,' said Hippolyta helpfully, nodding back over her shoulder.

'True,' said Susanna. She turned herself and Hippolyta. Elphick hesitated, and Susanna waved the pistol towards him again. 'Stand over there,' she said, 'where I can see you clearly. Mrs. Napier, I need my hands free. Please go and stand beside him: I'll still shoot you if I have to.'

Rubbing her arm where Susanna had clutched it, Hippolyta slipped gratefully over to stand beside Mr. Elphick.

'Have you a plan?' she whispered urgently.

'A plan? Why should I have a plan?' he asked, puzzled.

'Oh, well. Never mind.' She looked about the yard. Surely someone would be here soon? One of the stable lads? But again, she did not want anyone else hurt.

'Could we ... Susanna, it might be better if we moved a bit that way,' she called quietly, waving towards the stables. 'If Mrs. Broughton comes along the road here, she'll see Mr. Elphick and me straight away, and wonder why we are standing here doing nothing, don't you think? If we go that way we're better hidden.'

Susanna considered.

'Yes, all right,' she said. She backed cautiously across the yard, and gestured to them to move forward. They did so. Hippolyta had a think. Time was running short, though.

'Look,' she said, moving forward again a few paces – not too many, not all at once. 'Why not just leave it at this? You've dealt with Mr. Broughton, and you've dealt with his clerk.'

Susanna backed a few steps further.

'Keep back, Mrs. Napier. I've made up my mind.'

'And Clara,' said Hippolyta, edging a tiny bit further forward, more a matter of adjusting her feet than actually taking a step. 'Clara hasn't murdered anyone, has she? You don't want to get her into more trouble. She's the – well, you're the clever one, aren't you? You've looked after Clara all this time. You can't have her charged with murder, too.' Another couple of inches forward, and Susanna took another step back, almost unaware of what she was doing. 'Poor Clara – and you even hit her on the head to make it look as if she and I were attacked by the same person. But you're left-handed, Susanna: Clara's been hit on the other side of the head from me. Clara attacked me and – oh! Clara, did you kill Mr. Worthy? I thought it was Susanna!'

The two sisters glanced at each other, and Hippolyta took another step forward. There was no chance that she would be able to grab the pistol without Susanna anticipating it: the gap was too wide. But that was not her plan.

'But Susanna killed Mr. Broughton. There, it was both of you!'

Smiling as if she had just lost her senses, Hippolyta took another step forward. Had she pushed it too far? She saw, as if it were lit by gaslight, Susanna's finger tighten on the trigger. Then there was a cry of pain, a bang, and a shocked shout from the street, and the pistol clattered to the cobbles.

'Hippolyta, my dearest,' said Patrick, once more comfortable with his foot up on the sofa, 'please don't tell me that you steered Susanna back into our misbegotten pony on purpose!'

'Of course I did,' said Hippolyta. She poked a finger at her bonnet, which lay on the parlour table. 'I wasn't sure what else to do.'

'It was extremely dangerous, Mrs. Napier,' said Durris. 'If we hadn't come along –'

'But she had fired her one shot by then, when the pony nipped her,' said Hippolyta. Then she added sadly, 'Fired it through my bonnet, as it happens.'

'It could as well have been through your head,' said Marcus from his place by the fire.

'No need to sound disappointed, brother dear!' said Hippolyta.

'Or she could have hit Mrs. Broughton by accident, if we had not had her wait,' said Durris.

'After all, it seemed obvious that that was why you were all off to the inn,' said Patrick. 'Mrs. Broughton was the obvious next victim. It was pure good luck that we saw her coming out of the kirk just after you left: if I had not been hobbling we might have been away before she appeared, in fact.'

'Well,' said Hippolyta, 'and I was glad enough to see all of you at the gate, for Mr. Elphick is no use in a crisis. I believe Mrs.

Broughton was more comfort to him than he to her. And you were able to stop Clara from running.'

'We have our uses, Mrs. Napier,' said Durris solemnly. 'She attacked you because she thought you had begun to realise it was them – something from George Broughton's past, she said you said.'

Susanna had not run, though, Hippolyta remembered.

Susanna had dropped the pistol from her left hand as if it were hot, jumped away from the pony and stopped. Her body had jerked oddly, as if someone were pulling the wrong string. Then she crumpled to her knees, and began to cry.

Hippolyta had found herself crouched by her, holding her tight, feeling the wracking pain of loss crashing through the girl. She pulled her close and stared past her, seeing not the snow-patched cobbles of the stable yard but a crowded courtroom, a small, thin form in the dock, and a glorious, proud lawyer condemning her, sweeping her to her doom for the sake of his own power and might.

'The Trowell sisters are off to Aberdeen in the morning,' Durris added. 'As for McTavish and Halloran, well, the incident with the buckets of slurry has not helped them with Sir Holroyd. But they helped to catch the women. They'll go on a separate cart, for now: whether they had a part in the fire raising at Dinnet House or not is a matter for further investigation.'

Hippolyta slipped down from her seat at the parlour table and knelt by Patrick's sofa, gathering one of the cats into her arms. She leaned into the upholstery, glad to feel Patrick's hand on her shoulder.

'And Mrs. Broughton?' she asked.

'She is leaving with Mr. Elphick tomorrow, she says,' said Durris, giving no sign of any feelings on the matter. 'They will travel together as far as Edinburgh, anyway.'

'Good luck to them,' said Marcus. 'For myself, I shall wait until the snow melts.'

'And then?'

'And then I shall go and do my best to campaign for reform. If Sir Holroyd is staying for the winter, you can tell him: he will have no peace from me!'

'Oh,' said Patrick. 'Just what we wanted.'

Hippolyta reached for his hand, and smiled.
'No peace for anyone – not even in Ballater!'

Scots and other perhaps unfamiliar words in *A Murderous Game*

Ahint	behind
Bairnikie	little child (Doric diminutive of the already small bairnie)
Bide	dwell (your bidie-in is your live-in lover)
Birl	spin
Braw	strong and healthy
Cankert	ill humoured
Chitter	be afraid
Claik	gossip
Cludgie	chamber pot
Clype	betray, tell tales about
Cry	to call a name (to be cried in church: to have the banns read)
Finey, laney	Doric diminutives for fine and lane (no, really)
Fit wye	what way, how
Fly cup	a quick cup of tea, nothing formal (accompanied, if your luck is in, by a fauncy piece, or a bun)
Forbye	as well
Gang	go
Garron	a sturdy Highland pony, most often seen hauling stags off the hills or barrels of whisky over them
Gollar	shout incoherently
Gowf	golf
Guddle	muddle
High heidyin	person in charge, or who thinks they are
Hirple	limp
Howff	a low drinking house
Limmer	scoundrel
Loon	boy or man
Neb	nose
Oxters	armpits (in many dialects)
quine, quinie	girl or woman (and its inevitable diminutive)
risp	metal bar to rattle in place of ringing a doorbell

in room of	in place of
Teuchter	country bumpkin
Thole	put up with
Thrawn	stubborn
Turk	angry
Wabbit	pale and tired, washed out
Yett	gate

About the Author:

Lexie Conyngham is a historian living in the shadow of the Highlands. Her Murray of Letho and Hippolyta Napier novels are born of a life amidst Scotland's old cities, ancient universities and hidden-away aristocratic estates, but she has written since the day she found out that people were allowed to do such a thing. Beyond teaching and research, her days are spent with wool, wild allotments and a wee bit of whisky.

You can follow her meandering thoughts on Facebook or Pinterest or at www.murrayofletho.blogspot.co.uk, and if such a thing appeals you can even sign up for a quarterly newsletter by emailing contact@kellascatpress.co.uk. And if you enjoyed this book, please leave a review where you bought it!

The Hippolyta Napier books:
A Knife in Darkness
Death of a False Physician
A Murderous Game

The Murray of Letho books:
Death in a Scarlet Gown
Knowledge of Sins Past
Service of the Heir (An Edinburgh Murder)
An Abandoned Woman
Fellowship with Demons
The Tender Herb (A Murder in Mughal India)
Death of an Officer's Lady
Out of a Dark Reflection
Slow Death by Quicksilver
Thicker than Water

Standalones
Windhorse Burning
The War, The Bones and Dr. Cowie
Thrawn Thoughts & Blithe Bits (short stories)
Jail Fever

Printed in Great Britain
by Amazon